Brides of the Kindred

Book 5: Revealed

Evangeline Anderson

PUBLISHED BY:

Evangeline Anderson

Brides of the Kindred

Book 5: Revealed

Author's Note #1: To be the first to hear about new e-book releases, join my new newsletter by going to *www.EvangelineAnderson.com.* I promise no spam – you will only get email from me when a new book is out for either preorder or for sale.

Author's Note #2: I'm happy to let you all know that I am going into Audio in a big way. I put **Claimed** , **Hunted**, and **Sought** into the audio format and I had such a great response from readers and listeners, that I have decided to put ALL the **Kindred** books, plus all my **Born to Darkness** books into audio as well as my standalone book, **Purity.** If you have a long commute or you'd like something new to listen at the gym or just around the house, give it a try. The Kindred books are performed by the very talented Anne Johnstonbrown whom I hand-picked to read the series and she really brings the characters to life.

Author's Note #3: I'm trying to find out which of my readers are also listeners. For a chance to win a free audio book, sign up for my new **Audio book newsletter** by going to *www.EvangelineAnderson.com.* It's the same as my e-book newsletter, but only for audio. And as always, I promise not to bother you unless I have a new audio book out or I'm running a contest with an audio book as one of the prizes.

Author's Note #4: This is the fifth book in the Brides of the Kindred series. I recommend that you read Claimed, Hunted, Sought, and Found before starting Revealed.

Hugs and Happy Reading and Listening to you all,
Evangeline Anderson

Table of Contents

Brides of the Kindred

Book 5: Revealed

Evangeline Anderson

Chapter One

Detective Adam Rast stared down at the limp form of the girl in his arms in horror. "Nadiah?" he said, patting her cheeks urgently. "Nadiah, come on—wake up. Please."

But she just lay there, barely breathing, her lovely deep blue eyes rolled up to show the whites. She looked like a life-sized doll, her head rolling limply from side to side on his arm.

Rast couldn't figure out what was going on. Nadiah had come down to the Sarasota HKR building at his request to see if she could "feel" anything about the AllFather's last victim, Elise Darden. In the past, she'd been able to tell the whereabouts of a missing person just by touching her clothes, and Rast had hoped she would be able to do it again.

But he'd be lying if he said the still-open case was the only reason he'd asked her to come down from the Kindred Mother Ship to Earth. He'd heard from Commander Sylvan that Nadiah would be leaving soon, going back to her home planet of Tranq Prime, and he just couldn't let her go without seeing her one more time.

It was a stupid impulse and he knew it. They'd started off with a bang during the mistaken luck kiss at Commander Sylvan's wedding, but after that things went downhill fast, thanks to his own stubbornness and stupid pride. To be honest, Nadiah didn't like him at all—a fact she'd gone to great pains to make very clear during some of their earlier meetings.

Rast didn't blame her—he'd been a real jerk. First he'd refused to believe in her gift of "The Sight", as she called it, and then he'd called her crazy to her face. By the time Nadiah had proved to him beyond the shadow of a doubt that she really was experiencing a genuine psychic phenomenon, it was too late. As his mother liked to say, "You never get a second chance to make a first impression."

But even though he had blown it with the beautiful alien girl with exotically tilted dark blue eyes and long golden hair, Rast couldn't stop thinking about her. Couldn't stop wanting to see her again—just one last time. So he'd called on the viewscreen to ask for her help and to his surprise and gratification, she had graciously agreed.

"Should have known something was wrong," Rast muttered, patting her cheeks again. "I could tell she didn't feel well."

It was true—Nadiah had been unnaturally pale as she stepped through the sliding glass doors of the Human/Kindred Relations building. Her skin, always a delicate, translucent porcelain, had been paper white. Her eyes, a deep shade of mysterious blue Rast couldn't name because they didn't seem to match any Earthly color he'd ever seen—had been large and haunted. He'd also noticed dark circles beneath them that hadn't been there during their last meeting.

He'd thought about saying something then—considered asking if she was all right. But he'd assumed she was just having more nightmares. Visions of the AllFather's victims had plagued her in the past, no doubt turning her gift into a curse. Rast had hated like hell to put her through more of the same, but he genuinely needed her help.

Elise Darden hadn't had any family step forward to question her disappearance—in fact, all they'd been able to turn up were a few worried coworkers in the Tampa State Attorney's office. But even though she didn't seem to have any nearest and dearest, Rast still cared. Cared a hell of a lot that an innocent young woman had been taken and possibly tortured and killed. Something similar had happened to his beloved older sister, Jessie, when he was just a child, and as an adult he'd made it his life's work to find and rescue such victims if he could. Or to see their remains safely home if he couldn't.

Nadiah had greeted him in a low, colorless voice and they sat together on one of the HKR building's numerous gray couches. Rast had noticed that her hands were shaking when she reached for the bag of evidence he held out to her. He hadn't been able to help himself then.

"Hey," he said. "Are you okay? You don't mind me saying so, you don't look so good."

Nadiah had brushed his question off. "I'm fine. Just give me the clothes."

Against his better judgment, Rast had done as she asked. Nadiah had hesitated, then took a deep breath and plunged her hand into the plastic evidence bag as though it contained hot coals instead of discarded clothing.

"Well?" Rast had asked, looking at her anxiously. "What do you see?"

Nadiah had opened her mouth to reply and then everything had happened at once.

One minute she'd been touching the clothes he'd brought from the crime scene—the ones Elise Darden had been wearing on the day of her abduction—and the next minute she had given a cry and clutched at her chest, just below her heart. Then her eyes rolled up and she collapsed like a marionette whose strings had been cut.

It was a good thing he was there to catch her, Rast thought grimly as he shifted his arm to cradle her neck more securely. She would have slid right off the nondescript grey couch they were sitting on and banged her head on the floor if he hadn't grabbed her. But now what was he going to do?

Several of the Kindred warriors in the HKR building had come to his harsh shout and one of them had called Commander Sylvan on the viewscreen. Rast had wanted to call nine-one-one but apparently Sylvan was a doctor—his instructions were to sit tight until he appeared. But how long is he going to take? Rast wondered, looking anxiously down at Nadiah's lovely but unconscious face. She didn't seem to be having any kind of seizure or attack but her pulse was weak and thready and her respiration was light and quick—not to mention faint enough to worry the hell out of him.

Rast knew he should probably lay her down on the couch but somehow he couldn't bear to stop holding her. He needed her in his arms—needed to keep her safe any way he could. It was stupid but he had a fear that if he stopped touching her she would disappear, that her lovely porcelain skin would melt away to nothing like a princess in a fairy tale and he would never see her again. So he held her carefully but firmly to him and continued to pat her cheeks and murmur her name.

"Nadiah? Nadiah, please…"

"I'm here. What happened?"

Rast looked up in relief to see Sylvan standing there. The tall, blond Kindred had a small silver satchel slung over one broad shoulder—obviously the alien equivalent of an Earth doctor's little black bag. He pulled a tiny credit card sized scanner from it and began waving it over Nadiah's face without waiting for an answer.

"She fainted," Rast said, still holding Nadiah's still form close to his chest. "The minute she touched the evidence I asked her to look at." He shook his head. "It's my fault—I could tell she wasn't feeling well. I never should have asked her to put herself through that."

Sylvan finished the scan and put the tiny instrument back into his satchel. "It's not your fault, Rast," he said grimly. "This has nothing to do with your search for the missing girl."

"What does it have to do with, then?" Rast demanded. "Is she sick? Diabetic or something? Is she…" There was a sudden lump in his throat but he forced himself to go on. "She doesn't have anything…anything terminal, does she?"

Sylvan shook his head. "Not in the way that you mean, no. Though I do fear the long term effects of what is troubling her may eventually kill her." He sighed. "To form a blood bond in one so young, before the heart's true desires can manifest is reckless and cruel. But then, no one ever accused my people of being too compassionate."

"What are you talking about?" Rast felt himself go cold. "She said something about that to me before — something about a bond — but she would never go into detail. What does it mean?"

"Never mind." Sylvan shook his head again. "Just give her to me. I'll take her up to the Mother Ship and tend to her." He held out his arms for the limp form.

Rast started to hand Nadiah over…and stopped. "No." He heard the stubbornness in his own voice but he didn't care. "No, I…I can't."

Sylvan raised one dark blond eyebrow at him. "What do you mean you can't? Nadiah is my kinswoman — I am charged with her safety, not you. Give her to me so that I can take her for treatment."

"I'll go with you." Rast held her closer, cradling her small head with its luscious spill of long golden hair close to his chest. "But I won't give her up."

"Rast—"

"No!" Rast felt something like a growl rise in his throat and swallowed it back down again with difficulty. What was wrong with him? Everything Commander Sylvan said made sense. He was a doctor and related to Nadiah. By all rights he should be the one to care for her.

But Rast found himself completely and utterly unable to give her up. She was helpless in her unconscious state—totally vulnerable. And though he knew that Sylvan would never hurt her, he somehow couldn't bear to see her in another man's arms, even her married cousin's. Something inside him urged him to hold her—to guard and protect her and never let her go. It was an instinct too strong too fight.

"No," he said again, attempting to keep his voice low and even. "I can't let her go. We can go wherever you want but I'm going to carry her."

The big Kindred stared at Rast in evident surprise. He looked like he was going to say something but instead he simply nodded. "Very well. Come with me."

"Of course." Rast rose easily, holding Nadiah's unconscious form in his arms like a baby. "Let's go."

* * * * *

The trip up to the Kindred Mother Ship was a nearly silent one. The human detective seemed completely preoccupied with his precious burden and Sylvan was too busy piloting to speak.

Looking up from the controls, he cast a sidelong glance in Rast's direction. The male was cradling Nadiah in his lap, a look of concern on his usually stoic features. Sylvan wondered if Rast had any idea that the way he was acting was a classic Kindred mating behavior. The possessiveness, the unwillingness to trust her safety to another male, even one he knew to be trustworthy... Sylvan could almost swear he smelled a mating scent drifting from Rast's direction—something that only Kindred males exuded when they were trying to bond a female to them.

That, of course, was nonsense. Despite his truegreen eyes—(a green so dark it was almost black with a paler ring of green around the iris,) and his size (the detective was every bit as big and muscular as any Kindred warrior)—Rast was human. He'd been born and bred on the tiny blue and white planet called Earth and that was that, Sylvan was sure.

To be honest, he didn't like the human detective very much. Oh, he admired the dedication to duty that drove Rast to search for lost and hurting females, all right. But the male had started off on the wrong foot with him, as Sophia was wont to say. He'd refused to believe in Nadiah's gift of the Sight and had even accused her of being connected to some of the disappearances of the AllFather's intended victims. Lately he seemed less contentious but Sylvan still didn't like anyone who made slurs against his loved ones.

Of course, to look at Rast, anyone would think Nadiah was his loved one—his beloved. He held her as gently and anxiously as a new father holds a precious baby and the look of fear in his eyes when he's asked if she had a terminal disease had touched Sylvan against his will.

What's going on between the two of them? he wondered uneasily. Is Nadiah doing something she shouldn't? Sophia accused him of being a "cave man" but the fact was, Sylvan had been charged with maintaining and safeguarding his younger kinswoman's virtue and he took that charge very seriously. Virginity, while not essential to the Kindred, was highly prized on Tranq Prime. If Nadiah lost hers she would be nothing—less than nothing in the eyes of their people. Not to mention that her parents—his aunt and uncle—would disown her without it. She would be an outcast—the worst kind of pariah.

Sylvan didn't think that she'd been indiscreet with the human detective—Nadiah's eyes remained the same dark blue they had always been—but he couldn't help wondering what had brought about the change in Rast. Why else was he acting like a male about to enter the Claiming Period if he and Nadiah hadn't formed at least some kind of physical relationship?

He'd better not have touched her, Sylvan thought grimly, frowning at the other male. Rast, however, was completely oblivious to his scrutiny. He was still whispering Nadiah's name and stroking her pale cheek.

Sylvan shook his head and made a mental note to warn the human detective off once Nadiah was awake. Being human and not Kindred, he would only complicate the already complicated matter of the blood bond she had back on Tranq Prime. Only a Kindred male was strong enough to challenge such a bond and win—Rast would only get in the way.

But despite his doubts and worries, Sylvan couldn't help hearing the soft, coaxing way Rast spoke his kinswoman's name. "Nadiah," he murmured, brushing a strand of gold from her forehead and tucking it behind her ear. "Nadiah, come back to me. Please."

Chapter Two

Nadiah was dreaming—either that or she was having another vision. The Sight, that peculiar gift given by the Goddess to a chosen few of her daughters, had become such an ingrained part of her life that it was becoming difficult to tell the difference between precognition and a simple dream.

"Sometimes dreams and visions are one and the same," whispered a soft, soothing voice in her ear. "Watch and learn, daughter. Watch and learn and above all, remember."

Obediently, Nadiah turned her head in the direction the voice seemed to indicate. To her surprise, she saw this was a scenario she'd seen before—right before Sylvan and Sophia's bonding ceremony, in fact. Though at the time she had assumed the male in her dream was Merrick, Sylvan's friend, she now knew it was none other than the human detective.

Just as before, she saw Detective Rast standing before a throne in the Goddess's temple. Somehow, though she had never been there, she knew this was the original throne—built millennia ago on the original Kindred home world. The human was standing tall, his head thrown back, truegreen eyes blazing as though in response to some challenge. As in her previous vision, he was wearing the ceremonial robes of the First Kindred. But this time the robes were split in back, the soft white material ripped and hanging in ragged shreds to show the broad, tan expanse of his muscular back.

Nadiah had a spasm of horror. *Why am I seeing this? Is he about to be punished for some reason? Whipped or branded?*

Why—? Before the question could finish forming in her mind, she saw the tan skin along his shoulder blades ripple, almost as though something inside was trying to force its way out. Rast threw back his head, his face a mask of agony and then—

"Nadiah? Oh, thank God, she's waking up."

Nadiah, blinked and caught a fuzzy image of Olivia's pretty face hanging over her like an anxious moon. "Wha?" she whispered, her mouth too dry to speak properly. "Wha…what's wrong?"

"You fainted." It was Sylvan, also leaning over her and studying her with his cool, blue clinician's eyes. But far back in their icy depths there was worry as great as Olivia's, Nadiah could tell.

"I did?" She struggled to sit up—someone had brought her to the med station and put her in a healing cot for some reason—but many hands pushed her back down.

"Lie still. You scared me to death." It was Detective Rast, frowning at her sternly. "You were out like a light and I didn't know what the hell happened." He gave Sylvan an unfriendly look. "I still don't."

"You don't need to, Rast." The normally cool and collected Sylvan looked annoyed. "It doesn't concern you."

"The hell it doesn't." Rast glared at the other male. "It happened right in front of me. I'd say I have a right to know exactly what's going on."

"And I'd say you're wrong about that." Sylvan frowned. "Continuing in that vein, now that Nadiah is awake, I need to have a word with her. Privately. So if you could just step outside…?" He raised an eyebrow at Rast, who looked prepared to be stubborn. But before the human detective could open his mouth, Olivia took his arm.

"Come on, Detective. Let's tell everyone that Nadiah's going to be all right. They're all worried to death out there and I need someone to help spread the good news."

Rast frowned at her, obviously knowing he was being manipulated but not quite sure how to handle it. Finally he put a hand on Nadiah's knee and looked into her eyes directly. "Are you all right?" he asked, his deep voice surprisingly gentle. "Just tell me, sweetheart. I need to hear you say it before I go."

For some reason, Nadiah's heart started thudding in her chest and she found it hard to meet those truegreen eyes of his. "I...I'm fine," she finally managed to say. "Just fine."

"That's bullshit, but at least you're conscious." He frowned. "I get that I'm not wanted and your cousin here wants me to keep my nose out of your business, but if there's anything I can do—"

"Thank you, but no." Nadiah shook her head. "There's nothing you can do." Unless you can break a long standing blood bond, that is... But she didn't say it out loud. Rast was human, not Kindred. Of course he couldn't break the bond that bound her inextricably to her home world, so many thousands of light years away.

"All right, then." He patted her knee once and then withdrew. "I'll be outside if you need me. For anything." With a last frown at Sylvan, he followed Olivia out of the room, leaving Nadiah alone with him.

"Well?" Sylvan rounded on her the minute the door to the small exam room snicked closed. "It's the blood bond, isn't it? It's pulling you back toward Tranq Prime."

Nadiah sighed in defeat—there was no use denying it. "Yes," she whispered, nodding wearily. "I've been feeling it for awhile but lately it's getting worse. It's almost like he's yanking on it—trying to pull me back to him across space."

Sylvan frowned. "That's possible, I guess. Depending on the strength of the bond."

Nadiah laughed bitterly. "It's strong, all right. Mamam and Patro made sure of that when they linked me to Yo-dah." She sighed. "I guess I should stop calling him by that childhood nickname—it always makes him so mad. I'd better use his formal first name since it seems I have no choice but to join with him. Y'dex." The name tasted bitter on her tongue. "Y'dex, the one my parents chose for me. And they bound me to him as tightly as they could—that way they could be sure I wouldn't run off."

A reluctant grin twitched the corners of Sylvan's mouth. "I guess you proved them wrong on that score."

"Only for a little while." Nadiah's chest felt tight and there was a lump in her throat she couldn't swallow. "But now…now I'll have to go back. The pain is getting worse—it's like someone is twisting a knife right under my heart."

"I could tell you were hurting but I had no idea it was getting so bad." Sylvan sat on the edge of her cot, concern clear on his chiseled features. "Why didn't you tell me?"

"Because…" Nadiah's eyes burned and she blinked them rapidly, hoping to hold back the tears. "Because I knew you'd send me back. And I just wanted a little more time. I kept hoping I'd start dream sharing with someone—anyone. Because anyone would be better than Yo-dah—I mean, Y'dex. But…" The tears came now, she couldn't stop them. "But the only person I ever seem to dream about is Detective Rast."

Sylvan frowned and shook his head. "You can't dream share with a human, Nadiah. And even if you could, it wouldn't do you any good."

"I know." She sniffed and blotted her eyes on the sleeve of her tharp. It nuzzled her cheek comfortingly. "I know but it's like he's gotten in my head somehow and he doesn't...doesn't leave room for anyone else."

He sighed. "I'd tell you to make room but I'm afraid it wouldn't do any good. I can't let you stay here on the Mother Ship any longer—not when you're in so much pain."

"I know." Despair welled up inside her, threatening to drown her like a salty, bitter wave. "I know, Sylvan but it's so hard to go back. So—ahh!" Her words ended in a gasp as a bright bolt of pain stabbed her. It slid between her ribs like a red hot blade, just below the heart, and ripped downwards. Nadiah doubled over in agony, clutching futilely at her chest and belly. The searing pain took her breath away and for a moment the room around her went gray and pinpoints of light danced in front of her vision.

"Nadiah?" Sylvan pulled her upright, his deep voice filled with fear. "Are you all right?"

She tried to laugh but the sound came out sounding rusty and weak. "Never better, son of my mother's sister. I'm ready for a stroll around the sacred grove, can't you tell?"

Sylvan frowned. "This is no time to joke. We need to get you back to Tranq Prime and soon."

"I know." The pain had dissipated but Nadiah's forehead was damp with sweat and her mouth was dry. "I know it, Sylvan. I just hate to let him win—hate the fact that he has so much power over me."

"I hate it too," Sylvan said grimly. "If it were up to me, the whole practice of blood bonding would be abolished. It's archaic and cruel. And—"

"Sylvan?" Sophia's voice from the other side of the door interrupted his thought.

"What is it, Talana?" he asked. "You can come in."

Sophia slipped into the med room and closed the door behind her. "It's a call on the viewscreen," she said, and Nadiah saw that her green eyes were troubled.

Sylvan frowned. "A call from who? Whoever it is, tell them I will get back to them."

Sophia bit her lip. "I don't think this can wait. It's a call for Nadiah from her parents and..." She looked at Nadiah directly. "And I think your fiancé."

Nadiah felt her heart drop like a lead weight. "They're all calling me at once?"

Sophia nodded. "I'm afraid so. But, Nadiah, you're not well— you don't have to take the call."

"Yes, I do." Nadiah crossed her arms over her chest and shivered. This was the call she'd been avoiding—the moment she'd been dreading from the first second she stepped foot on the Mother Ship for Sophia and Sylvan's wedding. Now it could no longer be put off. "It's not just a call, Sophie," she said quietly. "It's a summons. And I must go."

* * * * *

Rast kept his head low and his eyes trained on the crack between the two medical drapes which shielded the cot where he was hiding. After leaving the room in the first place, he'd convinced Olivia that he needed to use the john and then slipped back to listen at Nadiah's door the minute she started talking to Lauren and Kat.

Eavesdropping wasn't exactly the most honorable way to get information but his time as a private detective had taught him that sometimes you got the intel anyway you could. Nadiah had a secret—a secret that was hurting her—and he intended to find out what the hell it was. When he was sure that Nadiah and Commander Sylvan and his wife were far down the corridor, he risked following.

As he slipped down the long curving metal hallway, he thought about what Sylvan and Nadiah had said. He hadn't gotten the specific details but it was clear she was being hurt by someone— being forced to go back to her home planet where she obviously didn't want to go by this blood bond, whatever it was.

The question is, who's hurting her? And how can I get to the son of a bitch to hurt him back? He didn't question the protective instinct that rose in him or the animal rage at the idea of someone causing Nadiah pain. He only knew that it needed to stop, now. And if no one else intended to do anything about it, he sure as hell would.

There was something else she'd said too—soft words that echoed in his heart as he jogged quietly along behind his targets. "...the only person I ever seem to dream about is Detective Rast," Nadiah had told her cousin. But there had been despair in her voice when she said it, as though that was a bad thing. And then Sylvan had said something about how she couldn't dream share with a human—whatever that was.

Rast couldn't figure out what dreaming had to do with anything. Come to that, he'd had a few interesting dreams about Nadiah as well. Most of them were ordinary enough—he saw her talking to her friends or walking down the halls of the Mother Ship. But there had been one where she was in the shower with hot, soapy water running down her small but firm breasts...

Stop it, he told himself sternly. No time for that now.

And indeed, there wasn't. Just ahead, he saw Nadiah, Sylvan and Sophia turn into the viewing room—a place he recognized from seeing it from the viewscreen of the Sarasota HKR building down on Earth. His first impulse was to go in with them and confront whoever was calling her. He'd threaten to pound them flatter than a pancake if they didn't leave her alone. But years of detective work and caution made him pause.

Get the facts first, he thought grimly, settling in the recessed doorway of the viewing room, just out of sight. Know your enemy.

Since the three people appearing on the large, rectangular viewscreen were obviously aliens from Nadiah's home world of Tranq Prime, he thanked fate he'd gotten a shot of the translation bacteria only offered on the Kindred Mother Ship. Originally he'd gotten it to help him understand different languages on Earth, now it appeared the bacteria would be much more helpful away from his home planet.

Two of the people were older and dressed in furs—obviously Nadiah's parents. Rast could see the family resemblance in their tall, slender bodies and blonde hair, not to mention the mother's aristocratic features. But there the resemblance ended. The coldness in their blue eyes was nothing like the lively warmth that animated Nadiah's—at least when she wasn't at death's door. And the look of stern disapproval on their haughty faces made it clear that she was in some kind of trouble.

But as compelling as the parents were, Rast found his gaze drawn to the young man who stood between them the most. He was tall and thin but there was a wiry strength to his muscles that couldn't be discounted—obviously he was stronger than he looked. His hair was a blond so fair it was almost white and his eyebrows and eyelashes were even lighter. They seemed to melt into his pale skin giving him the odd, lashless look of a white rabbit.

Like Nadiah's father, he was wearing the traditional male attire of Tranq Prime—a furry skirt looking thing Rast had learned was called a tharp and fur boots made from the hide of a vranna. The boots and tharp were both dark purple and they should have looked ridiculous on his thin, pale form. But the young man wore them with a patrician air of belonging, an unconscious arrogance that somehow put him above common concerns.

Know your enemy, Rast thought again, studying the young man closely. Could this be Nadiah's intended—the one called Yo-dah or Y'dex that she'd spoken briefly about back in Sarasota? Rast had thought the guy's name was unintentionally hilarious but he had no urge to laugh now.

There was a greedy look in Y'dex's pale, bulging blue eyes as he looked at Nadiah's slender form. The look of a rightful owner about to claim his property. And the property, apparently, was Nadiah.

Chapter Three

"Mamam… Patro," Nadiah greeted her parents. "And Yo-dah—I mean, Y'dex," she added reluctantly, nodding at the tall, lanky figure of her fiancé. "How are you?"

Y'dex sneered at her, his thin face twisting in an ugly way. "I think the question is how are you, my dear one? Are you feeling quite well, lately?"

Nadiah lifted her chin. "Yes, perfectly well, thank you."

He glared at her. "You're lying."

"Of course not." Nadiah shook her head, determined not to let him know how she really felt. "I'm fine. So if you simply called to ask about my well being, you can be assured of my health and we can end this conversation now."

Y'dex's face twisted into an angry sneer. "You know that isn't why we called."

"Nadiah, it's time you came home," her mother cut in. "We let you go to attend Sylvan's bonding ceremony but that was ages ago. Now that it's over, you need to get back to Tranq Prime."

"You didn't let me go—I escaped." Nadiah crossed her arms over her chest. "What makes you think I'm in a hurry to come home again?"

Her father frowned. "You will come home, young lady. We have your bonding ceremony all planned."

"For the second time," her mother emphasized, frowning. "And we expect you to be here this time."

Nadiah's heart fisted in her chest, but she tried to keep her voice even and light. "Let's be reasonable about this, Maman, Patro. Times have changed. I don't want to be bonded to Yo—Y'dex anymore and I'm sure he doesn't really want to be bonded to me."

"That's where you're wrong." Y'dex smiled at her nastily. "I very much want our bonding to take place, my lovely Nadiah. I am anxiously awaiting it—almost as anxiously as the bonding night that will follow."

"Never." Nadiah couldn't keep the revulsion out of her voice. "I will never give myself to you."

"Oh, you won't have to give yourself, my lovely." Y'dex's grin turned suddenly malicious and cruel. "I'll be more than happy to take you."

"Maman, Patro, do you hear this?" Nadiah appealed to her parents. "Do you hear what he's saying? He's planning to rape me. Don't you care what's going to happen to me once your precious bonding ceremony is completed?"

Her father looked uncomfortable but her mother merely frowned. "Our law recognizes no such crime after bonding. As your mate, Y'dex may do what he wishes and you must not complain."

Sophia, who had been standing beside Sylvan and squeezing his hand convulsively, could apparently no longer be silent. "So you're saying that once they're married, he can do whatever he wants to her and nobody cares? What's wrong with you people?"

Nadiah's mother sniffed. "If it isn't Sophia Waterhouse from that barbaric little backwater of a planet, Earth. What right have you to judge us, surface dweller?"

Sophia's cheeks turned pink with anger. "I have every right! You're forcing Nadiah into a loveless marriage where she's going to be abused. Now who's barbaric?"

"Talana..." Sylvan stroked her hair soothingly. "Gently, my darling," he murmured. "Let me try." Stepping forward, he nodded at Nadiah's parents. "Greetings, Zeelah, Grennly."

Nadiah's Maman and Patro nodded back genially enough and for a moment Nadiah felt a stab of hope. Maybe they would listen to Sylvan—he was older, an adult in their eyes instead of a naughty, wayward child who had run away from home—which was how they viewed her.

"Nadiah is happy here on the Mother Ship," Sylvan began, obviously trying to pick his words carefully. "And she's safe, under my protection. I do not think she wishes to return to Tranq Prime to be bonded. And since the blood bond was made when she was still a child, before she knew her own mind and heart, I think you should cancel the commitment you made on her behalf and let her go."

"Let her go?" Nadiah's mother looked horrified. "And dissolve the connection we've planned with the Licklow family for years? Lose the status of joining with such a prestigious clan and adding our bloodline to theirs? Never!"

"Besides, Kindred," Y'dex put in. "You know as well as anyone else you can't simply cancel a blood bond. It must be challenged and broken." He raised one nearly-white eyebrow at Nadiah. "Have you found a Kindred champion to challenge me, my lovely one?"

Nadiah hung her head. Goddess, how she wished she could answer that question in the affirmative. But there was no one to help—no one to undertake the burden she'd had thrust upon her at such an early age. She was on her own.

Y'dex laughed hatefully. "I'll take your silence for a 'no.' Not that I'm surprised—why would anyone but me bother with the likes of you? You're lucky, you know. I could have been blood bonded to any female in our grotto but my parents chose you."

"Oh yes, I'm so lucky. My whole life is about to be taken from me—I'll live in bondage to a male I hate just because our parents want to keep our bloodlines pure." Hot tears of rage and despair were rising in her eyes but Nadiah blinked them back fiercely, not wanting to let him see her cry. "Can't you...can't you just let me go?" she asked, trying to make her voice softer. "I don't want you, Y'dex. And deep down, I don't think you really want me. Please, go find someone else and let me live my life."

"And live with an unfulfilled blood bond hanging over me for the rest of my days?" He glared at her. "I think not. Besides, Nadiah, I do want you. I intend to show you just how much in the very near future."

The greedy, leering way he was looking at her made Nadiah's stomach lurch, and her skin turned cold with fear. "I'll fight you," she whispered, clenching her hands into fists at her sides. "Every step of the way, I'll fight. I swear to the Goddess if you lay so much as a finger or anything else on me I'll cut it off—I don't care if we're bonded or not."

Her fiancée's expression went from greedy to enraged—his nearly white skin flushing an angry red. "You think you can fight me? You think you can fight this?"

He made a motion with his right hand. Curling it into a fist, he dragged it back toward himself, almost as though he was yanking on a rope. At once Nadiah felt the burning blade slip between her ribs again. It was worse this time, like someone was stirring her guts with a red hot spoon.

She wanted to stand straight and tall, to stare into those hateful, bulging blue eyes defiantly, but she couldn't—the pain was too great. With a low cry, she doubled over, fully expecting to hit her head on the floor and not caring if she did.

Instead, a pair of strong arms caught her and she was picked up and held against a muscular chest.

Sylvan? she thought hazily but the male holding her smelled wrong—Sylvan's scent was sharp and this male had a deep, dark musk that was somehow familiar though she had a feeling she had never smelled it quite so strongly before. Also, she could see Sylvan and Sophia standing there arguing angrily with her parents and fiancée on the viewscreen. They seemed to be telling Y'dex to stop his assault on her, to stop yanking on the blood bond. But her fiancée only laughed and twisted his fist some more, causing a fresh wave of agony to roll over her. Her back arched helplessly and she gasped, tears pouring from her eyes.

"Stop it!" The full throated roar was coming from the male who was holding her. It echoed through her skull and rattled her bones as her ear was pressed to his deep chest. "You fucking stop it right now you little bastard!"

Nadiah felt herself being carried closer to the viewscreen, close enough to see the shocked looks on her parents' faces and the angry sneer on Y'dex's.

"And who is this?" her fiancée demanded, staring at her rescuer. "I thought Nadiah couldn't find a Kindred to be her champion."

"She found me." The pain was less now, allowing Nadiah to think. Could it be…was it Detective Rast holding her and shouting at Y'dex? She looked up at him in wonder and saw that his truegreen eyes were burning with rage. They seemed almost to glow in his face with a strange, protective light.

"One of the First Kindred. Imagine." Y'dex raised an eyebrow. "I thought your kind had all but died out."

"You're the one who's going to die out, buddy," Rast snarled. "I'll come with Nadiah and meet your challenge but I swear to you here and now, if you ever inflict that pain on her again I will end you. Do I make myself abso-fucking-lutely clear?"

Y'dex's already pale face went even whiter but there were still spots of angry red on his thin cheekbones. "How dare you speak to me in that manner? I am her intended."

"No, you're not. She never intended to marry you—she never wanted you." Rast glared at him and Nadiah thought she saw murder in his truegreen eyes. "And I don't really think you want her either—except the way a mean little boy wants a pet so he can beat it and hurt it. Well, Nadiah's not going to be your pet. Her life is worth more than that—a hell of a lot more."

Y'dex's face grew dark red but his voice was calm. "We'll see about that, won't we Kindred? I will meet you in my home grotto in one standard week. There I will best you in the three sacred challenges. Do you accept?"

"Rast," Sylvan murmured urgently, plucking at the human detective's elbow but Rast shook him off.

"I'll be there," he promised grimly. "And in the mean time, keep your psychic paws off Nadiah. No more pain—got it?"

Y'dex grinned nastily. "As to that, she is still my...what did you call her? Oh yes, my little pet until you attempt to break out bond. And as such, I can do with her what I want." He made another twisting, yanking motion with his fist and Nadiah cried out as the burning knife stabbed her again.

"You son of a bitch." Rast's voice was thick with rage. "I'll make you pay for that. I swear to God I will."

"Come and try. I look forward to it." And with that, the connection was broken and Nadiah's fiancée and parents mercifully disappeared from the viewscreen. She gasped in relief—and then fainted.

* * * * *

"Well this is a hell of a mess. Do you realize what you've done?" Commander Sylvan was clearly upset but Rast didn't care.

"Yeah, I know what I did. I stepped up and challenged the bastard who was hurting her which is more than you were doing." Rast cradled Nadiah protectively close to his chest. "What the hell, Sylvan—she's your baby cousin. Could you do more than just ask nicely?"

"Don't you think I wanted to help her?" Sylvan's normally impassive face was nearly anguished. "Of course I did, but I couldn't. Only an unmated, unrelated male can break the blood bond. A Kindred male—which you are not."

"You think I give a damn about that?" Rast demanded. "Besides, I don't have to be Kindred to take on that little bastard. I'll snap him over my knee like a twig."

"Just because you have Kindred size and strength doesn't mean you have Kindred blood." Sylvan ran a hand through his spiky blond hair impatiently. "There is more than just the challenge of strength to get through, Rast. You'll also have to endure the challenge of wills and the challenge of blood. Which you will almost certainly lose."

Rast frowned. "What makes you so sure? You know, you guys talk a good fight and you're eager enough to get married to Earth women but you clearly have some kind of superiority complex going on."

"The weakness isn't in your heart—you clearly have the courage of a vranna." Sylvan sighed. "But your blood—Kindred blood has special compounds in it that give extra strength of will and mind as well as physical strength. They're also what enable a Kindred to break the blood bond—one of the strongest symbiotic soul bonds in the known universe."

"Great—so you have superhuman blood and I don't." Rast shrugged. "What harm can there be in me at least trying?"

"The harm is that you could die trying." Commander Sylvan looked at him soberly. "And even if you did somehow manage to break the bond, there's a small but real chance that Nadiah could die as well. She's been bonded to Y'dex since she was six cycles old. If her soul becomes untethered from his and has no other, stronger soul to anchor to, it's possible she could lose consciousness and literally drift away."

Rast felt sick. "You mean even if I succeed I could kill her?"

Sylvan nodded. "Unfortunately, yes. It's not likely but there is that possibility."

"I don't care about that."

The soft voice came from the girl in his arms. Rast looked down in surprise to see that Nadiah's lovely deep blue eyes were open. She struggled slightly against him and he helped her stand, keeping an arm around her shoulders just in case.

"Now, what did you say?" he asked, frowning.

"I said, I don't care if I die." Her face was filled with calm desperation. "I'd rather die than live with that horrible male the rest of my life." She looked up at Rast earnestly. "Are you serious? Will you really act as my champion and challenge the blood bond on my behalf?"

He nodded slowly. "Yes. Absolutely."

Nadiah sighed, looking troubled. "I know I should ask you why or try to change your mind but I'm desperate."

"I can see that," Rast said dryly. "He's literally got you on the end of a leash."

A spasm of hatred passed over her delicate features. "As you said, I'm his pet. But I don't want to be—not any more."

"Of course you don't, honey!" Sophia came forward and gave Nadiah a quick hug. "But you shouldn't say you want to die—that isn't right."

"How could I live as Y'dex's mate?" Nadiah demanded. "Being abused every day and...and raped every night?" She looked ill. "That's no kind of life."

Rast felt a surge of protectiveness for the slender alien girl at his side. "That's not going to happen, sweetheart. I won't let it happen."

Sylvan sighed and shook his head. "I hope you can prevent it, Detective Rast—I really do. Though I don't see how you can without Kindred blood in your veins."

"I'll find a way." Rast squeezed Nadiah's shoulders gently. "Believe me, I will."

She looked up at him, her blue eyes troubled. "There's something else you should know before you commit yourself to my cause. While I was unconscious just now, I had a vision."

In the past Rast would have ridiculed her statement but now he knew she was the genuine article—an actual, honest to God psychic—so he listened with respect. "Tell me about it," he said quietly. "What did you see?"

Nadiah shook her head. "It wasn't a seeing exactly—not like when I saw you with your sister. It's something I know—a premonition. "

"Okay then." Rast stroked a strand of golden hair out of her eyes and looked at her seriously. "What do you know?"

"That if you do this—if you leave Earth and come with me—you may never return to your home planet again." Nadiah looked at him with troubled eyes. "I don't know if it's because you might die or just that you'll be busy with other matters. But I thought you should know before you committed yourself to my cause."

Her statement shook him—there was no hiding that. But Rast had no doubt whatsoever. For some reason he belonged with the slender, blonde alien girl. He couldn't explain it, even to himself, but the idea of leaving her, or of letting her leave without him and go millions of light years away to get married to a man she didn't love, made him cold inside. "There's nothing to think about," he said firmly. "I'm coming with you."

Nadiah smiled at him gratefully and Rast though he would walk over hot coals barefooted to see that warm, lovely expression on her face. It occurred to him that he'd never felt this way about a woman before—what was going on? He didn't know and at the moment, he didn't really care. He just knew he wanted to make Nadiah happy so he could see that look on her face forever.

"Thank you, Rast," she murmured." But I think you should go down to the surface one more time and say goodbye to anyone you might miss before we go."

He nodded reluctantly. "Okay, you're right about that. I should probably see my folks one more time."

"I'll come with you," Nadiah said but Sylvan shook his head.

"No, you won't. Not when Y'dex could attack you through the blood bond again at any moment. I don't want you down on the surface of a strange world in your condition."

Rast shook his head. "It's all right—I can go by myself. Just get me a driver and promise not to leave without me. It shouldn't take long."

"I'll fly you down myself." Commander Sylvan stepped forward, frowning. "And you'll fly us both back. Some of the smaller Kindred ships aren't much more complicated than an Earth car to drive but if you've never flown before, you're going to need some lessons before you start out for Tranq Prime."

Rast grinned. "I've always wanted to fly."

"Now's your chance." Sylvan clapped him on the shoulder. "Come on. We can talk as we go, but first I want a small sample of your blood. I'll get the lab working while we're gone and see if there's anything I can give you to increase your chances."

"Sounds good to me—let's go." He nodded and Sylvan led the way out of the viewing room. As they left, Rast cast one last look over his shoulder and saw Nadiah watching him. Her deep, otherworldly blue eyes were filled with emotion—nervousness, fear, uncertainty, but most of all hope. *She's counting on me, Rast though, and the idea made his heart swell in his chest.*

He swore to himself then and there, that he wouldn't let her down. That Nadiah's hopes and the trust she had placed in him would be fulfilled in every way, even if it killed him to do it.

Chapter Four

"I still don't understand why he's doing this." Olivia looked perplexed. "I thought he didn't like you."

Nadiah looked down at her hands. "I didn't think he did, either. I guess maybe he was just so angry at the way Y'dex was treating me that he couldn't stop himself."

"He was really angry," Sophie, who was sitting on the other side of Nadiah, put in. "You should have seen him—he looked like an avenging angel when he scooped her up and started shouting at that nasty Yo-dah…er, Y'dex."

"That's his formal first name," Nadiah said tiredly to answer the other girls' confused looks. "Yo-dah is a childhood nickname. But we're not children anymore."

"Tomato-tomahto," said Olivia. "I'm still wondering about Rast."

"Me too," Kat said. "So let me get this straight…Rast got so angry at the way Y'…Y'…Y'whatever-his-name-is was treating you, he decided to risk his life and maybe never see his home world and loved ones again just to get even? Sure, that's one explanation." She lounged back against the cushions scattered on the floor, looking skeptical.

They were all in Sophia's suite, spending a few more hours together before Nadiah had to go. But the thought of going back to Tranq Prime, even with a champion to challenge the blood bond, was making her more and more nervous.

"What do you mean, Kat?" she asked, frowning.

"Do I really have to spell it out?" Kat raised one auburn eyebrow at her. "I think Detective Rast has the hots for you, hon."

"The 'hots'?" Nadiah shook her head, frowning. "You mean you think his internal temperature rises when I'm around?"

Kat looked like she wanted to laugh. "Among other things."

"He was giving you some pretty significant looks," Sophia said thoughtfully. "Maybe Kat is right."

"I don't think so." Nadiah shook her head. "I mean, I don't see how he could, um, feel that way about me. You should see the way I've treated him. I shouted at him and slapped him. And then I had a vision where I brought up his beloved older sister who died. After uncovering a wound like that, I'm surprised he'll even talk to me, let alone act as my champion."

"Well you must be doing something right." Lauren came bustling up with a tray of homemade muffins. "Otherwise he wouldn't be willing to risk life and limb to save you."

"Here's an idea," Olivia said thoughtfully. "Didn't you say he's dedicated his life to saving women?"

Nadiah nodded. "Ever since his sister was killed."

"My mom said he was tireless when he was investigating my disappearance," Lauren put in. "He really takes a lost or hurting female very seriously."

"Maybe that's it then," Liv said. "Maybe he sees all women — you included — as extensions of his sister. He couldn't save her but maybe he feels that if he saves enough other women, he'll get over it." She shrugged. "Or something like that."

"Thanks Ms. Pop Psychology for that interesting analysis," Kat said dryly. "But I still think the simplest solution is the right one — Detective Rast has ants in his pants for Nadiah, here."

Nadiah shook her head. "My translation bacteria must be acting up. Did you just say that Detective Rast has insects in his trousers?"

Kat wiggled her eyebrows. "Among other things," she said again.

Sophie laughed and shook her head. "Kat's just being silly, Nadiah. Don't pay any attention."

"All joking aside, do you really think he'll be able to help me?" Nadiah asked her friends. "I mean, without any Kindred blood in his veins?"

"In my experience when a man is determined enough, he can do anything." Lauren patted her shoulder and offered her a muffin. "And from what you've said, Detective Rast is plenty determined."

"Amen to that." Kat popped a bite-sized muffin into her mouth. "Lauren, these are to die for."

Lauren smiled. "Thanks—they're made with tanka berries from Rageron. I kind of think they taste like a cross between a hazelnut and a cranberry. Zairn loves them."

"I just bet he does. You've really mastered this recipe." Kat grinned at her. "I mean, do you just chop the nuts up or do you have to grind them into submission or something?"

Lauren's creamy light brown cheeks turned dark pink in an obvious blush. "Stop being so bad, Kat!"

"Sorry, doll, I just have to get in a few digs wherever I can." Kat popped another muffin. "You have to understand that before you came along, my love life with the whole ménage thing was the kinkiest thing going. Now you get to wear the kinky crown for awhile."

Liv raised an eyebrow. "The kinky crown? Seriously, Kat, that sounds like a bad romance novel."

"Or a really cheesy Lifetime movie," Sophie put in.

Olivia laughed. "Yeah, something about beauty pageants gone bad, with all the contestants forced to be sex slaves to really stern but extremely hot masters. Awful."

"Yeah, but you know you'd watch it if it came on," Kat pointed out. She looked back at Lauren. "So does this recipe call for any whipping cream?"

"Kat!" Lauren threw a still hot muffin at her and Kat ducked. Olivia caught it instead and took a bite.

"Yum! Delicious but it needs dill pickle icing."

"Ugh, I wish you'd never started with that," Sophia made a face and looked at Lauren. "Seriously, she wants to eat it on everything now."

Nadiah laughed along with them as the topic of conversation turned to Olivia's pregnancy and her strange food cravings but inside she was still troubled. Why was the human detective willing to risk his life to save her from a lifetime of bondage? Was she really just another part of the quest that had started for him when his beloved sister, Jessie was murdered? Or could there be another, deeper reason? Did he care for her as Kat seemed to think? And more importantly, did she want him to care for her?

I've always dreamed of bonding with a Kindred warrior, she thought, chewing one of Lauren's muffins thoughtfully. Living aboard the Mother Ship, seeing new things and new people all the time as the ship moved on to new trades. Would she really be willing to give that up to be bonded to a human? Would she want to live on the little blue and white ball called Earth for the rest of her days?

Once again she tried to picture her ideal life, the one with a handsome Blood Kindred husband and two or three little boys that looked just like him running around. But somehow, she could only see Rast—his stern features looking like they'd been carved from granite, his truegreen eyes narrowed as he roared at Y'dex to leave her alone. Just remembering how it had felt to be held against his chest, his warm, masculine musk invading her senses, made her heart start to pound and her palms damp.

Stop being so stupid, she lectured herself, taking another bite of the muffin, which she hardly tasted. Olivia is almost certainly right—he's helping me because he sees me and all females, really, as an extension of his sister.

For whatever reason he was helping her, Nadiah felt extremely grateful. But she couldn't help wondering if she was just a symbol to Detective Rast...or if she meant something more to him.

Chapter Five

"You're picking this up remarkably fast." Sylvan eyed the way Rast was handling the controls with reluctant admiration. He'd given the human a brief demonstration before they left the docking bay and Rast had showed such instinctive skill that he'd decided to let him take the steering yoke on the way down to Earth as well as on the trip back.

The human detective shrugged, his eyes fixed on the blue and white ball of the Earth, growing rapidly in the viewscreen. "Not much different than driving a stick. I've been doing that since I was fifteen."

"I see." Sylvan nodded. "Ah, who are you going to visit, if you don't mind me asking? Just your parents?"

Rast nodded. "That's about all there is. I have an ex but we lost touch after the divorce. Even if I could to find her, I'm sure she wouldn't care if I decided to go to a galaxy far, far away." He barked a laugh. "Hell, she'd probably be glad to hear it."

Sylvan frowned. "So you've been bonded before?"

"Yeah, but for less than a year. It was ages ago, back when I was still with the PD. She claimed I was married to my work." He sighed. "Sad to say, she was probably right. I don't blame her for leaving my sorry ass—I never really did right by her. Never gave her the attention she deserved, so she found somebody who would."

Sylvan shook his head. "I've heard that humans do such things—that they abandon their mates and find new ones on a regular basis. But to hear you talk about it so casually..."

"Why?" Rast shot him a look. "You guys don't have divorce or separation?"

"We form a bond—both mental and emotional with our females," Sylvan explained. "Breaking it is nearly impossible."

"So you're stuck for life with one woman with no way out?" Rast frowned. "You know, if you'd told me that a month ago I would have thought it was a nightmare. Now...now I'm not so sure."

"If you're thinking of Nadiah when you say that, you can forget it," Sylvan said flatly.

"Oh yeah?" Rast shot him an angry glance. "And why is that? Because I'm not Kindred I'm not good enough for her?"

"Being Kindred or not has nothing to do with it," Sylvan said coolly. "Tell me why you're doing this. Why are you undertaking Nadiah's cause and challenging her blood bond?"

"I, uh..." The human detective looked uncomfortable. "It's the right thing to do, all right? I couldn't just let her go off and get married to that snot nosed little punk who's obviously going to beat on her the first chance he gets. Just thinking about..." He shook his head. "I just couldn't let her go. I mean, I couldn't let her face him alone."

Sylvan raised an eyebrow. "So you're only concerned for her safety? You have no other motives for championing her cause?"

"I don't know, all right?" Rast squeezed the steering yoke in obvious frustration, causing the little ship to wobble alarmingly. "I've never felt this way before about a woman—not even my ex. Especially not my ex. It's goddamn confusing."

"And that's why I don't want you forming a permanent relationship with Nadiah." Sylvan pointed a finger at him. "Confusion and a vague desire to do the right thing aren't enough to base a lasting relationship on—especially since you've already abandoned one mate."

Rast groaned. "Look, I told you—she left me. Besides, what is this, The Scarlet Letter?"

"I know the book you're speaking of," Sylvan said. "And it was the male—the one who abandoned his pregnant female—who should have been shunned and cast out of society. What he did was shameful and wrong—she was blameless."

"Blameless, huh?" Rast's eyes flashed. "It takes two to tango, buddy."

"Well you're not going to be giving Nadiah any dancing lessons—understood?" Sylvan pinned him with a cold glare. "I mean it, Rast, she's a virgin and she's going to stay that way. Do you understand?"

The human's eyes widened with surprise. "You sure about that? I mean, she's what—twenty-three? Twenty-four? Most women have done some exploring by that age."

Sylvan felt red rage rising up in him but somehow he held onto his temper. "Nadiah just came of age recently," he said in a slightly strangled voice. "And yes, I'm sure her virtue is intact. Look, Rast..." He turned fully so he could give the other male the full weight of his glare. "Virginity is very, very important to my people. If Nadiah loses hers to anyone but her bonded mate...well, let's just say what happened to Hester Prynne would look mild in comparison to what will happen to her. The entire community would shun her and on Tranq Prime, that is no laughing matter. She'd be cast out in the cold—literally."

"Okay, okay, I get it. Hands off." Rast raised one hand in a conciliatory gesture that made the ship sway again. "But how would they even know?" he asked. "I mean, unless Tranq Prime females get pregnant every time or something."

"Her scent would be altered—that's immediately obvious to a Kindred," Sylvan said, still frowning at him. "But beyond that, her eyes would also change color."

"Her eyes?" Rast looked at him as though to be sure he wasn't joking. "Seriously? Would they turn green or orange or something?"

"No." Sylvan shook his head. "They'd either get darker or lighter—only by a shade or two but enough to make it obvious to anyone who knew her before what had happened."

"Wow." Rast shook his head. "That's bizarre. So her family would take one look at her eyes and know right away she'd been, uh, up to something."

"I would know," Sylvan emphasized. "And as her protector, I would certainly take action."

"I said I wouldn't touch her, didn't I?" Rast shot him an unfriendly look. "Look, Sylvan, I'm not the type to take what isn't offered. You ought to be a hell of a lot more worried about that little bastard waiting for her on your home world. It's pretty clear what he has in mind if he gets his hands on her."

"I know." Sylvan felt like someone had dumped a fist-sized lump of ice in his stomach. "I can't bear to think of her being treated like that. Taken that way," he confessed in a low voice. "She is, as you say, my baby cousin. I used to watch her while her parents were away at functions and sing her to sleep when she had nightmares. The idea of that Goddess-forsaken son of a motherless vorteg hurting her makes me so angry I could kill."

Rast squeezed the steering yoke until his knuckles went white. "I know the feeling," he growled. "That's exactly what I was thinking when I agreed to take the challenge—that I wanted to kill that little son of a bitch for hurting her. Well, except for the vorteg part." He looked at Sylvan. "What the hell is a vorteg, anyway?"

"A low, stinking creature that looks like a cross between a snake and a spider," Sylvan explained. "It's about as long as your forearm and covered in greasy brownish-gray hair."

"Ugh." Rast frowned. "Okay, your cursing just took on a whole new meaning. I get it now." He gave Sylvan a look. "And I get the idea that Nadiah is off limits. So don't worry—I'll take good care of her."

"You'd better," Sylvan said grimly. "If I find you've changed the color of her eyes, you'll have more than a blood bond challenge to worry about. No other male from Tranq Prime will have her if she's defiled—especially by an off worlder."

"Defiled, huh?" Rast shook his head. "You know, Sylvan, back on Earth we humans always thought that when we finally made contact with an alien race, they'd be amazingly advanced. But the things I'm hearing from you—arranged marriages, women are worthless without their virginity—well, it sounds more like the dark ages to me." He frowned. "It's a hell of a shame."

"I never said I agreed with such ideas," Sylvan said tightly. "I only said that they're prevalent on my home planet. A planet that Nadiah may well have to return to and live on the rest of her days. I just want to be sure she can do that without shame or regret."

"I understand" Rast said tightly. "And you have my word I won't, uh, change the color of her eyes. All right?"

Sylvan stared at him a long time. "All right," he said, nodding at last. "I believe you're a male of your word. So I am charging you with my kinswoman's safety and virtue. Please know this is not a charge I make lightly—nor should you take it lightly. Nadiah's death, injury, or deflowerment will be on your head, no matter who commits the acts that lead to such consequences."

"You Kindred play hard ball, don't you?" Rast muttered. He cleared his throat and spoke formally. "I accept your charge, Commander Sylvan. I swear to guard your cousin's life and virginity with my life."

"Thank you." Sylvan felt marginally better.

"Shake on it?" Rast held out a hand and Sylvan clasped it briefly, feeling the steady pressure of the other male's grip. Then he let go.

"You're going to need both hands for landing," he said, pointing at the curving, blue side of the Earth which now filled the viewscreen. "Pay attention—this is the tricky part."

Rast sat up straighter and took a firm grip on the steering yoke. "I'm ready—let's do this."

As they hurtled downward, into the Earth's atmosphere, Sylvan instructed him on landing procedure and watched the human male react with fluid grace and speed as each new challenge was thrown in his path. Rast seemed to handle himself with a natural ease that stood him in good stead while dealing with dangerous situations.

Sylvan only hoped it wouldn't desert him when it really counted and Nadiah's life was on the line.

Chapter Six

"Hi, Mom, it's me," Rast called, stepping into the large white Victorian house on Baker street where he'd lived as a child. His voice echoed in the hallway and he wondered for a moment if his parents were out. But his mom's car was in the driveway and she usually parked it in the garage when they were going somewhere. She must be home. "Mom?" he called again, walking deeper into his house...deeper into his childhood.

There was the bright, sunny kitchen where Jessie had made him pancakes in the shape of Mickey Mouse on Saturdays. And the breakfast nook with its built in circular booth and worn plaid cushions where she had tutored him in math. One of the paintings she'd done in art class—a watercolor field of jewel-tone flowers—was still hanging above the nook. Rast felt his heart throb when he saw her familiar loopy initials, J.R., scrawled in one corner.

God, Jessie, he thought. You're still here. Everywhere I look it's like you never left. Like you might walk right back in at any minute and call me "kiddo" and ruffle my hair.

There was a lump in his throat he couldn't swallow and suddenly his eyes were burning. How long had it been since he'd been back to this house? Five years? Ten? He usually made it a point to meet his parents out somewhere—take them to a nice, fancy restaurant, eat and catch up and little—then leave. That way he could keep things calm and impersonal and he didn't have to visit his old home or remember that the entire house was a shrine to his dead sister.

Touches of Jessie's bright personality were everywhere. Rast saw another as he walked into the music room—a framed picture of her laughing smile and long auburn hair standing on the baby grand piano where she'd practiced constantly. But despite her ghostly presence, her death was a forbidden topic of conversation. His parents didn't speak about it to anyone, and they didn't want anyone else to talk about it either.

"Jessie..." he whispered thickly, picking up her picture and looking down at it. He remembered the pose well—it had been taken in their backyard just days before her death. How happy she had been—how alive.

I took this picture to bed with me for an entire year after you died. After he killed you, he thought, tracing the bright arch of one auburn brow with his thumb. That and the shirt you were wearing before you went to the party. It still smelled like your perfume—like fresh cut flowers. I wrapped it around me and pretended it was your arms, hugging me. Oh, Jessie...

Droplets of moisture fell on his dead sister's face and slid down the shining glass, making it look like Jessie was crying. Crying for all the years she'd missed. For the little brother she'd left behind, so lost without her...

"Adam? Whatever are you doing here at this time of day?"

Rast nearly dropped the picture in surprise. Holding it tightly, he turned to see his mother standing there to one side of the piano.

Carolyn Rast was getting along in years but she still stood tall and straight, unstooped by age. Her hair, once as red as Jessie's, was now a lovely silvery-white. It was swept into an elegant coif at the back of her head and the suit she was wearing wouldn't have been out of place in an upscale business meeting.

"I said, what are you doing here?" she repeated. "And what are you doing with that?" She gave the picture of Jessie in his hand a disapproving look, as though she'd caught him bringing something dirty into the house.

"Just remembering," Rast said. He put the picture back on the baby grand carefully. "Look, Mom, I came by because we need to talk."

"Oh?" She raised an eyebrow at him. "Very well. Come into the study."

Rast followed her into the bookshelf lined room with its sober, overstuffed leather furniture. The study was where his father had always doled out punishment. Being summoned there to talk made him feel like a kid all over again—one who had transgressed one of the many house rules and was soon to be spanked or grounded.

"Where's Dad?" he asked as his mother settled herself into a deep leather armchair with brass buttons and indicated that he should take the one across from it.

She sighed and steepled her fingers. "Well, that's something I need to talk to you about. I kept meaning to call you and somehow I just never got around to it…"

Rast felt a quick spasm of panic. "Is he sick? Is he in the hospital or something?"

"No, I think he's in the Bahamas. Or wherever it is old fools go to chase young women." His mother shook her head. "Anyway, the point is, we're getting a divorce."

"What?" Rast couldn't have been more shocked if she'd told him his father was down at the funeral home and she hadn't gotten around to picking a casket yet. "You're what?" he said again.

"Honestly, Adam, I don't know why you're so surprised. You know things haven't been right between us for a long time. Not since..." His mother shook her head. "Not for a long time."

"Not since Jessie was killed, you mean," Rast said in a low voice. "Don't make that face, Mom—you know it's true."

"That doesn't make it a polite topic of conversation." She frowned at him reprovingly. "So kindly stop talking about distasteful subjects and tell me what you came to say."

Rast took a deep breath and tried to clear his head. "I...I'm leaving,

he said at last. "Not just the city or the country. I'm leaving Earth. I'm going in a Kindred ship thousands of light years away and I don't know when I'll be back. In fact, someone told me I might...might not be back. I'm sorry, Mom."

For a moment she just sat there, staring at him. Then she seemed to shake herself and sighed. "Don't be, Adam. You barely come around anyway—I'm sure we'll manage without you."

Her accusation was true but it still stung. "Thanks, Mom. I'll miss you too," he said dryly.

She nodded. "I'm certain you will."

"Don't you want to know why I'm going?" He felt like a little kid asking for approval, showing her the A plus on his math test or the Excellent on his book report and hoping for a positive response—any response. But as usual, his mother didn't give him one.

"I'm sure you have your reasons." She looked down at her steepled fingers and then up at him again. "Adam, if you're serious about leaving I feel there's something I ought to tell you. Something you should know."

"What?" His heart was suddenly beating in his throat. "Is it about Jessie? Something you didn't tell me when I was a kid?"

"Something like that but not what you're thinking." His mother gave him that reproving look again. The look that said he was discussing "distasteful" matters and should let them drop.

"What then?" Rast was genuinely bewildered.

She took a deep breath. "Adam, I don't know how to tell you this so I'll just say it. You were adopted."

"What?" The word should have come out as a full throated roar but it was a bewildered whisper instead. "What?" he asked again, feeling sure he must have misheard.

"It's true." His mother nodded briskly. "We got you for Jessie. Your father and I were both so busy with our careers and she wanted something to play with—something to love. We offered her a cat or a dog but what she wanted most was a baby—a little brother."

Rast shook his head in disbelief. "So you took her down to the local adoption agency and let her pick me out like a puppy in a pen?"

"Something like that." His mother flicked an imaginary piece of lint off her skirt. "Of course she was in school so we didn't want a baby in arms. I had already gone through the whole tiresome mess of potty training once with Jessie—I had no intention of doing it again."

Rast's lips felt too numb to speak but somehow he managed to force words out anyway. "How...how old was I when you got me?"

His mother shrugged. "Around three, we think—no one really knew for sure."

"No one knew? What about my real mom—my biological mother, I mean?" Rast demanded. "She would have known."

"I'm sure she would have if they could have found her," his mother said tartly. "But no one could. You were picked up wandering naked in a field outside the city. The woman who brought you in said you were right by a huge sink hole and it was a wonder you hadn't fallen into it and killed yourself."

"So she just took me?" Rast demanded. "How could they be sure my real mother wasn't there somewhere and too afraid to come forward?"

"To my understanding they did an exhaustive search of the area," his mother said. "But even if one or both of your biological parents had been around, there was no way they could have stepped forward to claim you."

"What? Why not?"

"Because of the scars." She gestured at him. "You had two terrible scars running parallel to your shoulder blades. It was clear you'd been abused—anyone who dared to claim you would have been blamed for that. So no one did—claim you, I mean."

"Except for Jessie," Rast said in a harsh whisper. "She claimed me when she picked me out."

"We tried to change her mind, your father and I." His mother shook her head. "We told her you'd had a traumatic past and there were likely going to be behavior problems as a result. Problems she was going to have to deal with because we made it very clear that you were her responsibility, right from the start."

"Jesus, Mom." Rast didn't know what to say—it was too much to take in at once.

"Well, nothing we could say would change her mind," his mother continued, either oblivious or uncaring of his shock. "She just had to have you. Said she would heal you and she wanted to be your mom. We took you as a foster child at first—as a trial to see how well she'd do, you know."

"Yeah?" Rast whispered numbly.

"Oh, yes." His mother nodded. "But she proved to us she was responsible after all. That's why we ended up adopting you." She looked thoughtful. "And I must say, you were a remarkably well adapted child. Jessie used her own allowance to buy the special skin cream the doctor recommended and even the scars faded over time." She cocked her head. "I dare say you never even noticed them yourself."

Rast frowned. "My...my shoulders feel tight sometimes. And sometimes I get kind of an...an itching, tingling sensation along my shoulder blades but no, I never would have guess that someone..."

"Abused you," his mother finished for him. "Yes, well, we assumed the scars were from some kind of belt. But as I said, they faded in time. And you made Jessie very happy." She looked down at her hands. "I've always been grateful for that. That she had some happiness before...before she had to leave us."

Rast was suddenly angry. "She didn't leave, Mom—she was murdered. Murdered."

"Adam, please." His mother looked up at him, frowning. "That is not—"

"A polite topic of conversation, I know," he finished for her savagely. "Nothing about Jessie is a polite topic of conversation. Do you know how much I missed her? How awful it was to know she was never coming home again and not even be able to talk about it?" He ran a hand through his hair. "Hell, this is the most you've mentioned her name in twenty years."

"We all deal with grief in our own way, Adam." His mother's lips were a thin, tight line. "I did the best I could for you after Jessie left. I never really wanted the responsibility of raising another child. You were hers...the same way she was mine. After she was gone I didn't...didn't quite know what to do with you."

"You sure as hell knew what not to do, though, didn't you?" All those lonely nights after Jessie died. Crying myself to sleep and waking up with bad dreams. Wishing Mom would come in like Jessie used to. His sister had always stroked his back or held him tight when the nightmares came. His mother simply opened the door briefly and told him to go back to sleep. There were no comforting touches, no soothing whispers, no love at all from that direction. Now he realized there never had been. There had only been Jessie and when she died, there was nothing left.

"What are you talking about, Adam?" Her prim, brittle voice brought him back from the past with a snap.

"Nothing." Standing, he straightened his jacket and looked down at her. "I think we're done talking now. Thanks for telling me about...about my past."

"I thought it was about time you knew," she said gravely. "Are you leaving now?"

He nodded. "I'm getting in a Kindred shuttle almost immediately."

"Well then, I hope you have a pleasant flight." She nodded at him, as though he was planning to fly across the state instead of thousands of lightyears away to a place he might never return from.

She really doesn't care, Rast thought, despair filling him. Honestly doesn't give a damn that she might never see me again. His throat felt tight.

"Mom..." Reaching down he took her hand and saw her flinch with surprise and perhaps distaste. He almost never touched her except to give her a stiff little hug and a dry peck on the cheek on

Mother's Day and her birthday. Carolyn Rast didn't approve of overt displays of affection. Or any kind of affection, for that matter.

"Yes, Adam?" she said stiffly.

"Mom," he said again. "Wasn't there any room in your heart for anyone but Jessie? You really never…never wanted me?"

She looked uncomfortable. "We always tried to do right by you, Adam. We kept you and raised you even after Jessie was gone. Isn't that enough?"

"No." He dropped her hand abruptly. "No, it was never enough. But it doesn't matter now — I'm going."

She started to rise. "I'll see you to the door."

"Don't bother." He turned away. "I'll see myself out."

"Have a safe trip," he heard her call as he left his childhood house for what he was sure would be the last time.

What does it matter if I'm safe or not? he thought, banging the gate savagely behind him. Why should it matter that I'm leaving when there's no one on Earth who'll give a damn if I ever come back or not?

Chapter Seven

"I wish you could come with us — both of you." Nadiah hugged Sylvan and Sophia again, a wave of sorrow washing over her. She wasn't even gone yet and she already missed them terribly. When would she see them again? The vast, echoing space of the docking bay seemed to be filled with foreboding.

"I wish we could too, Nadiah." Sylvan hugged her back gently, enfolding her in his arms in that warm, comforting way she remembered from childhood. "But the rules of the blood challenge clearly state that only you and your champion are allowed to return to the grotto."

"Stupid rules." Sophia looked like she was going to cry. "I don't understand the point of that at all."

"It's so the champion couldn't bring an army of his kin to kill and ravage the intended's family if he lost the challenge and take the girl anyway," Sylvan explained. "Not that we would do something so savage but the law was made centuries ago in less civilized times."

"Well then, we should come with them and stay in another grotto." Sophia lifted her chin defiantly. "At least we'd still be on the same planet."

"But where would we stay?" Sylvan asked. "We have no hotels or motels on Tranq Prime as you do on Earth. If you have no kin to stay with, you have no place to stay. And regrettably, my only kin are in Nadiah's home grotto."

Sophie sighed. "That's right. I'd forgotten what an inhospitable place Tranq Prime is."

"It's all right, Sophia." Nadiah hugged her again. "I'll have Rast with me. Everything is going to be okay…I hope." She bit her lip and cast a sidelong glance at the human detective who was standing by the small but surprisingly spacious ship they would be flying in. He had a brooding expression on his strong features, as though he was thinking about something that troubled him. "Um, he's kind of quiet," she murmured to Sylvan. "Do you think everything is all right?"

Sylvan shrugged, his broad shoulders rolling under his pale blue uniform shirt. "He's been like that ever since we left Earth. Maybe taking leave of his parents troubled him."

"Did you ask him about it?" Sophie wanted to know.

Sylvan shook his head. "I assumed that if he wished to talk about it, he would. He remained silent so I did as well."

Sophia rolled her eyes. "Men. There's obviously something upsetting him, Sylvan. You should have at least asked."

"I'm sorry, Talana, but it's too late now. They need to go." He looked at Nadiah. "Come on, I have to have a few words to say to you and Detective Rast together."

"Wait." Sophie clutched at his arm. "Are you sure he knows how to pilot well enough to get Nadiah all the way to Tranq Prime with no accidents?" she asked in a low voice. "I mean, he hasn't been flying that long at all."

Sylvan patted her hand comfortingly. "I'm positive. Actually, it's amazing how well Rast has taken to Kindred technology. He mastered flying faster than anyone I've ever seen. With a little more experience, I wouldn't be surprised if he could give Baird a run for his money."

"Really?" Sophie looked surprised. Baird was a master pilot — an instructor's instructor.

"Really," Sylvan assured her. "Now come, space is being folded as we speak and Nadiah and Rast can't miss the window of opportunity."

The three of them walked over to the sleek silver ship and Rast turned to meet them. "Ready to get going?"

"Not at all." Nadiah took a deep breath. "But I don't think we have any choice."

He nodded shortly. "Good enough. Let's go."

"Wait." Sylvan put up a hand. "I have something to tell you and something to give you before you go."

"All right." Rast nodded respectfully. "Shoot."

Nadiah was certain that was just an expression — he didn't actually mean that Sylvan should shoot him with his blaster. It seemed odd to her but her cousin had clearly heard it before because he nodded back before speaking.

"I just want to go over the route with you one more time." He looked at Rast. "You know that because of where Tranq Prime is in its orbit, the fold won't put you directly by it. You'll be almost five standard days out but the autopilot is configured to take you straight to it. All you have to do is help with the landing."

Rast nodded. "No problem. Can do."

"I know you can," Sylvan said gravely. "I was just telling Sophia and Nadiah what a good pilot you are."

"I know." Rast flashed them a sardonic grin. "I heard."

Sylvan frowned. "You have hearing like a Kindred."

"Reflexes too." Rast cracked his knuckles. "Don't worry. Nadiah's in safe hands. I promise to protect her with my life — all of her."

The emphasis he placed on the last words made Nadiah frown. Had Sylvan said something to him on their trip to Earth? If so, what? "We'll be fine, Sylvan," she told her cousin. "Thank you."

"You're welcome." Sylvan brushed her cheek lightly with his knuckles.

"And what do you have to give us?" Rast was clearly impatient to be gone.

"This." Raising a hypo-blast to the human's muscular arm, Sylvan injected him with a hiss, before he could protest.

"Ouch!" Rast complained, rubbing his shoulder. "What the hell was that?"

"A hemo-booster with some Kindred compounds in it to strengthen your blood." Sylvan put the hypo-blast away. "The lab isn't done with the full analysis of your blood — that will take more than a week because it goes all the way down to the molecular and genetic level. But early analysis suggest that this booster should at least give you a fighting chance against Nadiah's intended."

"Thank, then." Rast nodded. "I guess I can use all the help I can get." He twitched uncomfortably. "But... are you sure you didn't give me something I'm allergic to?"

Sylvan frowned. "Of course not — the hemo-booster was specifically formulated for your body — it should have nothing in it that your system would reject or react to. Why?"

"Because my back is itching like crazy." Rast twitched again. "Right along my shoulder blades — ouch!"

"Let me have a look." Sylvan made a motion with his hand. "Raise your shirt."

"You're the doctor," Rast muttered. Lifting his shirt, he turned so that Sylvan could see his back. "Well?"

"Oh!" Nadiah couldn't help gasping. Right along Rast's shoulder blades, running the length of his muscular back, two long, red welts had appeared. *Just like my dream,* she thought, remembering the nightmare she'd had earlier. *I foresaw this. But why would the Goddess send me a vision of an allergy attack?* Unable to stop herself, she touched one thick red welt lightly. It seemed to throb under her fingertips and Rast jumped.

"What?" he demanded, turning his head. "What do you see?"

"I'm not sure exactly." Sylvan frowned. "I suppose it could be an allergic reaction but I've never seen anything like it. Most of the time a patient will break out in hives all over or—oh!" he ended in surprise.

"They're disappearing!" Nadiah exclaimed and indeed, the long red lines running along the human detective's shoulder blades were fading as suddenly as they had appeared. Soon they were nothing but faint, white scars no thicker than a thread.

"You never told me what they were," Rast complained. "I can't see my own back, you know."

Sylvan shook his head. "It appears you might have had an allergic reaction of some kind but it seems to be over now. Is your skin still itching?"

Rast frowned. "No...no, it's fine now. That's weird." He pulled down his shirt. "My, uh, mother told me when I saw her last that I had an injury there, on my back, when I was a kid. "You think whatever you gave me might have reacted to the old scar tissue somehow?"

"I suppose it's possible—you are human, after all and I injected you with Kindred compounds." Sylvan sounded thoughtful. "We heal faster and better than you do—perhaps the Kindred components were simply trying to heal the old wound."

Rast shrugged his shoulders experimentally. "Well it feels find now. You think everything is okay?"

"I think so, yes. But if you want to stay another day and let me observe you..."

"No." Rast shook his head decisively. "The longer we stay the longer that Y'dex bastard has to yank on the blood bond. We need to go get this over with." He looked at Nadiah. "Don't you think?"

Reluctantly, she nodded. She would have loved to have another day or two with her friends and family aboard the Mother Ship but Rast was right—they needed to confront her intended and get the challenge over with. Besides, Y'dex had given them exactly one solar week to get back to Tranq Prime. If they took more time than that, her parents might declare a forfeit and hand her over to her fiancée the minute she stepped off the ship.

"All right." Sylvan sighed. "I suppose there's nothing left to say except safe journey. May the Goddess, the Mother of All Life, hold you safe in the center of her palm and give you victory in your quest." He hugged Nadiah one last time and despite herself, she felt hot tears leaking from the corners of her eyes. "Goodbye. Be well," he murmured in her ear.

"I'll miss you." Nadiah clung to her cousin in desperation and then hugged Sophia again too. "Both of you—so much."

"We'll miss you too!" Sophia was openly crying, which made Nadiah feel a little better about her own tears. "I'll pray you come back to us soon."

"Me too," Nadiah whispered. With a last, backwards glance, she climbed into the small silver ship and strapped herself into the passenger seat. All her other goodbyes had already been said back at Sophie and Sylvan's suite—there was nothing left to do now but go.

Rast pumped Sylvan's hand once more in the human gesture of friendship Nadiah was beginning to recognize and then climbed into the ship beside her.

"All right," he said, working the controls with smooth efficiency. "Let's go. Time to face the music."

Nadiah didn't know what that meant but she did understand that she was leaving the one place in the galaxy where she'd been happy and truly free for the first time in her life.

And though she prayed to come back to the Mother Ship soon, she feared desperately that she might never see it or her beloved Sophia and Sylvan again.

Chapter Eight

Merrick twisted the steering yoke on his small star-duster, aiming in the general direction of the tiny blue and white dot his star charts assured him was the planet called Earth. He'd heard it was nothing much to look at but he'd still been hoping to get there before this—a long time before.

"Goddess damn it," he muttered, running a hand over his shaved head. He kept his hair convict short because it was easier to deal with that way. Along with his massive seven foot seven frame and mismatched eyes—one gold and one blue—it made him look like what he was. A thug.

Or that was what they called him growing up on Tranq Prime. Thug, low life, half breed, scum—you name it, he'd heard it. The good folks on TP weren't known for their tolerance of anything different, especially if that difference was Kindred in nature. And Merrick had not one but two Kindred bloodlines in his heritage— the fiery Beast Kindred line that filled him with bloodlust and urged him to kill, and the chilly Blood Kindred line which made him cold as ice when he did so. The killing frost which came over him in times of violence and his huge size made him a male to be feared and avoided.

Hybrid vigor—the scientific term for a half breed growing bigger, stronger, and faster than its parents. If you cross a lion and a tiger, the resulting offspring will dwarf every other animal around it. That was the story of Merrick's life. Even in a room filled with Kindred warriors, he stood head and shoulders above the rest. And thanks to his mixed heritage, he had sexual attributes of both

Kindred races—the mating fist of a Beast Kindred and the fangs of a Blood Kindred. Unfortunately, while a true Blood Kindred's fangs only grew when he was angry or aroused, Merrick's fangs were permanently elongated. They served as a constant reminder of what a freak of nature he was—a half breed that should never have been born in the first place.

Despite the chilly temperature in the little star-duster, he wore only a black tank top over his tight black flight pants. The scars on his broad, bare shoulders proved his life hadn't been easy but they were nothing compared to the scar on his face, a twisted white line that bisected his left eyebrow and narrowly missed his eye—the blue one—before continuing on down his cheek in a broken squiggle. That one had been done by his own father—or at least the man his mother had been living with at the time. Merrick had left Tranq Prime soon after that and he'd been on his own ever since.

His childhood on the frozen planet was something he would rather forget. Back then, Sylvan had been the only bright spot in the black pit of his existence. The only true friend Merrick had ever had.

"So what do I do to thank him for standing by me?" he growled to himself as he twisted the steering yoke again. "I go and fuck up his joining ceremony. Some friend I am."

He had been right on schedule until the Trissian pirates caught him in their energy web. They wanted him dead but Merrick wasn't one to roll over and die. He hid in the guts of the ship, a one-male ambush, and waited for them to board his little star-duster. He wasn't going down without a struggle— and it was a struggle which left every last one of the damn Trissies in a mangled, bloody heap at his feet. Only their pilot, who had stayed on their ship while the rest boarded his star-duster, had lived to tell the tale.

Merrick didn't remember much of the conflict. When the killing frost was on him, he saw nothing but red. Using no weapons but his fangs, which grew even longer when he was enraged, he ripped the pirates apart, tearing out their throats with his teeth and disemboweling them with his bare hands. And he didn't stop—couldn't stop—until every last one of the thieves who had dared to invade his ship was dead.

Afterwards, his arms red to the elbows and his face smeared with their blood, he regretted killing them all. Not because of the pain he'd caused—they had wanted to cause him the same and worse. But because he wondered how much information they'd gotten. How much had their scan of his star-duster revealed? Their spy-probe had read all his ship's data and scanned all its systems for anything of value. Has it revealed his secret? It was too late to find out—when the killing frost left him, the Trissian ship was already speeding away into the blackness of space, putting as much distance between itself and his star-duster as it could.

He was angry at himself for not being better prepared for the attack. Of course, who could have predicted that Trission pirates would come after him in the Centauri system? Honestly, he couldn't even figure out why they bothered with him— Trissies typically went after fat cat merchants with huge space yachts, not ragged mercenaries like himself. Merrick didn't have much—he traveled light through life because he never knew when he was going to have to pick up and leave.

He only had one thing of value and there was no way the pirates could have known about it. Under the hull of his small star-duster was a small but ingenious mechanism that generated wormholes—tears in the fabric of space-time which allowed him to jump from one spot in the vast universe to another in the blink of an eye. Considering that even moving at light speed, it could take millions of years to travel across a single galaxy, the wormhole generator was an invaluable tool.

Of course it was temperamental and didn't work all the time. In fact, it had been giving him trouble since the Trission attack which was why he was in manual mode as he flew through the Earth's solar system.

Part of the problem might have been the fact that the wormhole generator had been built using alien technology Merrick had scavenged from an abandoned wreck. He didn't completely understand it to be honest, although it had been immediately apparent to him what it did. What he needed was time to assess the damage and work on the star-duster, but he wanted to wait until he was safe on the Mother Ship to do it.

But though the pirate attack had been brutal and bloody, it wasn't what currently occupied Merrick's thoughts as he flew toward the Kindred Mother Ship. No, what he couldn't stop thinking about, what his mind kept prodding the way a tongue will prod a loose tooth, was what had happened before the ambush, on First World—the home planet of the Kindred race.

Before running into the Trissians, Merrick had made a pilgrimage to the Kindred home world—a foolish and pointless quest as it turned out. He'd gone to try and clear his mind of the constant conflict his two natures caused, and to ask forgiveness for the bloody deeds of his past. The pilgrimage hadn't been so much for himself as for Sylvan—Merrick hadn't wanted to bring bad luck to his old friend's joining ceremony.

"So stupid," Merrick muttered to himself, as he steered the star-duster through the Earth's solar system. "So fucking stupid to think going there would help…"

* * * * *

He'd approached the temple, a vast white marble structure with ceilings so high he couldn't see the murals painted on them, with more than a few misgivings. Like all Kindred, he believed in an all knowing Goddess, the Mother of All Life, but unlike most of his kin, Merrick didn't think she was particularly benevolent or kind. His own sorry existence proved that.

The temple was housed within the holy mountain and hundreds of white marble steps led up to it. Merrick climbed them, two at a time, and saw a line of priestesses in simple white robes. Most had their heads bowed reverently and the dim light of the elegantly tapered torches glimmered in their green streaked hair. It reminded him of his mother, who had also been one of the rare female Kindred as most priestesses were. They stood before the raised dais which housed the Empty Throne—the seat which had been empty since the last Counselor had died centuries ago and his only son and heir had been lost.

One of the priestesses stepped forward as he came to a stop before the white marble throne. "Why do you come here, Warrior?" she demanded, frowning in a most unwelcoming way. "Kneel as you speak. And remember when you answer that you speak to none other than the High Priestess of the Empty Throne—the mouthpiece of the Goddess herself."

Unwillingly, Merrick had knelt before the Empty Throne. He couldn't place the priestess's age. Her long, curling hair was pure green and worn loose around her shoulders and her eyes were a solid emerald with no pupil, iris, or white to interrupt their blank, unbroken expanse. That blind yet knowing stare was strange and otherworldly and the high priestess's demeanor was anything but welcoming. But Merrick hadn't come all the way to First World just to turn around with his tail between his legs.

"I come asking forgiveness for my past misdeeds," he rumbled, bowing his head in reluctant submission. "My past has not been a kind one."

"Your past or your present either," the priestess said, frowning. "Oh yes, Warrior, I see into you with no effort at all. You are a killer. A murderer many times over."

"I am," Merrick acknowledged, nodding coolly. "I don't deny it. But I'm going to be a part of an old friend's joining ceremony and I don't wish to bring him bad luck. I need—"

"You need much more than I can give you." The priestess made a dismissive motion. "Be gone. Bloody hands are not welcome at the Goddess's table, nor bloody boots on her sacred sands."

"What the fuck?" Merrick growled. "I came asking for forgiveness. And you'd damn well better believe this is the first and last time I've ever asked for that."

"It is just as well. Some sins cannot be forgiven." The high priestess wrinkled her nose, as though she smelled something bad. "You would do well to remember that in future. And furthermore—"

But her words ended in a choked gurgle. Suddenly her strange blank emerald eyes had gone pure white and her voice dropped into a low, sing-song tone as words that didn't seem to be her own poured from her throat.

"You shall find your bride on your journey to help a friend seal his love. She who is meant for you waits wrapped in darkness— waits for your kiss to awaken her, warrior. You shall be her light and she shall be yours. You will heal each other, body and soul, though the path to that healing will be long and thorny. Go now and find your female. Only then will your troubled soul find peace."

Her eyes changed back to green and she looked at him. "You are blessed indeed, Warrior—the Goddess has gifted you with a prophecy though I cannot imagine why. Do you understand it?"

"No," Merrick snarled. He was so tall that even with him kneeling and the priestess standing, they were still eye to eye. "You've got it wrong, your Holiness," he said sarcastically, ignoring the gasps of the other, lesser priestesses at his blasphemy. One did not tell the High priestess of the Empty Throne that she was mistaken but Merrick didn't give a damn about protocol. This female had treated him like shit she'd wiped off her shoes and then given him a ridiculous, unwanted prophesy he hadn't asked for. In the light of those circumstances, he felt no more need to bow and scrape.

The strange, blank emeralds of her eyes blazed. "How do you mean, warrior?" she asked, her voice cool and forbidding.

"You prophesied that I would meet someone—a female."

"Indeed, and what is wrong with that?"

He shrugged. "To begin with, I'm not looking for any fucking female to complete me—I'm not like the other pathetic Kindred, all searching for their brides. I don't need anyone but me to get along." He spat on the temple floor, drawing more gasps from the other priestesses. "And second, even if I wanted to find a bride, it's not possible. I'm a half breed—a hybrid. I'm not able to connect with a female and form a bond. Not that I want to."

"Oh?" She raised one pale green eyebrow at him. "Do you dispute my prophecy?"

"Hell yes, I dispute it. There hasn't been a female born yet who would take one look at this..." Merrick pointed at himself—his massive frame, scarred face, and mismatched eyes. "And not run for the hills."

"It is difficult for me to believe too, but the Mother of All Life does not lie. There is a bride for you." The high priestess sniffed disdainfully. "Though Goddess knows I feel sorry for her."

Merrick's hands clenched into fists at his sides. He would never hit a female but this bitch was really pushing it. "That's enough," he growled. "I came here for absolution—not to hear your fucking false prophecies and insults. I'm leaving."

"Not yet!" Raising one arm, the priestess pointed at him with an accusing finger. "I have words for you, Hybrid. Turn back and hear them or face the consequences."

Merrick looked at her in disbelief. "Are you threatening to curse me?"

"You curse yourself, warrior." The priestess's strange eyes had grown cold by now. As cold as the frozen exterior of his home planet, Tranq Prime. "Hear me well—there is a bride awaiting you. Her love will prick your heart like a thorn, giving you pain such as you have never imagined."

Merrick feared nothing—surviving what he'd been through as a child left little room for fright. But at her words a cold finger touched his heart and he knew he would pay for the disrespect he had shown her.

Still, he lifted his chin. "Look at my scars, Holiness—I've known pain. Plenty of it."

"Not like this. I say to you now, Hybrid—the knife of love will twist in your heart and will you know true agony. Despite your mixed heritage you will form a bond—one which cannot be broken. A bond which will threaten your very life." The priestess raised her head, a look of regal displeasure written on her strong features. "I have given you enough of my time, warrior. Now go and be at peace...if you can."

* * * * *

Merrick shook his head as he remembered that meeting. The curse had been a bitter benediction and his parting with the high priestess still made him uneasy, although he didn't like to admit it, even to himself.

He'd tried not to think about the foolish prophecy but it wouldn't leave his mind. He had been going to Sylvan's joining ceremony, and since his old friend had told him he intended to include the luck kiss in the ceremony, Merrick had assumed that the girl he performed it with would be the female the priestess spoke of. Hadn't the prophecy included something about waking her with a kiss? But of course it turned out to be a moot point, since the run-in with the pirates had forced him to forgo his place in Sylvan's joining.

Despite his anger and frustration at missing the ceremony, Merrick had to admit to a sneaking sense of relief, too. To be honest, he'd been dreading the luck kiss. Dreading the look of fear and horror in the poor, hapless girl's eyes as he gathered her to him for a kiss she surely didn't want to give. There was no way she would have gone to him willingly, no way she would have kissed him without recoiling, without blanching in fear as all females did when faced with his massive, muscular frame and scarred visage…

"Goddess damn it, stop thinking about it!" Merrick muttered savagely to himself. He gave the star-duster a little more juice, scooting past a small rust-red planet his star charts informed him was called Mars by the humans. It looked barren to him— apparently Earth itself was the only planet located in the temperate zone and suitable for habitation in the entire solar system.

Despite his best efforts, his thoughts returned once more to the prophecy—to the curse. The high priestess had to be mistaken—of that he was certain. There wasn't any willing female waiting for him out there in the vast reaches of the universe. Even his own mother had feared him before he left home—how could he expect anything different from any other female he met? Just as well, he thought, urging the ship to an even higher speed. Don't need a female. Don't need anyone. Need is weakness and I'm not fucking weak.

Earth was coming into view now, as well as its one lonely moon. Circling the pale, pocked lunar surface, he saw two massive ships. One, which had smaller vessels hustling back and forth between its docking bay and the Earth below, was obviously the Kindred Mother Ship. The other was the abandoned hulk of the Fathership— all that remained of the once malevolent Scourge.

Merrick shook his head in awe as he looked at the dark and drifting Fathership. He'd heard that the Kindred's old enemy had been destroyed with the help of the AllFather's own son but it had been difficult to believe. Seeing the proof brought home the truth that the Scourge threat really was no more.

He was about to turn his star-duster toward the Mother ship when a sensor on his console beeped. Looking down at it, Merrick frowned. "A life pod, huh? Tell me more." His little ship had a built-in scavenger function that was always scanning for valuable finds. That was how he had had found the equipment which became his worm hole generator—the star-duster had detected the long lost alien technology and brought it to his attention.

He hit a few buttons and swiped the info-panel with his thumb, requesting a more detailed scan. The read-out came back at once and Merrick's mismatched eyes raced as he read it.

"Scourge life pod—probably jettisoned from the Fathership— but no vital signs aboard. Just a bunch of old equipment and…hmmm, that's interesting." His super sensitive scanners had picked up a signal so faint he was certain anyone else would have missed it. It was probably just deep space parasites but something about the signal piqued Merrick's interest.

Going after the abandoned life pod might take awhile. It appeared to be floating in a huge cloud of debris and sorting through the lot would be a time consuming process. Merrick almost passed it up—his finger hovering over the autopilot control that would lead him directly to the Mother Ship's docking bay.

But something made him stop. Call it intuition or hybrid luck or whatever you wanted, but something about the signal from the life pod called to him.

The skin at the back of his neck prickled and a chill ran down his spine. It was the same, strange feeling he'd had when he had found the alien tech which eventually became his wormhole generator. Something different here, a little voice seemed to whisper at the back of his brain. Something that might be important—damn important.

Merrick let his finger drop and grabbed the steering yoke with both hands instead. Sylvan had waited this long, he was sure his old friend wouldn't mind waiting a little longer. Before he went to the Mother Ship to make his apologies, he wanted to find out what was in that pod.

Chapter Nine

They were about three standard days away from Tranq Prime when the next spasm of pain hit.

Nadiah had been expecting it — dreading it — since before they'd left the Mother Ship. After all, her fiancée had made it abundantly clear he didn't intend to stop pulling on the blood bond until she submitted to him and agreed to their bonding. Still, she'd gone several days without pain, which had made her start hoping that maybe her parents had taken a hand in the matter. Possibly her mother had complained or her father had instructed Y'dex not to hurt her any more. She had even begun to relax a little — had stopped fearing that sharp, burning stab beneath her heart quite so much.

So when the flaming knife slid between her ribs, it came as an unwelcome, though not completely unexpected surprise.

When it happened, Nadiah was in the tiny food prep area of the small ship, making herself a cup of hot chocolate. It was a sweet, creamy Earth drink she'd learned to love while aboard the Mother Ship. As a parting gift, Sophia had made sure she had a large supply of the tiny packets filled with light brown powder for which Nadiah was eternally grateful. The warm, soothing drink seemed to ease her mind and make her feel less unhappy somehow, and just at that moment she felt a great need for what Kat called "the healing power of chocolate."

It wasn't just the upcoming challenge that made her upset and anxious—it was the state of her relationship with Rast. Not that what they had could even properly be called a relationship.

In every old book and story Nadiah had read as a child, the male who dared to challenge the blood bond was passionately in love with and utterly committed to the female he was challenging for. The stories seemed to indicate that it was the intensity of the challenger's love as much as the strength of his blood that broke the bond. But there was nothing like that between herself and the human detective—nothing but a vague uneasiness and uncertainty.

Nadiah had tried talking to him but their conversations always came out awkward and stilted. He never seemed to look at her, even when he was talking to her, and he never initiated the conversation. She was growing tired of seeking him out and trying to exchange pleasantries, hoping that they might turn into something more meaningful, which they never did.

Even worse than their stilted conversations was the fact that Rast seemed to go out of his way not to touch her. If their hands touched by accident or their bodies brushed against each other in the ship's single, narrow corridor, he jumped away as though he'd been stung. It was painfully obvious he wanted nothing to do with her—not even in a friendly way.

Back on the Mother Ship, Nadiah had wondered if Rast was acting as her champion because he felt something for her...or simply because of his own sad past experiences. Now she was sure she had her answer. It was time to face the facts—Rast didn't actually like her very much. He was acting as her champion out of pity and his own past pain. And how could he possibly win the challenge if he didn't really care? If he had no love or passion for her with which to break the bond?

She had been mulling over this depressing thought, and filling a mug full of steaming water for hot chocolate, when the pain hit. It stabbed her so suddenly that she couldn't even scream. Instead, she gave a high, breathless gasp and fell to the floor, spilling the scalding water all over her tharp.

The knife twisted and Nadiah doubled in agony, the pain sinking its claws into her like an angry beast. Such torture left little room to think of anything else but one corner of her mind was still clear enough to fear for her delicate, one of a kind tharp. It was still young and tender—easily hurt. She could feel it writhing against her skin, in as much pain as she was, from the scalding water she'd spilled on it. But until the spasm from the blood bond passed, she could do nothing to ease it.

Then, though she would have sworn she'd fallen almost soundlessly, Rast was there. He'd been up in cockpit in the pilot's chair studying star charts earlier and several doors and rooms were between that area of the ship and the food prep area. Still, there he was, holding her and looking anxiously into her eyes.

"Is he doing it again? The pain's back?" he demanded.

Nadiah nodded, unable to speak as another bolt of pain shot through her.

"That bastard!" Rast looked angry enough to kill and Nadiah had a brief, hazy thought that she was glad that look wasn't directed at her. Then he asked, "What can I do?"

"Th-tharp," she gasped, plucking at the wounded garment which still writhed against her skin.

Rast looked down at it. The tharp was changing colors rapidly, unable to hold any particular shade or form due to its pain. "What the hell is wrong with it?"

"Take...off," Nadiah managed to gasp. "Spilled...hot on it. Put...cold water."

He looked doubtful. "How will stripping you naked and dunking your dress in cold water help?"

Nadiah was out of breath for talking and out of patience for explaining. Reaching up, she grabbed a handful of Rast's shirt and yanked him down. "Just...do it," she panted. "Hurry!"

His eyes widened but he didn't ask any more questions. Quickly, he jerked the wounded tharp over her head and stood to push it under the cold tap at the sink unit. Nadiah lay naked and shivering on the floor as he doused it thoroughly.

"There." Rast knelt beside her, his eyes filled with worry. "It's soaking in cold water in the sink. Better?"

She nodded. "Thank you."

"Welcome." He didn't seem to know where to look and she realized she was still naked. She was about to ask for some clothes when another spasm of pain hit.

"Ahh!" It was a moan of pure anguish and Nadiah couldn't stop the hot tears that came to her eyes. They spilled over her cheeks, adding humiliation to her agony. She didn't want Rast to see her crying. Didn't want him to pity her or see how weak she was...

"Son of a bitch!" Rast growled, scooping her up. "Come on, I'm taking you to the bed."

Stripped of her dignity as well as her tharp, Nadiah could do nothing but cling to him as he settled on the bed in one of the two tiny sleep chambers at the back of the ship.

"I'll get you something to wear." Rast started to put her down but then another spasm hit and another. Nadiah's fingers clenched in the material of his shirt and she couldn't make herself let go.

"Sorry," she gasped, looking up at him. "Know you don't like...don't want..."

"Don't want what?" He frowned down at her, stroking her damp hair away from her forehead.

"Don't want to touch me," Nadiah whispered, looking away as the pain lessened somewhat. "I'm sorry. I'll get up."

"No." He pulled her closer. "No, stay right where you are." He rubbed her back gently, his large hand soothing and warm. "Does this help?" he murmured.

Strangely enough, it did help. The warmth of his big body surrounding hers and his dark, masculine scent seemed to ease the tremors of pain that still echoed through her body.

"Yes." Nadiah nodded, her cheek pressed to his chest. The low, steady rhythm of his heart was comforting. "I...I don't know why but it does."

"Then just relax." Rast stroked her hair. "We'll wait it out together. Here." He pulled the blanket at the foot of the small bed over her, covering her nakedness and making her feel more at ease. Not that the hideous knifing pain had left much room for modesty but still, she had never exposed her body to a male before and she was shy.

They stayed like that for a long time, long after the sharp, burning spasms of pain had past and Nadiah found herself feeling strangely comfortable in his arms. She should have felt self-conscious about being naked in the arms of a male but somehow she didn't. Rast rocked her gently and stroked her hair, as though she was a fretful child wakened by a nightmare. After awhile, she became aware that he was humming in a low, tuneful voice under his breath.

"What's that you're humming?" she murmured, feeling too warm and sleepy to speak up. "It's beautiful."

"Just a song from Earth."

"What is it about? Does it have words?"

Rast shifted a little. "It's, uh, about love. A man telling a woman how much he loves her and how he'll do anything to prove it." He sighed. "And yeah, it has words."

"Sing them to me," Nadiah begged. "Please," she added, when he seemed to be hesitating. "I think it might help me feel better."

"Yeah, right," Rast muttered but then he began to sing anyway, in a warm baritone that seemed to echo through Nadiah's entire body.

"When the rain is blowing in your face,

And the whole world is on your case,

I could offer you a warm embrace

To make you feel my love…

When the evening shadows and the stars appear

And there is no one to dry your tears,

I could hold you for a million years,

To make you feel my love…"

There were several more verses along the same lines and Rast sang them softly, still rocking her. Nadiah found herself charmed and strangely touched by the soft refrain. It was almost as though the words had been written just for her, as though Rast really meant what he was singing.

Don't be stupid, she told herself sternly. He doesn't really feel that way about you—it's just a song, a silly Earth song that doesn't mean anything. But if it didn't mean anything, then why did her heart feel like it was going to burst? Why did she wish that she would never have to leave the comforting circle of his arms? Why did...

"Hey..." Rast's soft voice got her attention and she looked up.

"Yes?"

"Is he hurting you again?" He cupped her cheek and swiped a thumb under her eye. "You're crying."

"No." Nadiah shook her head and rubbed at her eyes briskly. "The pain has stopped for now. It was just...just that your song touched me."

"Oh." Rast didn't seem to know what to say. "Uh, well..."

"I'm better now. I'll get up." Determined to regain her dignity, Nadiah pushed out of his lap and wobbled to her feet. She tried to take the blanket with her but it slithered out of her hands and fell in a heap at her feet. "Oops!" She reached for it, her cheeks hot with embarrassment, but Rast was too quick for her.

"Here." He grabbed the blue blanket and whisked it around her shoulders. "I'll get you something else to wear. Where are your clothes?"

"I don't have any." Nadiah shook her head. "I only brought one tharp with me."

He raised an eyebrow. "Seriously? You only brought one outfit? Tranq Prime women must be more different from Earth females than I thought."

"My tharp is one of a kind. It configures itself to any form or color I want," Nadiah explained. "It can even imitate the clothing others are wearing. I used it as my bridesmaid's dress during Sophia and Sylvan's joining ceremony."

He frowned. "Wow—that's some talented dress. Well…I guess I can try to dry it out."

"No, don't." Nadiah put out a hand to stop him and nearly lost the blanket again. "It's been injured. It needs time to heal."

"Well you can't go walking around the ship wearing next to nothing." He eyed the slippery blue blanket clutched around her shoulders balefully.

Nadiah stiffened. "I'm sorry if you find the sight of me naked distasteful. I'll be sure to stay in my room where you won't have to look at me until my tharp is healed."

"No, damn it—that's not what I meant!" He shook his head. "It's not that I don't want to see you naked. It's that I—" He stopped abruptly, his face going red. "Never mind. You can borrow some of my clothes."

He stalked abruptly from the room, leaving Nadiah to stare after him and wonder what had happened. How could he be so sweet and gentle one minute and so gruff the next? And what had he been about to say when he stopped himself and went for the clothes?

* * * * *

Rast cursed to himself under his breath as he rummaged in the small duffle of extra clothes he'd picked up while on Earth. So Nadiah thought he didn't want to see her or touch her? How in the hell had she gotten such a crazy idea in her head when the exact opposite was true? When all he could think about was her soft, ripe breasts moving under the thin tharp, when even the slightest brush of her hand against his sent his body into overload? He felt like a horny teenager, walking around with a hard-on most of the time. To put it bluntly, she was driving him crazy.

Only her obvious suffering had kept his body from reacting when he'd held her earlier. His anxiety for her pain and his anger at the evil fiancée who was doing this to her had completely overridden any sexual urges he might have had at the time. But now that she was better, he could feel himself reacting again. Now that he'd held her warm and naked in his arms, he wanted her more than ever.

And it wasn't just the physical desire that was tormenting him — there was a dark, possessiveness that seemed to be growing like a weed inside him. He'd told Sylvan that he didn't know how he felt about Nadiah but that was no longer true. Now, when he looked at her, there was no doubt what he felt. Mine, whispered a voice in the back of his head whenever he saw her. She's mine and no one else had better touch her or I'll fucking kill them!

It was crazy and Rast knew it. Nadiah didn't belong to him — he had no claim on her at all. But no amount of reasoning with himself seemed to help. He wanted her, wanted to protect her, possess her, provide for her. I want to be the one she comes to if she's hurt, the one she shares her joy with when she's happy. The one she tells her troubles to. The one she curls up with at night.

The one she loves.

Rast shook his head. But if I tell her that, what will she think? What will she say? I'll scare the hell out of her, talking like that, saying that I want to own her, to possess her. I haven't even known her that long, I can't dump all these crazy, strong emotions on her out of the blue.

He felt like an idiot. Best not to say anything, he decided as he finally found something in his duffle he thought might fit her. Best to just go back to normal — or what had become normal for them — which was mostly avoiding each other while they waited to get to Tranq Prime and get on with the damn challenge.

"Here," he said, striding across the narrow corridor and handing Nadiah the bundle of clothes. "These should work." He turned his back to let her change and nearly jumped out of his skin when he felt her small, soft hand on his shoulder a moment later.

"Thank you," she said when he turned around. "But I'm afraid only half of it works."

Rast took a look at her and nearly groaned aloud with sexual frustration. Had he thought the thin tharp she had been wearing was bad? This was a hundred times worse.

He'd given her a pair of his old sweatpants and a white button down dress shirt he'd packed in case he found himself in a formal situation. She was holding the former and wearing the latter—with nothing underneath it.

Rast didn't remember his shirt being so see-through but he could clearly make out the tight pink points of her nipples pressing against the white cotton material. The shirt was long enough to cover her, at least—it fell to mid thigh—but when his eyes moved down, he saw that her long, shapely bare legs were exposed and the faint shadow of her sex was visible through the hem.

"I'm sorry if you don't like the way I look," she said stiffly, obviously misinterpreting his gaze. "But the pants won't fit—they just keep falling down."

Her soft voice made him realize that he'd been ogling her like a schoolboy. Quickly, he jerked his eyes upwards to meet hers. "Don't be stupid," he said roughly. "You look...fine. And don't worry about the pants." He took them from her and threw them back into his own room, directly across from hers. "I'd, uh, better go check the star charts."

"Wait..." She put out a hand but at her soft touch on his shoulder, Rast flinched away. Nadiah pulled back at once, a hurt look on her face. "I'm sorry. I didn't mean to…to touch you when you didn't want to be touched."

The innocence and pain in her deep blue eyes moved him. She wasn't to blame for his crazy feelings, he reminded himself. Nadiah was innocent—a virgin. She truly didn't know how desirable she was and probably had no idea of the effect she was having on him, just by being near.

Part of Rast thought it might be best to keep it that way. After all, what good could it do for him to admit how much he desired her? Commander Sylvan had made it abundantly clear that she was off limits. Letting her know he wanted her would only make things difficult between them. But the look in her eyes was breaking his heart. Would it be possible to let her know how beautiful he thought she was without actually admitting how desperately he wanted her? Rast hoped so.

"I'm sorry," Nadiah said again, turning away from him. "I'll go lay down on my bed and you can study the charts."

"No, wait." Rast put a hand on her arm. "I'm the one who ought to be sorry."

She turned back and frowned. "What for?"

He sighed and ran a hand through his hair. "For avoiding you. For keeping you at an arm's length all this time when we should have been getting ready for what's waiting on Tranq Prime together. For not…for not telling you how I really feel."

Her breath seemed to speed up and her cheeks got pink. "What do you mean? How…how do you really feel?"

"Come on." Rast tugged her into the small sitting room across from the food prep area. "We'd better sit if we're going to talk."

Chapter Ten

Nadiah couldn't believe that they were finally going to have a real conversation—one that Rast himself had actually initiated. But what exactly was he going to say? She felt like her heart was pounding in every part of her body at once as she sat down beside him on the tiny, plush love seat which was barely big enough for two—especially when one of them was as big and muscular as Rast.

He settled across from her and took one of her hands in his. "I haven't been fair to you, Nadiah," he said, looking at her directly. "I've been avoiding you, trying to keep my distance, never really talking. But not for the reason you think."

"What—?" Nadiah started but he shook his head.

"Please, just...let me finish. You somehow have the idea I don't like the way you look, that I don't want to see you or touch you." He brushed her cheek lightly with his fingertips. "Nadiah, sweetheart, nothing could be farther from the truth."

Nadiah's heart seemed to stop in her chest. "What...what are you saying? That you feel something for me?"

"More than something. And a hell of a lot more than I should." Rast sounded grim.

"Then...you don't dislike me?"

He frowned. "What the hell would give you that idea?"

"Because of the way I treated you before, when you didn't believe in my gift." Nadiah looked down at their joined hands. "I shouted at you...slapped you..."

"I deserved all that and more," Rast said firmly. "I was being a bastard—I don't blame you for being upset."

"But I...I brought up your sister. Jessie...And I know you'd probably rather not talk about her..."

"Not true at all." Rast squeezed her hand. "You don't know how many years I went wishing I could talk about her. Wishing I had anyone to listen."

"Really?" Nadiah looked at him doubtfully. "But your parents— you said before it was a forbidden subject in their house but would they really never even mention her?"

Rast laughed bitterly. "Whenever I try to bring Jessie up, my mother just frowns and says it's not a polite topic of conversation." His eyes took on an inward looking expression. "I thought she was my mother, anyway," he muttered.

"What?" Nadiah asked but he shook his head.

"Never mind. We're getting off subject—way off subject. The point is, I've been treating you the way my parents treat anything they want swept under the rug. I've been avoiding you because it was easier to do that than to admit what I feel. What I think."

Nadiah's heart was thudding so hard she could hear it in her ears. "What...what do you think?"

Rast looked her in the eyes. "I think you're beautiful, Nadiah. Fucking gorgeous, to be exact. And please don't think I don't want to touch you—I do. Uh..." He cleared his throat. "I, uh, hope that doesn't make you feel uncomfortable."

Biting her lip, Nadiah shook her head. "No, I don't mind. It's better than thinking you found me repulsive."

He laughed and shook his head. "I could never do that. You're really have no idea how beautiful you are do you?"

Nadiah felt her cheeks getting hot. "I've never had a male tell me that before, if that's what you mean. Y'dex was always more interested in talking about himself."

Rast looked angry. "That kind of guy always is. He's a selfish bastard—not good enough for you."

"I wish my parents could see it that way." Nadiah sighed. "I'm so glad you challenged him for me. You don't know the nightmares I've had, imagining what my first sex would be like if I had to have him as a partner."

"That's not going to happen," Rast said grimly. "You're not going to have to give yourself to him—I swear it, Nadiah."

"I couldn't, even if I had to," she confessed in a low voice. "I can't stand the thought of his hands on me. I'd fight him, even if it didn't do any good. Even if he…took me anyway. I'd still fight."

"Good for you." Rast nodded. "I like a girl with spirit."

"I've got plenty of that, as long as he doesn't yank on the blood bond." Nadiah sighed again. "The thing is, I've been promised to him for so long I've never even had any hope of escaping before. I try but I can't…can't even imagine what…what making love with someone I actually cared for and wanted would be like." She looked up at Rast shyly. "What is it like?"

"What is what like?"

"You know…making love." Nadiah nudged him. "I've talked a lot about it with my girl friends back home but none of us really has any first hand experience. I've always wanted to hear about it from someone who's actually, uh, done it."

He looked startled. "What—you want me to describe it or something?"

"That's exactly what I want." Nadiah scooted a little closer, looking up at him eagerly. "You've done it before, right?"

Rast cleared his throat. "Uh, you could say that, yeah."

"So you know what it's like." Nadiah leaned forward and put a hand on his knee. "Tell me what happens. What do you do when you…when you take a female? When you make love to her?"

"Um…" Rast's cheeks were dark red now and he seemed ill at ease. "I don't know…know if that's something we ought to be talking about, sweetheart."

"Please," Nadiah begged. "It's not like I'm asking you to show me. I just want to hear about it, that's all."

"Well…" Rast seemed to be wavering.

"I want to know what to expect," Nadiah said, pushing a little. "For when I actually do give myself to someone. To the male I'm bonded to."

He sighed. "All right. But stop me if anything I say bothers you. I don't want to shock or offend you."

Nadiah shook her head. "You won't, really. Just tell me…what do you do when you make love to a woman?"

"All right, then." He shifted a little and then seemed to settle into a more comfortable position. "Well, first I kiss her. Taste the flavor of her lips. Stroke her hair." Rast brushed a strand of hair from her face and tucked it behind her ear. "No rushing, I want to build up slowly. That way things are even more intense when we get to where we're going."

"Oh?" Nadiah's breath seemed to catch in her throat. Rast seemed to have lost his embarrassment for the subject. He was looking at her intently as he spoke. "And then?" she asked softly.

"Then I like to take my time undressing her. Slipping off her skirt, unbuttoning her blouse…" He ran one finger down the row of white buttons on the dress shirt Nadiah was wearing and she bit back a soft gasp. "I pull her bra off slowly, revealing her breasts. If she's excited her nipples should already be tight and pink. Sometimes I'll blow a little cool air over them, to make them even tighter."

"R-really?" she asked.

"Mmm-hmm." Rast nodded. "Then I take off her panties very, very slowly. I want to give her time to get used to being naked. Some women are shy about that."

Remembering how he'd held her naked against him made Nadiah blush. "Yes, I…I can see that. Go on."

"By this time I have her completely naked. But remember…" Rast raised one finger. "I haven't actually touched her yet—not really. I like to go slow in case she's shy. Maybe…maybe inexperienced. I want to let her know I'll be gentle, that I won't hurt her."

He held her gaze with his as he spoke and Nadiah knew they weren't talking about a hypothetical situation anymore. Rast was describing what he would do if he was making love to her—if he was taking her for the first time. It was both frightening and incredibly stimulating. She never wanted him to stop.

"Tell me more," she breathed. "What would you do next?"

"Look at her." Rast's truegreen eyes burned down her body in a scorching gaze. "Have her lay on the bed, open for me, so I can just drink her in."

"Wouldn't…wouldn't she be shy to have you look at her like that?" Nadiah asked softly.

Rast shook his head. "Maybe a little. But I'd be telling her all along how beautiful she is, how much I want to touch her, to taste her and give her pleasure."

"How...how would you give her pleasure?" Nadiah couldn't seem to pull her eyes away from his.

Rast smiled. "Slowly. Always slowly. First I'd caress her, pet her like a cat, with long, slow strokes down her arms and legs and belly. I wouldn't touch her breasts or her pussy just yet."

"Pussy?" Nadiah bit her lip. "Like a cat? I'm sorry, my translation bacteria..."

"It's a name for your sex—the place between your legs," Rast explained. "There are a lot of names for it but most of them are too technical or too crude. Pussy sounds like what it is—soft, warm, something that loves to be stroked and pleasured."

"Oh." Nadiah nodded. "I...I like that."

"I do too," Rast's murmured, his eyes half-lidded as he looked at her. "I like looking at it, touching it, and most of all, tasting it."

"T-tasting?" Nadiah's eyes flew open. She had heard of such things in secret whispers from her girl friends but no one had actually come out and talked about it to her before.

Rast nodded. "Yeah, but I don't start with that. First I like to kiss her, to press my body against hers and feel her against me while I explore her mouth. Our bodies touching, skin to skin, the soft press of her breasts under my chest and her thighs against mine..." He stroked her cheek gently. "Have you ever been kissed? I mean, except for the, uh, luck kiss thing we did at Sylvan's wedding?"

Biting her lip, Nadiah shook her head. "I'm not...not supposed to because I'm promised to Y'dex. And he, well, I never wanted him to kiss me. So no, no I haven't, other than the luck kiss."

"I never would have known." Rast smiled, as though remembering. "Not from the way you kissed me. Definitely the hottest kiss I've ever had."

"Really?" Nadiah asked doubtfully. "You're not just saying that?"

"I swear," Rast murmured. Cupping her cheek, he ran the pad of his thumb over her trembling bottom lip. "I remember thinking during the ceremony that your lips were gorgeous—so full and pink. Thinking they looked just made to be kissed."

She laughed shakily. "You know, when I first kissed you I didn't think you were going to respond. You seemed...I don't know, frozen to the spot."

"I was surprised, that's all." Rast stroked her cheek. "Here I was, dressed up in some ridiculous outfit and forced to be part of a wedding I knew nothing about when suddenly this gorgeous girl walks up and kisses me."

Nadiah smiled. "I suppose it must have been...what's the word...weird for you."

"Only at first," Rast assured her. "I caught on pretty quickly to what was happening."

"You certainly did." Nadiah felt her cheeks get hot as she remembered the passionate, possessive way he had kissed her back.

Rast was obviously remembering as well. "I was thinking I'd never wanted a woman so much in my life," he said softly. "It's a good thing we got interrupted when we did or—"

"Or what?" Nadiah prompted him.

He shook his head. "Let's just say I wanted to do a hell of a lot more than kiss you."

Nadiah's heart was pounding and her face felt like it was on fire but she didn't want him to stop taking—she wanted to hear more. "Tell me," she urged. "Tell me what you wanted to do. What you would do if we were...were making love."

Rast arched an eyebrow at her. "Want to stop pretending then? Because you know I was talking about you earlier, don't you? When I was describing the way I like to make love."

Biting her lip, Nadiah nodded. "Yes, I...I thought as much. But I still want to hear more."

"I'll tell you then." Rast put an arm around her and pulled her closer. His warm, masculine scent seemed to fill Nadiah's senses and the heat of his big body was comforting and exciting at the same time. He took her hand once more with his free hand and looked into her eyes. "Where was I?" he murmured.

"You were saying that you wanted to lay her—me—down and...and touch me all over," Nadiah breathed. "I...I think, anyway."

"That sounds about right." One corner of Rast's mouth curved up in a sensuous smile. "I'd want to kiss you for a long, long time, sweetheart. Then, when I was sure you were comfortable, I'd touch you—the parts I hadn't touched before."

Nadiah's breath caught in her throat. "My breasts you mean. And my...my pussy."

Rast shifted on the couch. "God, you don't know what it does to me to hear that naughty little word from your sweet pink lips."

"Does it..." Nadiah tried to think how to put it. "Does it make you hot? Aroused?"

"You're damn right, it does," Rast growled. "Everything about you makes me hot."

"I...I feel the same way about you." Nadiah dared to reach up and stroke his cheek. It felt rough and warm against her hand.

He caught her hand and laid a hot, gentle kiss in the center of her palm. "Then do you want to hear more?'

Wordlessly, Nadiah nodded.

"I'd want to stroke your breasts, maybe tease your nipples a little." Rast's eyes were half-lidded with lust.

"Tease them? How?" she whispered.

"Lick them." His eyes strayed down to the cleavage displayed at the v-shaped opening of the white dress shirt. "Suck them. I'd take my time about that."

"Y-you would?" She felt suddenly self conscious, aware of her breasts in a way she hadn't been before. Her nipples felt tight and achy and when she shifted, the thin white material of his shirt rubbed against them in a way that was both irritating and pleasurable at the same time.

He nodded. "Oh yeah, I definitely would. I'd suck them until they were tight and dark pink and very...very sensitive. I might even nip them, very gently, like this." Raising her hand to his, he nipped lightly at the end of her index finger to illustrate.

Nadiah had to swallow a moan and shifted, trying to get comfortable, but for some reason she couldn't. Her skin felt too tight and her breath was coming too short. Still, she wanted more. "Go on," she managed to say. "What...what would you do next?"

He kissed her fingertip—the one he'd nipped—and smiled. "Well, when I was sure you were ready, I'd slip my hand down and cup your sweet little pussy."

Nadiah pressed her thighs tightly together, feeling a surge of heat that nearly made her gasp. No one had ever spoken like this to her before. And the way Rast was looking at her—like he wants to eat me up!—was making her feel incredibly warm and flushed.

"What...what next?" she asked. She could almost feel his large, hot hand cupping her there, holding that most sensitive and secret part of her as though it was a delicate treasure he didn't want to injure.

"I'd cup you...and then I'd spread you." Rast's voice was a low, lustful growl. "Spread you open so I could slip my fingers deep inside your pussy and feel exactly how wet you were."

"W-wet?" she murmured.

He raised an eyebrow at her. "You know what I'm talking about. Your pussy gets wet when you're turned on—when you're aroused. I'm sure it does when you touch yourself at night, right?"

Nadiah looked down at her lap. "I've never...that's forbidden."

He frowned. "Forbidden by who? It's your body, Nadiah. You have the right to give yourself pleasure."

She shook her head. "I...I guess I never thought of it that way. On Tranq Prime we're taught to believe our bodies belong to our mates. It would be like...using someone else's property for an illicit purpose."

"Sounds to me like Tranq Prime could use a good does of women's lib," Rast muttered.

"What?'

He shook his head. "Never mind. Just...don't be afraid or ashamed to touch yourself, all right? There's nothing wrong with it—nothing to feel guilty or ashamed about."

Since she'd been taught differently her whole life, Nadiah had a hard time wrapping her head around that idea. She filed it away to think about later. "I'd rather hear about how you want to touch me," she murmured, feeling bold. "I mean, if you don't mind."

"Of course not. Sorry we keep getting off track." He shifted toward her, his voice dropping into a lower, softer register. "Where did I leave off?"

"You...you were touching me here." Nadiah nodded at her tightly clenched thighs. "Between my legs. You were touching my...my pussy."

"That's right." He shifted again. "God, I can almost feel how wet and slick and soft you'd be. So hot and ready to be touched. To be tasted..."

Nadiah felt like her heart was going to beat out of her chest. "You...you said something about that earlier. Do you...would you really want to..."

"Taste your pussy?" Rast finished for her. "Absolutely, sweet heart. And I'd want to take my time about it too. First I'd pull you down to the end of the bed so your legs were hanging over. Then I'd get on my knees on the floor in front of you, so I could get right between your thighs."

Nadiah bit her lip. "You seem to have it all thought out."

He raised an eyebrow at her. "If you're asking if I've fantasized about this—about tasting you—the answer is hell, yes. And the position I'm describing would be the best because it's comfortable for both of us. So you can watch and I can spend a long, long time eating your pussy."

The area between her thighs that he was talking about—her pussy—was throbbing in time with her heartbeat by now. Nadiah squeezed her thighs together even more tightly, though what she really wanted to do was part her legs and let him in. "Do you...would you have a special technique for...for tasting me?"

He nodded. "I certainly would. I'd want to rub my cheeks against you first, to feel your warmth, soak up your scent. Nothing smells better than an aroused female—I'd want your scent all over me. And I'd want to put mine on you, too...but later."

It sounded like something a Kindred would say, Nadiah thought distractedly. She knew that scents were very important to them—maybe humans were the same way? She didn't know and didn't care, she just wanted him to go on. "And then?" she prompted.

"Then I'd kiss you—kiss the outside of your pussy. Slowly and gently, the same way I'd kiss your mouth." Rast ran a thumb over her bottom lip again, making her moan softly. "I'd go as slow as you wanted me to, I swear it, sweetheart. I'd take time and make sure you were ready before I spread open you open and tasted the inside of your pussy."

"How...how would you know I was ready?" Nadiah asked softly.

"Just like before—I'd be able to tell by how wet you were." Rast caught her eyes with his. "Tell me, Nadiah, are you wet right now?"

Nadiah bit her lip and squeezed her thighs together. "I...I don't know."

"Will you let me see? If I promise not to touch?"

"I...I guess that would be all right." Slowly, feeling more self conscious and aroused than she ever had in her life, Nadiah leaned back and spread her thighs.

"That's good." Rast's deep voice was rough with lust. "Now just lift up the hem of the shirt and let me look at you."

He'd seen her naked just a few moments before but this was entirely different—it was sexual. Before he had been trying to comfort her. Now, he wanted to really look at her, to see how hot she was. How wet. Feeling exposed in a whole new way, Nadiah raised the hem of the white shirt and pulled it high, almost to her belly button. Rast leaned forward but, true to his promise, he didn't touch her.

"God," he groaned softly. "Just look at you, Nadiah. Look how hot and wet and swollen your pussy is."

Nadiah followed his gaze and saw that he was right—her pussy, which still throbbed with desire—was slick with her juices. In fact, even her inner thighs were shiny and wet with them. And that wasn't the extent of it. She was, as Rast had said, swollen with need. The outer lips of her sex were puffy and hot and the act of spreading her legs had also spread them open, revealing a glimpse of the tight little button she'd heard her friends call a clit.

"So slippery and wet. So beautiful," Rast murmured hoarsely, pulling her out of her self contemplation. He looked up at Nadiah. "You have no idea how badly I want to go down on you right now, sweetheart. Want to get on my knees in front of you and clean all that sweet cunt honey off your thighs and pussy."

Again, Nadiah felt like her clit was throbbing in time to her heart. "But wouldn't...wouldn't the feeling of having you licking me...tasting me...just cause me to make more. More...honey?"

"Oh yeah." He nodded, his eyes half-lidded with desire. "It sure as hell would. So of course I'd have to stay there. Stay between your thighs to keep on licking and sucking and cleaning away your sweet honey until you came for me...came all over my face. God." He shook his head and seemed to force himself to look away. "Better put the shirt down now, sweetheart," he said in a thick voice. "I don't...don't want to lose control but you're so goddamn beautiful I don't think I can keep it together if I keep on looking at you."

"All right." Slowly, Nadiah closed her legs and draped the hem of the white shirt modestly over her thighs. "Better?"

"Not really." Rast shook his head. "I can still see it—see you, all wet and hot—in my mind's eye. But at least it takes away some of the temptation to touch...to taste."

"Goddess," Nadiah whispered breathlessly. She sensed he was about to stop them, to stop this little talk they'd been having and she didn't want him to. "Tell me more," she begged. "Tell me what you'd do when you...when you penetrated me."

"You mean when I fucked you?" The word itself was harsh and rough but the low, purring tone in his deep voice made it sound like an act of love.

"Yes." She nodded. "How would you do that? Would you...I don't know...get on top of me?"

He surprised her by shaking his head. "Not for your first time, no. Your first time it would be better for you to be on top."

"Really?" Nadiah widened her eyes in surprise. "Why?"

"So you can be in control," Rast explained. "If you're on top of me, lowering yourself down so that my cock slides up into your pussy, you can control how much you take at a time. How deep I go, how fast or slow I enter you—you see?"

Nadiah nodded. "Yes, I guess so."

"That way it wouldn't hurt you." Rast stroked her thigh lightly, making her jump. "I would never want to do that, Nadiah. Would never want to hurt you. I'd make your first time special, I swear."

"I know you would," she whispered, touching his hand with her fingertips. "And that's why you want me on top?"

"That and so I can watch your breasts bounce and see the look on your face while I fill you." Rast stroked her hot cheek. "I want to see it in your eyes when my cock touches bottom inside you, when I'm all the way inside your tight little pussy, taking you for the first time."

"Would it feel good?" she asked softly.

"As good as I could make it for you, sweetheart." Rast shifted. "I'm, uh, kind of big if you know what I mean. But as long as you were wet enough and hot enough, I know you could take me." He sighed. "It would be a fantasy come true."

Nadiah felt her cheeks getting even hotter. "You…you fantasize about doing that with—to—me? Making love to me? Fucking me?"

Slowly, he nodded. "God help me, I know I probably shouldn't. Nothing's going to come of it but—"

"Wait a minute." Nadiah held up her hand to stop him. "What do you mean 'nothing's going to come of it?'"

He sighed again. "Exactly what I said. Look, Sylvan warned me off you before we left. He told me that no matter what happened, I'm not allowed to, er, change the color of your eyes. And I swore I wouldn't."

"What?" Nadiah felt like someone had dropped a cold lead weight into the pit of her stomach. "So even if you win the challenge you're not going to…to take me?"

"I can't, sweetheart. Try to understand," Rast pleaded. "I gave my word. Besides, Sylvan told me how important virginity is on your planet. I can't take that away from you—no matter how much I might want you."

Nadiah pulled away from him and sat on the edge of the couch. "So all that…that talk about it being my body to do with as I pleased, that wasn't true, was it?"

Rast blew out a breath in obvious frustration. "Of course it was true. It is your body to do what you want with."

"Unless I want to give it to the man I lo—a man I care for," she said, hoping he didn't notice her blunder. "Is that right?"

He ran a hand through his hair. "Look, I didn't mean—"

"You didn't mean any of it." Nadiah stood abruptly, suddenly furious. "I guess I should go. You and Sylvan have already decided between the two of you what's best for me so there's nothing for me to do here."

"Nadiah...sweetheart," he begged but she shook off his restraining hand and marched back to the end of the ship. Locking herself in her tiny, closet-sized bedroom she threw herself on the narrow bed and put her arms over her head.

Her body was still throbbing with desire but now her head was throbbing too—with a whole different kind of ache. As much as she tried to push them back, she could feel hot tears coming to her eyes. Lies, everything Rast had been telling her was lies. *For a minute there I thought he really cared for me. Maybe even loved me. But if he really wanted me, if he really cared, he wouldn't let anything stand between us,* she thought miserably. She forgot she didn't want to be bonded to anyone but a Kindred, forgot that she'd hated Rast when she first met him.

All she could remember now was his soft, low voice as he described all the things he wanted to do to her...and the look on his face when he'd explained that no matter how much he wanted her, he was never going to do them.

Chapter Eleven

It took almost three solar days to sort through the shifting debris jettisoned from the Fathership but at last Merrick found what he was looking for. The pod was a sleek, elegant cylinder not much bigger than a coffin and like all Scourge equipment, it was dead black with glowing green etching on the sides. He pulled it inside with his energy net, barely fitting it in the cramped confines of the airlock.

Once the ship's hull was sealed again, he opened the inner door and dragged the pod inside, careful not to touch the poisonous runes that ran along its black sides. They were made of the metal which filled the core of the Scourge home world—he knew of few things more deadly.

Taking his time, he popped the seals along the side of the long black pod and was rewarded with a faint hiss. So at least the inner contents, whatever they were, hadn't been compromised. That was good. If it was some kind of equipment he could probably sell it or maybe even modify it to fit his star-duster. The Scourge had been evil bastards but their gear was always top notch. Also—

But his train of thought was abruptly cut off when he swung open the pod's lid and saw what was inside.

A smaller, semi-transparent cylinder was nestled inside the life pod like an egg within an egg. This one was made of a pure, milky-white crystal and it hummed very faintly, a soft musical sound that even Merrick's sharp ears could barely detect. But it wasn't the cylinder itself—which he recognized as a rare and expensive stasis chamber—that held his attention. It was what lay inside it.

Curled inside the translucent crystal shell, like a baby bird waiting to hatch, was a small, fragile looking human female.

Merrick's breath caught in his throat with surprise and knelt to get a closer look at her. She was completely naked and so petite that at first he thought she must be a child. But the full curves of her breasts and her softly rounded hips convinced him otherwise. There was also a tiny, neatly shaved mound of dark curls at the apex of her sex—oh yes, she was fully mature, a perfect, exquisitely formed female.

She no longer reminded him of a baby bird, now he thought of the fanciful stories his mother had told him when he was little—stories of a beautiful young girl charmed into a magic sleep within the heart of a jewel that couldn't be broken until the right male came to free her.

He ran one hand over the thin crystal shell—it hummed, vibrating faintly under his fingers. Merrick shook his head. A stasis chamber—no wonder his instruments hadn't detected any life signs. The chamber had slowed down all her vitals until they were almost nonexistent. She probably only drew breath once or twice a day—if that. And her heartbeat had been slowed too, probably to a single beat per hour.

He wanted to see her face but a cloud of long black hair obscured it. There were a series of buttons on one side of the crystal chamber and he pressed them carefully, in the order that was indicated. A faint, musical chime sounded and the top shell of the chamber melted away, like snow in strong sunshine. Finally, the female's form was completely revealed.

What Merrick saw when the stasis chamber opened made him frown grimly. Someone had been beating this female—maybe even torturing her. The semi-transparent crystal had hidden what he could now clearly see as bruises on her upper arms and inner thighs. Also, her pale, porcelain skin was marked all over with tiny, cruel wounds.

Merrick felt a surprising surge of pity in his gut. Gods, what the fuck had been done to her? And who had done it?

Though he wasn't known for his people skills, Merrick didn't approve of harming females. Though they were frightened of his scarred visage and rough ways, he had never touched a woman in anger in his life, and he had only contempt for anyone who would. It was beneath a male to hit or hurt one who was powerless to defend against the attack. Only scum would do such a thing.

Of course, opening the chamber broke the stasis. The female began breathing again and the pink flush to her skin proved her heart was pumping blood at a regular rate. But though her vital signs were returning to normal, she still hadn't woken up. Wondering if her face had been marked, Merrick brushed the silky, black strands of her hair away.

There were no wounds on her cheeks but someone had blacked one of her eyes for her—a ring of dark purple that marred the delicate perfection of her features. His big hands curled into fists at the sight and he felt a strange stirring in his chest. Could it be…pity he felt? It wasn't an emotion he was familiar with but he thought it must feel something like this. Against his will, he was moved by the map of abuse he saw written on the small female's pale skin.

She stirred and this time he thought of a doll, one with perfectly painted features. But no doll he knew of made faces of fear and pain in its sleep. And no doll shivered and cried out, begging to be left alone.

"No," the girl moaned, in a soft contralto. "No, please…not again. I'll do anything but don't…" Her last words were lost in a mumble of sleep talk but she had begun to thrash inside her crystal shell, her face a mask of agony. It was almost as though she wasn't just remembering the pain that had been done to her—she was still somehow feeling it. He didn't know how he knew that, but Merrick was sure of it.

Concerned that she would hurt herself, he reached down to gather her into his arms. She was so light and small it was almost like holding nothing. To his surprise and discomfort, she quieted at once and cuddled close to his chest. Her long black hair draped like a shawl over his arm as she nuzzled her cheek against his shoulder.

Now what the fuck am I supposed to do? Merrick looked down at the girl in his arms uncertainly. She had to wake up sometime but he didn't want her to be upset when she did. And let's be honest, if she gets a look at me, she's gonna be upset. True. Any female waking up from a traumatic experience and seeing his scarred face and mismatched eyes would be terrified, not comforted. Better put her back down. He started to put her back in the chamber…and stopped. She felt so small and fragile in his arms—a delicate ornament that might break if he wasn't very, very careful.

Don't be stupid, he told himself roughly. She's just a female like any other. Put her down before she wakes up and screams bloody murder. Then she stirred against him, nestling closer to his warmth, and his heart seemed to skip a beat. Goddess, what was wrong with him?

She stirred again and this time her bruised eye and cheekbone pressed against his arm. A faint cry came from her lips and an expression of pain passed over her delicate face. Though he usually didn't give a damn for the suffering of others, the soft sound of distress moved something inside Merrick.

A memory, long buried, surfaced in the back of his mind. He remembered himself running to his mother with some small wound — so long ago it was, back when his true father still lived. And his mother...She kissed it better. She kissed it better and it didn't hurt after that.

Merrick frowned. How long had it been since he'd thought of that — since he'd let himself remember that perfect, early time in his life before everything went to the seven hells? Years, probably. Dwelling on the past was yet another weakness he didn't permit himself. And sometimes it hurt more to remember the good times than it did to remember the bad.

Merrick looked at the Earth girl's black eye again. Without thinking about it, he leaned down and pressed his lips to the dark ring of bruised skin. Then he asked himself why the hell he'd done such a thing — especially with a female he didn't even know.

At the brush of his lips, the girl in his arms stiffened and then stretched, like a cat waking up from a nap. Merrick pulled back quickly and got ready to put her down in a hurry. She was about to open her eyes and see him for the first time, and that was never a good thing as far as females were concerned.

But when her eyelids, ringed with thick, black lashes, finally fluttered open to reveal large, dark brown eyes, there was no fear in them. Instead, Merrick saw only relief.

"Oh, thank God!" she whispered hoarsely. To his surprise, she threw her arms around his neck and held him close. He felt hot tears on his neck and then she was whispering again. "Thank you, thank you for coming. I thought no one would. I thought he'd kill me. Oh God..."

Merrick was bewildered. She had seen him but hadn't screamed or tried to get away. Instead, she was hugging him tight enough to cut off his circulation. "Wait a minute," he protested. "Wait a fucking minute, uh..."

"Elise," she finished for him. "Thank you, thank you so much!"

"Elise," he began. "I'm not sure who you think I am but I don't even know who you are." He frowned. "I don't know who hurt you either but I'll be happy to kill the son of a bitch for you if you'll point him out."

"Then...then you're not here to take me away? To save me?" She pulled back from him, her delicate features twisted into a knot of pain and fear. "Please don't leave me here—please. He'll kill me—I know it!" She hugged him again, her grip around his neck panicky-tight, and he could feel fresh tears against his shoulder. "Please," she whispered. "Please, just take me away from here, away from him. Please."

Merrick reflected that it was a good thing he didn't share the weakness other Kindred had—that urgent need to find and claim a bride. If he had, the feel of the tiny, fragile female in his arms and the sound of her soft, desperate pleas in his ear might have been his undoing.

As it was, he wasn't quite sure what to do. The role of comforter wasn't one he'd ever played. Most females got away as quick as they could when they met him—not a single one had ever sought shelter in his arms.

"Calm down. It's all right," he said roughly and patted her gingerly on the back.

"But he'll get me! He'll find me!" The little female was getting more hysterical, not less. Something else was needed—he had to reassure her somehow or she was going to completely lose it. And the last thing he needed on his star-duster was an out of control female.

"No, he won't," Merrick rumbled in her ear. Being careful not to hurt her, he held her firmly to him, restraining her as gently as he could against his body. "It's all right, baby," he said, keeping his voice low and reassuring. "I've got you now. I won't let him hurt you anymore."

"You won't? Oh, thank you!" He felt something soft brush his scarred cheek and was surprised when he realized it was her lips—she'd kissed him there. "Thank you so much. And…" she pulled back to look at him. "And you'll take me away from here?"

"Far away," Merrick said firmly. "I swear it."

Her big brown eyes filled with relief. "Thank y—" she started to say again. But then her lovely eyes rolled up in her head and her small body went suddenly limp in his arms.

"Goddess!" Merrick stared with horror at the lifeless form in his arms. She wasn't breathing and this time the stasis chamber had nothing to do with it.

Chapter Twelve

The descent to Tranq Prime was easy. Despite the fact that he'd only had a few lessons, the Kindred ship seemed to respond to his hands as though he'd been flying for years. Rast wished he could say the same about the way Nadiah responded to him. Ever since their fight, two days before, she'd been distant and cold—as cold as the frozen wasteland they were about to land on.

Shouldn't have told her how I felt. Shouldn't have started anything with her in the first place, Rast told himself for the hundredth time. But he hadn't been able to help himself. When he got around Nadiah, everything practical and sensible flew out of his head, leaving only ridiculous, useless emotion. And when he looked at her, one word throbbed behind his eyes in glowing red letters— *Mine.*

She's not mine and she never will be, he told himself sternly as the craggy white peaks and snow-covered tundra of Tranq Prime grew larger in the viewscreen. *Even if I win the challenge, she's still off limits. It's clear Sylvan wants her to marry a Kindred or one of her own kind and I'm neither. I made him a promise and I'm not going to break it.*

Despite his determination, the thought of relinquishing Nadiah to another man made him feel sick. *So don't think about it,* he told himself as he went through the landing sequence. *Just concentrate on the matter at hand—getting her out of the blood bond so she doesn't have to marry that bastard of a fiancée.*

The sequence went smoothly and before long the little ship was touching down on a landing field covered with short, bluish-gray vegetation. Rast sighed and rose, cracking his neck and stretching to get rid of the kinks in his shoulders. Despite the way Kindred technology came so naturally, he'd been nervous about the landing and he was glad it was over. Of course, performing a smooth, safe descent wasn't nearly as difficult as what was to come.

Now comes the hard part, he thought grimly. Taking a deep breath, he called, "Nadiah — we're here."

He wasn't expecting much of a response — since their fight she'd mainly kept to her room and when she did come out, she refused to talk to him. Rast was certain she'd had endured several other blood bond attacks in the past few days but though he ached to hold her and ease her pain, she denied him access when he knocked at her door. So he was surprised to see her suddenly standing in the doorway, dressed in her newly healed tharp, which had configured itself into the shape of a warm winter coat.

"I'm ready," she said flatly. "We can go as soon as you put on the vranna skin coat Sylvan packed for you." She held it out to him — a huge bundle of turquoise fur which looked like it would just fit his big frame.

"Vranna skin, huh?" Rast took it from her and shrugged into it, feeling nearly suffocated by its furry warmth. "Ugh, this is fucking hot. Maybe I should just carry it."

Nadiah shrugged. "Suit yourself. But off-worlders have been known to freeze to death in the time it takes to get from their ship to the grotto door." She nodded at the viewscreen which showed an arched doorway in the side of a mountain a few hundred yards away. "Sophia almost did."

"Thanks for the warning," Rast said dryly. "I guess I'll keep it on then."

"Do what you like." She shrugged. "I don't care either way." She started to turn away but Rast grabbed her shoulder and pulled her back.

"Nadiah!"

"What?" She looked down at his hand on her shoulder as though it was a dead spider. "We're not bonded, Rast. You should probably stop touching me."

"Is that what this was about? Because I refused to take your virginity?" he demanded. "Because I told you I could never fuck you?"

Her pale cheeks blushed scarlet at his rough words but she held her head high. "You figure it out."

"If I could figure it out—if I could figure you out—I'd be a very happy man," he growled, glaring at her. "Unfortunately, I have no clue and you're not giving me anything to go on."

"That makes two of us, Rast." She put a hand on her hip. "Because I can't figure you out either. I don't even know why you're here challenging for me."

The words, Because I love you! trembled on his lips but Rast clamped down on them hard. She'd think he was crazy if he declared himself like that. Not to mention the fact that it didn't matter how he felt about her—she was never going to be his.

"Because…" he said at last, lamely, "Because uh, it's my fault you're having this problem in the first place. If it hadn't been for me distracting you and asking for your help with the missing girls you would have had time to meet a nice Kindred guy to challenge for you. So I feel, I don't know…" He shrugged. "Responsible."

Nadiah's full pink lips had narrowed down to a thin white line. "Is that all you can come up with? You feel responsible? Really, Rast?"

"What do you want me to say?" he exploded. "Damn it, Nadiah, I'm here, aren't I? What more do you want?"

"Too much apparently." Her lips trembled and for a moment he thought she was going to cry. Then she lifted her chin and frowned. "Forget what I want, Rast—it doesn't matter. Let's just go, I'm sure my parents are waiting for me." She grimaced. "Along with my intended."

His hands clenched into fists at the mention of her fiancée's name. "If he hurts you—"

"You cannot interfere," Nadiah interrupted, frowning. "As far as my people are concerned, Y'dex has a perfect right to 'punish' me with the blood bond if he sees fit. The only way you can stop it is by breaking the bond."

"I'll do it, then," Rast vowed grimly. "I swear I'll do it, even if it kills me, Nadiah."

For a moment her eyes were filled with emotion that made his entire body throb. "Thank you, Rast," she whispered. A single silver tear slipped from the corner of her eye and slid down her cheek. "But it might, you know. Trying to break the blood bond might kill both of us."

Then she turned and hit the door lock, letting in a rush of the coldest air Rast had ever felt in his life. Without waiting for him to answer, Nadiah stepped out onto the frigid crust of her home world and headed for the grotto.

As he followed her, Rast couldn't help thinking she didn't look at all happy to be home.

* * * * *

As she walked, Nadiah barely felt the chilly wind swirling around her face, trying to pry icy fingers between her skin and her sheltering tharp. She usually found the cold of the surface of her home world bracing but today she didn't even care. Hot or cold, what did it matter? Rast didn't care for her—he was only doing this out of pity. And of all the forbidden romance stories she had read and all the holo-vides she'd watched, the hero never broke the blood bond and won the heroine out of pity.

He's going to fail, she thought miserably, as she trudged along, her face bent against the stinging ice needles in the wind. We both are. We can't break the bond with anything less than true love. And even though I care for him, he doesn't feel the same for me. So it's never going to work.

Despite the efforts of her tharp to warm her, she was half frozen by the time she got to arching wooden doorway that served as the entrance to the Lanash grotto. A quick look behind her showed that Rast looked all right—better than any human not used to the extreme cold of Tranq Prime had a right to, actually. Nadiah felt a flash of hope. That injection Sylvan gave him must really be working. Maybe we can get through this after all.

But the moment she pushed open the grotto door, any optimism she felt faded. Standing there, waiting, were her mother and father and her hated fiancée.

Rast came in behind her, stamping his feet and blowing on his hands. "You weren't kidding—it really is cold out th—" He stopped abruptly when he saw her parents and Y'dex. "Well, well, if it isn't the welcome wagon," he muttered, shoving the door shut behind them. "Real friendly of you folks to come down to meet us."

Nadiah realized it was up to her to make introductions. "Mamam, Patro," she said, ignoring her intended. "This is Detective

Rast. I mean, Rast," she said quickly, trying to cover for herself. But it was too late.

"Detective?" Y'dex stepped forward, frowning, his white-blond brows pulled down over his pale, bulging eyes. "Not 'Commander' or 'Warrior'? What kind of Kindred designation is 'Detective?'"

"It's not Kindred, it's human." Rast stepped forward. "I'm human. Got a problem with that?"

"None at all." Y'dex grinned. "Without the Kindred compounds in your blood, it should be even easier to best you." He laughed nastily. "I have to hand it to you, Nadiah, you certainly know how to pick yourself a champion."

Nadiah lifted her chin. "He's a better male than you'll ever be, Y'dex, no matter what type his blood is."

"Nadiah, please, such insults to your intended are rude and unnecessary." Her mother frowned disapprovingly.

"No, what's rude and unnecessary is the way this little bastard has been yanking on the bond between them, putting your daughter through excruciating pain." Rast fixed both her parents with a glare and then looked at Y'dex. "That stops now by the way. You might have gotten away with it before because I couldn't reach you. But I'm here now and I give you fair warning—you hurt Nadiah again and you'll have me to answer to."

Y'dex's pale face twisted into a sneer. "Nadiah is my property to do with as I please."

"Your law may say that, but where I come from we believe that no one has the right to own another person." Rast frowned. "Understand me on this, buddy—I'm not just threatening to make you sorry if you hurt her. I'm promising."

"Threaten or promise whatever you like—Nadiah is mine as the challenge will soon prove, weak-blooded human." Y'dex turned to

Nadiah, "This is a joke, my lovely—there's no way your champion can best me. In fact, why don't we just call the challenge over and start the first night of our bonding together right now?"

"You won't be spending tonight or any other night with Nadiah." Rast stepped in front of Nadiah protectively, his voice a low, menacing growl.

"We'll see about that, won't we?" Y'dex smiled coolly.

"That's enough of this male posturing. Nadiah, come with us." Her mother made a preemptory gesture with one hand. "Though your father and I don't approve of what you're doing, you'll be staying in our domicile until after this whole unpleasant business is finished."

Nadiah crossed her arms over her chest, refusing to budge. "Where is Rast going to stay?"

"With me, of course." Y'dex gave the human detective a nasty smile. "Unless he'd rather take shelter in the public reflection area." He looked at Rast. "Your choice."

"You can't expect him to stay with you!" Nadiah exclaimed. "You're rivals... enemies."

"Of course we are but there's no reason why we can't be civilized about it, is there?" Y'dex's smile abruptly turned into an ugly frown. "Besides, female, it's not your place to say where a male stays or what he does. Now go home with your parents until I see fit to claim you."

Nadiah lifted her chin. "You don't tell me what to do. I am not your slave."

Y'dex spit on the ground at her feet. "You are less than a slave. You're...what did this human champion of your call you? Oh yes, you are an animal—my pet. And a pet has to be taught to obey." He closed his hand into a fist and made a twisting motion.

Nadiah's whole body clenched, getting ready for the burning blade to slide between her ribs. She felt it come and fought not to double over, fought to stand her ground despite the fiery agony...

And then Rast took a step forward and punched Y'dex in the face. There was a crunching sound and the sharp pain beneath her heart ended as abruptly as it had begun.

"Ahh!" Her fiancée staggered backward, his long, beaky nose pouring blood. "You!" He glared balefully at Rast. "You...human. I think you broke my nose!"

"Yup." Rast wiped his bloody hand casually on the vranna hide coat. "And there's more where that came from if you do it again. Remember, buddy, a promise is a promise and I always keep mine."

"Well!" Nadiah's mother looked incensed and her father was obviously aghast.

"This...this is unacceptable," he blustered. "Completely unheard of."

"You're going to hear a lot more of it if tall, pale, and nasty over there doesn't mind his P's and Q's." Rast gestured at Y'dex and then frowned at her parents. "You know, I shouldn't have to do this. You two should be the ones protecting Nadiah—you should never have given that weak, pasty little bastard so much power over her. She's your daughter for God's sake."

"As our daughter she is bound to obey our parental orders," Nadiah's father said, frowning. "We hand picked Y'dex for her. If she would be more obedient he would not feel the need to punish her."

"Let me tell you something about your hand-picked son-in-law." Rast took a step forward and her father fell back, dithering nervously. "He's the kind of guy who's always going to want to hurt or punish whether he has reason to or not. I know — I've seen his kind in my line of work more times than I can count."

"In your human employment, you mean, off-worlder?" Nadiah's mother raised an eyebrow at him.

"Yeah, that's right. But unfortunately this behavior isn't limited to Earth." Rast pointed at Y'dex. "He's a coward and a bully and he's going to be a wife-beater if you give him the chance. I think maybe you two should ask yourselves if a little social status is worth seeing your only daughter black and blue every damn day of her miserable married life."

"Well, really!" Nadiah's father drew himself up, throwing out his thin chest in anger. "I cannot allow you to talk to myself and my mate in such a fashion!"

"I don't really see how you can stop me." Rast gave them both a lazy grin. "And by the way, Nadiah stays with me."

Nadiah's heart leapt at his words but regretfully, she had to shake her head. "I can't Rast — it will cause too much talk."

"Why?" He frowned. "Anyone who looks at you can see your eyes are the same color they've always been."

Her parents and Y'dex all gasped simultaneously. "Young man! That is not polite conversation!" her mother protested, turning red. "And my daughter must stay in our domicile with us or the challenge will be considered void and Y'dex will win her by default."

Rast frowned and looked at Nadiah. "Is that true?"

Reluctantly, she nodded. "Any female challenged for must be a female of virtue. If I stay with you — even if nothing happens between us — I could be considered unvirtuous."

"Unvirtuous, huh?" He nodded and looked at her parents. "All right, she stays with you. But I want to see her during the day so I can ask if you're treating her right and be sure idiot boy over there isn't messing around with the bond." He nodded at Y'dex, who was still cupping his wounded nose, his pale face painted with bloody red streaks.

"I don't think—" Nadiah's father began.

"I'll bring you your meals," Nadiah interjected quickly. "That will give us a chance to talk."

Rast nodded. "Sounds good to me." He looked at Y'dex. "Well let's go home, buddy. I assume your offer still stands?" His smile was friendly enough but his truegreen eyes were as hard and flat as emeralds. Her fiancée must have seen the danger in those eyes because he recoiled and shook his head.

"I rescind my invitation. By law I am not required to offer hospitality to anyone who has done me violence."

Rast cracked his bloody knuckles. "What a shame. Guess I'll be camping out in the public reflection area then." He nodded at Nadiah. "Lead the way, it looks like I'll be roughing it."

"This way." Not caring what anyone said, she took his hand and pulled him down the long underground corridor that led to the main grotto. Behind her she could hear her parents and Y'dex muttering in outrage and disapproval but she no longer cared. Nor did she care about the many curious eyes of her fellow Prime citizens as she led Rast into the vast, arching cave and down into the quiet meditation area with its grove of snowflower trees and the large, steaming purple-blue lake.

"Here we are," she said at last, spying a small cloth lean-to someone had built in the shelter of one of the supporting pillars. In it were a rolled up sleeping mat and a thin pillow.

"Hmm." Rast nodded his approval. "Looks like they weren't expecting me to stay with your boyfriend after all."

"Very funny," Nadiah said dryly. But inside she was feeling cautiously hopeful again. She liked the way Rast had stepped in and taken charge of the situation, refusing to let her parents and fiancée dictate to him. Of course, there was more to winning the challenges than just being stubborn but Rast's irascible, indomitable attitude was certainly a good start.

"Well, I guess this is me." Rast shrugged and looked around the grove. "Nice place you got here. The outside part of it, anyway."

Nadiah felt a surge of shame for her family's poor hospitality. "I'm so sorry we have no guest house or zotel to put you in like you have on Earth."

"Zotel?" Rast grinned. "You mean hotel or motel?"

"Whatever." Nadiah waved a hand. "I'm sorry you have to stay out here instead of in someone's domicile."

"It doesn't matter." He looked up. "At least I don't have to worry about being rained on, right?"

"It's not right." Nadiah sighed fretfully. "The more I examine it, the more I realize there are a lot of things that aren't right with my home world — with my culture."

"Don't worry about it." Rast squeezed her hand comfortingly. "As soon as this is over you can leave and go wherever you want, sweetheart."

I want to go with you, Nadiah thought longingly. Wherever you are, that's where I want to be. But Rast had made it clear that even if he won the challenge and broke her blood bond, he wasn't interested in taking things any farther between them. So she just bit her lip and nodded. "Thank you."

"You're welcome." He nodded.

"I mean it," Nadiah hugged him impulsively. "Really, thank you—for everything. For coming here in the first place. For fighting for me."

He hugged her back and kissed the top of her head. "You're worth fighting for, sweetheart."

He's being so sweet and kind, even after the way I treated him! Nadiah felt suddenly ashamed of herself. "I'm sorry I was cold to you earlier, Rast," she murmured.

"It's all right, honey." He stroked her hair. "You were just scared and I don't blame you—this is a hell of a scary situation we're in here." He pulled back to look in her eyes, a much softer expression on his granite-hard features. "The thing to remember is that we're in it together. And I swear to you, I'll see it through to the end and make sure you get free of that little bastard."

"I know you will." Nadiah's heart swelled and suddenly she felt sure that Kindred blood or no Kindred blood, Rast would be able to keep his word. "And I know I told you not to interfere if Y'dex hurt me through the blood bond but, well, thanks for doing it anyway."

"Any time," he murmured, looking into her eyes. "Any time at all, sweetheart."

"Rast..." she whispered and then couldn't think of anything to say. She was lost, drowning in his dark green eyes, unable to look away.

"Nadiah," Rast said softly. He cupped her cheek and leaned down, his eyes still locked with hers. Nadiah could feel his warm breath on her lips and her heart leapt crazily in her chest. For a moment the entire world around them seemed to disappear and there was nothing but the two of them standing so close she could almost feel his pulse in her veins.

But just before their lips met, a hard hand grabbed the crook of her elbow and dragged her away.

"What is wrong with you, young lady?" her mother demanded in a shrill, outraged voice. "How dare you make such a display of affection with a strange off-worlder male in the middle of the public reflection area?"

"Maybe because you didn't give me any place private to stay," Rast said mildly, but his eyes flashed dangerously as he took in the way Nadiah's mother was pinching her arm. "I shouldn't have to tell you this, but you'd better treat her right."

"Our daughter's welfare is not your concern," Nadiah's father told him stiffly. "And it won't be until the very unlikely event you win the blood challenge."

"You're wrong about that." Rast took a step forward and pointed at Nadiah's parents and Y'dex, who was hovering in the background, glowering. "Nadiah is under my protection and anyone—I mean anyone—who hurts her will answer to me. Understand?"

Nadiah's parents nodded stiffly but Y'dex just glared. "Strong words are well and good off-worlder. We'll see if you can back them up tomorrow in the challenge grotto." He nodded at her father. "Let's go."

As she was dragged off by her parents, Nadiah cast a last look over her shoulder. Rast was standing there quietly, looking at her, a steadfast look in his eyes. Stay strong, those eyes seemed to say. I'll fight for you. I swear it.

Nadiah's eyes filled with tears and she blinked them back rapidly. "I love you." It was just a whisper, barely a breath but she said it even though she knew he wouldn't hear it. Said it because it was true.

No matter what Adam Rast might think of her, Nadiah had given him her heart and there was no taking it back now.

* * * * *

"How dare she? How dare she?" Y'dex Licklow paced back and forth, his vranna hide boots thumping on the solid stone floor with rage. "How dare she bring such an inferior off-worlder male here to challenge me?"

"We're very sorry, Y'dex." Nadiah's mother and father looked besides themselves and Y'dex's own parents had looks of steely disapproval on their faces.

"It's unheard of—ridiculous!" he sputtered. "Really, Father, can he get away with hitting me? Can't we put him out on the surface to freeze for daring to perform violence on a citizen of the grotto?"

"That rule only applies during the challenge itself, unfortunately." Magistrate Licklow frowned. "But I wouldn't worry, son. If he's not even Kindred, you'll win the challenges easily. What did you say he was again? Hooman? Is that the word?"

"Something like that." Y'dex waved one hand in the air dismissively. "But he's a Goddess damned big human, father. He may not have true Kindred blood in him but he's certainly as massive as one of them." He touched his throbbing nose gently with the tips of his fingers. "Strong, too."

"Y'dex, I'm certain you'll do fine." Nadiah's mother spoke in a fawning tone. "You're as tall as he is and with his inferior blood lines…"

"I think we're all overlooking something quite important, here." Lady Licklow, who had been silent through most of the exchange, spoke up.

"Oh?" Y'dex's father looked at her respectfully. "And what is that, my love?"

"Why that you are the magistrate who will be presiding over the three challenges." Lady Licklow put a hand on her husband's shoulder and smiled, an expression which didn't reach her pale blue-grey eyes. "You are the one who will be inspecting and qualifying all the equipment. You are the one who will judge each match."

"The goldurs for the challenge of strength," Nadiah's mother looked excited. "If one of them was off balance..."

"And the magistrate judging the match failed to notice it," Nadiah's father chimed in.

"Or the mud worms for the test of wills," Nadiah's mother said. "They don't have to be of exactly equal potency, now do they?"

"Exactly." Lady Licklow nodded, her smile widening. "I see you're all beginning to take my point."

"But...but my love..." Magistrate Licklow looked ill at ease. "Judging a blood challenge is a sacred duty. I really don't think –"

"That we should leave anything to chance. Isn't that what you were thinking, my dear? Oh, thank you, Lydiah," she added, as her daughter came through the assembled guests quietly, refilling drinks from a black stone pitcher. "That's most refreshing."

Lydiah nodded and went to refill Y'dex's mug but he put her off with a frown. "Get out of here, sister. Can't you see we're discussing important matters?"

"I see." Lydiah bowed her head quietly and backed away. "I'm sorry, brother."

"As well you should be," he sneered. "Now go on, run away and leave us."

"You heard your brother, Lydiah." Lady Licklow nodded at her sharply, her good humor entirely gone. "Scamper away now and don't bother us again."

"As you wish." Lydiah bowed again and left the room swiftly. She ducked into the food prep area just long enough to put down the stone jug and then slipped quietly out of the domicile.

Nadiah was one of her best friends and she wanted to tell her that her off-worlder champion wasn't going to be playing on a level field.

Chapter Thirteen

"Are you ready for this? Truly ready?"

The deep, commanding voice made Lauren shiver with mingled fear and anticipation as she knelt in the middle of the bedroom floor. "Yes," she whispered, bowing her head submissively.

"Yes, what?" the voice rapped out.

"Yes...Master." God, she still got hot calling him that. Then again, she and Xairn hadn't been together sexually that long and they were still feeling their way through this new and exciting aspect of their relationship.

Xairn had been taking things slowly, very slowly, because he was still a little afraid he might hurt her. His Scourge urges to dominate and possess were as strong as ever but little by little, Lauren was proving to him that there was nothing to fear. That she could take whatever he could dish out.

"Very good." One large, warm hand reached down to caress her hair and Lauren leaned into it, like a cat that wanted to be stroked. "We will have a human bonding ceremony—a wedding—if you like," Xairn continued. "There we will exchange rings and vows of eternal love. But this is the mark of my people—the final mark of possession which I give you tonight. If you are willing to receive it."

Lauren shivered at the meaning in his deep voice. The final mark—the one that would make her his beyond the shadow of a doubt. She'd had her nipples pierced and his initial tattooed on her body. And just the week before, she'd gotten the hood of her clit pierced with a tiny silver ring as well—by a female technician, of course. Lauren didn't want another man's hands on her, especially in such an intimate place. Now there was only one mark of possession left—the most visible one of all.

The collar.

"I am willing, Master," she said, looking up at him, letting the adoration and love shine in her eyes as she took in his tall, muscular body and red-on-black eyes. "More than willing—I am eager."

"Lauren...my Lauren." He stroked her hair again, his voice filled with tenderness and love. "And I am eager to fasten it around your neck. To mark you as mine forever."

From behind his back, Xairn produced a slender black leather collar with a gleaming silver buckle. Dangling from the center of the collar was a single blood-red ruby, as large as her thumb. It was cut in a perfect square and it gleamed in the dim, romantic light cast by the small fire crackling in the fireplace.

Lauren gasped when she saw it. "It...it's beautiful." She could see that once the collar was buckled in place, the ruby would nestle in the hollow of her throat perfectly. "But...why a square?"

"Each side represents one of the four Scourge marks of possession." He handled the ruby carefully, cupping it in his palm to show her. "It doesn't have to be a ruby—traditionally any jewel will do. But I thought the blazing red would look lovely against your skin."

"I'm sure it will." Lauren was already picturing the sparkling red stone against her creamy, mocha skin tones. It would look amazing. But she didn't just want to wear the collar because of its gorgeous jewel—she wanted to wear it as a sign of her submission and her love for her man. As a public reminder of what they did when they were alone together in private.

"I know you're ready to wear it. But there is one final test." Xairn placed the black leather collar carefully on the mantelpiece above the fireplace. There was, of course, no need for fireplaces on a spaceship. But since the Kindred catered to their women's wishes as well as their needs, almost every suite had one.

"A test?" Lauren frowned. "But I thought...I've taken all the marks now, haven't I?"

"You have. You have endured pain to show your love for me." Xairn's voice was slightly hoarse as he knelt on the rug, facing her.

"No more than you endured for me," Lauren murmured, tracing the raised letters of her name which were branded across his broad, bare chest.

"I would endure that and much more to be with you always," Xairn assured her softly. "But in order for you to wear the collar, I must link the other marks and then take you with them linked."

"Link them?" Lauren frowned. "I don't understand."

"I'll show you." From a pocket of his tight, black leather flight pants, Xairn produced a slim golden chain. "This is the first," he said mysteriously. "Raise your arms."

Lauren did as he commanded and he fastened the chain around her hips. The tiny gold links felt cool against her skin and she couldn't help noticing that the chain fell squarely in the center of the large capital X for Xairn she'd had inked on her skin even before he had bonded her to him.

Before she could ask what was next, Xairn produced another chain, or rather, three chains all hooked together with a single gold ring at one end. "What's that?" She frowned as he spread the three golden strands apart.

"You'll see." The gold ring clipped to the chain he'd put around her hips, leaving the three strands dangling. Xairn took one of them and hooked a tiny clip on its end to the silver ring piercing her right nipple. He took a second strand and hooked it to the left. "Like this," he murmured and plucked lightly at both golden chains which stretched in taut lines from her tight, berry dark nipples to the center ring at her naval.

"Oh!" Lauren moaned softly as the slender gold chains pulled at her pierced nipples. God, if she'd had any idea piercing her intimate areas could make her so deliciously sensitive she would have done it years ago. But then, it wouldn't have been as special. As pleasurable as it was, she was glad she'd had herself pierced just for Xairn.

But as good as her nipples felt, she still felt a surge of uncertainty and nervousness when Xairn reached for the third and final golden chain and began to stretch it down to the tiny silver ring between her legs.

"Xairn," she whispered uncertainly. "I mean, Master, I'm still kind of…tender in that area. I haven't had that piercing as long as the others."

"I know, Lauren." He stopped what he was doing and stroked her cheek lightly with the back of his hand. "And I swear to be very, very careful. But this is part of it the ritual and I didn't want to wait anymore. I'll tell you what…" His hand dropped from her cheek and slid down her trembling abdomen to cup her pussy. "I'll check your piercing before we proceed to make sure you're ready. Would you like that?"

As he spoke, one thick finger slipped between the swollen lips of her cunt and stroked delicately over the pierced hood of her clit.

Lauren, who was already wet and hot from wanting him, moaned. "Che-check it?" she stuttered. "How? With your fingers?"

"No." Leaning forward, Xairn kissed her gently on the cheek and murmured in her ear, "With my tongue." He kissed her again and his voice turned hard. "Now, up on the bed."

Lauren bit her lip in anticipation and nervousness as they got onto the vast king-sized bed together. Xairn didn't have much Kindred blood in him but he had enough to give him the Kindred pleasure in going down. The only thing the huge warriors loved more than licking a woman between her legs was bonding her for all eternity—commitment issues weren't usually a problem within the alien race.

She started to lie on her back and spread her legs for her master, but Xairn shook his head. "Not that way. Like this." He lay down with his head on a pillow near the headboard of the bed and then motioned for her to join him.

Lauren frowned. "I'm not sure exactly how…"

"Straddle me—my head." Xairn beckoned her to come closer. "Then spread your legs wide and come down to ride my tongue."

The position sounded simple enough, although she'd never done it before. But Lauren couldn't help thinking how vulnerable she would feel, how uncertain lowering herself down until he could reach her pussy with his tongue. "I…I don't know," she whispered, hesitating.

Xairn's red-on-black eyes grew stern. "Did I ask you what you wanted to do, Lauren?"

She bit her lip, her pussy getting even wetter at his strict tone. "No," she admitted.

"No," he echoed. "I told you what to do. And in the bedroom, I expect you to obey me without question. Do you understand?"

"Yes." Lauren nodded. "I mean, yes, Master."

"Good." He nodded and beckoned for her again. "Then come here."

Obediently, she came to him and straddled his face with her knees as he had commanded. "I'm here, Master," she said, looking down to meet his eyes. "But I have to be honest—I don't understand why you, uh, want me this way. Wouldn't it be easier for you if I was lying on my back?"

Xairn's eyes softened a bit. "Easier for me, Lauren but not easier for you. This position is for your own protection—to keep me from hurting you."

She shook her head. "I still don't understand."

"It's like this," he explained. "I'm going to start out slow and gentle, caressing your pussy and clit with the tip of my tongue, just barely tasting you. If it hurts, you can pull away. If it doesn't, I'll expect you to come further down, and give me deeper access to your pussy." He arched an eyebrow at her. "Do you understand?"

Laurens' heart pounded in her chest. "Y...yes, Master," she murmured softly.

"Good." He kissed her inner thigh, making her jump a little. "The let's begin. Come down, Lauren. Let me taste you."

Disobedience wasn't a choice unless she wanted to be spanked. And while part of her did, indeed, enjoy the slap of her master's hand against her bare ass very much, right now Lauren simply wanted to do as he said. Gripping the headboard tightly in both hands, she started to lower herself.

"Wait." Xairn stopped her.

"Master?" she asked, wondering if he had changed his mind. But she needn't have worried.

"Come down to me," he directed. "But first spread your pussy lips open. Let me see the inside of your cunt."

The hot, dirty words given in that harsh, commanding tone of voice made her even wetter. Slipping her hand between her thighs, Lauren spread her outer pussy lips with her middle and index fingers, baring herself completely for her master. Then, holding onto the headboard with the other hand for balance, she began to lower herself again.

True to his word, Xairn was incredibly gentle. She shivered as she felt just the tip of his tongue inside her, outlining her slick petals slowly but never touching her center. The lengthy, ticklish exploration seemed to take forever and the more he avoided her clit, the more anxious Lauren was to have him there. But just as she thought she was going to go crazy, she felt his tongue slide inward to circle her throbbing button.

"Xairn..." she whispered and gripped the headboard tighter as he traced the tiny silver ring piercing her hood. "Oh, Master..."

"Does it hurt, Lauren?" he asked, using the mind link all males with Kindred blood develop with their bonded females.

"No," she answered aloud. "Not...not at all."

"Then come lower. Let me taste you more deeply."

Yielding to her master's will, Lauren lowered herself more fully, giving him greater access to her open pussy. When she felt Xairn's hot tongue flatten out against her slick, inner cunt she moaned in pleasure. And then he was lapping her hard, sucking and licking and teasing the tiny silver ring which sent shivers of pleasure to the tiny, hot bundle of nerves at her center.

"Oh God...Oh Xairn..." she gasped, and found she was gripping his coal black hair with both hands and pressing down, trying to get as much contact between her sensitive pussy and his hot mouth as possible.

Xairn seemed to welcome her loss of inhibition. Two strong hands gripped her hips as he guided her, urging her to ride him, to grind her pussy against his mouth while he serviced her with his tongue. The whole time while he lapped and sucked her eagerly, Lauren could hear him whispering through their link.

"Goddess, love to eat your sweet pussy. So sweet and salty and perfect. Love the feel of you riding my tongue, letting me tonguefuck you from below like this…"

"Xairn," she gasped, gripping his hair tighter. "God, baby…Oh, I think I'm going to…I can't hold back. Have to…have to come."

She felt a surge of pleasure through the link and the tip of his tongue flicked the silver ring that pierced her. With a gasp that might have been his name, she felt her orgasm finally hit, rushing over her like a warm wall of water, drowning her in Xairn's intensity and love.

"Oh…Oh, God," she whispered, sliding to one side as the last tremor finally passed through her. She felt lightheaded, almost dizzy—but she put that off to the intensity of the experience. The feel of her man tasting her from below while she rode his face had been incredibly different and delicious. In fact, the only thing that could have made it better was penetration. She felt so empty inside.

"We can fix that," Xairn murmured and she realized he must have heard her thought through their link.

"I'd like that," Lauren murmured, rolling over on her side to face him. "Do you wish to take me now, Master? To fuck me?"

"I am going to fuck you, long and hard and deep," Xairn promised, his voice a low, possessive growl. "But first the last piercing must be linked. Do you feel ready to let that happen?"

For an answer, Lauren lay on her back and spread her thighs. "Link me," she said, nodding at the last slender golden chain still dangling free. "Link me and then put me in whatever position you want to fuck me, Master."

"Lauren." Leaning down, Xairn kissed her long and deep, sharing her own taste on his tongue. Lauren kissed back eagerly, loving the sweetly intimate kiss and the promise of what was to come. Finally, he broke the kiss and looked into her eyes. "It is time," he murmured and then, gently, he hooked the final golden chain in place.

Lauren moved her hips experimentally and had to bite back a gasp as the gentle tugging sensation electrified her already over-sensitive clit. Xairn was watching her closely and he raised his eyebrows in a silent question.

"It feels good," Lauren assured him, moving her hips slightly again. "Oh. Intense but really, really good." She looked at him. "So…what position do you wish me to assume, Master? How will you take me?"

"I want you on your hands and knees for this." Xairn stroked her side, urging her up. "And I'm only using my secondary shaft this time. I don't know if you're ready to have my thick primary shaft in your ass, even if you have been eating bonding fruit."

Lauren bit her lip, uncertain how to feel about that. On one hand, she loved the feeling of double penetration her man's two shafts gave her. Because of their configuration, the primary shaft was the one that pierced her pussy when they were facing each other while the secondary shaft slid deep into her rosebud. It was a delicious sensation, being so filled in every possible way and Lauren never worried about being hurt because of the elastic qualities the bonding fruit gave her more intimate areas.

Oh the other hand, it was going to be nice to be able to really concentrate on feeling his cock in her pussy. And he was right—

even with bonding fruit taking his huge, thick primary shaft deep in her ass was a frightening idea.

"Up," Xairn demanded, and she realized she'd been thinking too long. "Up on your hands and knees and spread your legs for me."

Lauren scrambled onto her hands and knees at once, enjoying the feeling of vulnerability it gave her to get into such an exposed position. She loved belonging to her man in the bedroom, loved submitting to his orders and giving him her body in any way he pleased.

"Beautiful," Xairn murmured, running a large, warm hand up and down her bare back and over her ass. "So very beautiful and submissive. Now…arch your back."

Without thinking about it, Lauren obeyed at once. A moan of surprised pleasure was torn from her lips as the gesture tightened all three golden chains and tugged at all her piercings simultaneously. She started to relax her posture, wanting to ease the intensity of the feeling but Xairn stopped her.

"Keep your back arched," he commanded in that low, dominating voice she'd come to love. "And spread your thighs wider for your master's cock."

"Yes, Master," Lauren whispered submissively. Spreading her thighs even wider caused another tug on the chains and she couldn't help moaning as she opened herself for him.

"Such a good girl," Xairn murmured, stroking her back in a long, sensuous caress. "Such a submissive female to open herself so wide for her master's cock."

"Please, Master," Lauren begged breathlessly. "Please, I ache for your cock. Please fill me up and make me yours."

"That is exactly what I plan to do." As Xairn spoke, she felt him get into position behind her, his huge, muscular body looming over hers, his body heat climbing her spine like an open flame. There was a soft rustling sound of leather opening and she knew he was baring the thick club of his sex. "And when I fuck you," he continued, the broad head of his secondary shaft nudging the entrance to her pussy. "And fill you with my cum, only then will I put the collar on you."

With all the pleasure and submission going on, Lauren had completely forgotten about the collar. Now she remembered it and what it stood for—her desire to give herself completely to Xairn to do with as he pleased. God, how she wanted to wear it! How she wanted to show how she felt, how much she loved him.

"Yes, Master," she moaned softly as she felt the head of his cock pierce her pussy entrance and begin to slide inside, stretching and opening her cunt channel. "Yes, please, fuck me...take me...make me completely yours."

His answer was a low groan and then a long, hard thrust deep inside her pussy. Lauren cried out in surprised pleasure as the abrupt movement tugged on her chains again. God, her clit and nipples were throbbing and it didn't look likely they would stop any time soon. With every long, hard thrust into her body, Xairn tightened the chains, stimulating her to even higher and higher reaches of pleasure.

"Master," Lauren gasped, spreading her legs wider and gripping the bedspread hard. "Please, Master, please fuck me!"

"I will fuck you, Lauren." Xairn's deep, growling voice was filled with promise. "Fuck you and come in you to make you mine. Mine always and forever. The only female who wears my collar and all the marks of my possession on her skin."

As he spoke, his tempo increased, his thick shaft thrusting harder and faster into her body, increasing the delicious friction between them until Lauren felt ready to scream. God it felt so good, so incredibly right to give herself to him this way. To open herself and let her master fill her with his cock and his cum. Speaking of which, she could feel her mate's thick secondary shaft swelling within her and she knew it wouldn't be long before she felt his hot essence bathing the mouth of her womb.

"You're right, Lauren. I'm going to come in you soon, come in your tight little pussy," he murmured through the link. "But first I want to feel you coming all around me. Want to feel your sweet, soft pussy tremble around my cock."

His hands, which had been gripping her hips, slipped down to explore her body and Lauren moaned when she felt him pluck gently at the silver rings in her nipples, increasing the tension caused by the gold chains.

"Master," she whispered. "Master, please. It's too much...too intense..."

"Then you will learn to bear it, for me, because I ask you to," he murmured. Lauren felt one of his large hands trace down the length of the golden chains until he came to the one attached to her clit ring. "I'm going to rub your sweet little clit, Lauren," he told her, his fingers tracing lower. "Going to rub it while I fuck you, do you understand?"

Biting her lower lip, Lauren nodded. "Yes, Master."

"Good, then open yourself even more for me. I want you to spread your cunt again."

It was harder this time, spreading open her pussy lips for him. Lauren lost her balance and was forced to go from her hands and knees to her elbows as she did as he asked. The change in position forced her ass even higher into the air, giving Xairn better access to her pussy.

Lauren moaned as his thrusts deepened and then gave a low cry when she felt the blunt pads of his fingers circling her silver clit ring. God, she was going to come again, come so hard while he fucked her and fingered her…she couldn't help it. Didn't want to help it. She just wanted to give in to the intense pleasure that was peaking inside her and let her mate mark her as his forever.

"Come for me then," he whispered through their link. "Come and let me feel your pussy clenching all around me."

With a low cry, Lauren did exactly that, giving in to the pleasure of her master's cock pounding inside her pussy and his fingers caressing her clit. Giving in to the pleasure of being taken and claimed.

Xairn allowed her orgasm to trigger his own. With a low roar, he fucked as deeply into her as he could and then held rock solid and still, pressing the head of his cock to the mouth of her womb as spurt after spurt of hot cum bathed her inner pussy, filling her and marking her as his for all eternity.

The pleasure was so intense that Lauren felt light-headed again. No, more than light-headed, she realized as her orgasm peaked. She was really dizzy. So dizzy she could no longer remain upright. With a little gasping cry, she fell over on her side as the world spun around and around.

"Lauren?" Xairn had finished coming and was instantly alert to her condition. "What's wrong?" he asked anxiously, cradling her close. "Are you feeling all right?"

"I feel…strange." Lauren put a hand to her head and tried to sit up but the world started spinning again and she had to lie back down. "That was intense, really intense, but I've never felt like this afterwards before," she admitted. "I'm not sure what's going on."

Xairn rolled her over onto her back and stared into her face, his eyes filled with worry. "Was I too rough? Did I hurt you?"

"No, no, it was nothing like that." Lauren was seeing double, two sets of anxious red-on-black eyes looking down at her. She closed her own eyes, trying to block out the strange vision. God, what was wrong with her? Rather than getting better, she seemed to be getting worse. Much worse.

"Come on." Xairn fastened his flight pants and then gathered her into his arms. The world spun again as he lifted her off the bed.

"Come on? Where…where are we going?" Lauren protested.

"To the med station to see Sylvan. I think something is wrong."

"I can't go like this," Lauren protested, motioning down at herself. "I'm still all…all linked. Not to mention completely naked."

"Here, then." Swiftly he removed the chains and somehow managed to wrap her in a red silk robe at what seemed to Lauren the speed of light. "Now, let's go."

"Really, Xairn, I'm fine," she protested. "Let's just stay here and take it easy."

"Fine, are you?" he growled, setting her on her feet. "Let's see you walk a straight line, then."

"All right." Lifting her chin, Lauren tried. But with her first step, the world swayed around her and she nearly fell.

"See?" Xairn swung her up in his arms again, his eyes anxious. "Your balance and equilibrium are completely off. We have to get you checked out."

Reluctantly, Lauren agreed. "All right." She sighed. "But I bet I'm just hungry. It's been hours since the last time I had anything to eat. In fact, I'm starving." And suddenly she was—completely and totally ravenous. "Xairn, let's skip the med station and go out for a bite," she begged, her stomach growling. "I feel like I'm going to faint if I don't get something in me right now."

But Xairn shook his head. "Let's see what Sylvan says first."

And he carried her, still protesting, out of their suite and down the long curving corridor to the med station.

Chapter Fourteen

"You did the right thing, putting her right back into the stasis chamber," Sylvan said. "It probably saved her life."

Merrick felt like a huge weight had been lifted off his chest. The minute he'd landed in the Mother Ship's docking bay, he'd put in a call for Sylvan. Now the two of them were crammed into his little star-duster, staring down at the milky, once more opaque stasis chamber. "So then...you think she'll be all right?" he asked, trying to keep his voice indifferent. "Not that it matters—I don't even know the female. But I do feel responsible."

"Responsible, hmm?" Sylvan gave him a sharp look which Merrick returned with a scowl.

"Yeah, responsible and that's fucking all." Merrick wanted it to be true but try as he might, he couldn't get her out of his head. The way she'd cried and clung to him, her petite body shivering against his much larger frame...the warm, feminine scent of her hair, the feel of her trembling against him...somehow it had gotten to him.

"Her vitals appear to be good," Sylvan said, frowning at the blinking lights on the chamber door. "So that's a good sign. But..."

"But what?" Merrick frowned. "What's wrong with her?"

"There may be...complications," Sylvan said reluctantly. "Depending on how long she's been in that chamber and what exactly was done to her, she may have stasis sickness when we bring her out of the chamber the second time."

"Stasis sickness?" Merrick shook his head. "What the hell is that?"

Sylvan clapped him on the shoulder. "Nothing for us to worry about right now. I'll call a team and have them move the life pod and stasis chamber down to the med station. I, myself will open it and personally oversee her recovery. Will that be all right?"

"It's all right with me." Merrick shrugged. "As I said, I don't even know her."

"No, but you brought her in and if what you told me is right, you comforted her when she was upset and confused. That puts you in the roll of her protector." Sylvan frowned. "I know it's not a roll you're comfortable with so if you'd rather I found someone else to speak for her and watch out for her interests —"

"No!" The word was out before Merrick could stop it. "No," he said again, frowning. "You're right. I brought her in — I'll be responsible."

"Very well." Sylvan nodded gravely. "I know you have her best interests at heart, Brother."

"I do." Merrick frowned. "I don't know why but..." He shook his head and looked at his friend. "Thanks for taking care of her yourself, Sylvan. I appreciate it — especially after I ruined your joining ceremony."

Sylvan laughed. "You didn't ruin it, Merrick! I would have rather had you there but as it turns out, Nadiah had someone else to perform the luck kiss with so it all worked out in the end."

"Nadiah? I've never met her but do you mean the daughter of your mother's sister?" Merrick asked.

Sylvan nodded. "Yes, that's her."

"Then I'm glad I wasn't here after all. Forgive me, old friend, but I wouldn't have wanted to frighten your kin."

Sylvan frowned. "Don't be silly, you wouldn't have frightened her."

"With this face?" Merrick pointed at himself. "Hell yes, I would have frightened her," he growled. "I frighten any female that looks at me. Except..." His eyes went to the sleeping girl with her cloud of midnight black hair.

"Except who?" Sylvan urged softly. He obviously saw the direction Merrick's gaze was taking because his voice got even softer. "Except her?"

Merrick scowled. "It means nothing but..."

"But what?" Sylvan asked.

"Well...when I first got her out of stasis I was sure she would scream the minute she opened her eyes and saw me. She's obviously been through a lot—there are bruises and wounds all over her." His hands clenched into fists. "I'd like to catch the son-of-a-bitch who did that to her, who hurt her."

Sylvan shook his head. "I'm afraid there's no catching him—he's dead."

"What?" Merrick demanded. "How do you know?"

"Because it was the AllFather. If I'm right, and I think I am, this female is the last one he abducted before his son, Xairn, went to confront him. We looked everywhere on the Fathership for her and couldn't find her. She must have crawled into the stasis chamber before the life pod deployed." Sylvan shook his head. "If you hadn't found her, she might have been lost, floating in deep space forever."

"The AllFather, huh?" Merrick shook his head. "No wonder she looks like she does. That sick bastard must have tortured her."

"I think that's a pretty safe bet," Sylvan said quietly. "She was missing for awhile before he was defeated. It's hard to say what he did to her but I'm sure it wasn't pleasant."

Merrick looked at the fragile form of the girl and something like awe crept into his heart. "She was abducted and tortured and

Goddess knows what else. But despite all that, she wasn't scared of me when she saw me. She...she clung to me. Wrapped her arms around my neck and didn't want to let go." He gave a harsh laugh. "Thought she was going to fucking strangle me before I calmed her down."

"It sounds like she knew a good male when she saw one," Sylvan said, smiling. "You see? You're not so frightening to females after all."

"Yes, I am—to most of them," Merrick objected. "Which is why I'm damn glad the daughter of your mother's sister didn't have to perform the luck kiss with me."

Sylvan looked troubled. "There isn't much that frightens Nadiah. In fact, sometimes I think she's too fearless for her own good."

"What do you mean?"

His old friend sighed. "Just that things with Nadiah have gotten...complicated lately. She's back on Tranq Prime now, challenging the blood bond her parents set up for her when she was only six cycles old."

"Challenging a blood bond?" Merrick, who had been raised on Tranq Prime, knew exactly what that entailed and how risky it was. He gave a long, low whistle. "That's bold, all right. What kind of warrior did she get to challenge for her?"

Sylvan frowned. "That's the thing—the one who is seeking to break the bond isn't Kindred. At least, I don't think he is."

"What's that supposed to mean?" Merrick asked, perplexed. "How can you not know if he's Kindred or not?"

Sylvan shook his head. "I really shouldn't say any more. He's not exactly my patient but—"

"But you're worried about your kinswoman and you need to unload." Merrick squeezed his shoulder. "Come on, old friend—say what you need to. I'm as silent as the grave and you know I'll be leaving as soon as I meet your bride and my duty to this little female is discharged." He nodded at the shape in the stasis tube. "I'll probably never even meet the male you're speaking of."

Sylvan sighed. "All right. Well, he comes from Earth, just like my female, Sophia. But he looks Kindred—that's how the mix-up at my bonding ceremony occurred. Deep and Lock, my second brothers, mistook him for you, since they'd never met you before and didn't know you're a hybrid. They forced him into the ceremony and Nadiah kissed him."

"Some mix-up," Merrick agreed. "The poor male must have been pretty fucking confused."

Sylvan nodded. "He was—although he rose to the occasion admirably. Later, when he offered to challenge for her, I took some of his blood, trying to find a way to strengthen it and him for the coming conflict." He rubbed the back of his neck, as though to ease tension. "At first blush, it appears to be completely human which would be in keeping with the fact that he was born and raised on Earth. But the results of the long term analysis are starting to come in and they're so strange that—"

Suddenly he broke off, his head cocked to one side in a listening gesture.

"Sylvan?" Merrick frowned. "You all right?"

"Forgive me." Sylvan shook his head. "But I'm getting an urgent message from Sophia. Apparently there's an emergency down at the med station."

"Then go," Merrick urged him. "The girl will be all right as long as the stasis chamber is sealed, right?"

"Right." Sylvan nodded. "And I'll send a team to bring her right away—as soon as I finish dealing with this. He turned to go but Merrick put a hand on his shoulder.

"One more thing, Brother, since you know about this little female. What's her name?"

"Oh, um..." Sylvan frowned, obviously concentrating. "Elise, that's it. Yes, Elise."

"Thank you." Merrick looked back at the girl.

"You're welcome and now I really must go. I'll talk to you later." Sylvan clapped him on the shoulder once more and then left the star-duster in a hurry.

"Elise," Merrick murmured to himself, staring at the fragile form still cradled in the dreamless sleep of stasis. "Elise..."

* * * * *

"I'm sorry to have Sophie call you, Sylvan, but nobody seemed to know where you were," Olivia greeted Sylvan anxiously as he burst into the small exam room near the back of the med station. She and Sophia and Kat were all huddled anxiously on one side of a cot which held Lauren. On the other side of the cot, Xairn hovered anxiously, holding his female's hand and looking as worried as a male could look.

"It's all right," Sylvan assured her. "I was with Merrick in the docking bay—he finally got in." He looked at Lauren. "Now what seems to be the matter?"

"She's very faint and weak. So dizzy she can't even sit, let alone walk. I had to carry her here." Xairn sounded near panic. "This came on very suddenly—I am extremely worried."

"Of course you are," Sylvan said soothingly. "All right, you say it came on suddenly. What was she doing when the symptoms hit? Any kind of strenuous exercise?"

"Um..." For some reason both Xairn and Lauren looked embarrassed and while it wasn't easy to tell with the Scourge warrior's gray skin, Sylvan was almost positive he was blushing.

"We were just...Well, actually we were, um..." Lauren shifted in the cot and the scent of sex wafted to Sylvan's sensitive nose. Oh.

"Never mind," he said briskly. "Let me just draw some blood and run a few tests. We'll see what's going on."

"I really don't think there's anything wrong with me except I'm hungry," Lauren protested, holding out her arm for the needle he was preparing. "Seriously you guys, I feel like I could eat an entire week's worth of cupcakes right now. And I bake a lot of cupcakes in a week."

Olivia frowned. "You have a really strong feeling of hunger? Like you have to eat right now or you're going to be sick or faint?"

Lauren nodded. "Exactly." She looked at Sylvan pleadingly. "Please, can't one of the girls get me something to eat? I swear I'm starving over here."

Sylvan frowned as he collected the blood sample. "I don't know if that would be a very good idea. If, Goddess forbid, something was truly wrong and we needed to operate, we would want your stomach to be empty."

"That's what I feared," Xairn said, his face turning pale. "Which is why I refused to let her eat before I brought her here."

"Just let me run those tests," Sylvan began but Olivia shook her head.

"There's only one test you need to run, Sylvan."

"What?" He finished taking the sample and sealed the small wound in Lauren's arm with flesh glue. "What are you talking about?"

"Come here." Olivia beckoned to him and whispered in his ear.

After a moment Sylvan nodded. "All right. We'll do it at once." He looked at Lauren and Xairn. "Just sit tight for a moment. I'll be back in five standard minutes."

* * * * *

Lauren watched fearfully as Sylvan left the room and went to run whatever tests he needed to find out what was the matter with her. Could it be that there truly was something really wrong? Was she dangerously ill? Was she—

"Stop worrying, doll." Kat patted her on the arm comfortingly. "You're going to be fine—Sylvan's the best doctor on the whole Mother Ship. Isn't that right, Liv?"

Olivia nodded. There was a secretive smile playing around the corners of her mouth that Lauren couldn't understand. "Absolutely. And I bet he'll come back with good news."

"Good news?" Xairn growled. "How in the seven hells could anything which makes Lauren faint and sick good news?"

"We don't know for sure yet so I'm not saying anything," Liv said. "But just wait—it shouldn't take long to check."

"What shouldn't take long to check?" Sophie sounded exasperated. "Honestly, Liv, why are you being so secretive? Would you mind telling us exactly what's going on here?"

"I'm not saying anything until we know." Olivia looked stubborn. "I don't want to raise any false hopes."

"False hopes?" Lauren shook her head. "Now you've lost me completely, cuz. Seriously can't you just tell me—"

"I'm not saying anything," Liv repeated. "Just wait."

The time seemed to crawl, and Lauren swore that the five minutes Sylvan had asked her for had turned into five days or possibly five years. But just as she couldn't take it anymore and was about to grab her cousin and demand an explanation, Sylvan came back inside the room. Olivia looked at him and he nodded once, a small smile on his lips.

"I was right then?" she asked.

Sylvan nodded again. "You're quite the diagnostician, mate-of-my-kin."

"Right about what?" Lauren nearly yelled. "Come on, you guys, I'm dying over here. Well, not literally, I mean…that is, I hope," she added, feeling suddenly uncertain. "But I—"

Olivia laughed. "You're not dying, Lauren. You're pregnant. Sylvan, show her."

With a smile, Sylvan produced a small, perfectly formed pink flower and handed it to Lauren who took it and stared at it. She'd heard about the Kindred pregnancy test from her cousins and Kat but the results were almost always a blue flower. A pink flower meant…

"A little girl! Oh my God, you're going to have a little girl!" Kat yelled. With a squeal of excitement, she rushed to hug Lauren who accepted the gesture and then hugged her friend back as the reality of the situation began to sink in.

"A little girl," she whispered. "I didn't…didn't think it was possible. Not after Xairn lost the human DNA he had from me when he went back to the Fathership that last time."

"Enough of it must have remained to make pregnancy possible." Sylvan smiled. "Congratulations, Lauren, Xairn. In about a year you're going to be parents."

"And you're only a quadmester or two behind me." Liv grinned. "My little boy and your little girl will grow up together."

Sophia spoke up suddenly. "It's the prophecy," she said, her face strained and white. "The one the AllFather was hunting Liv and me for in the first place. It said that a female would come who would regenerate their race by having girls—isn't that right?"

"That's right." Xairn nodded slowly and Lauren couldn't help noticing that his face was paper-pale as well. "The prophecy has come true. My female...my female is with child. I am going to be a...a..." He shook his head, clearly unable to finish.

"Honey?" Lauren said anxiously, looking up at him. "Are you all right?"

"I...I'm fine." He took a single, weaving step toward the door and then another. "I just can't believe...I...I need some air." He opened the door and was halfway out before he wobbled and his knees crumpled.

"Oh my God, catch him!" Kat shouted at the same time Liv yelled,

"He's going down!"

Unfortunately, none of them but Sylvan was close enough in size to catch the huge Scourge warrior without being completely flattened. And Sylvan was on the other side of the room. He ran to catch Xairn but Lauren could see he wasn't going to be in time.

"Oh, no!" she gasped, hoping her man wouldn't fall flat on his face and break his nose. "Xairn, honey!"

But disaster was averted at the last moment by the biggest, scariest looking male Lauren had ever seen. He appeared, seemingly out of nowhere, and caught her man under the armpits just before Xairn hit the floor.

"So this is the Scourge who helped defeat the AllFather," he rumbled, turning to Sylvan. "Where do you want him?"

There was shocked silence for a moment and then Sylvan smiled. "I'll have another cot brought in until he recovers," he said, leaving the room. "Thank you Merrick—good catch."

"A very good catch." Olivia looked at him with one eyebrow raised. "You must be Sylvan's friend, the one we were expecting for the bonding ceremony."

"Yes." He nodded and Lauren noticed that he had mismatched eyes—one bright blue and the other gleaming gold—and fangs like a Blood Kindred. A long, crooked scar bisected one side of his face, adding to his frightening appearance. But it was his size and strength she couldn't get over. He was still supporting Xairn's full weight without the least sign of any effort and his shoulders completely filled the doorway. Good Lord, he's big! Even bigger than the Kindred and the Scourge, she thought wonderingly. I've never seen anyone that tall outside the pro Basketball circuit and none of them are nearly as massive as he is. How the hell did he get like that?

"It's very nice to meet you, I'm Sylvan's wife." Sophia nodded politely at the stranger holding Xairn, but Lauren thought she had a troubled, strained expression on her face. "Don't worry about the ceremony, it went perfectly well without you." She blushed. "Oh, no offense."

Merrick's mismatched eyes flashed. "None taken," he rumbled.

Sophia's cheeks went pink. "I...I mean, not that we didn't want to have you in it because we did, very much! But we were still okay and...and..." She shook her head. "Could you excuse me, please?"

"Sophie?" Kat touched her shoulder. "Are you okay?"

"Yeah, womb mate—what's going on?" Liv asked.

"Nothing. I'm fine." Sophia nodded briskly but Lauren saw that her big green eyes were suddenly filled with tears. "I'm fine," she repeated, even though it was clearly untrue. She took a long look at the pink flower in Lauren's hand and then nodded. "Congratulations again, cousin. I'll see you later."

With a stifled sob, she slipped out the doorway, leaving Lauren to wonder what in the world could be wrong.

Chapter Fifteen

"They're going to what?" Rast demanded.

"Shhh!" Nadiah put a finger to her lips as she handed him the steaming hot bowl she'd brought for his dinner. "Not so loud. This is a public area — anyone could be listening." She looked around the grove of snow flower trees as though an army of spies was hiding behind their slender, pale trunks.

"Tell me again," he growled. "Tell me what your slimy fiancée and his parents and your parents are up to."

"They're going to try and fix the challenges." Nadiah looked miserable. "It's completely unacceptable, I know, but there's nothing we can do about it."

"How about if we confront them with it — tell them we know what they're doing?" Rast said.

"And get Lydiah in trouble?" Nadiah put a hand to her hip. "She risked everything to tell me what she heard, Rast. She could be severely punished or even lose her own chance to be bonded if her parents decide to declare her rebellious and unbondable."

"All right, all right," he muttered, picking up the carved wooden spoon she'd provided with the bowl. He poked morosely at the steaming mass of gray pudding that was his dinner. "I don't want to get your friend in trouble but I don't see what else we can do. I'm already playing against a stacked deck here."

Nadiah bit her lip. "You could…could withdraw from the challenge, if you want," she offered in a small voice. "I know it isn't fair to ask you to do this, especially when you don't even really care for me in a romantic way."

"Don't care for you? I 1—" Rast stopped himself abruptly. "I mean, I like you just fine, sweetheart. And you deserve someone who isn't going to cut and run when things get a little tough." He put down the spoon and took her hand in his. "I'm not quitting—no matter what."

Nadiah looked relieved. "Thank you, Rast. Thank you so much."

"Anything for the sweet little lady who brings me oatmeal for dinner." Rast picked up the spoon again and took a big bite...then nearly spit it out. He took a quick look at Nadiah and swallowed with difficulty. "That tastes like...like raw liver or something. What the hell is it?"

"Steamed vorteg brains." Nadiah looked at him anxiously. "Is it still too hot to eat?"

"A vorteg? Isn't that the animal that looks like a cross between a snake and a spider?"

She looked at him, surprised. "Why yes, I guess it does look like a mixture of those two Earth animals. Have you been studying my planet's fauna?"

Rast shook his head. "Nope—just something Sylvan said."

"I made it the traditional way," Nadiah told him. "Seasoned with the venom of a tis'rock and cooked in a vranna skull cooking pot. It's this whole long recipe that every Tranq Prime female is supposed to learn before she's bonded." She blushed. "I'm only supposed to make it for my intended but I wanted you to have it instead. Mamam always says I'll never master it but I'd like to think I proved her wrong."

Rast was touched. "I'd say you mastered it all right."

She smiled. "It's one of our most famous dishes. Well, aside from fleeta pudding. But I didn't think you'd like that—it's made of fleeta beetles."

"Mashed up beetles, huh?" Rast shook his head. "Kind of puts the whole brains thing in perspective."

"Don't you like it?" Nadiah asked anxiously. "I can bring you something else if you don't."

"No, no, it's delicious. Absolutely the best brains I've ever put in my mouth, really." Manfully, Rast took another big bite and swallowed as quickly as he could while trying not to grimace. *The things I do for love.* "It's just…a little rich," he improvised, taking another spoonful. "I, uh, don't want to be weighed down during the challenges tomorrow."

"Good thought." Nadiah nodded. "I'll get your some billa bread to go with it later."

"Bread—that sounds great." Rast smiled and put the bowl down as unobtrusively as he could. "I'm too worried to eat right now anyway. What are we going to do about tomorrow?"

"Well, I do have a few ideas." Nadiah's voice dropped to a whisper. "If they want to fix the challenges, there are a few fixes of our own we can make…"

They talked for the entire hour Nadiah was allowed to be away from her parents' domicile and then she left to get him some bread. She returned with a round, flat loaf that reminded Rast of pita bread only it was three times as big and bright blue. He sniffed it experimentally and then took a small bite from one side. To his surprise, a rich, mellow flavor like a cross between good coffee and a Krispy Kreme donut filled his mouth.

"Mmm, this is delicious!" Rast tore into it, his appetite renewed. The bread's texture reminded him of Cuban bread back home—crispy and chewy at the same time.

Nadiah flushed with obvious pleasure. "I'm so glad you like it. I made it just for you."

"What's it made out of? Wait—" He put up a hand. "Don't tell me. I just want to enjoy it without thinking about that."

Nadiah watched, smiling as he polished off the whole thing and then took back the thin stone platter she'd brought it on. "I'm so glad you enjoyed it."

"Sweetheart, I didn't just enjoy it—I loved it." Rast smiled at her. "So much in fact that you can bring me more of it for breakfast—a lot more."

Her face fell. "I'm afraid I won't be able to see you tomorrow morning. That is, I'll see you but I won't be able to talk to you. Someone else will bring you your breakfast and a tharp and boots to wear, but you and I will have to maintain silence during the first two challenges. Not until the third challenge when…when you give me your blood, will I be allowed to address you." She blushed as she spoke and looked down at her hands, making Rast wonder if there was something more than a blood transfusion going on in challenge number three.

"Is that a big deal?" he asked softly, ducking to look into her eyes. "Me giving you blood?"

"Letting another drink of you…it's a very intimate thing," Nadiah admitted. "And my people also consider it very, um, sexual."

Rast finally got it. "Because of the whole Blood Kindred thing with their fangs and biting, right?"

She nodded, her porcelain cheeks still rosy. "Yes."

"Well, then…" Rast lifted her chin and held her eyes with his. "It will be my pleasure to let you drink of me, Nadiah."

His words seemed to have the desired effect. Her lovely dark blue eyes with their exotic tilt were dilated and her cheeks were flushed — clear signs of arousal. Rast was struck all over again by her gorgeous, otherworldly beauty. God, how he wanted her! Wanted to take her in his arms and kiss her and mark her as his own so that no other male would dare to come near her…

Nadiah frowned and sniffed the air. "What's that scent?"

"What scent?" Rast sniffed as well but didn't smell anything. "What are you talking about?"

"It's dark and masculine…really nice but…" She sniffed again. "Actually, it smells like you. Like your scent. But I've never smelled it so strongly before."

Rast frowned. "Um, well, I don't know what to tell you. Is there anyplace to get a shower around here?"

"No, it's not bad." She put a hand on his arm. "I actually really like it. A lot. I didn't think human males had mating scents — that's all."

He shook his head. "We don't. I don't. So I'm not really sure what's going on."

Nadiah sighed. "Never mind. Maybe it's just my imagination." Leaning forward, she kissed him lightly on the cheek. "I'd better go so you can get some sleep. I'll see you in the challenge grotto in the morning."

"All right, see you. Nadiah…" He caught her hand before she could go.

"Yes?"

"I am going to see this through tomorrow," Rast told her seriously. "No matter what it takes, no matter how hard it is, I'm not giving up until you're free or I'm dead."

"Oh, Rast!" Impulsively, she threw her arms around his neck and hugged him hard. "Thank you," she whispered in his ear. "I don't care why you're doing this just...just thank you so much for caring."

"I do care for you, sweetheart. So much." The words sounded lame and inadequate coming out but he didn't know what else to say. He couldn't admit his true feelings, couldn't declare his love so he was reduced to mouthing empty pleasantries. To let her know how he really felt, he crushed her soft, slender body to his and gave her a slow, hot kiss on the cheek. "I can't wait for you to drink of me tomorrow," he murmured in her ear.

"Rast..." Nadiah stiffened, then melted against him. Rast could feel her pulse racing and her cheek flushing against his own. "I want that too," she whispered. "That and...so much more."

"Me too, sweetheart," he growled softly, stroking her hair. "Me too."

Chapter Sixteen

"So everything is going according to plan?" Nadiah murmured, keeping her eyes forward as she spoke. She was sitting by herself on a low platform that faced the pit in the challenge grotto. Half of the pit was filled with glowing hot coals and the other half with icy water. Directly between the two sides ran a narrow walkway — little more than a beam actually, since it was only about six inches wide.

"Everything's fine," Lydiah assured her, speaking out of the corner of her mouth as she poured water into Nadiah's cup. "He put it on, no questions asked."

Nadiah sighed in relief. "That should help with the challenge of strength, at least."

"At least." Lydiah gave her a fleeting smile. "And I've got something lined up for the challenge of wills too so don't worry."

"Thanks, Lydiah." Nadiah wanted to hug her friend but she was afraid the spectators sitting in the seats on the other side of the pit might suspect something. Instead, she squeezed Lydiah's arm. "I really appreciate this."

"I'll do anything I can to keep you from having to bond with Y'dex," Lydiah said seriously. "He may be my brother but he's also the cruelest male I know." She shivered. "I can't wait to be bonded myself just to get away from him."

"Is Havris excited too?" Nadiah asked, indicating Lydiah's intended, who was sitting among the spectators.

Lydiah smiled. "He is. I'm so lucky I was blood bonded to a male I actually care for." She looked at Nadiah. "I wish the same for you, my dear friend. That your champion will win the challenge so that you two can bond."

Nadiah tried to smile. "That's very kind of you, but even if he wins, Rast won't be bonding me."

"What?" Lydiah frowned. "But then...who will your soul anchor to?"

Nadiah shrugged uncomfortably. "I don't know. No one, I guess."

"But why—?"

"Even if he wanted to bond with me—which he doesn't—Rast made a vow to my kinsman, Sylvan that he wouldn't change the color of my eyes or tie me to him," Nadiah explained. "He's an honorable male—he won't break his vow."

"But Nadiah, surely Sylvan didn't know how strong your bond with Y'dex is when he made Rast take that vow. You have to have someone to replace my brother or you could die."

"I know," Nadiah said seriously. "But even death would be better than being bonded to Y'dex. I decided that long before Rast offered to challenge for me."

"But does Rast know? Know the consequences of breaking the bond without forming a new one will be your death?"

Nadiah shook her head. "He knows it's a possibility but I don't think he realizes how strong the bond is and I didn't want to tell him. I was afraid he'd feel pressured to do something he didn't want to do—something he wasn't ready to do."

"But, Nadiah—"

"That's enough chit-chat, girls." Lady Licklow suddenly appeared at the foot of the platform, frowning at them. "Lydiah, let Nadiah rest and meditate. Your brother and the human challenger will be here shortly." She sniffed. "At least he's not Kindred even if he does look like one of them."

Nadiah stiffened. The Licklows were deeply into the Purist movement which stated that no off-worlder should be able to marry into a Tranq Prime family and "pollute" their bloodlines. They had a special hatred of the Kindred for doing just that.

"The Kindred are an honorable people," she said. She was going to add something pointed about how the Kindred would never try to cheat on a contest but the sight of Lydiah still standing by her elbow stopped her. Whatever else happened, the Licklows and her parents must have no idea she knew what they were planning.

Lady Licklow simply sniffed again and moved off. Lydiah followed her mother, whispering a soft farewell as she went. Nadiah twisted her fingers together, wondering when the challenge would start—but she didn't have long to wait.

"Attention. Attention, please." Magistrate Licklow was standing in front of the assembled spectators, looking extremely self-important. His rotund figure was draped in a deep purply-blue tharp and he wore vranna hide boots of the same color. "Attention," he called again even though everyone had already stopped talking.

Seeing that every eye was firmly fixed on him, the magistrate began. "Ahem. We gather here today for a blood challenge between the esteemed Tranq Prime male Y'dex Licklow and his off world competitor, the human called Rast."

At this point, Y'dex and Rast both entered the challenge grotto from a small, side tunnel. Nadiah was angered to see that Rast was flanked on both sides by guards. As if he was some kind of criminal, just because he's an off-worlder!

Both the competitors were wearing the traditional Tranq Prime male costume of furry boots and a tharp wrapped around the waist, leaving the chest bare. Nadiah was proud to see that Rast filled out his outfit much better than her intended. Seeing him in the dark green tharp and boots reminded her of when they'd first met, during the luck kiss at Sylvan's bonding ceremony. *I fantasized about this,* she remembered. *Imagined that he would be the handsome male who would sweep me off my feet and challenge Y'dex for me.* Of course, in her fantasy he had also declared undying love for her and that certainly hadn't happened. But still, at least part of her dream was coming true.

Tearing her eyes from Rast, Nadiah examined the tharp Y'dex was wearing as well. It was a brilliant blue which looked too bright against his pasty skin. *Perfect,* she thought, staring at it. *A perfect match* — the exact color of his best dress tharp. *Now if only* —

"The challenge of strength is about to begin," bugled Magistrate Licklow, interrupting her thoughts. "I will now recite the rules. Ahem. The competitors will each be given a goldur with which to do battle over the pit of ice and fire. The one still standing on the beam at the end of the challenge is the winner. Falling off on either side constitutes a loss and the end of the match."

At this point, he reached for two long staffs which were lying at his feet. He seemed to take a moment handling them before giving one to his son and one to Rast.

Nadiah studied the ancient weapons with a kind of dreadful fascination. The goldur was straight out of Tranq Prime history texts — used only for kin feuds and blood challenges. Each three foot long staff had a heavy, battering-ram type knob attached to one end and a thin, circular blade attached to the other.

Supposedly each goldur was perfectly weighted so that the contestants could keep their balance while fighting on the narrow walkway that ran over the pit, between the hot coals and the icy water. Supposedly. But she saw Rast hefting his goldur with a frown—from the way he handled the weapon it was plain to see that one end was much heavier than the other.

It was no more than Nadiah had expected. Still, it made her angry to see Magistrate Licklow pronounce both weapons sound and fit for battle when the one he'd given Rast had obviously been tampered with.

"And now," the magistrate said in his pompous, nasal tone. "Let the contestants cross the pit and the challenge of strength begin." He nodded at Rast, who hefted his obviously overbalanced goldur in one hand and stepped onto the narrow beam across the pit.

Rast walked carefully but with a natural agility Nadiah couldn't help but admire. He might be human but he moved like a Kindred, with inherent grace despite his large, muscular frame. In fact, she was so busy watching Rast she almost missed what Y'dex was up to.

Her fiancée followed Rast across the pit, holding his goldur in both hands, obviously using it to balance himself as he walked. Just as both of them had reached the center of the pit with the hot coals to one side and the icy water on the other, Y'dex hefted his goldur and used the blunt end of it to strike at Rast's unprotected back.

Rast hadn't yet turned around and Nadiah saw what was happening just a split second before it did. She gave a little a cry as Y'dex struck with his weapon. The soft sound wasn't much but it warned Rast and he braced for the blow. Instead of toppling over into the pit of fiery coals as Y'dex had obviously intended, he jumped lithely and turned to face his opponent, his own goldur held at the ready.

An angry murmur was heard from the crowd at the cowardly move and Rast spared a moment to look up at Magistrate Licklow.

"Hey, is that how you guys play it here? Hit your opponent in the back before he gets a chance to turn around?"

"Both contestants were in the center of the beam and the challenge had begun," Licklow said, frowning. "Y'dex's move is perfectly legal."

"Yeah, I'm sure," Rast muttered. "Just remind me not to do any real estate deals with you guys."

"What is that supposed to mean, off-worlder?" Y'dex sneered, swinging the sharp end of his goldur in a dangerous arc.

Rast gave him a grin that didn't reach his eyes and jumped back. "Just that I don't trust you any farther than I can throw you, cave boy." He swung his own weapon but it was clear the poor balance was affecting his aim and he missed.

"Ha!" Y'dex laughed triumphantly. "Is that the best you can do?"

"With this thing, yes." Rast raised an eyebrow at him. "Care to trade weapons?"

"That is against the rules of the contest!" Magistrate Licklow declared before his son could answer. "The contestants must keep the weapons they were given at the start."

"Well, isn't that convenient?" Rast muttered. He used the blunt end of his goldur to poke at Y'dex but the other male moved back in time to avoid it and parried with his own, balanced weapon.

For a moment their weapons locked and then Rast broke free with a jerk and retreated a step to be out of reach. Laughing nastily, Y'dex pressed his advantage. He came after Rast, swinging his goldur until the sharp edge whistled through the air.

Nadiah gasped as she saw the cutting edge connect and leave a long, nasty looking slash across Rast's broad, bare chest.

"First blood!" Magistrate Licklow trumpeted triumphantly. "Y'dex has drawn first blood."

"Yeah and it's gonna be last blood if I have anything to say about it," Rast muttered. "Hey Y'dex, think fast." With a quick advance, he swung his own goldur, causing Y'dex to hop backwards, losing his balance. One of his feet slipped off the beam and landed in the hot coals below. With a howl, he pulled his burned foot up, pivoted, and splashed it through the icy water on the other side.

"You off-worlder human scum," he growled, stalking towards Rast, his wet boot squelching as he went. "You'll pay for that."

"Oh yeah? Come at me." Rast spread his arms. "Come on, I'm waiting."

Y'dex glared at him but didn't move. Instead, he looked up at Nadiah and made a fist. Then, with a cruel smile, he made the twisting gesture that had become so horribly familiar.

She barely had time to think, Oh no! before the burning blade slid between her ribs, robbing her of breath and doubling her over with pain. A cry of agony escaped her—she couldn't help it.

"Nadiah!" Rast turned to her, his face filled with concern. "Nadiah, are you alri—?"

At that moment, when Rast's head was turned, Y'dex rushed forward, goldur swinging wildly. Rast turned back just in time to parry the attack but his opponent's momentum tore his weapon from his hand and flung it far out into the bed of hot coals.

"Now then, off-worlder." Y'dex laughed unpleasantly as he advanced on his unarmed opponent. Rast backed slowly away, trying to stay out of reach of the other male's weapon without getting either sliced or pounded. He was scowling and there was murder in his eyes.

"I warned not to hurt her again. Didn't that broken nose I gave you yesterday teach you anything?"

"You talk bravely for an unarmed male." Y'dex swung his goldur in a slow, taunting arc. "Come on, human, which do you prefer—fire? Or ice?"

With Y'dex's attention centered on Rast instead of herself, Nadiah felt the pain ease and then release her completely. She sat up, glaring at her fiancée. Concentrating fiercely she stared at the bright blue tharp wrapped around his waist and muttered, "Now."

Slowly, almost imperceptibly at first, the blue tharp began inching its way higher up Y'dex's long, skinny body. Soon the top edge of it was at his armpits. Which meant the bottom edge was considerably higher too.

Rast, who had been scowling as he ducked the other male's swinging weapon, began to grin. "Hey, buddy," he said. "You feeling a breeze?"

"What are you talking about?" Y'dex demanded haughtily. "If you think you can trick me with your false words—"

"It's no trick, cave boy—your ass is hanging out. Uh, among other things." Rast laughed. "I'd ask if you were a boxers or a briefs kinda guy but I think it's pretty clear you're neither."

Y'dex risked a quick glance down. When he saw his exposed genitals, an outraged expression of embarrassment crossed his face. "How dare you? What have you done to my tharp?"

Rast lifted his hands. "Not a damn thing—maybe it just doesn't like you. Or maybe it would rather be a scarf than a skirt—I don't know." He shrugged. "Bad time to go commando, though, with everyone from your home cave watching."

There was a faint sound of laughter coming from the assembled crowd and Y'dex's normally pale face went blood red. Still holding the goldur with one hand, he yanked futilely at the creeping tharp with the other. Nadiah couldn't help noticing that he wasn't nearly so well endowed as Rast appeared to be—at least from the bulge she'd seen in his pants from time to time.

"Down, get down," he muttered angrily. "What's wrong with you? You've never behaved this way before."

Rast shook his head and made a tsking sound. "It's always sad to see a boy who can't control his skirt."

"You off-worlder bastard!" Y'dex nearly screamed, his eyes bulging with rage. "You did this somehow, I know you did!" He turned to his father. "Father, he's cheating! I don't know how but he is!"

"Cover yourself, son, for Goddess's sake!" Magistrate Licklow was as red in the face as Y'dex. "Have some decorum. This is not the proper place for such a display."

"I'm trying! Get down!" Y'dex implored the tharp again.

Nadiah couldn't hide a smile as she leaned forward and concentrated on the tharp again. "Down," she murmured to it, sending a message only it could hear. "Go down. All the way."

At her soft words, the tharp started creeping down her fiancée's body, much to Y'dex's evident relief. But though it soon reached its correct position around his hips, it didn't stay there. Y'dex gasped with wordless outrange as the bright blue living wrap slid suddenly down to his knees, baring him once more to the gaze of the entire grotto.

"Guess I was wrong," Rast remarked, still grinning. "Looks like your tharp would rather be a pair of leg warmers than a scarf."

"You...you..." Y'dex swung at him and missed, nearly overbalancing. The tharp was wrapped securely around his knees now and with another soft command from Nadiah, it began to tighten, effectively hobbling him.

"Look at that," Rast said. "The incredible shrinking underwear. I've heard of tighty-whitys but that, my friend, is ridiculous." Reaching out, he plucked the goldur out of the distracted Y'dex's hand. "Uh-oh. Look who's unarmed now."

"Human scum, give me that back!" Y'dex clawed forward, snatching for the goldur and missing.

"Ah-ah-ah," Rast admonished. He twirled the goldur like an oversized baton. "You know, I could be wrong but I think this one has better balance than mine did. Think I'll keep it. I know there are regulations against us switching weapons but I assume there's nothing in the rule book about disarming your opponent?" Rast looked over at Magistrate Licklow who said nothing. "Didn't think so." He looked back at Y'dex and leveled the goldur. "So which do you prefer, cave boy? Fire? Or ice?"

Y'dex blanched. "You wouldn't. You can't strike an unarmed male."

"Oh no?" Rast frowned. "So you can do that but I can't? Is that how it goes?"

"Bastard!" Y'dex hobbled backwards and then began yanking at the tharp with one hand as he tried to keep his balance with the other. "Make it stop!" he shouted at Rast. "Make it stop or I swear to the Goddess I'll give Nadiah more pain than she's ever felt in her whole miserable existence."

Rast's face went dark. "If you so much as give her a dirty look—"

"I'll do it! I swear!" Y'dex looked up at Nadiah and made his free hand into a fist. But before he could twist his arm and yank on the bond, she made contact with her tharp once more.

"Leave him," she told it. "Go before he hurts you. But give him something to think about first."

A bright blue fabric arm flowed from her fiancée's knees up to his unprotected testicles. The tharp—the same prototype tharp she'd taken and imprinted before she ran away to Sylvan's bonding ceremony—gave Y'dex's balls a mighty squeeze. Then, as he howled and toppled over into the icy water on one side of the pit, it flowed off his body and disappeared from sight.

"Be careful," Nadiah whispered, knowing that wherever it was it could hear her. "You did well. Just stay hidden and find me later."

She felt the tharp's assent and thanked the Goddess she had thought to take it in the first place. Having a tharp which could mimic any other garment in the universe was coming in handy for much more than good fashion sense. Doubtless Y'dex's own dress tharp was still lying unused in one of his drawers at his domicile.

Of course without Lydiah to smuggle her tharp into his room and let it see which garment to emulate, the plan would never have worked. Nadiah risked a glance at her friend and gave her a very small smile. Lydiah smiled back and gave her a sly wink before going back to refilling someone's cup.

"I declare the off-worlder challenger the winner of the challenge of strength." Magistrate Licklow didn't sound very happy as he announced the outcome but there was nothing else he could do.

"It's not fair, Father! Not fair—he cheated!" Y'dex protested from the freezing water. It was clear he wanted to climb out of the icy side of the pit but couldn't since the bright blue tharp had deserted him completely.

"Hush yourself." Magistrate Licklow glared at his son. "You cannot blame another for your own failure to control your tharp."

"But, Father—"

"Y'dex!" Lady Licklow came bustling up, holding out a thick, purple tharp to wrap her son in. "Come out right now," she hissed. "Everyone is watching!"

Y'dex exited the icy water with poor grace. "You'll be sorry, offworlder," he snarled at Rast, who was still standing calmly on the beam, twirling his goldur. "I'll make you pay during the next challenge. You'll see."

Rast didn't answer but he turned a troubled gaze on Nadiah. She wasn't allowed to speak to him but some silent communication seemed to pass between them anyway.

"What next?" his deep green eyes seemed to be asking. "What next?"

Chapter Seventeen

Rast had no idea what the next challenge—the challenge of wills—involved, but he told himself he was ready for anything. He retreated from the narrow beam and watched as the partition between the hot coals and the icy water was lifted. The water flowed into the hot part of the pit, putting the fire out with a hiss. A vast cloud of steam rose and when it cleared, he saw that the enterprising Tranq Prime males who seemed to be in charge of setting everything up had fitted a long, flat slab of stone in place, obscuring the pit completely. Pretty good, he thought admiringly. You can't even tell it was ever there. It just looks like part of the floor now.

Nadiah had excused herself for a moment and by the time she returned, several rocks of varying sizes had been placed along the edge of the new floor. Rast looked at her anxiously, searching for any sign that Y'dex was hurting her but she seemed fine. She nodded at him, smiling as she sat back on the low platform, and he nodded back, wishing they could actually talk.

He wanted to tell her that the thing with the tharp was pure genius and let her know how much he admired her for thinking it up. Something like that never would have occurred to him but then, he didn't own a sentient fur blanket that was capable of emulating any other garment in the universe. He only hoped the tharp had managed to make its way safely back to her after it finally left Y'dex.

"It is time for the second challenge—the challenge of wills," Magistrate Licklow announced, breaking Rast's train of thought. He was standing in the exact center of the new floor, looking as self important as ever. "Challengers, come forward."

Rast came to the center to stand in front of the magistrate. Y'dex was already there. He was wearing a purple tharp and he was dry, except for his white-blond hair which had been slicked from his forehead. Rat thought the new 'do made him look like an albino hairless cat. Y'dex shot Rast a look of pure, unadulterated hatred and Rast responded with a little grin.

"Hey, how you doing, buddy?" he murmured. "I like your new skirt. Is this one going to stay on?"

"Silence!" Magistrate Licklow thundered, frowning. "The second challenge is about to begin." He turned and nodded at two attendants who were standing on the far edge of the new flooring. "Bring out the mud worms."

"Mud worms?" Rast muttered. "What the hell are those?"

He got his answer soon enough as the two female attendants — one of whom was Nadiah's friend — stepped forward. Both of them were holding a long, thin stone platter and on each platter was a thick black earthworm-looking creature as long as Rast's forearm.

Though both worms were the same length, Rast couldn't help seeing that one was much livelier. It writhed and wiggled so much it nearly escaped its stone platter twice and the girl holding it had to push it back.

In comparison, the other worm was limp and sluggish. It barely lifted its head and couldn't be bothered to move an inch in one direction or another. Magistrate Licklow examined both worms, pronounced them "equal" and gave the lively, wiggling worm to his son.

This meant, of course, that Rast got the limp, tired looking worm which, now that he looked more closely at it, seemed obviously sick. But sick or well, what the hell was he supposed to do with the damn thing? Were they going to have some kind of a worm race? If so, he was going to protest because Y'dex had obviously been given the worm to beat. In fact—

His thoughts were cut off abruptly as Y'dex lifted his own, writhing black worm, and bit off one end. He grinned at Rast fiercely, black slime dribbling down his chin, and swallowed with obvious enjoyment.

"What the hell?" Rat demanded, repulsed, as the Tranq Prime male took another big bite of the still wiggling worm. Was the contest of wills about who could do the most disgusting thing? Watching Y'dex chow down on the oozing, thrashing worm made him feel like he was on some kind of sick reality show. Suddenly, he felt a soft nudge at his elbow.

"Huh?" he looked down to see Nadiah's friend, Lydiah motioning at the limp worm on his platter.

"Eat it," she hissed. "Quickly—you will not be able to compete in the challenge of wills unless you do."

"Eat it?" Rast's stomach rolled in protest. He'd had some more of the excellent bread Nadiah had brought him for breakfast but now, at the thought of eating the live worm, it had decided it wanted to come back up. With a grim effort, Rast held it down. "Look," he muttered under his breath. "How in the hell is eating a live worm going to help me compete in a challenge?'

"The mud worm gives limited short term telekinetic ability," she replied in a low voice. "The male who is able to lift the largest boulder with his mind will win the challenge."

"Seriously?" Rast looked at her in surprise. "Eating one of these suckers makes you able to move things with your mind?"

She nodded. "And the more lively the worm, the greater your ability."

Rast frowned. So that explained the fact that Y'dex had been given the wiggly worm while he got the limp noodle.

"Don't worry," Lydiah hastened to assure him. "Y'dex and my father think Y'dex has been given the worm with the most life, but it is untrue. Look closely at yours—examine it."

Hesitantly, Rast poked at the limp worm, causing it to roll over. What he saw made his gorge rise again. The entire underside of the worm's belly was writhing and bulging. It was as though there were hundreds of tiny things in there, trying to get out.

"What the fuck?" he whispered, grimacing at the disgusting sight. "Is it pregnant or something?"

"No. Your worm has been stung by a marlot."

"A what?" he demanded.

Lydiah looked impatient. "A marlot. A creature that usually lives in harmony with the mudworms and endows them with their telekinetic abilities. But when one spawns, they inject their eggs into a mudworm. When the neophyte marlots mature, they eat their way out. This worm is about to burst—the larvae inside it will give you uncharted abilities!"

"Let me get this straight," Rast muttered. "You're saying that this worm is filled with other worms? And you want me to eat them all?"

"Yes!" Lydiah nodded her head eagerly. "It took me hours to find one like this for you—the marlots spawn only rarely. Eat it quickly before Y'dex gains the upper hand."

The idea that he had to eat not only the thick black worm but also its contents of writhing larvae nearly made Rast puke on the spot. He didn't consider himself a squeamish man—he'd eaten everything from blood sausage to haggis in the past. But at least all of that was dead, he thought, looking at the worm in dismay. Y'dex, meanwhile, was nearly halfway finished with his own worm and still grinning fiercely as he chomped.

Rast was about to refuse when he looked up and saw Nadiah watching him with anxiety. She was twisting her fingers together the way she did when she was nervous, and the look in her deep blue otherworldly eyes was one of fear and concern. Suddenly his own words came back to him. "No matter what it takes, no matter how hard it is, I'm not giving up until you're free or I'm dead," he had told her. Of course, when he had made that vow, he'd imagined some kind of duel to the death—not eating live animals. But that didn't matter—a promise was a promise.

I have to do it, Rast realized. No matter how disgusting or repulsive it is, I have to do this for Nadiah. He sighed. And to think after all this is over, I don't even get to stay with her in the end. But that doesn't matter—what matters is freeing her from that bastard of a fiancée of hers.

Speaking of Nadiah's fiancée, Y'dex was starting on the last third of his worm and Lydiah was tugging at his elbow anxiously.

"Eat," she whispered. "Please, off-worlder. You must eat!"

"You're right." Not giving himself time to think about it, Rast grabbed the worm and took a huge bite from one end.

The taste was even worse than he'd imagined. It was a cross between mud, blood, snot, and rotting fish—a dirty, salty metallic flavor with a rotten, bitter aftertaste as though he'd been chewing aspirin. The texture was fleshy and sandy at the same time, a little bit like eating soft-shelled crab that had been severely undercooked.

But worse than the taste was the sight. After Rast bit off the end, grayish-red larvae came writhing out the ragged hole in the weakly struggling worm. They were bathed in a coating of slimy black mucus and making a faint, high pitched sound as though to protest the invasion and destruction of their home.

"Excellent! Look how many of them there are!" Lydiah sounded excited for him. "Quickly, off-worlder—eat them! Eat them all!"

Rast wanted to gag but he knew if he did, he'd never be able to start eating again. Grimly, he swallowed the bite he was chewing, closed his eyes and dove in again.

The larvae writhed against his tongue, making him feel like he had a mouthful of bugs. Which I basically do, he thought, feeling sick. Heedless of their struggles, he ground them between his teeth where they popped like rotten grapes and released a liquid that tasted like stale urine which ran down the back of his throat.

His stomach rebelled but Rast refused to throw up. This is for Nadiah, he told himself. All for her. I have to do it, I can't quit now.

Closing his eyes he took another bite. And another, and another. He told himself that after this, he would never complain about anything that was served to him ever again. Not that he was usually a picky eater but anything would taste better than a live worms stuffed with baby bugs.

Rast didn't know how he did it but somehow he finished the worm, right down to the last wiggling end. His chin was dripping with black mucus when he was done, his stomach was rolling and his eyes were watering fiercely but somehow he managed to keep the nauseas mess down.

"Water," he begged hoarsely. "Can I get some water?"

"Here." Lydiah poured him a cup and handed it to him quickly. "This is a cleansing drink—it will remove all traces of the worm from your palate."

"Thanks." Rast took a huge gulp of the minty tasting stuff, trying to get the rancid taste out of his mouth. Then he wiped his chin on the steaming cloth she was holding out to him which seemed to be saturated in the same stuff. "Needed something to wash down the worm chunks," he told her, handing it back.

"Certainly." She smiled at him as she folded the black streaked cloth. "You did excellent, off-worlder. I think Nadiah thinks so as well."

Rast looked up to where she was sitting and noticed a sick expression on her face and a faint greenish tint to her skin. Was it possible that on this world where they ate steamed brains and bug pudding, eating a live worm was pushing the envelope? Rast didn't know and he didn't care. He was just glad it was over. He gave Nadiah a thumbs up gesture and she gave him a ghostly smile and nodded encouragingly.

"Are you ready for the test of wills, human?" Y'dex finished wiping his chin on a cloth napkin and tossed it to the other female attendant who caught and whisked it away. "Are you feeling the worm's strength? But perhaps your worm wasn't very strong…"

Rast realized that no one but himself, Lydiah and Nadiah knew he'd gotten a special worm. Good, he didn't want to get anyone in trouble.

"I do feel…something," he said, which was true, actually. Now that his stomach had begun to settle, he felt a strange tingling sensation at the very top of his head, as though tiny, invisible fingers were massaging his scalp and playing with his hair. "It's weird…like someone's messing with my hair."

Lydiah's eyes widened. "Already you feel the fingers of the mind? So quickly! I have never heard of any but a Kindred feeling the worm's power so fast."

Y'dex scowled. "I feel it as well. Father," he said, turning to Magistrate Licklow. "Hurry, we must begin the challenge while the worm's essence is strong within me."

"Of course, my son. Of course." Magistrate Licklow cleared his throat importantly. "And now for the challenge of the wills. I will state the rules. Ahem. Each challenger will attempt to lift the rocks from smallest to largest using only his mind. The male who is able to lift the largest rock and hold it aloft the longest will be declared the winner. Esteemed challenger Y'dex Licklow will take the first turn." He nodded at his son. "Go ahead. Start with the smallest rock first."

"I know what to do, Father," Y'dex snapped. "Haven't we been working on this for weeks ever since the bride you picked for me ran away?" He sneered at Rast. "Don't worry thought—she'll be coming home with me shortly."

"Been practicing, have you?" Rast tried to sound casual. "I guess you knew Nadiah didn't want anything to do with you early on."

"Of course I've been practicing." Y'dex frowned haughtily. "The hand of the mind is like any other muscle—in order to use it effectively you must flex and test it." He smirked at Rast. "Good luck lifting anything at all with your puny human mind, off-worlder. It is I who have the advantage in this challenge." Then he glared at the line up of rocks.

They ranged in size from a pebble all the way up to a boulder taller than Rast and were arranged in a neat row about ten feet away. Rast remembered that it had taken four of the largest Tranq Prime males to get the largest into place. How was Y'dex going to lift that behemoth using only his mind? And more importantly, how was he going to do it?

But for the present, his rival wasn't trying to lift anything nearly so large. Instead, he was gazing steadily at a pebble which would have fit easily into the palm of his hand. He looked at it for a long time — so long that Rast began to wonder if the whole challenge was just a joke. Maybe it was all an excuse to see who could eat a live worm and keep it down. Maybe —

Suddenly Y'dex's face turned red and the pebble began to rise into the air. It rose a foot, then two feet, then three and kept going until it was eye level. Then, with no warning, it sliced through the air straight at Rast's head. He ducked just in time to keep from losing an eye and heard the pebble clatter to the ground behind him.

"My apologies." Y'dex bowed, an unpleasant little smile playing around the corners of his thin mouth. "I must have lost control of it. The hand of the mind is a tricky thing." He nodded at the pebble, which had been put back in its place in the line-up by one of the female attendants. "Your turn, human."

"Right. My turn. My turn to move things with my mind." Rast took a deep breath and stepped up.

He hated to admit it but he was beginning to feel nervous. The tingling at the top of his head aside, he had no idea how to go about lifting anything with his mind. And if what Y'dex said was true, the skinny worm-eating bastard had been down here tossing rocks around with his "hand of the mind" for weeks — possibly months. For Rast, this challenge was like going to the gym and being expected to dead-lift five hundred pounds on the first try with a muscle he'd never used before. And in this gym, he was the ninety pound weakling. How the hell was he going to win this challenge?

Then he looked up and saw Nadiah watching him with a mixture of hope and fear on her face. That was all it took to give him strength. I can do it, he told himself. If I ate the damn worm, I can sure as hell do this.

Glaring at the pebble he whispered, "Move."

Nothing happened.

"Move!" Rast told it again, clenching his hands into fists. Still the pebble remained motionless.

"What a pity." Y'dex yawned loudly, as though bored. "It appears I ate my entire worm for nothing. I could have beaten you with one bite."

Lydiah, who had struck Rast as quiet and unassuming until now, faced her brother with hands on her hips and fire in her eyes. "He's only having trouble because no one had explained to him how the hand of the mind works."

"The rules state—" Magistrate Licklow began but Lydiah shook her head.

"No, Father. There is nothing that states an off-world contestant may not at least hear an explanation of what he is expected to do to complete the challenge." She looked at Rast. "Listen carefully—the hand of the mind is not moved by words but by thoughts. Imagine yourself lifting the pebble, picture it in your mind as you would hold it in your hand. Then will it to move and it will happen."

"Stupid female!" Y'dex glowered at his little sister. "Whose side are you on, anyway?"

Lydiah lifted her chin. "I am on Nadiah's side. She is the one who will have to bond with you if her challenger loses. And I wouldn't wish that fate on an animal I liked, let alone my best friend."

"Lydiah!" Magistrate Licklow looked aghast. "How can you speak so to your own brother?"

"After all the cruelty he has visited upon me? I would rather be related to a mud worm." Lydiah spat at her brother's feet, spun on her heel, and left the challenge grotto.

"Wow." Rast shook his head. "When your own kin feel that way about you…"

"Be silent," Y'dex snarled. "The challenge is still in progress and yet the pebble has not moved. Father," he said, turning to the magistrate. "How long does the off-worlder have to try? Isn't his time almost up?"

"Indeed it is. Indeed it is." The magistrate nodded, smiling. "In fact, if he doesn't move it within the next—"

Rast turned them out and concentrated on the pebble. As Lydiah had directed, he imagined holding the pebble, pictured closing his fingers around it, feeling its smooth surface and slight but substantial weight in the palm of his hand… and then he imagined lifting it into the air.

To his surprise and relief, the pebble moved. More than moved, actually—it shot into the air as though a major league pitcher had decided to throw a fastball at the high, vaulted ceiling.

"Oh!" he heard Nadiah gasp behind him and there was a smattering of applause from the spectators as he let the pebble hover in midair for a moment and then lowered it gently to the ground.

"A lucky fluke," Magistrate Licklow muttered but Rast didn't think so. He felt an overwhelming mixture of exhilaration and relief—he was actually going to be able to do this. Despite his inexperience, he was going to make it work!

"I'll lift a larger one this time," Y'dex said. Bypassing some of the smaller rocks, he concentrated on one about the size and shape of a bowling ball. For a long moment, nothing happened and then his face turned red and the ball rose slowly but steadily into the air.

Rast watched alertly, trying to be sure that Y'dex wasn't going to lob the damn thing in his direction. To his relief, his competitor simply lowered the ball-sized rock after holding it aloft for two minutes and then looked at him. "Your turn."

"All right." Looking at the rock, Rast concentrated hard. He imagined hefting it in his arms, lifting it high into the air. It was harder this time but not too much—about as hard as lifting an actual bowling ball with his hands, he thought as he held it steady in midair. He made sure to hold it for a full four minutes—doubling Y'dex's time—then let it go gently back down to the stone floor.

Y'dex frowned. "Most impressive for an off-worlder. But let's see if you can manage this." He turned to stare at the largest rock at the end of the line—the one that was more of a boulder than a rock.

How the hell is he going to manage this? Rast frowned. From what he could feel, lifting something with his mind took about the same strength as lifting with his physical body. Was Y'dex really strong enough to heft a boulder it had taken four large men to move? For that matter, was Rast? Then again, he didn't really have to lift it high or hold it long—he just had to lift it higher and hold it in the air longer than Y'dex could—if the Tranq Prime male could lift it at all, which was beginning to look doubtful.

Y'dex stared at the boulder, his fists clenched, his red face frozen in a sneer of effort. But the huge rock didn't budge an inch.

"My son..." Magistrate Licklow spoke in a low, worried voice. "My son, do not attempt such a huge burden. You will strain your mind."

"Quiet....Father," Y'dex ground out. "Let...me...work."

The Magistrate fell silent though he continued to watch his son anxiously as he shifted from foot to foot. At last when Rast was sure nothing was going to happen, the massive boulder shifted and then wavered about an inch into the air. It stayed there for only about thirty seconds before it came crashing back down, but there was a murmur of approval from the audience anyway.

Panting and sweating, Y'dex turned to him. "Your...turn," he said, and armed sweat off his pale forehead. "Let's see you...top that, off-worlder."

Rast took a deep breath. "I'll sure as hell try, you can bet your ass on that." He looked briefly up at Nadiah and saw that she was sitting on the edge of her seat, twisting her fingers together anxiously. This one's for you, sweetheart, he thought and then turned his attention to the massive stone.

Taking a deep breath, he pictured himself wrapping his arms around its stony sides. The thought was so deep and the image so vivid he could almost feel the rough coldness of it against his arms, could almost touch its surface, his fingertips searching for a grip on its ungiving hide.

Lift with your legs, not with your back, he thought irrelevantly, then he closed his eyes and pictured himself heaving the huge thing up into the air.

It was immensely heavy and he could feel himself straining, feel the newfound muscles in his mind protesting against such treatment. But he was determined to do it. He ignored the silent pain which felt like a burning that started at the top of his head and ran down all the nerves in his body. He pressed on, imagining the feel of the monstrous stone in his arms rising higher and higher.

There was an awed gasp from the spectators and Rast dared to open his eyes. What he saw almost made him lose his concentration—the stone was up in the air at least a foot and it was rotating there silently, like a giant pendant twirling on an invisible chain.

Only the chain is my mind, Rast thought with cautious enthusiasm. I'm doing it—I'm actually doing I—"

A scream directly above his head nearly caused him to drop the boulder but he held on tight and looked up instead.

Hovering near the top of the high, vaulted ceiling, was Nadiah. She was at least three stories up but Rast could still see the terror in her dark blue eyes. Beside him, he heard a low, nasty laugh.

"Which would you rather keep in the air, human?" Y'dex asked him. "The rock or the girl? Better decide—now!"

Suddenly, Nadiah was falling, her piercing screams echoing against the rocky grotto walls.

Rast had no time to think. He knew instinctively that he couldn't hold the boulder up with his mind and catch Nadiah at the same time. He let the huge rock drop with a resounding thud and reached for her with his new muscle as though he was reaching for a fly ball. Yes, like a ball, he thought wildly. Running with the idea, he imagined catching her in a giant, cushy baseball mitt.

To his unspeakable relief, Nadiah landed with a gasp in the invisible mitt he'd imagined when she was barely three feet from the ground. The impact seemed to knock the breath out of her but she didn't appear to be seriously harmed in any way.

Rast ran to her and took her in his arms, hugging her tight. Nadiah hugged him back, her slender frame shaking with sobs.

"It's okay, it's okay. You're safe now," Rast soothed her. He stroked her long blonde hair and held her trembling form against him, trying to surround her with his body, to make her feel safe. "Are you all right?" he murmured after a moment.

Nadiah seemed to make an effort to bring herself under control. Taking a deep breath, she pulled back from him and wiped her eyes. "I...I'm fine," she whispered brokenly. "I just don't...I've never liked heights. They frighten me."

"Anyone would be frightened after that." Rast glared at Y'dex who was still smirking at him. "That's it, buddy, you and I are gonna dance and this time I'm going to break more than your nose."

"Any challenger who physically attacks another challenger during the course of the blood challenge shall be summarily dismissed in defeat and cast out of the grotto into the wild lands above," Magistrate Licklow intoned, obviously quoting from the official rules.

"What?" Rast glared at him. "So it's not against the rules for him to nearly murder an innocent girl but I can't punch his lights out for doing it?"

"Precisely." The magistrate gave him a cruel smile that didn't reach his bulging eyes. "And I'm afraid that Y'dex wins this challenge. He held the boulder aloft for thirty seconds while you, human, only managed twenty."

"What?" Rast was really getting angry now. "I had to drop it to catch Nadiah. And he knew I would."

"That doesn't change the fact that he is the official winner." The magistrate cleared his throat. "I declare the honorable Y'dex Licklow as the winner of the challenge of wills," he announced loudly.

There were some angry murmurs from the stands which made Rast feel a little better. At least all the people of Tranq Prime weren't corrupt—they knew injustice when they saw it. Unfortunately, the crowd's reaction didn't help him. He and Y'dex were now one to one with a single challenge left to decide the winner.

The challenge of blood.

Chapter Eighteen

"Are you ready for the challenge of blood?" Lydiah rubbed her shoulders comfortingly and Nadiah looked up at her friend gratefully.

"I think so," she said, trying to keep her voice from trembling. "I mean, I have to be, don't I? If I'm not, I don't have a chance of getting free and after what Y'dex just did…" She trailed off, shaking her head.

"Did he truly lift you with his mind and let you drop?" Lydiah sounded upset but not surprised. "Havris said he did but I didn't see it."

Nadiah nodded. "Yes. If Rast hadn't dropped the boulder in order to catch me I would be dead now, I'm certain of it. He lost the challenge in order to save my life." She shook her head. "I knew your brother hated me but I never thought he wanted to kill me." Despite knowing what kind of male her intended was, the near death experience had still shaken her to the core.

"I don't think he wants to kill you so much as that he feels if he can't have you, no one can." Lydiah sounded thoughtful. "It was always that way when we were children too. If Mamam gave me a toy for my own to play with and I refused to hand it over to him, Y'dex would take it and break it. He used to say, 'If I can't have it, neither can you.'"

"I am not some toy to be broken and cast aside," Nadiah cried passionately. "I am a living female with feelings. And now more than ever I want to be free of him!"

She could tell by the lifted heads in the audience that some of the spectators had caught her words, or at least the gist of them, but she didn't care. Didn't care if the whole of Tranq Prime knew how she felt—she was tired of being held in thrall to the blood bond, tired of being tied to a cruel and pitiless tyrant who cared so little for her life he would kill her out of spite. She just wanted to be free to do as she pleased with her life. Free to live it with Rast.

Forget that, she told herself sternly. It's not going to happen, even if you do break the blood bond and manage to survive being bondless. But she couldn't help remembering the way he'd saved her from certain death and the look in his eyes when he held her close. The way his big, muscular body had seemed to surround her, making her feel safe as he soothed and comforted her. Oh, she thought desperately. I wish I didn't love him so much—this would be so much easier if I didn't!

Then again, without her love for Rast, how would she ever find the strength to break free of Y'dex? I have to use my love, she thought, staring at the center of the challenge floor where Rast was waiting quietly for the new challenge to begin. And I have to cherish these final moments with him. One way or another, this is all we have left.

"Do you have any idea how this will turn out?" Lydiah asked, breaking her train of thought. "I mean, you do have the Sight so I thought maybe—"

Nadiah shook her head. "That's not how it works. I can't see things just because I want to." She frowned. "In fact, I haven't had a single vision or al'lei since I stepped foot back on Tranq Prime. It's strange."

"Maybe the Goddess wants you to trust in her," Lydiah said. "To have faith that she will see you through this trial no matter what occurs."

Nadiah sighed. "Yes, I think you're right. Although it would be nice to know everything will work out well."

"It will," Lydiah said soothingly. "They're setting up a privacy curtain for your blood sharing," she said, changing the subject. "I'm certain you'll be glad to hear that."

"I am." Despite herself, Nadiah felt a warm blush creeping into her cheeks. "I would not…wish for everyone in the grotto to witness such a private moment."

"Of course not." Lydiah's cheeks were pink too. "I cannot wait to share blood with Havris," she admitted in a low voice. "He has promised that we will, even though we are already blood bonded."

"Will you still be allowed to bond with him permanently so that you can share your lives together?" Nadiah asked anxiously. "I mean, after the way you helped Rast during the challenge of wills, I was afraid your Mamam and Patro—"

"Havris had promised to take me to the priestess for a private bonding ceremony as soon as the challenge is over." Lydiah's pretty face glowed with excitement. "I am not even to go back to my domicile. This very night we will seal the bond between us—when next you see me, my eyes will be a different color."

"Oh, Lydiah!" Nadiah pressed her hand. "I'm so glad! Havris is truly a worthy male."

Lydiah nodded. "He is. And he says he won't take a chance on losing me just because my family is angry at me." She looked suddenly serious. "I just hope this last challenge goes well. I hope that by nightfall we will both be sealing our bonds to the males of our choice."

Nadiah shook her head. "You know that is not to be. Not for me, at least."

"You must tell him," Lydiah urged. "Tell Rast what will happen if you have no one to anchor your soul to once your bond is broken."

"I won't," Nadiah said stubbornly. "And I want you to promise you won't tell him either. I don't want him to feel pressured into a relationship he doesn't want."

Lydiah frowned mutinously. "Nadiah..."

"Swear!" Nadiah crooked her pinky finger and held it out. "Heart and hearth, blood and bone, keep my secret as your own."

"That old promise we used when we were children? Oh, Nadiah..." Her old friend looked torn between laughter and tears. But at last she crooked her own pinky around Nadiah's and repeated the words. "Heart and hearth, blood and bone, I'll keep your secret as my own. There — are you satisfied?"

"Yes." Impulsively, Nadiah hugged her. "No matter what happens, always remember I love you, dear Lydiah. I will never forget our time together as girls and your kindness to me today."

"I love you too." Lydiah hugged her back tightly. When they finally broke the embrace, both their cheeks were wet. "Now go," Lydiah ordered, trying to smile through her tears. "You're about to share blood with the male of your dreams. Make it count."

Nadiah lifted her chin. "I will." *If this is all I can have of the male I love, I will make the best and the most of it I can. I will take this sweet memory with me into the grave if necessary.*

Rising, she left her childhood friend behind and went to the small, circular curtain which had been erected in the center of the challenge floor. Beside it, Rast, Y'dex, and his father were standing in readiness, waiting for her. The spectators in the stands were silent, staring at the little tableau in breathless anticipation.

"This is the beginning of the third and final challenge – the challenge of blood." Magistrate Licklow spoke in a low voice, obviously embarrassed by the intimacy of the first part of the challenge. "Since Nadiah has already had her rightful fiancée's blood at the age of six cycles, she will now take some of the challenger's blood in order to form a tie to him. If the new connection proves strong enough to break the existing bond, she will be free to go." The sneering look on his face made it clear he considered that highly unlikely. "If it is not, then she will be bonded this very night to Y'dex who may claim her as is his lawful right."

"It is also my lawful right to punish her for her insolence in putting us all through this in the first place," Y'dex snarled, glaring at her. "I swear to you, my lovely, you'll pay triple for every bit of humiliation I suffered today."

"You won't touch her." Rast's voice was a low, menacing growl. "I'm taking her back with me."

"Only if you win the challenge which is very unlikely, off-worlder," Magistrate Licklow interjected. "The bond between Nadiah and Y'dex was formed when they were children – it has had years to strengthen and grown. Now, let's get this over with, shall we?"

"I still think she should have to take some of my blood as well," Y'dex protested. "She hasn't had it since she was six cycles old."

"The bond between us is already strong enough," Nadiah said bitterly. "Our parents saw to that. They gave you dominion over me but no more – I'm going to be free of you tonight, one way or another."

Y'dex gave her an unpleasant grin. "Keep telling yourself that, my lovely. We'll see what happens when I twist the bond and pull you to me. You'll come running like a pet on a leash."

At the promise of pain in his voice, Nadiah suddenly felt cold and shaken. She had been putting it to the back of her mind as much as she could but now she couldn't help thinking, *this is going to hurt. Hurt more than anything I've ever done or had done to me.*

"Nadiah?" Rast touched her elbow. "Are you all right? Don't let him get to you—he's full of hot air."

The human expression made her smile just a bit as she pictured Y'dex puffed up with air like a yarber toad during mating season. "I'm fine." *I won't think about it. Won't think about the pain. I don't want it to ruin my time with Rast.* She raised her chin and gave her intended one last, disdainful look before turning back to Rast. "Let's go into the tent, shall we?"

"Absolutely." Taking her hand, he led the way.

Inside the privacy of the small tent, she settled herself onto the tiny padded bench barely big enough for two and looked up at Rast. "Are you ready?"

His eyes, which had been blazing with possessive rage at Y'dex just a moment before, were suddenly half-lidded with desire. "More than ready." He produced a small silver ceremonial knife about as long as her palm. It was intricately carved with a curving blade. "Just tell me how you want to do it."

Nadiah bit her lip. "I've only shared blood once before and that was when I was a child, with Y'dex. Thank the Goddess they just had him bleed into a cup and made me drink it—at least I didn't have to take it from his arm." She clenched her fists. "I'd sooner eat a live mud worm than taste his blood again."

Rast made a face. "I wouldn't be too quick to say that if I were you. Have you ever tasted one of those things? They're not exactly fine dining."

Nadiah put a hand over his. "I saw the look on your face when you took the challenge. I know how distasteful it was to you."

"That's all right, sweetheart." He cupped her cheek gently. "Anything for you. I mean that."

Nadiah flushed with pleasure. "I know you do." She looked down at her hands shyly. "I...I think we'd better get going. They probably won't give us much time for this."

Rast sighed. "Unfortunately not. Okay, how does this go?"

"I...I believe you cut your wrist and let me drink of you," she murmured.

He raised an eyebrow. "And that's going to form a bond between us?"

Nadiah nodded. "But it will be fresh and young and the bond I have with Y'dex is old and hardened. Sort of like the difference between a sapling and a fully mature tree."

"But if I'm the sapling and he's the tree, how the hell—"

She squeezed his hand. "Don't be discouraged, Rast. Trees can rot away from the inside out and saplings can have more strength than you can imagine."

"I'm sure." Rast smiled and squeezed her hand in return. "So that means Y'dex and I are going to put you between us and do a psychic version of tug-of-war?"

"If you mean that you will both be pulling on me, trying to draw me to you then yes, you're right," Nadiah said.

He frowned. "But won't that hurt you?"

She took a deep breath. "It will be agonizing. But not nearly as painful as spending the rest of my days with Y'dex. So please, Rast, pull hard."

"I will," he promised grimly. "But first I've got to get something to pull with." Raising the tiny silver knife, he sliced firmly across the blue bracelet of veins that ran along the underside of his wrist.

Nadiah bit her lip when she saw the rich crimson begin to flow from his skin. "Oh Rast, you shouldn't have sliced so deep!"

"Don't worry about me." His deep voice had taken on a soft, sensual tone that made her feel like her skin was prickling all over her body. "Just drink of me, Nadiah." He held his bleeding wrist to her lips, his eyes half-lidded with lust again. "Drink deep."

Feeling hot and cold at the same time, Nadiah flattened her tongue and pressed it to the warm flow, lapping long and slow as she took his blood into herself. She'd expected the salty, metallic taste she remembered from the time she'd been forced to drink Y'dex's blood but somehow, it wasn't like that. The scarlet ribbon that flowed from Rast's arm into her mouth tasted sweet and spicy and hot at the same time—as though he had fire wine flowing through his veins. It went to Nadiah's head at once, as though she'd been drinking a rare and expensive liquor and made her feel warm and tingly all over.

She drank for what seemed like a long time but Rast didn't seem to mind. In fact, he stroked her hair and murmured encouragement, urging her to take more, to take as much as she needed. Somehow Nadiah found herself in his lap, with her mouth still locked to his wrist. If she'd had any doubt about how he felt about this, the hot hard lump of his cock pressing against her ass erased it. Rast wanted this as much as she did and he was getting just as much pleasure from the intimate act, if not more.

Goddess, she thought, as the new bond began to form inside her, like a sapling putting down roots. He feels so good, tastes so right. If only we could seal our bond after this as a bonded couple is supposed to. Of course, to seal the bond with Rast, she would have to let him change the color of her eyes and Nadiah knew they couldn't do that. But, gods, how she wanted to. Wanted to feel that hot, hard ridge of his shaft thrust deep inside her pussy, filling her up, making her Rast's forever…

"One minute. You have one minute remaining." Magistrate Licklow's pompous voice through the curtain shattered her sweet fantasy. Nadiah sighed and, with a final lick, released her beloved's wrist. "Oh!" She looked at it in surprise—now that she was finished sucking, the slice was already beginning to seal itself. "It's already closing."

"I've always been a fast healer," Rast said dismissively. He shifted her on his lap, allowing her to feel his throbbing cock pressed against her once more. "Uh, are you sure you got enough? I'll be more than happy to cut myself again if you need me to."

"I got enough," Nadiah assured him. "But there is one more thing I'd like to do," she added with sudden inspiration. "Give me the knife."

"What for?"

"Hurry—we don't have much time!"

Rast handed her the small silver knife hilt first. "All right. Sorry."

"It's all right." Bracing against the pain, Nadiah stabbed herself in the pad of her right index finger and watched as a single crimson drop welled up.

"Wait a minute." Rast turned her so he could see her face. "What are you doing?"

"I want you to drink of me too," Nadiah told him breathlessly. "To remember me always in case…just in case," she ended lamely.

"You think I could ever forget you, sweetheart?" Rast's voice was low and demanding. "Because I'm telling you now, that's not gonna happen. You're burned into my heart forever."

"Oh, Rast…" Nadiah had to blink back tears at his sweet words. "That's wonderful but I still want you to. Please?"

"As you wish," he murmured. Taking her hand in his, he brought her finger to his lips. Then, keeping their eyes locked the entire time, he slipped her wounded fingertip into his hot, wet mouth and sucked gently.

Nadiah's breath caught in her throat at the erotic promise in his eyes and the soft suction of his lips. I want you, the look on his face said. You and only you.

Goddess, Rast, I want you to, she wanted to say. Want you and love you so much. I want to spend the rest of my life with you, showing you how much…

"Time," Magistrate Licklow declared, once again interrupting her fantasies. "You must now exit the tent."

Rast didn't stop sucking at once. He took his time, swirling his tongue around her finger and lapping gently at the wounded tip before slowly letting it slide from his mouth. "Delicious," he murmured, placing a soft kiss on her finger before giving her back her hand. "I bet all of you tastes good. Sure would like a chance to find out."

Nadiah blushed when she realized what he was talking about. He wants to taste me, she thought, her cheeks getting hot with pleasure and embarrassment. Wants to taste more than my finger— wants to taste me there, between my legs. Gods, how she wished it could be so. That they were together alone after their bonding ceremony and Rast was about to change the color of her eyes.

But the sound of Magistrate Licklow clearing his throat impatiently popped her bubble. With a sigh, she realized there was no escaping the harsh reality of the situation. She was about to undergo the most agonizing process a Tranq Prime female could be subjected to, aside from childbirth. And some who had endured both said even childbirth was better. But since there was no way to the end of her road except through the fiery curtain of pain, Nadiah resolved to grit her teeth and go through it, no matter what the cost.

"We have to go," she told Rast.

He sighed. "I guess we don't have a choice."

"Unfortunately not." Reluctantly, Nadiah rose from his lap. "Do you feel the bond between us?"

He nodded. "It's like…like someone tied a rope around both of us but the rope is somehow alive. Maybe more of a vine than a rope…" He shook his head. "I can't describe it but it's there, all right."

"Good," Nadiah felt a surge of relief. Up until this moment she hadn't been completely sure if his human blood would allow them to form a bond or not. It was good to know that it was possible to forge a psychic tie between the two of them. Now if only she knew if it was strong enough to defeat Y'dex…

"I like it," Rast said in a low voice. "It feels…right somehow. Like we're, I don't know, plugged into each other."

"I like it too," Nadiah admitted, blushing.

He frowned. "But aside from being newer, isn't it the same as the bond you have with Y'dex? I remember Sylvan saying that if your blood bond came loose and you didn't have a soul to anchor to you might…might die." He cleared his throat. "Of course that can't happen now, can it? Now that we're bonded too?"

Nadiah bit her lip. For a moment the truth almost came out…but no, she didn't want Rast bonded to her permanently out of a sense of duty. "The bond between myself and Y'dex is very old and very strong," she said carefully. "It's difficult to replace such a bond."

In fact, it was impossible but she didn't want to say that. The weak, new bond she had with Rast was only surface deep—like a plant which had rooted itself in loose, sandy soil. Her bond with the hated Y'dex was more like a mighty giant of the forest, a tree whose roots went miles underground. Trying to fill the gap those roots would leave when she pulled out his half of the bond with a newer, weaker connection would be like… It would be like trying to seal a gaping hole in my heart with one of Rast's tiny human Band-Aids, she thought grimly.

The only solution was to anchor her half of the stronger bond to another soul, to put those same roots deep down in the soil of another being, but she could not do that without Rast's permission. And she wasn't about to tell him that.

"Difficult but not impossible, right?" Rast frowned. "Just tell me you'll be all right, Nadiah."

She shook her head. "I can't—not absolutely. But please, Rast, don't let that stop you—pull on it as hard as you can to bring me to you. And while you're doing that, I'll be trying to rip the roots of Y'dex's half of our bond from my soul."

He looked at her doubtfully. "Can you do that?"

"I hope so," Nadiah said grimly. "I certainly intend to try."

"Good." Rast pulled her to him suddenly and gave her a long, hard, hot kiss, his mouth demanding and receiving entrance to hers as he claimed her for his own. At last he pulled back. "Don't worry about anything, sweetheart," he murmured, looking into her eyes. "We're going to get through this together."

"I know." She smiled at him gratefully and then lifted her chin. "I know we'll get through it because I'd rather die than be bonded to Y'dex. No matter what it costs me, I will be free of his bond. Even if it means my death."

* * * * *

Seeing the set of her chin and the grim determination in her eyes reminded Rast again of why he loved her so much. On the outside she looked so fragile and feminine, so delicate and lovely. But inside she had a soul of steel—a cool determination to do whatever it took to get the job done. He admired that in a woman—admired the hell out of it. But he still didn't like her fatalistic attitude toward breaking the blood bond.

"Hey, don't talk like that," he protested as they exited the tent together. "Everything's going to be fine and nobody's going to die. Except that idiot fiancée of yours if he dares to lay a finger on you again." He gave Y'dex a glare as he said it, letting the other male know what was coming.

"I hope you're right," Nadiah murmured but there was still something in her dark blue eyes Rast didn't like. Something that looked like a mixture of determination and resignation. But that didn't make sense, did it?

He wanted to ask her about it but they were already taking their places for the final part of the blood challenge. The line-up of rocks had been cleared away and Magistrate Licklow had Y'dex stand on one end of the challenge floor and Rast stand on the other. Nadiah, he positioned exactly between them.

Well, maybe not exactly between them. Actually, Rast saw, he put her a foot or two closer to Y'dex. But she shook her head firmly and said something to the magistrate under her breath. Frowning, he nodded reluctantly and called for one of the male attendants.

The male ran up, bringing something that looked like a tape measure only instead of tape, it laid down a long, thin, glowing blue trail marked at intervals with vertical red lines. He ran between Y'dex and Rast, obviously taking measurements and when he was finished, Nadiah went to stand in the exact center of the blue line, on the widest red marking. Turning to Rast, she gave him a wink and he grinned and gave her a thumbs up. Leave it to Nadiah to keep the magistrate from cheating any way she could.

"And now," Magistrate Licklow intoned. "We are finally ready to begin." He looked at Y'dex and Rast. "Challengers, please remember that you must stay in your places and you may pull on the contested female using only your blood bonds. Physical touching is not allowed unless she touches you first. The moment she does, you may claim her." These last words he directed solely to Y'dex, obviously ignoring Rast. "Is that clear?"

"Crystal," Rast said loudly, letting the pompous bastard know he refused to be ignored. "Let's get going."

"Very well." Licklow gave him a disgusted look and then stepped back. "Begin...now."

Even before he uttered the last word, Rast saw the look of pain appear on Nadiah's face. That bastard, he thought angrily, looking down the glowing blue line to where Y'dex was standing, his hand already curled into a fist as he twisted the bond. He started early. Still trying to cheat. Well, let's see how he likes this.

Closing his eyes, he concentrated on the newly formed bond between Nadiah and himself and gave a gentle tug. It was like pulling on a slender, silk cord that was somehow wrapped around her—around her heart or soul, he supposed.

To his dismay, Nadiah responded to his tug with a hurt cry. It was clear she was already fighting the pain Y'dex was inflicting on her and now…Now, I'm adding to it, Rast thought, feeling sick. He let the silk cord slide through his mental fingers…and Nadiah suddenly stumbled several steps in Y'dex's direction.

"No!" It was a cry of agony, straight from her heart. "No, Rast, please!" she gasped, her blue eyes filled with pleading. "Please don't give up on me. Please bring me to you."

"But it's hurting you," he objected, even as he mentally felt for the silk cord of their bond again. It seemed to throb in his hands, echoing her pain with every heartbeat.

"I don't care." Nadiah's voice was a breathless whisper. If it hadn't been so quiet in the vast, echoing room he never would have heard it. "I don't care, just pull."

Bracing himself, Rast took another tug on the cord connecting them.

Nadiah's hands clenched into fists. As she took a single, staggering step toward him, she bit her lip hard. So hard, in fact, Rast saw a thin trickle of blood on her chin. She's trying to hold back for my sake, he realized. Trying not to scream so I won't feel bad about hurting her. God what a beautiful, brave, amazing woman!

"You'll never win her that way, human," Y'dex called from the other end of the glowing blue line. Rast looked up and saw he was smirking, obviously enjoying every ounce of pain inflicted on Nadiah. "Watch and learn," he told Rast. "This is how it's done."

Clenching both his hands into fists, he twisted and pulled back toward his body with a cruel smile on his face.

Nadiah shrieked, her slender body contorted with pain. Rast thought with horror that she must look the same way someone who is struck by lightning does at the very moment of impact. It was clear she didn't want to but this time she moved towards Y'dex. It was almost like some invisible hand had her by the hair and was dragging her. Dragging her closer and closer to her doom…

"What's wrong with you?" Nadiah's friend Lydiah was suddenly at his side. Hands on her hips, she glared at him furiously. "Why aren't you fighting for her? Why aren't you pulling?"

"I'm trying, damn it!" Rast growled. "It's just…I knew Y'dex would hurt her when he pulled. But I didn't think I'd be hurting her too."

"Nadiah would rather suffer the agony of being burned in a thousand suns than give herself to Y'dex." Lydiah spoke in a low, intense voice. "So pull. You didn't come all this way and go through so much just to give her up to my tyrant of a brother, did you?"

"Hell, no." Gritting his teeth, Rast dug in and pulled — really pulled on the slender cord between himself and Nadiah with all his might.

Nadiah gasped, her face going paper-pale. But she managed to stagger several steps closer to him and away from Y'dex. And despite her obvious pain, she somehow managed to smile at him.

Oh Nadiah, I'm so sorry. Forcing himself to do it, Rast pulled again and she came a few steps closer. Though he could see what it was costing her in pain, he knew he couldn't stop. This was his only chance to claim her, to save her from what she had told him was a fate worse than death. He had to bring her to him no matter how much it hurt her physically or him mentally to give her such anguish.

"That's right, you're doing it. You're bringing her to you!" Lydiah sounded excited. "You're...oh..." Now she sounded surprised and a little worried. "Off-worlder, you're crying."

"Am I?" Rast swiped at his eyes briefly, making sure to keep his hold on the bond.

"Are you well?" Lydiah asked.

"I don't like hurting her, goddamn it," Rast snarled. "Not even for her own good."

"But it's almost over," Lydia said coaxingly. "Just a few more feet and she'll be able to reach out and touch you..."

But just as she spoke, Y'dex redoubled his efforts, yanking on the bond with both hands. Nadiah gave a sharp, breathless cry and Rast watched in dismay as she was dragged within three feet of her cruel fiancée.

"Just a little closer, my lovely," he heard Y'dex crooning. "Just a little bit closer and you'll be mine for the rest of your life."

"No!" It was a shout of agony from the bottom of his soul. Suddenly Rast knew what he had to do. He had to pull Nadiah to him, yes. But he also had to give her a reason to come. Had to give her the strength to break the bond with her evil fiancée and come to him forever.

"Nadiah," he called, yanking on the cord as hard as he could. "Nadiah, come back to me right now. Come back to me because I love you!"

Her eyes flew wide and she turned her attention from Y'dex to him. "Rast," she whispered uncertainly. "Do you...do you really mean that?"

"Of course I fucking mean it!" he shouted, angry and desperate with love for her. "Now get back here so I can prove it!"

Nadiah closed her eyes tightly for a moment. Though Y'dex was twisting with all his might, doing the double-pump fist and arm gesture Rast had grown to hate, she was still, like a slender tree withstanding a storm. Then she lowered her head and took a single, staggering step in Rast's direction. Then another and another. She looked like a person walking against the wind—a hurricane force wind, actually. Her whole body leaned forward, clearly past her center of gravity as she pulled away from the bond that had held her most of her life. The look on her face was one of anguish and yet she came, step by step, towards Rast.

"Stop!" Seeing what was happening, Y'dex left his place at the end of the glowing blue line and jumped toward her. Grabbing her arm, he spun her around and shook her. "You're mine, you little bitch! Mine!"

"No!" Nadiah's voice cracked like a whip as she faced her tormentor. "No, I'm not yours, Y'dex and I never will be. I will be…free…of you…now!"

On that last word, Rast felt something give inside her—a quiver like the first tremblings of a killer earthquake came shivering along the cord of their bond. He looked at Nadiah with fresh respect and wonder. I'll rip his bond out by the roots—that's what she said, he thought. And I think she just did it. No, I know she did.

Y'dex staggered, his face filled with pain as he clearly felt it as well. "You bitch, that hurt!"

Nadiah laughed grimly. "Good. Now you know how it feels." She tugged at the arm he was still holding. "It's over, Y'dex—let me go. Let me go to the male who loves me as you never did."

"Never." Y'dex's pale face was a mask of animalistic hatred. "Never. I'll never let you go."

"Oh, yes you will, you son of a bitch!" Rast had been holding himself back up until now, trying not to break the rules and give the magistrate any reason to invalidate the challenge. But now he couldn't stand it anymore. He strode down the glowing blue line, reaching out for Nadiah as he went.

But before he got to her, she pulled back her free hand and slapped Y'dex as hard as she could. Her handprint stood out red on his pale face and he staggered backwards, a look of disbelief in his eyes. "You…you struck me! I can't believe you actually struck me." His fingers stole up to his reddened cheek. "How dare you?"

"I warned you." Nadiah was panting with exhaustion but her words were still firm. "I warned you to leave me alone. I'll never be yours." She turned toward Rast, took a stumbling step and fell.

Luckily, she fell right into his arms. Rast scooped her up and cradled her tenderly against his chest. He could still feel the bond between them but it seemed weaker somehow, the throbbing heartbeat that ran through it was fainter. He told himself it was nothing—only that she was no longer in pain. But one look at her face made him wonder if that was right.

"Nadiah?" he asked, looking anxiously down at her. "Sweetheart, are you all right?"

"Fine." She smiled up at him, her eyes half closed in fatigue. "Now that you've got me I'll be all right forever."

"Oh, sweetheart…" He bent to kiss her cheek…and realized that it was ice cold. Surely that couldn't be normal, could it? "Nadiah?" he asked, trying to keep the panic out of his voice but this time she didn't answer. "Nadiah!" Rast shook her gently and then with more force but her eyes—those lovely, otherworldly blue eyes—were closed and her head rolled limply against his arm. "Help!" He looked around wildly. "I need a doctor over here—help me!"

Suddenly Lydiah was pulling on his arm again. "Off-worlder?"

"What? Do you know a doctor? Where's the fucking hospital around here?" Rast demanded, all in one breath.

"Do you truly love her?" Lydiah was looking at him steadily. "You weren't just saying that to help her break the bond?"

"What? Yes, of course I love her!" Rast said wildly. "I'm out of my goddamn mind in love with her, all right?"

"And you want her with you?" Lydiah persisted. "You want to be tied to her for always and spend your whole life with her and only with her?"

"Yes, yes, yes! What is this, twenty questions? Just tell me where to find a doctor!"

"You don't need a doctor—you can heal her yourself. If you're willing."

"Willing to do what?" Rast begged. "Please, just tell me, she's barely breathing."

"Close your eyes, calm yourself, and feel for the broken bond—the one she tore away from Y'dex," Lydiah instructed.

Rast forced himself to do as she said. He'd always had a cool head under pressure. This was no time to panic—not when Nadiah's life might hang in the balance.

Closing his eyes, he reached along the slender cord that connected him to Nadiah. He could barely feel it now—it was like a ghost, a whisper of silk that passed right through his mind's fingers as he searched. But there was something else in there—something big—he could sense it. Big and hurt and throbbing, like a cut artery pulsing away the life's blood of its victim.

"Do you feel it?" Lydiah asked anxiously. "I don't want to rush you, off-worlder, but Nadiah seems to have stopped breathing."

"Yes." Reaching out mentally with everything in him, Rast grabbed the severed cord. It was more like a rough rope or a vine in his hand and unlike his own, slender connection, it was still throbbing with life. Even as he held it, though, the throbbing grew weaker and the cord felt less and less substantial. "I've got it," he told Lydiah, still not opening his eyes. "I've got it — now what?"

"All right, feel for the end," she instructed. "The broken end."

Rast felt for it and found it soon enough. It came to a sharp and jagged point, like a limb torn away from a tree by lightning. Like holding a dagger in my mind, he thought and felt a strange comfort in the thought. "I've got it," he said grimly. "Just barely. It won't last long. Now what do I do?"

"Now you must stab it into your heart."

"What?" Rast's eyes flew open and he almost lost his mental grasp on the slippery, jagged bond. "What did you say?"

"If you want to save her, you have to anchor her to you," Lydiah explained patiently, as though speaking to a young child. "The only way to do that is to push the bond deep into the core of your soul — your psychic heart. Close your eyes and imagine pushing it into yourself — stabbing the root deep in your heart. It's the only way."

"Of course it is," Rast muttered. Suddenly, it all made perfect sense.

"One thing, off-worlder," Lydiah said. "This will hurt. And if Nadiah is too far gone, she may take you down with her to death's doorway."

"You think I give a damn about that?" Rast growled. "I don't care where she takes me as long as we're together."

Lydiah smiled at him. "Then you are truly worthy of her. I am glad I broke my vow."

Rast didn't know what she was talking about and he didn't care. Closing his eyes, he took a firm grip on the jagged, pulsing root. Then, with no hesitation, he pictured himself driving that wickedly sharp point firmly into his own beating heart.

Chapter Nineteen

Nadiah was in a long, dark tunnel. So long and so dark she was almost afraid. But when she looked up, she saw a light at the end—a light that dispelled all her fears. So beautiful, she thought as she drifted towards it. So perfectly peaceful. So right...

The light grew closer and now she could see a figure standing there in the center of it, the figure of a person who was somehow familiar, though Nadiah had a feeling she hadn't seen whoever it was in a long, long time.

"Nadiah? Nadiah, my child." The figure became clearer and suddenly Nadiah recognized her Grandmaman—the one who had told her about her gift—about the Sight. She had warned Nadiah before she died that she might inherit the gift and told her what to expect. But that had been years ago. And now...

"Grandmaman?" Nadiah could hardly contain her joy. "Oh, Grandmaman, I'm so happy to see you!"

"And I'm happy to see you as well, child. But it's too soon. You're early."

"Early?" Nadiah frowned. "What do you mean?"

"I mean the Goddess says it's not your time yet. You must go back, child. The one you left behind loves you dearly—so dearly he is willing to risk his own life for yours. You must go back to him."

"Rast?" Nadiah asked. "Are you talking about Rast?"

"He has a hard road ahead of him child—the wellbeing of First World will rest in his hands." Her grandmaman shivered. "I wouldn't wish that heavy a load on anyone but his shoulders are broad enough to bear it—if he has the right female to help him, that is. So you see, you must go back to him and face the Empty Throne. You must."

"I must," Nadiah repeated softly. Faintly, so faintly she could barely hear it, the sound of voices drifted up to her. One of them belonged to her friend, Lydiah and the other, deeper one was Rast—she was sure of it. He seemed to be panicked or upset about something. He was calling her name, asking for help and it sounded like Lydiah was answering him.

"Go..." Her grandmaman's voice was softer now and when Nadiah looked up, she saw that the older female was fading back into the brilliant, warm glow at the end of the tunnel. "Go now, my child. Go and do what you must do."

"Wait," Nadiah pleaded. "What is it I must do?"

"When the time is right, you will know, child."

"Will I see you again?" Nadiah asked.

"Of course you will." Her grandmaman's voice was fainter still and the sound of Lydiah and Rast talking was growing louder. "We all come to the Goddess in the end," her grandmaman said. "But first you must fulfill your destiny. Goodbye, Nadiah. Goodbye..."

"Goodbye, I love you," Nadiah called after her. By now the circle of light was no more than a pinprick. Suddenly, she felt a rushing sensation, as though she was falling—no—flying downwards. Diving from a great height down to something or someone who was terribly important to her.

The darkness cleared and she caught a glimpse of her own lifeless body, cradled in Rast's muscular arms. And then—

* * * * *

Nadiah jerked in his arms like a heart attack patient being shocked by a defibrillator. A ragged gasp tore from her throat and her eyes flew open, staring up at him in wonder.

"Rast?" she whispered, reaching up for him. "Rast, is that you?"

"Nadiah!" It was impossible to put the relief he felt into words. His heart throbbed in his chest and he could feel the newly connected bond throbbing with it, beating in time to his pulse and hers. "Oh, sweetheart," he whispered and crushed her to him.

She wrapped her arms around his neck and held on, weakly at first but then tighter as strength seemed to pour back into her limbs. Strength that he was giving her, Rast realized. She's getting better. Thank God! Or the Goddess, or whoever, I don't care! She's going to be all right.

"I love you," he heard her whisper timidly as he pressed his cheek to hers. "Love you so much, Rast."

"I love you too, sweetheart." He drew back and studied her lovely face, cherishing every detail of it from her exotic eyes to her full, pink lips. "I'm sorry I was too much of a coward to say it before," he said hoarsely. "It's just, I know Sylvan wants you with a Kindred and he made me swear not to touch you."

Nadiah smiled. "Sylvan will just have to understand."

"Yes." Rast kissed her deeply and then pulled back, smiling as well. "Yes, he will. I mean, I'll call him and tell him what's going on. We can ask for his blessing but if he doesn't want to give it, I'm still going to make an honest woman out of you."

Nadiah frowned. "What exactly does that mean? I'm already honest. Well, mostly."

Rast started laughing, so full of relief he thought he might burst. "It's a human saying. It means I want to marry you."

Her eyes shone. "You mean like a bonding ceremony?"

"Exactly." Rast bent to kiss her again but a heavy hand fell on his shoulder.

"Just a moment, off-worlder. I don't believe this challenge is over."

Rast looked up to see Magistrate Licklow standing there glowering at him. Behind him, a very pissed-off looking Y'dex was doing the same.

"What the hell are you talking about?" he demanded. "It's finished—done. Nadiah's bonded to me now—I won fair and square."

The magistrate's face got red. "You most certainly did not. You had help from Lydiah in the form of verbal direction. And you left your spot to go to Nadiah as I specifically directed you not to."

"Y'dex left his place too—before I did as I matter of fact." Rast was really beginning to get angry. "He grabbed her and wouldn't let go."

"All the more reason to declare this challenge void and start from the beginning," Licklow said pompously. "Now, then, Nadiah will have to be re-bonded to Y'dex so she has a connection to both of you, just to make things fair. And then—"

"No!" Rast interrupted. "Hell no. Nadiah is my female now. She's mine. And I'm not letting any male—let alone your slimy, hairless-cat-looking, fucked up son get anywhere near her."

The last words were a full throated roar of aggression, like an enraged lion fighting for its mate. Rast suddenly knew that something strange was happening to him—something he'd never felt before. His eyes felt hot in their sockets and a red veil seemed to have dropped over his vision, painting everything in tones of bloody crimson. Every muscle in his body was tense and his shoulder blades itched and burned horribly, like someone was running a red-hot knife over them. The pain only added to his rage and he took a step forward, a menacing growl rising in his throat.

Magistrate Licklow's face grew pale and he fell back a step. But he was still frowning as he spoke. "I'm sorry you're upset, off-worlder, but rules are rules."

"I don't give a flying fuck about your damn rules. Nadiah is mine," Rast growled. He was beginning to see that this might come to a fight, which worried him. Not because he didn't think he could take the pudgy magistrate and his son, but because he'd have to put down Nadiah to do it. And something told him the bond between them was still incredibly fragile. The least little mistake might tear it lose and he might not be able to reattach it this time.

Licklow was still talking, clearly ignoring the warning look Rast was giving him. "As I said, rules are rules. And if I have to, I will bring in guards to help me enforce them."

"Be quiet about the damn rules for once, why don't you, Licklow?" A new male had showed up—a tall, lean fellow with a rugged swimmer's physique and light brown hair. He had one arm firmly around Lydiah which told Rast that he, at least, was not a threat. Still, he backed away warily, holding Nadiah close to his chest to protect her and the fragile bond.

"I beg your pardon, Havris," Magistrate Licklow blustered, frowning. "What are you talking about and how dare you interfere?"

"I'm interfering because I can't stand to watch any more of this blatant favoritism." Havris frowned. "The off-worlder won the blood challenge fairly and you know it. It was Y'dex who attempted to cheat over and over. And every time, you helped him."

"I...I don't know what you're talking about!" But the magistrate's face was almost purple and he was slowly backing away.

"The hell you don't," Havris said angrily. "Lydiah told me that she overheard you and Nadiah's parents plotting to fix the challenges. And believe me, I'll be more than happy to go to the Elders with that information if you don't let Nadiah and her male go right now."

"You wouldn't dare!" Y'dex exclaimed, stepping forward with an outraged look on his face. "Not if you want my sister for your wife."

"You're the one who had better not dare anything, Y'dex." Havris's voice was low and cold and he looked at his future brother-in-law as though Y'dex was a bug he wanted to squash beneath his boot. "After the way you treated Lydiah for all these years, the cruelty and humiliation you subjected her to, I'm itching to put my fist through your face. Just come one step closer and try me."

"Traitor!" Y'dex screamed, but Rast noticed he didn't come any closer. "You're a traitor to the Purist cause. A traitor to Tranq Prime," he accused.

"No, I'm just someone who won't stand by and let you cheat anymore." Havris frowned. "You've gotten away with everything your whole life because your father was magistrate. Well, no more! You're going to let Nadiah and her off-worlder go right now with no interference from you or the guards." He turned to the magistrate. "And as soon as they're safely gone out of orbit, Lydiah and I will be having a private bonding ceremony. You and Lady Licklow are invited if you can keep civil tongues in your heads. If not, don't come. I don't care either way."

"I...I...you can't..." For once Magistrate Licklow seemed to be at a loss for something to say.

"Oh yes I can," Havris said grimly. He gave Lydiah's shoulders a squeeze. "Run say goodbye to your friend, darling. She and her male are leaving."

Lydiah gave him a radiant smile and then ran up to Rast. "Can you put her down, just for a moment so I can say goodbye?" she begged.

Rast looked uncertainly at Nadiah but though she looked extremely fatigued, she nodded. "All right," he said at last. "But be careful not to joggle her too much. I'm worried the bond will shake loose."

Lydiah laughed. "Silly off-worlder—it's not that easy to get rid of a deeply rooted blood bond. Although you do need to seal it as soon as you can."

For some reason, this statement made Nadiah's cheeks turn red. "Lydiah!" she exclaimed.

"Well, it's true." Lydiah pulled her into a gentle hug and Rast heard her say, "Sorry I had to break my vow."

"That's all right." Nadiah hugged her back and kissed her cheek. "I'm glad you did."

"All right, no time for long goodbyes." Havris had a wicked looking gun-type thing in one hand and his eyes on Magistrate Licklow and Y'dex. "Let's go," he told Rast tersely. "Lydiah and I will escort the two of you to your ship."

Nadiah tore herself away from her friend and Rast picked her up again over her feeble protests.

"Be quiet," he ordered tenderly. "You're in no shape to walk. Besides, I want to carry you."

"All right." Sighing, she relaxed in his arms and rested her head on his chest. "Let's go then. I want to get out of here."

"You and me both, sweetheart," Rast murmured. "You and me both." Holding her carefully, he turned to follow Havris and Lydiah who were headed out of the challenge grotto. But just as he reached the high, arching exit, he heard someone calling his name. Turning his head, he saw Y'dex still standing there, his pale face purple with rage and both hands clenched into fists.

"You'll regret this, Rast," he howled, his voice echoing through the cavern. "I swear it on my soul! If I can't have her, no one can!"

In his arms, Nadiah shivered. "Oh, Rast..."

He held her closer and walked faster, following Havris. "Don't pay any attention, sweetheart. He's just a sore loser, that's all. After this you'll never have to see him again, I swear."

"I hope you're right." Her face was pale and drawn. "Oh, Rast, I really hope you're right."

They made through the main grotto and down the long tunnel that led to the frozen landing area. Only when they were standing right by the door that led out into the chilly tundra did Rast breathe a sigh of relief. He turned to Havris and nodded at the other male.

"Thank you. I appreciate your help."

"You're more than welcome." Havris nodded back. "I've been aching to tell Lydiah's father off for years but I had to wait until she came of age."

"Yes, so you could whisk me away and bond me." Lydiah looked up at him, her face glowing with love and adoration. She grinned at Rast and Nadiah. "But I think the two of you have some bonding to do too."

Nadiah blushed again. "Lydiah, really."

"Well, you know it's the truth! Oh, and before I forget, here." She stepped forward and pressed something into Nadiah's hands.

"My tharp!" Nadiah hugged the furry garment to her excitedly and it ran through a rainbow of colors, obviously as glad to be back with her as she was to have it. "Where did you get it?" she asked Lydiah. "I was afraid it was lost. I told it to find me but…"

"Well, it couldn't do that without attracting attention," Lydiah said. "Besides, if it had come back to you, how would you have explained it? Didn't your mother drag you off and ask you about a thousand questions after that first challenge?"

"Yes, she did." Nadiah shuddered. "She demanded to know where the tharp was and everything else. If she'd caught me with it…"

"But she didn't because it was smart enough to come to me." Lydiah stroked the living garment affectionately. "But it belongs with you. Keep it safe, dear friend. It has served you well."

"It certainly did and it will again." Nadiah looked up at Rast. "Hold me closer — I'm going to wrap it around both of us."

He started to protest, then realized that he was still wearing the traditional Tranq Prime outfit of a fur skirt and furry boots. His chest, legs, and arms were bare and it was past nightfall outside, so the temperature was going to be in the double digits below freezing.

"All right," he said, pulling her closer. "Do it."

With a little help from Lydiah, they got the tharp wrapped around themselves. Either it was bigger than Rast remembered or it was stretching itself to cover them both. Whatever the reason, once it was fastened securely around them, only their faces stuck out. Nadiah murmured some words to it and it puffed out, putting any down jacket Rast had ever worn to shame.

"Wow, that's warm!" he exclaimed. "Let's get out of here before I fall over from heat exhaustion."

"You'll need every bit of heat you can muster to get from here to your ship," Havris said grimly. "Winter is coming—its chill is already in the air." He raised an eyebrow at Rast. "Are you ready? You'll have to run for it."

Rast took a firmer grip on his precious burden and Nadiah squeaked with protest. But she was smiling so he knew she was all right. "Ready," he said, nodding. "If you'll open the door we'll get out of here."

"On the count of three then," Havris said. "One...two..."

"I love you, Lydiah! Be sure to call me when you're bonded," Nadiah said, smiling at her friend from the cover of the tharp.

"I love you too, dear friend. You do the same." Lydiah's eyes shone as she waved a last farewell.

"Three!" Havris called and flung open the door.

A blast of icy wind so cold it nearly stole his breath away hit Rast like a slap in the face. And then he was off and running.

Chapter Twenty

"Please, please help me. I'm begging you. I've tried everything but nothing works. I don't know where else to turn. Who else to ask."

Sophia fell on her knees in the green and purple grass of the sacred grove. She lifted her hands in supplication to the priestess who towered over her, a forbidding look on her face.

"Of what do you speak, human female? What troubles do you bring before the Mother of All Life this day?" she asked, her green-on-green eyes flashing.

"I am...barren." Sophie could barely get the word out—it stuck in her throat like a bone. But it was the only way to describe her situation. The only word that fit.

"Barren, you say?" The forbidding look in the priestess's strange eyes softened a bit. "How do you know this? You have only been bonded to your warrior a little while, have you not? Perhaps a few more months of trying..."

"That's not going to help," Sophie told her. "After my cousin, Lauren, got pregnant I had Sylvan run some tests. I...my eggs actually reject his seed. They repel it for some reason—some kind of syndrome. And even though he's been working at the lab day and night, he can't find any way to solve the problem." She put her face in her hands and sobbed. "I just want a baby so badly. A little boy I can love and care for and raise."

"I see." The priestess nodded. "And how does Sylvan feel about this?"

Sophie shrugged helplessly. "He says he'll love me no matter what. But I know he wants a son of his own as much as I do. There's so much sadness in him since we found out. It's like...like he's grieving for the son he'll never have. The son we'll never have."

She broke down crying again, all the stress and pain and worry of the last few days catching up to her. Sylvan believed that their problem might be due to a rare disorder which sometimes ran in Kindred bloodlines and became active when introduced to the right stimulus. When a male with the condition came into contact with a female who activated the disorder, the very genes which enabled him to trade with other species somehow got flipped, causing them to do the exact opposite and reject a pairing with an alien female. Which in this case is me, she thought miserably. I'm the one who set him off, it's my fault we can't have a baby!

"If you will allow me, I must lay hands on your head and try to see into this matter," the priestess said.

Though that feeling of cool fingers rifling through her mind was on Sophie's list of top ten hated things, she nodded humbly. "Yes, of course."

"Very good." Two strong hands descended onto her hair and Sophia held her breath and closed her eyes, waiting to feel the strange tingle of an invading mind inside her own. But somehow, it never came.

She opened her eyes again and dared to look up. The priestess, her hands still buried in Sophie's hair, was staring up at the artificial green sun which hung above the sacred grove and chanting something under her breath.

At last, after what felt like a very long time, she removed her hands from Sophie's head and looked down at her. "Rise, daughter of another star. I believe I have your answer."

"You do?" Sophia looked at her with hope. "Oh, thank you! Thank you!"

"Silence!" The priestess's voice cracked like a whip. "You may not be pleased with what you hear."

"I...I may not?" Sophie faltered. "Oh, please —"

"The Goddess has revealed to me that your womb has been closed for a reason."

"What?" Sophie said doubtfully. "I mean, what does that even mean? For what reason?"

"To prove that he who was lost has returned."

"But who? Who was lost and when is he coming back?" Sophie wished the Kindred priestesses wouldn't always talk in riddles but there seemed to be nothing to do but try and follow along.

"One who comes from the mists of time to claim the Empty Thone." The Priestess's voice had taken on a hollow, ringing tone and when Sophie looked at her she saw that the woman's strange green-on-green eyes had rolled up in her head. It reminded her a little of what had happened to Nadiah when she had an al'lei or waking dream.

"Uh...are you all right?" she whispered, taking a step back. "Do you want me to get you a doctor?"

"Be silent," hissed a voice in her ear and Sophie turned to see another priestess standing barefoot on the holy grass beside her. This one was younger — only the irises of her eyes were green, not the whites — but she was somehow no less forbidding than the older one. "The high priestess is having a vision," she told Sophie, taking a firm, pinching grip on her arm. "Kindly be silent and let her continue."

"I'm sorry," Sophie whispered. "I didn't mean to —"

"You must go to him," the first priestess intoned. "Go and stand before the Empty Throne which shall be empty no more. Now it shall be filled as the Goddess decrees it must." Her eyes rolled further up in her head and a narrow stream of spittle started to leak from the corner of her thin-lipped mouth. "They are coming...The Blackness which Eats the Stars...the nameless horror from ancient times. Something has awakened it, has awakened them. They are evil, horror...they are legion. And when they come all of creation will be devoured by their insatiable hunger. The Blackness...it comes...ahhh!"

Suddenly she fell to the ground and began to convulse. With a little cry, Sophie shook off the younger priestess and ran to her. "Get some help," she yelled. "Somebody help me—call the med station!"

But before the words completely left her mouth the seizure or vision or whatever it was stopped completely and the priestess was still, her long, green streaked hair spread on the grass around her.

"Priestess?" Sophie looked down at her anxiously, but sightless eyes stared back into hers. "Your Holiness?" she said. Timidly, she touched the woman's arm, then her cheek. "Oh, her skin is so cold."

"That's because she's dead." The voice of the younger priestess was flat and calm but the grief in her eyes was terrible to see. "Dead!" she cried, rising to shout the news to the entire sacred grove. "The high priestess is dead!"

* * * * *

"Now, tell me again what happened?" Sylvan held her trembling form close to his chest and tried to speak soothingly.

"I...I k-k-killed the high priestess." Sophia was crying so hard he could barely understand her. He held her tight, feeling helpless to end her grief and terror. All he could do was stroke her back and try to soothe her until she cried herself out.

At last the worst of the tears seemed to be over and he was able to get the story out of her. In a shaky voice, Sophie admitted what she had done and told him exactly what had happened.

"So she had a vision and fell over dead?" he demanded. "That doesn't sound like anything you could have done, Talana."

"It was my fault," Sophia insisted. "If I hadn't gone to her asking for help, she never would have had the vision that killed her. I did it, Sylvan—me."

He shook his head. "No, you didn't. It sounds to me like the vision she had was a very serious one. Whether it was responsible for overloading her brain or heart or whether it was simply her time to go to the Goddess, it wasn't your fault. If the message is that important, the Goddess would have sent it sooner or later anyway."

"Do...do you really think so?" Sophia's voice still wavered but there was hope in it now, which made him glad.

"Really, Talana." He kissed her tear stained cheeks gently and brushed a strand of her chestnut brown hair away from her forehead. "And you didn't have to go to the priestess in the first place. You know I'll love you no matter what. Even if we can never have sons, it doesn't matter to me as long as I have you."

"Oh, Sylvan, I know that." Her eyes filled with tears again. "It's just...I want a baby so much. And I know you do too. We can adopt, I guess—I know you'd love any child we chose like your own. But I can't help myself...I want a little boy who looks just like you. With blond hair and blue eyes and that serious expression you get when you're thinking..." She sniffed and blotted her tears with her sleeve. "I'm sorry, I should have told you what I was going to do. I just thought, you know, if the priestess had a solution for me I could surprise you with it."

Sylvan frowned. "We may be able to find some hope in her words. Tell me again, if you can, exactly what she said."

Sophia shook her head. "I can't really remember it all but I'll try. First she said my, uh, womb had been closed for a reason. Then she said I have to go stand before the Empty Throne."

Sylvan was surprised. "The Empty Throne? You're sure that's what she said?"

Sophia nodded. "Reasonably sure, anyway. I remember thinking how weird and spooky it sounded. What is the Empty Throne, anyway?"

"The seat of the Counselor — the rightful ruler and defender of the Kindred home planet—First World as we call it. But the last Counselor died thousands of years ago and ever since the Seat of Wisdom he sat on has been known as the Empty Throne."

Sophia frowned. "I don't understand. Why didn't they just elect another Counselor ?"

Sylvan smiled. "The position is not like your American President, Talana. Counselor is an inherited position. Only one who has a very specific genetic heritage and traits can take the Seat of Wisdom and see with the Eye of Foreknowledge."

"Okay." She nodded. "So this throne has been vacant for how long?"

"Centuries. Ever since the last Counselor 's blood line ran dry." Sylvan frowned. "It was said that he had one heir but the baby was lost somehow or else killed in the battle between the Kindred and the Grimlax."

"The what?" Sophia shook her head. "Could you repeat that? My translation bacteria didn't get it at all."

"That's because it's spoken in a dead language—the language of the Grimlax. They are a race so voracious in their appetites, so evil in their intent, and so mindless in their violence that they were simply called the Hoard." He shrugged. "Or sometimes in the ancient legends, they were referred to as The Blackness which Eats the Stars."

To his surprise, Sophia jumped as though she'd been stung. "The Blackness which Eats the Stars!" she gasped. "That's what she said—she said The Blackness which Eats the Stars was coming!"

Sylvan felt his heart clench in his chest. "Are you certain? Because if you're right, this is a very serious thing indeed."

"But…but I thought they were just an old legend. You just said so yourself."

"I said we had ancient legends about them but that doesn't make them untrue. A millennium ago the last Counselor of First World waged a mighty war upon them. He won, but at the cost of his own life and that of his female. Some say he killed every last one of their relentless number but others say a few survived to grow and multiply under the burned crust of their arid world. Hiding until their numbers were enough to wipe out the stars."

Sophia looked scared. "But that's still just a story, right? And besides, how bad could they be? I mean, the Kindred defeated the Scourge, right? The Hoard couldn't be worse than they were."

Slowly, Sylvan shook his head. "The Scourge were a dying race led by a mad male. The AllFather was sickened and corrupted by his own power. In the end, they had almost no true warriors left, only vat grown soldiers without the sense the Goddess gave a child. But the Hoard…" He looked down, trying to think how to put it. "Have you ever heard the expression, 'he fights like a demon?'"

Sophia nodded. "Sure. But it's just an expression."

"Not in this case. The Hoard are demonic, or what we consider to be demonic, anyway. They are soulless, seeking only to devour, to torture and maim and kill and ruin every living thing they come into contact with." He sighed. "The Scourge were a twisted race but they grew that way gradually, polluting their home world and selling their virtue for monetary gain. The Hoard on the other hand…they cannot be reasoned with, cannot be tamed or bargained with. They can only be killed."

Sophia bit her lip. "You make them sound like monsters."

"Let me put it this way," Sylvan said grimly. "The legends say that if a ship was boarded by a tribe of the Hoard, the passengers would be tortured, raped, skinned and eaten in that order—all while they were still alive."

"Tortured and eaten and sk-skinned?" Sophia's voice wavered. "That's horrible. So barbaric! But what…why did they skin them?"

"According to legends, the more primitive Hoard tribes delighted in making garments from their victims' skin." Sylvan said. "They wore their trophies as a warning to the next ship they boarded."

"Ugh!" Sophia shivered. "I'm so glad that all happened in the past and that it's far, far away from us, near the Kindred home world." She frowned. "What if by some chance they did come back? Would they be able to fold space and come get us?"

Sylvan shook his head. "The ability to fold space is a technology known only to the Kindred and the Scourge. So now, of course, only the Kindred have it. We guard its secret closely. But honestly, even if a hostile alien race were to get hold of it, it wouldn't do them much good."

"Why not?" Sophia asked.

Sylvan shrugged. "Because, it takes vast quantities of energy to create and sustain a controlled tear in the space-time continuum. Energy which now only Kindred Mother ships are able to make thanks to the artificial sun at their centers."

"I see." Sophia nodded. "So without the secret of the green sun and the technology to use it..."

"Any hostile race that wanted to spread through the universe would have to rely on existing worm holes," Sylvan said. "And they are mostly too narrow and unstable for anything but a small scout craft to fly through."

"So then we're safe, no matter what the priestess said. Aren't we?" Sophia looked at him hopefully.

"Yes, of course." Sylvan drew her to him again. "Of course we are, Talana," he murmured into her hair. But deep in his soul a stirring of unease had begun and he couldn't tell if he was telling his beloved wife the truth...or a lie.

Chapter Twenty-one

"All warmed up?" Rast asked as she stepped from the bathroom into the tiny living area of their ship.

"Yes, thank you. You were right—a hot shower was just what I needed." Nadiah smiled shyly. She had dried herself off already and had her tharp draped around her in what Kat had called "toga style" with one shoulder bare. "You, uh, can take one now too, if you like. There should still be plenty of hot water left," she said.

"Thanks." Rast nodded. "I think I will. And don't worry about anything, we're already out of orbit and the autopilot has all coordinates locked in for the fold."

"Will it take us five days to get back to it the way it took five days going?" Nadiah wanted to know.

"No, I don't think so. If the calculations are correct, it should only take three days or so, Earth time." He smiled. "So we'll be back on the Mother Ship with all your friends in no time."

"Oh. That's...nice." Nadiah tried to look happy but to tell the truth, she was rather disappointed. She'd been hoping for more time than that alone together with Rast.

He picked up on her mood at once. "What is it, sweetheart?" he asked, taking her hands in his. "Come on, we're bonded now. You can tell me."

Nadiah bit her lip. "It's true we have a bond but it's not...well, it's not sealed."

Rast frowned. "Sealing the bond—your friend Lydiah said that several times, didn't she? What was she talking about?"

"Um…" Nadiah felt her cheeks flushing. It was funny how easily she used to talk about sex with her girlfriends back on Tranq Prime. But now that she was alone in a ship with the man she actually wanted to give herself to, she found herself completely tongue-tied.

"Wow, whatever it is, it must be hot stuff. Come on, sweetheart, spit it out," Rast said, grinning a little. Nadiah realized she'd been stalling for long enough.

"In order to seal the bond between us, you'll have to change the color of my eyes," she murmured, looking down at her hands. "I think you know what that means."

"I know exactly what it means but I'm not going to do it. Not yet," Rast said.

"What?" She looked up at him in dismay. "Then you don't really love me? I thought you said—"

"Hey, whoa, slow down there." Rast put a finger across her lips to stop the flow of worried questions. "First of all, know this—I love you like I've never loved anyone before." He tilted her chin to look into her eyes and murmured, "To tell the truth, I'm fucking crazy about you."

Nadiah gave him a trembling smile. "I'm insanely in love with you too. I think I have been for awhile, I was just afraid to admit it."

"Me too," Rast admitted, smiling.

"So then why—"

"Because I haven't had a chance to talk to Sylvan yet."

"But I thought you didn't care what he said," Nadiah protested.

"I don't," Rast said seriously. "I'm going to marry you whether he likes it or not. But I'm not going to make love to you and change the color of your eyes until after we tie the knot. I promised your cousin you'd be a virgin on your wedding day and that's one promise I intend to keep."

Nadiah sighed mournfully. "All right. I knew you were an honorable male from the start. I just wish…"

"What?" he said, laughing. "That I wasn't quite so honorable."

"Exactly."

"Well, as it turns out, I'm not." He leaned closer and his eyes were suddenly half-lidded with lust. "Not quite."

"What…what does that mean?" The hungry way he was looking at her made Nadiah feel breathless.

"It means there are a lot of things we can do without taking that final step. Without changing the color of your eyes." Rast tilted her chin again and placed a hot, gentle kiss on her lips. "Do you know what I mean?"

"I…I think so." Suddenly Nadiah's heart was beating so hard she could feel it in every part of her body. It seemed to shake her with its excited rhythm.

"Good." Rast gave her a slow smile. "Then be ready for me when I come out of the shower. All right?"

"All right," she murmured nodding.

"See you in a few minutes, then." With a last, meaningful look, he headed into the bathroom.

Nadiah scrambled back to her tiny bedroom to get ready…then realized she really didn't have much to do. She was already clean and naked under her tharp, her still damp hair falling in blonde waves past her shoulders. She never wore make-up and she didn't have any perfume to put on. Still, shouldn't she do something?

Oh yes, of course! She whispered a command to her tharp and suddenly it went from being slightly a furry, opaque blue to a sheer, white silky material that draped seductively over her curves. Nadiah looked down in mingled embarrassment and satisfaction and saw that the pink points of her nipples and the plump V of her pussy were both clearly visible beneath the new gown. There, definitely sexier than blue fur, she told herself. But was it too much? After all, she didn't want Rast to think she was trying to make him break his vow. Although it would be extremely interesting to see how far she could push him…

Deciding to leave the tharp as the see through white gown, she tried to arrange herself in a seductive pose on the bed. Should she be lying on her back? No, too blatant. Sitting with her legs crossed? No, too demure. Well, what about on her side? Her breasts weren't as full as some females' she knew, but when she lay on her side, it formed some nice cleavage.

Just as she was deciding that the side was definitely the way to go, Rast suddenly appeared wearing only a towel slung low on his hips. His massive shoulders filled the doorway and droplets of water clung to his broad, bare chest. His eyes were burning as he took her in, naked beneath the silky, sheer tharp.

He didn't say a word, just stood there and looked at her but the hungry expression his face made Nadiah forgot to worry about what position she was in. She only knew she wanted him and she could tell that Rast wanted her too. She whispered his name and held out her arms.

That was all it took. Rast was suddenly on the bed with her, kissing her with an urgency that seemed to set her on fire. She could feel her nipples turning into hard little points beneath her tharp and her pussy was getting hot and wet and slippery too––ready for him. Ready to let him in, to let him take her.

That's not going to happen right now, she reminded herself. Not until we have an official joining ceremony. Silently she vowed to haul her handsome human to the sacred grove to say vows the minute they landed on the Mother Ship. And after that...

"What are you thinking?" Rast murmured, surprising her. "You have the naughtiest look on your face."

Nadiah blushed, then smiled, one corner of her mouth going up. "I was just thinking that I wish...wish we didn't have to wait. And the minute we get back to the Mother Ship—"

"We'll find the first handy priest. Or priestess or whatever to tie the knot," Rast finished her thought with a grin. "I'm with you on that. But for right now, I think we need to take it easy."

"You're not leaving, are you?" Nadiah asked. "Please, Rast, I promise I'll be good. You can trust me not to...not to do anything I shouldn't."

"The question is, can I trust myself?" He stroked her cheek. "But no, what I meant was let's go slow so you can enjoy it. I mean, this is your first time being with anyone—is that right?"

Blushing, Nadiah nodded. "I've been promised to Y'dex all my life so I never even got to hold hands with another male."

"Well, we're going to do a lot more than hold hands tonight, I promise you that," Rast murmured. "But slowly...I don't want to rush things. Don't want to scare you."

"What are you going to do?" Nadiah asked, feeling her heart begin to race again.

"To start with? Touch you. Just touch you." Rast smiled. "And I want you to lay there like a good little girl and let me do it. Can you do that for me, Nadiah?"

"I...I guess so." She nibbled her bottom lip. "Should I take off my tharp?"

"Not right away. You're naked under it, right?"

She nodded and he made a low noise of approval deep in his throat. "Good. Just lie quietly on your back and let me touch you, then."

Nadiah arranged herself as he directed, her heart thumping loudly in her ears. She expected him to touch her breasts or reach between her legs but Rast surprised her.

Starting at one of her burning cheeks, he stroked slowly downward, letting his fingertips trail over the sensitive side of her neck and down her bare shoulder. He did the same thing on the other side and then, starting at the point of her chin, he caressed down the pulse in her throat and the warm, bare skin between her breasts. His large hand came dangerously close to her curves but never quite touched them, making Nadiah feel like all her nerve endings were on fire with need.

"Rast, please," she whispered, attempting to catch his hand and press it over her breast.

"Ah-ah-ah." He shook his head. "Just lie still, all right?"

"But you're driving me insane," Nadiah protested.

He gave her a lazy smile. "That's the idea of taking it slow. Don't you like it?"

"I...I don't know if I like it or not," Nadiah admitted. "I only know I want more."

"And you'll get more — much more — in a little bit." He leaned down to kiss her gently on the mouth. "Don't worry, sweetheart. I won't leave you wanting. Just relax and try to enjoy yourself."

"All right." Biting her lip in frustration, Nadiah subsided.

"Good girl." Rast reached down to pull up her tharp and her heart started pounding again. *This is it. He's finally going to touch me there.*

But instead of cupping her pussy, as Nadiah had imagined he would, Rast only started the same, slow, stroking caress up and down her legs which he had performed on her arms and throat. Nadiah moaned and shifted restlessly as his big, warm hand slid from the ticklish inside of her ankle all the way up to her inner thigh. It hovered there, just for a moment, then slid across to her other thigh. His fingertips brushed teasingly close to her mound before continuing their journey down to her other ankle.

"God, your skin is like silk." His deep voice was hoarse with desire and Nadiah suddenly realized that this was almost as hard on him as it was on her. *Going slow wasn't easy, apparently. So then, why was Rast so insistent on it?*

"I...I'm glad you like it. My skin, I mean," she whispered.

"It's beautiful. You're beautiful." He looked into her eyes and stroked her cheek again. This time when his hand traveled down, it brushed lightly over the aching peak of her breast.

"Oh!" Nadiah gasped, straining upward to get more of his touch.

"This dress you have on is pretty damn sexy too," Rast murmured, casually brushing the other breast, as if by accident.

"It...it's just my tharp," she whispered breathlessly. "I...I told it to look like this. I thought...I hoped you might like it."

"I more than like it, sweetheart. I love it." At last his big hand slid down to cup her pussy, stroking gently through the thin, silky material.

Nadiah moaned and bit her lip. No one had ever touched her like this before, so intimately...so tenderly. It made her feel like her whole body was on fire with need. Suddenly, she couldn't wait to feel his hands on her naked skin any more. With a whispered command, the tharp parted, leaving her bare before him.

Rast groaned low in his throat. "God, Nadiah…"

"Is…is this all right?" she asked, hoping he wasn't upset. "I just thought…"

"You thought you'd speed up the process, didn't you." He smiled lazily. "Well guess what, it won't work. I'm not nearly done touching you yet. So you're just going to have to lay there and take it a little while longer."

And with that, he went back to caressing her in long, slow strokes but this time touching every part of her body. His fingertips trailed over her skin, not avoiding her breasts and pussy but not paying any special attention to those sensitive spots either. It went on and on until Nadiah honestly thought she was going to go mad.

"Please," she begged him, panting. "Please, Rast…don't you…isn't there something else you want to do?"

"Oh, there's a lot I want to do to you, sweetheart. Starting with this."

Bending over her, he lapped gently at one tight nipple. Then, almost before Nadiah could moan he was sucking it deep into his mouth, drawing hard on the aching peak until she felt like she was going to come out of her skin.

"Rast, oh Goddess!" she moaned brokenly, her hands squeezing into fists at her sides. She arched her back, pressing her breasts up to him, begging for more as he turned his attention to her other nipple as well.

Rast seemed to take forever, licking and kissing her breasts. He sucked gently at first and then increased the suction until she felt she couldn't stand it any more. He nipped her gently, too, sending little sparks of pleasure/pain from her tender nipples straight down to her pussy while she writhed and moaned under him.

At last, when Nadiah thought she really couldn't take it any more, he sat back, panting. "You like that, do you?"

"You know I do." Nadiah looked down at her breasts. Her nipples which were dark pink from his erotic attention. "But Rast, I want more. So much more."

He chuckled softly. "Eager little virgin, aren't you? Good, because we're only getting started."

Nadiah had no idea what was coming next but she hoped it involved his hands sliding below her waist. Rast didn't disappoint her.

"Spread your legs, sweetheart," he murmured as one large, warm hand stroked down her trembling abdomen. "I want to see if you're wet."

Nadiah was sure that she was. Her pussy had never felt so wet and swollen in her life—even during the conversation they'd had about sex on the journey to Tranq Prime. Then, Rast had only been looking at her. Now he was actually going to touch her—she hoped.

Slowly she spread her thighs, opening them wider when he directed. As her plump cunt lips came into view, she felt incredibly exposed and a little embarrassed to see that her honey had already coated her pussy and inner thighs.

"So wet," Rast murmured hoarsely. "God, I haven't even touched you yet and you're already so damn wet."

Nadiah bit her lip. "My people have a word for it—for a female who gets very wet for her male."

"Tell me," he commanded.

"Numala," she whispered, blushing at the forbidden word. "It means liquid pussy."

"Numala." He rolled the name on his tongue, making her blush again to hear it spoken in his deep, male voice. "I like that. It fits you."

"So your people like such females?" she asked.

"We do." He traced a pattern around her belly button and then his hand slid down to cup her mound. "I do. A hell of a lot."

"I...I'm glad," Nadiah whispered. "Glad you find me pleasing."

"You're a hell of a lot more than pleasing, sweetheart. You're incredible." Leaning down, he kissed her mouth, stroking her tongue with his possessively until Nadiah moaned. Finally he broke the kiss but continued to look into her eyes. "Last time I asked you to spread yourself for me," he murmured. "This time I'm going to spread your pussy open myself. Spread you open and explore your sweet little cunt."

The hot promise in his deep voice excited Nadiah more than she could say. "Yes," she whispered, spreading her legs wider. "Yes, Rast, please..."

"So wet and hot," he murmured hoarsely as he spread her open. "Just look, Nadiah. Even your little clit is swollen and hot." He brushed very, very lightly over the tiny pink nub at her center but to Nadiah the light touch felt like an electric spark. She gasped his name and arched her back...and Rast did it again. And again and again.

"Rast...Rast," she moaned as he slid one careful finger tip back and forth over her clit again and again. "Oh...oh, Goddess!"

She understood now why this act was forbidden on Tranq Prime. Nothing that felt this good could be anything but deliciously sinful. She'd often squeezed her thighs together for the pleasurable sensations it brought but never had she felt such pleasure as that slow, gentle fingertip strumming her clit.

But just as she felt like she was reaching some kind of a peak, Rast backed off and began exploring the rest of her inner pussy. Nadiah gasped when she felt two blunt fingers come to rest at the very entrance of her well.

"Not sure how far I can go here," Rast murmured, looking at her. "I don't want to break your cherry, uh, I mean change the color of your eyes by accident."

From speaking to her Earth friends, Nadiah understood what he meant. "Tranq Prime females have no barrier within," she explained in a breathy voice. "We...you can't change the color of my eyes unless you put yourself inside me and fill me with your seed. It's a biological reaction that takes place when my body senses your seed inside. Does that make sense?"

"Uh-huh." Rast seemed to like the idea. "So I'd have to be buried inside you, my cock balls deep in your tight little pussy while I filled you with my cum?"

His hot, dirty words sent a little quiver of pure lust through Nadiah's entire body. "Yes," she whispered breathlessly. "Ex...exactly."

"So, it's safe to do this?" Slowly, one thick finger breached her entrance and slid deeply into her slick inner pussy.

"Oh!" Nadiah bucked her hips, wanting more of the new, erotic sensation. "Yes," she moaned. "Yes, more, please!"

"I'll give you more, sweetheart. But not with my fingers." Giving her a heated look, Rast got off the bed and came around to the end. Kneeling, he motioned for her to slide down. "Come on, numala. I want to taste you."

This is what he talked about before…tasting me. Licking my pussy. Nadiah felt like she could barely breathe she was so hot. Her whole body trembled as she obeyed him, sliding down to the end of the bed until her lower legs from the knee down were hanging over the edge.

"That's good." His truegreen eyes were burning with desire but Rast still seemed to want to take his time. "Very good, sweetheart. Now spread your legs for me again."

Moaning softly, Nadiah did as she as told. Goddess, she felt like she was on fire and only Rast could put out the blaze. He didn't seem to be in any hurry to do so, though.

"God, you smell so damn good." With a low possessive growl, he rubbed his rough cheek against the soft curls of her mound, making Nadiah gasp. He did the same with the other cheek, rubbing possessively, as though he couldn't get enough of her. It was as though he was bathing in her scent, breathing her in, getting her feminine aroma all over him.

But Nadiah had begun to smell a new scent in the bedroom and it wasn't hers. Rich, and dark and masculine, it filled the small space, making her feel drunk with need. His mating scent, she thought, as she had before. But no, that was impossible — wasn't it? Nadiah didn't know and she didn't care, she only knew that his warm, male musk made her want to give herself to him completely, to spread her legs and open her pussy to be fucked by his thick shaft over and over until he filled her with his seed.

"Rast," she begged. "Rast, please take me. I need you in me — please!"

He looked up at her, his cheeks wet with her juices though he had yet to taste her, and his eyes burning with desire. "Can't do that yet, sweetheart. Can't make love to you tonight. But I can do this."

With that, he spread her outer pussy lips with his thumbs and leaned down to give her a long, hot lick.

Nadiah cried out, her hips bucking helplessly as he lapped her open pussy. His hot tongue seemed to be everywhere at once, licking her slowly one minute and then teasing her clit lightly the next. Her hands, which had been fisted in the covers on either side of her, crept up to grasp at his thick hair. Before she knew it, she was sliding her fingers through the silky-coarse strands and holding on tight while Rast continued to feast on her.

If he minded her death grip on his hair, she certainly couldn't tell by his reaction. If anything, her fingers against his scalp seemed to spur him on, to make him even more eager to pleasure her.

His big hands slid around her thighs, locking them open, and he redoubled his efforts, sucking her swollen clit into his mouth and tonguing it mercilessly until Nadiah cried out breathlessly with pleasure.

She could feel something inside her now. Something like a wire in the very center of her being. A wire that was slowly growing taut, winding tighter and tighter until soon it must snap. Nadiah wasn't sure what would happen to her when it did, but all the same she ached for it, needed it…needed something she couldn't name.

"Rast," she begged. "Rast, please, I need…I need…"

"You need to come," he said, panting, as he looked up momentarily from his labors. "You need to let yourself go and come all over my face."

Nadiah was filled with frustration and need. "But…but I don't know how."

"You don't have to," Rast assured her. "I'll show you. Just spread your thighs a little wider and let me work on you, sweetheart. Let me eat your sweet little pussy."

She tried to do as he said but it seemed like every muscle in her body wanted to tense up. Her stomach was fluttering and her skin felt incredibly sensitive, almost as though it was suddenly too tight for her body. But she knew that if she didn't let Rast finish, she would never reach that elusive peak. Never find out what happened when the wire inside her snapped.

Releasing her grip on his hair, she forced herself to relax and spread her thighs wider, giving him even greater access.

"That's good," Rast murmured, kissing the inside of one thigh gently. "Very good, sweetheart. But you didn't have to let go of my hair—I like knowing how much you're enjoying yourself."

"Oh…I thought…though maybe I was hurting you." Nadiah slipped her fingers into his thick, light brown hair again.

He grinned. "I'll probably have a hell of a headache later but it's worth it. So don't worry—just do what feels good." With that, he lowered his head again and gave her another long lick, flattening his tongue so that he tasted every part of her pussy at once.

Nadiah moaned and prepared herself for more, waiting for the wire to snap. But this time, it wasn't only his tongue on her pussy that made her gasp and cry. As he started to tease her swollen clit again, drawing circles around it with his tongue tip until she thought she would go insane, she felt first one, then two of his thick fingers slide deep into her pussy and begin to move.

"Oh…oh, Goddess!" she gasped. This is how he'd do it, she thought as he continued the steady pumping motion, thrusting deeply inside her virgin pussy as he continued to lap and tease her clit. This is how he would make love to me…how he would fuck me.

The forbidden thought, almost as much as his careful penetration, was what finally made the wire snap and sent her spinning over the edge of pleasure. Her hands tightened in his hair and she wailed his name, her entire body arching in a spasm of pure need as he gave her what she'd been begging for.

"Rast...oh, Rast!" Nadiah chanted his name like a prayer, pumping her hips in time to the rhythm he'd started with his tongue and fingers. Pleasure washed over her like warm water, drenching her completely as her release went on and on. It was as though years of frustration and forbidden thoughts, over a decade of building sexual need had finally come to a single searing point in her soul and she was exploding from within.

Rast rode out her orgasm, the fingers of his free hand digging into her thigh as he stayed with her no matter how she bucked. He seemed to relish her pleasure almost as much as she did and he didn't stop licking and sucking and pumping his fingers inside her until Nadiah finally relaxed completely.

"Oh..." she whispered, her whole body feeling flushed and warm and totally relaxed. "Oh Goddess, that was unbelievable. Amazing."

"Fucking amazing," Rast agreed in a low growl. Holding her eyes with his own, he slowly withdrew his two fingers and sucked them clean of her honey. Then he was on the bed with her again, taking her into his arms. "You're gorgeous when you come, you know that?" he whispered hoarsely, and then took her mouth in a long, passionate kiss.

Nadiah moaned when she realized what he was doing—sharing her own unique and secret flavor with her, feeding it to her on his tongue as he penetrated her mouth the same way he'd penetrated her pussy.

I taste good, she thought deliriously. Who could have imagined? But she did. Hot and wet and sweet, she loved the flavor of herself mixed with the warm taste of Rast's tongue. Loved the intimate act of sharing this secret part of herself with him. It felt so good, so right…

And then suddenly, Rast broke the kiss and rolled away from her.

"What…what's wrong?" Feeling disoriented from the passionate kiss and the intense pleasure she'd just experienced, Nadiah looked at him in confusion. "What's wrong?" she asked again. "Why did you stop?"

"Had to stop." Rast's deep chest was heaving in and out as he dragged air into his lungs. "Can't…can't do anymore or I won't be able to help myself. To keep myself from…" He trailed off, shaking his head but Nadiah knew what he meant.

He's talking about taking me, she thought and a shiver of pleasurable fear ran through her. Making love to me right here and now, changing the color of my eyes even though he promised not to.

A single look down between Rast's muscular legs confirmed it. The towel which had been wrapped around his waist had come off and Nadiah could see his long, thick shaft pulsing between his thighs in time with his heartbeat. It was a darker shade than the rest of his body and the broad, blunt head was already leaking a slippery clear liquid.

His seed, she thought. That which could change the color of my eyes. Despite the inherent danger, she longed to stroke that angry looking shaft, to sooth and pleasure him as he had pleasured her. To taste his salty seed.

Without thinking about it, she reached out to wrap her fingers around his thickness and began caressing his cock.

* * * * *

Going down on her, hearing her cries and gasps and moans while he tasted her sweet, soft little pussy had almost been Rast's undoing. All he could think about was rolling her over, spreading her thighs and thrusting his cock as deep into her soft, unresisting body as he could.

Can't, he told himself, half delirious with lust. Can't. Have to stop. Have to — And that was when he felt her soft little hand on his swollen shaft.

Rast nearly jumped out of his skin. "God, sweetheart," he gasped, half sitting up. "Don't! You shouldn't!"

"Why not?" Nadiah looked up at him, her deep blue eyes sparkling. "Why can't I touch you as you touched me? Explore you as you explored me?"

"It's dangerous," he ground out. "You don't understand, Nadiah, I might lose control."

"Lose control and take me, you mean?" A naughty little smile curved the corners of her pink lips. "Well now, wouldn't that be a shame? I guess I'd have no choice but to spread my thighs and let you...let you fuck me."

The hot, dirty word coming from her sweet, innocent mouth nearly drove him over the edge. And it didn't help that she was basically saying she wouldn't try to stop him if he took her. That she would just lie back and spread for him, open herself and let him have anything he wanted.

"We need to stop now, while I still can." Rast reached for her wrist and pulled her small, delicate hand away from his cock. "Come on now, stop touching me."

"But you got to touch me." Nadiah gave him a disappointed look. "Please, Rast, can't I just touch you a little if I promise to be very, very careful? I've never seen a naked male before and I've certainly never touched one. Please?"

God, if there's anything more dangerous than a curious virgin I don't want to know what it is. But the pleading tone in her voice as well as the look on her lovely face finally convinced him.

"All right," he said with a sigh. "But just...be careful. Think of it this way—you're playing with a loaded gun. It might go off."

"That's what I'm hoping." Nadiah gave him a look that was half shy, half defiant. "I want to make you come the way you made me come. I want to give you pleasure, Rast. Please let me—please tell me how."

After that, there was nothing he could do but let her.

He watched, his hands fisted at his sides, as she stroked him, her small white hand caressing his entire rigid length from the sensitive crown all the way down to the thick root of his cock. After a long while, she looked up at him and smiled tentatively.

"Is this all right? Is this how you like to be touched?"

"It's more than all right," Rast assured her hoarsely. In fact, her soft, innocent exploration was doing more for him than the feel of a much more experienced hand would have. She was so beautiful, her cheeks still flushed pink from her orgasm, her dark blue eyes bright with curiosity and love, her long blonde hair hanging down over her shoulders like a bright, golden shawl. Watching her explore him, he thought his cock and his heart might burst at the same time. She was just too much, too perfect. It was hard to believe she was really his.

She's not yet, though, whispered a little voice inside his head—the voice of his intuition. Until you bond her completely and change the color of her eyes she can still be taken away from you. You should take her now, mark her so no other male can touch her.

But he couldn't do that—he'd made a promise to Sylvan and damn it, he wasn't a man who broke promises. *Everything's going to be all right,* he told himself uneasily. *I'll marry her and make her mine as soon as we get to the Mother Ship.*

It made him anxious and uneasy to ignore his gut instinct—all his life he'd followed it and it had never led him astray. But in this case, he had his honor to think about. He had given his word and he wasn't going to break it. Still, he couldn't help thinking he might be sorry...

"Oh, God." The surprised gasp was torn from his lips as Nadiah decided to try something new. Rast watched with a fresh surge of desire as she bent over him, the ends of her long, silky hair tickling his thighs, and licked the head of his cock again.

"Mmm." She looked up at him, a naughty glint in her dark blue eyes. "I love the way you taste."

"Sweetheart you...you don't have to do that," Rast told her in a strangled voice.

"But I want to. Want to taste you like you tasted me." She frowned. "Am I doing it wrong? Should I take it in my mouth instead?"

"You're doing everything right," Rast assured her. "Just...be careful. I'm right on the edge as it is."

She gave him a teasing smile. "Then you're right where I want you." Leaning down, she opened her mouth and sucked the head of his cock into her hot, wet mouth. He was thick and long so she couldn't get all of it in but it was clear she was taking as much as she could.

Rast cried out hoarsely and one hand stole down to caress her silky hair. God, she was a natural at this. She seemed to know instinctively to be careful of her teeth and the way she was swirling her soft little tongue around the pulsing head of his cock made him feel like he was going to come at any second.

Have to be careful, he thought hazily. Will getting cum in her mouth change her eyes? Better not risk it.

Reluctantly, because she seemed perfectly willing to keep on sucking him until he went over the edge, Rast decided he had to stop her. Gently but firmly, he pulled her away though it was the last thing he wanted to do.

"But…but Rast," she protested as he pulled her loose. "I wanted to taste your seed."

"That's exactly what I don't want to risk," he growled. "What if it changes your eyes?"

Nadiah frowned. "I don't think it would. I think it's only if you get it in my…my pussy." She still seemed a little shy saying the word, her cheeks flushing as she spoke. Rast found her embarrassment both charming and arousing.

"Well, let's not take a chance, okay? Come here." He pulled her up to lie against the side of his chest, leaving her right hand free. "You can finish me off with that soft little hand of yours. Okay?"

She sighed. "All right, I guess. But I wanted to use my mouth to make you come—the same way you did for me."

"There'll be plenty of time for that as soon as we're married," Rast said firmly and felt that little tingle of unease again. He pushed it away and stroked her hair. "Well? Come on, sweetheart, don't leave a guy hanging."

She smiled. "All right then. I'll do my best." Reaching down, she fisted his shaft again—or tried to. Her slender fingers couldn't quite fit all the way around the thick girth of his cock. "You're so big," she murmured as she stroked him up and down. "How will you ever fit inside me?"

"As wet and slippery as you get?" Rast kissed her hungrily. "I should be able to slide right in," he murmured. "But I swear I'll be very slow and gentle, you know that, right?"

Nadiah kissed him back and began pumping his cock in a slow, up and down stroke that drove him wild. "Yes, you're good at that. You were so slow and gentle touching me I thought I'd go insane."

"That's because sex isn't about the destination," Rast lectured in a hoarse voice. "It's about the...oh, God, sweetheart! It's about the journey."

"So that means I should go very slowly while I touch you too?" With a mischievous smile, Nadiah slowed her stroke considerably, until she was just barely touching him. "Is that right?"

Rast groaned and bucked up into her hand, trying to get more sensation, more contact with her slim fingers and soft palm. "You little tease. You're giving me a taste of my own medicine, aren't you?"

She laughed delightedly. "Yes, exactly. I want to make this last."

But he'd lasted long enough already. Rast was afraid that if he held out much longer, he would give in and let her suck him again. Or else roll her over and thrust his cock balls deep in her tight little pussy.

Wrapping his own, larger hand around her smaller one and taking a firm grip, he thrust up and down, using the delicious friction to finally achieve his release.

"God!" he gasped as he felt the orgasm rolling up from the base of his balls. He'd never been this excited by a simple hand job before. But then again, he'd never had the hand of the woman he loved and wanted to be with forever wrapped around his cock. Even with his ex, he hadn't had this sense of rightness...of belonging. The feeling that the woman in his arms was meant to be there, and that he would kill or die to keep her with him and protect her forever. Mine, he thought again and this time the thought came with no shame or guilt—just a complete and utter certainty. Nadiah's mine.

"Oh!" Nadiah gasped breathlessly as his cum jetted out in hard, hot spurts, covering both their hands and bathing Rast's flat belly as well. "Oh," she murmured. "It's so hot. And you're still hard."

"Uh, yeah. Sometimes it takes a little while to go down." Rast shifted uncomfortably. To tell the truth, he'd barely taken the edge off his lust and could probably go several more times if she wanted to. But he'd learned from experience that his peculiar gift—the fact that he needed almost no recovery time after coming—wasn't always welcome to the opposite sex. In fact, his ex had hated it.

But far from being upset, Nadiah's eyes were shining with excitement. She turned to Rast eagerly. "Can we do it again?"

"Sure." He grinned at her. "As many times as you want, sweetheart. But first, I think it's your turn—I want to taste you again."

"Only if I can taste you too." Nadiah looked at him shyly. "Do you think...could we taste each other at the same time?"

Rast felt a surge of lust pulse through his cock. God, he loved this woman! She was such a mixture of innocence and raw, hungry sexuality it made him crazy.

"Of course we can," he murmured. "I'll show you how in a minute. Just let me get cleaned up."

"I'll get you something." Nadiah started to hop off the bed but he stopped her for a moment.

"Wait," he commanded. "Let me look at you just for a minute."

She looked up at him questioningly. "What? Is everything all right?"

"Everything's more than all right." Rast searched her lovely face, memorizing the delicate lines and feminine angles. "You have beautiful eyes, you know that?" he murmured. "I don't even have a name for that color blue—I don't think there's anything like it anywhere on Earth."

"Oh, Rast..." She looked down, blushing, but he lifted her chin.

"I'm serious," he told her. "They're beautiful. But I can't wait to change their color. I can't wait to look at you and know you're mine forever and no one can take you away from me."

Her lovely eyes filled with tears for a moment. "You can know that now. I'm sure my parents will never want me back on Tranq Prime. But even if they did I wouldn't go. I'm yours and you're mine—we belong together."

"Together forever," Rast agreed, kissing her. The soft brush of her lips against his enflamed him all over again. "God, you taste sweet," he growled. "Everywhere."

"I like the way you taste too." Nadiah's voice had gone breathy and soft again. "Rast, please, I want you. Let's make each other come again."

They did.

Chapter Twenty-two

Sylvan waited anxiously for the small ship to dock. Solar flares from the Earth's sun had made communication patchy at best and he hadn't been able to get any details about what had happened on Tranq Prime. He did know two things for sure, however: one, Rast had somehow won the challenge because Nadiah was with him. And two, Rast has been true to his word—Nadiah's eyes were the same dark blue they had always been.

Sylvan was glad to see that Rast had kept his promise. He hadn't been greatly impressed with most of the human males he'd met and—-No, he told himself, frowning. Have to stop thinking of him like that. After seeing the final results on his blood test—

"Oh, look, they've landed!" Beside him, Sophia was nearly jumping up and down with excitement. Sylvan was glad to see her looking happy for once. Ever since the fertility tests he had run on the both of them had come back with the unhappy verdict of Tander's Syndrome, she'd been quiet and sad. And the strange, morbid outcome of her visit to the sacred grove hadn't helped a bit.

Sylvan wished, as he often had, that the priestesses would speak plain truth instead of couching their prophecies in riddles and enigmas. If he could, he would have gone to the sacred grove himself to demand an explanation. But in this case, it wouldn't have done any good since the one who had made the prophecy was dead, and all the rest of the priestesses were in mourning and would be for the next solar month.

They would see no one during this time and everyone else aboard the ship was ordered to avoid seeing them as well, to preserve their modesty. As a sign of their mourning for the high priestess, all of them would shave their hair and wear no clothing at all until the time of sadness had passed. It was a good thing the artificial green sun warmed the sacred grove, Sylvan thought. If they attempted to observe such a custom on Tranq Prime they would have all frozen to death in a matter of minutes.

"Here they come! Oh, Nadiah!" Sophia couldn't hold herself back anymore. As the hatch of the little ship opened, she ran forward and wrapped her arms around his kinswoman exuberantly.

Nadiah hugged her back and seemed to be laughing and crying at the same time. "I'm free," Sylvan heard her tell Sophia. "I'm free — Rast won my freedom for me."

"I knew he would!" Sophia smiled at the tall male who was climbing out of the ship after Nadiah. He smiled back, nodding. "I knew you could do it," Sophia told him.

And I know why he could do it, Sylvan thought to himself grimly. What I don't know is how in the universe he wound up on Earth in the first place.

Nadiah and Sophia seemed intent on catching up on all the details of the journey and blood challenge but Rast came right up to Sylvan, a determined look on his face.

"I have something to say to you," he told Sylvan, his eyes flashing.

"I have something to tell you as well," Sylvan said quietly. "And I think you should hear it before you speak further. In fact, I think it would be best if we went someplace private."

Rast shook his head. "Sorry to be rude, Sylvan, but I'm going first and what I've got to say can be said right out in the open." He took a deep breath and looked Sylvan in the eyes. "Nadiah and I are deeply in love and we're going to be married. Now, I know you don't like me for her because I'm human—"

"But, you're not," Sylvan said.

"But I went through the blood challenge and I feel I won the right to—excuse me?" Rast frowned. Apparently Sylvan's words were finally sinking in. "What did you say? I'm not what?"

"I said, you're not human," Sylvan repeated, frowning. "Do you understand?"

"No." Rast looked both confused and angry. "Of course I don't understand. What the hell are you talking about?"

"Yes, what are you talking about?" Nadiah came up behind them with a worried look on her face. Sophia trailed behind her anxiously.

Sylvan sighed. "Do you see why I wanted to speak about this in private? Come on, let's at least leave the docking bay."

"No." Rast planted his feet squarely and crossed his arms over his chest. "No, I want an explanation now. You can't just come up and tell me something like that and expect me to wait to hear the rest. So come on, Sylvan, spit it out."

Sylvan spread his hands. "Very well, if you wish to give up the privilege of confidentiality we can talk here. To be blunt, the deep analysis of your blood test shows that you're not human. Oh, you have human traits on the surface—it's almost as if someone engineered your DNA to appear strictly Earth-like to the casual observer. But more in-depth testing proves that your human façade is literally only skin deep."

"Only skin deep, huh?" Rast frowned angrily. "Well then what the hell am I?'

"You're Kindred," Sylvan told him, hoping he wouldn't be upset by the news.

"Kindred? I knew it!" Nadiah's eyes were shining. "I felt it from the very first."

"It's true Rast is Kindred," Sylvan said, trying to choose his words carefully. "But he's no species of Kindred I've ever seen before."

"But I thought you said he looked like a First Kindred," Sophia said. "Isn't that why everyone mistook him for Merrick at our ceremony? Nobody knew Merrick was a hybrid because Sylvan never thought to tell them so they just assumed because Rast had the truegreen eyes—"

"Merrick's hybrid status is a sensitive subject with him," Sylvan interrupted, frowning. "As for Rast's heredity, he is closer to the First Kindred than anything else. He is close...but not an exact match."

"Well, what the hell am I then?" Rast demanded, repeating his question.

"I don't know yet," Sylvan said evenly. "But I would like a chance to find out before you bond my kinswoman—my cousin, as you say—to you for life."

"You're too late for that—we're already bonded." Rast's eyes flashed like green fire. "I took over the blood bond she has with that Y'dex asshole."

"Yes, but the bond is not sealed," Sylvan said. "I can tell because Nadiah's eyes are still the same color."

Nadiah blushed but lifted her chin defiantly. "I don't care what you say, Sylvan and I don't care if Rast is human or Kindred or a

Hyperion shadow-caster. I love him. He saved my life—did you know that? You warned him not to touch me, not to bond with me but the bond I had with Y'dex was too strong. If Rast hadn't taken the severed end of it into his own heart, I would have died. In fact, I did die for a minute—I saw Grandmaman in a dark tunnel with a bright, white light at the end of it."

"Wait a minute…" Sophia grabbed her arm. "You actually saw your dead grandmother? What did she say?"

"Yes, what did she say?" Rast demanded. "And how come you didn't tell me about it?"

Nadiah looked down. "I guess I had…other things on my mind." She glanced at Rast rapidly and blushed. "Anyway, I don't remember it very clearly. Mostly I think she said it wasn't my time to go. Oh, and she said she loved me."

Sylvan felt his heart clench like a fist. To think that Nadiah had come so close to going to the Goddess! To think she had almost died because of his directions to Rast… "Forgive me, Nadiah," he said hoarsely. "I knew the blood bond was strong but I thought the chance that breaking it would hurt you was remote. I only spoke of such dangers to warn Rast off."

"Well, it nearly worked." Rast's eyes were suspiciously bright and he swallowed convulsively. "I'm telling you, when she went limp in my arms and stopped breathing…" He shook his head. "Look, the point is, I fought for her and won her. I hate to sound like a goddamn cave man but she's mine."

"And I agree with your claim wholeheartedly," Sylvan said quietly. "I'm only asking for a little more time to run a few more tests on you before you claim her."

"But I don't want to wait!" Nadiah declared. "I feel like I've been waiting my whole life while I was tied to that stupid Y'dex! I want to join with—uh, marry, Rast now. In fact…" She took Rast by one muscular arm. "We're going straight to the sacred grove and you can't stop us."

"Oh no, you can't go there now!" Sophia exclaimed. "Nobody can—the priestesses are all naked and bald."

Rast's eyebrows shot up. "They're what?"

"They're in mourning," Sylvan explained. "The high priestess has gone to be with the Mother of All Life."

"Meaning?" Clearly Rast still didn't understand.

"Meaning she's dead." Sophia bit her lip and Sylvan felt a flood of sorrow and guilt coming through their mental link. He wished she would stop blaming herself.

"It's all right, Talana," he said softly, putting an arm around her shoulders and drawing her close. "Everything is going to be fine. And for the last time, the death of the high priestess wasn't your fault."

"What?" Nadiah exclaimed. "How could the high priestess dying be Sophia's fault?"

Sophia sighed. "Because I…look, Nadiah, do you mind if we talk about this later? Maybe with all the girls together? There's something very difficult I have to say and I'd rather just say it once."

Nadiah's face was filled with curiosity but she nodded immediately. "Of course. And I won't say a word to anyone."

"I know you won't." Sophia smiled at her gratefully. "I'm sorry you have to wait to get married but at least this way we'll have some time to plan a truly fabulous wedding." She laughed. "Kat and Liv are going to be so jealous—you'll be jumping ahead of their joining ceremony and baby shower. Lauren will have to make the next cake for you."

"I don't want to upset anyone," Nadiah said, sounding anxious. "I'm just, well, I'm extremely eager to be joined to Rast."

"Not half as eager as I am," Rast growled, giving her a possessive look. "Are you sure we can't just go down to Earth and find a Justice of the Peace?"

"And be joined without a priestess to officiate?" Nadiah frowned. "We can if you like, Rast, but I have to be honest, I won't really feel legally joined to you unless we have the ceremony performed by a priestess."

He sighed deeply and Sylvan noticed a troubled look on his face. "All right, we'll wait. I just…don't want to lose you. And I don't like the fact that this damn ship is crowded with males— unmarried ones, especially."

"I don't think you have to worry about any unmated males bothering Nadiah," Sylvan said dryly. "I can smell your scent all over her and I'm sure every other male within a five mile radius can too."

"Sylvan!" Nadiah looked absolutely mortified. Her cheeks turned a dark pink and she put a hand to her chest. "Please!"

He smiled slightly. "I'm only telling the truth, Nadiah. Don't worry, as I noted earlier, your eyes remain unchanged. So I know your virtue is intact."

Sophia laughed. "Mostly intact, anyway. Come on, let's go find the girls. We have a lot to catch up on."

Nadiah looked anxiously at Rast. Not asking for permission, Sylvan thought, but offering reassurance and letting him know she still loved him even though she wanted some time with the other females.

Rast seemed to understand her perfectly. "Go on, sweetheart," he said gently. "Have some fun. I think Sylvan and I have some catching up to do, too."

Sylvan nodded. "Yes, I think we do."

"All right then." Nadiah kissed Rast lingeringly on the cheek. "I love you," she murmured. "Come find me in a little while and we'll get some dinner. Something that doesn't come from a dehydrated food cube."

"Or involve mud worms," Rast said and they shared a private smile.

Despite his worry, Sylvan couldn't help smiling himself at their exchange. The two of them were already in sync with each other—a perfect couple now that Nadiah's blood bond was broken and Rast had realized and acknowledged his true feelings for her. Yes, they were perfect together and perfectly happy as well. So why did Sylvan's heart tell him that something wasn't quite right? He watched Sophia and Nadiah walk away together, their light, feminine voices echoing softly in the vast space of the docking bay and wondered why he couldn't answer that question...

"Okay, now you want to tell me how the hell I'm not human when I was born and raised on Earth?" Rast demanded in a low voice, breaking his train of thought.

Sylvan turned to him. "Were you? Do you have a birth certificate or other proof showing the place of your birth? Of course, such things can be forged..."

A strange look had come over Rast's face. "Well now that you mention it, I don't. I mean, I have a birth certificate but I'm pretty sure it's a fake."

"A fake?" Sylvan frowned. "How so?"

Rast blew out a breath and ran a hand through his hair. "It's something my mom told me right before we left for Tranq Prime—when I was saying goodbye to her. She said…she told me I was adopted."

"Did she mention your original birth parents?" Sylvan asked. "I can't imagine how but I suppose a Kindred male and his female might have somehow made their way to Earth." He frowned. "Although, that was years before we discovered your planet…"

"She said she didn't know." Rast looked unhappy and the tone of his voice seemed to say his adopted mother hadn't cared either. "She said no one knew—that I was found wandering naked in a field somewhere and no one ever learned who my birth mother was."

"And she told you all this right before you left?"

Rast laughed humorlessly. "Hell of a goodbye, isn't it? I tell her I'm leaving the planet and she tells me…ah hell, never mind." He shook his head. "I'm over it now. No big deal."

Sylvan remembered how quiet the other male had been on their trip back from Earth to the Mother Ship and thought it was a big deal—a very big deal indeed. Sophia was right, he thought. I should have asked him what was wrong. Aloud he said, "I don't know how it's possible that you're of Kindred origin but what you're telling me certainly seems to make it more probable."

"Yeah. Yeah, I guess it does." Rast shook his head. "Don't get me wrong—it's not that I mind being one of you guys—I've always felt strangely at home on the Mother Ship. But it would be nice if you could tell me which one. Or which kind, I guess."

Sylvan sighed. "I wish I could. Your DNA almost matches that of a First Kindred but it's more primitive somehow—more basic and powerful. Also you have an extra gene on your Y chromosome which I have never seen before."

Rast's eyebrows shot up. "An extra gene? Doesn't that kind of thing usually cause a deformity?"

"I don't know what it's for," Sylvan admitted. "It appears to be dormant right now but if it should ever become active…" He shook his head. "I don't know what would happen. What you would become."

Rast crossed his arms over his chest. "You think I'm some kind of science experiment? Some kind of freak? Dr. Jekyll and Mr. Hyde—the minute that extra gene gets going I'll turn into some kind of a monster?"

"No, no—nothing like that!" Sylvan protested. "I don't think you'd be a danger to yourself or others or I would have taken much stronger steps to keep you away from Nadiah."

"Well…all right." Rast nodded grudgingly. "But you think you can find out what's going on if we run more tests?"

Sylvan nodded, relieved that the other male was willing to be reasonable. "I just need a little more blood."

Rast sighed. "All right then—no time like the present. Let's go."

Sylvan clapped him on the back as they headed for the med station. "You're doing the right thing. You need to know what's going on before you and Nadiah get joined."

"I suppose I do—I owe it to her." Rast ran a hand through his hair. "I just don't want to lose her, you know?"

"You won't," Sylvan promised. "I know Nadiah—she has a loyal heart. She'll never give you up, no matter what."

"But what if it turns out we can't have kids or something?" Rast asked. "Would she still want to stay with me then?"

Sylvan felt a surge of sadness in his heart. "Even then," he said quietly. "Even then."

Chapter Twenty-three

"Okay, Nadiah, spill," Olivia commanded. "Tell us all about the blood challenge and how Rast won your freedom and your heart."

They were all sitting around the low structure called a "coffee table" in Sophia and Sylvan's suite. Olivia, having another one of her cravings, had gotten a small machine which pressed two round, flat pieces of bread called tortillas together with various ingredients in the middle to create what the Earth girls called a quesadilla. The entire oblong table was covered with various foods chopped into tiny pieces, some of which Nadiah recognized and some which were completely foreign to her.

"Yes, come on," Kat urged. "And don't leave out any dirty parts. We love the dirty parts." She grinned and nudged Lauren who laughed.

"Kat, you're bad!"

Nadiah blushed and put down the triangular wedge of quesadilla. "I'll tell you everything, of course, but I think Sophia has something to say as well." She looked at her friend.

"No, hon, you go ahead." Sophia shook her head. "Take your time. It'll give me time to get my thoughts together. And besides..." She pressed Nadiah's hand and smiled. "I want to hear everything too."

Nadiah saw Lauren, Kat, and Olivia exchange glances but then they shrugged and nodded.

"Go on," Liv said. "And don't mind me—I'm just going to make another quesadilla while you talk, okay? I think this time I'll try a sweet one. Kat, pass the salsa, please"

"A sweet one?" Kat objected. "Then what do you want salsa for?"

"Never you mind," Olivia said crossly. "Just pass it. And the peanut butter and chocolate chips while you're at it."

Kat made a face but passed the requested ingredients to her friend. "Okay, now that Queen Olivia is happy, go on with your story, doll." She nodded encouragingly at Nadiah.

Nadiah wasn't sure where to begin but she found herself telling them how she'd realized that she was in love with Rast. The way he stood up for her against her parents and Y'dex, and the way she thought he could never love her back because of what Sylvan had made him promise.

Sophia let out a sigh at this point. "I love him with all my heart and I know Sylvan was just trying to look out for you but..."

"But men sure are stupid sometimes, aren't they?" Olivia finished for her, licking a mixture of salsa and peanut butter off her fingers.

Sophia gave her a mock slap on the arm. "Hey, that's my guy you're talking about."

"Yeah, yeah." Liv grinned unrepentantly. "Don't worry about it, I'm sure Baird would have done the same thing. Or any of the guys, really. It's not a Sylvan thing, it's a male thing." She nodded. "Go on, Nadiah. What happened next?"

"Well..." Nadiah told about the three challenges but when she got to the part about Y'dex's tharp inching up and falling down to expose him to the entire audience, the girls broke up into a fit of giggles.

"Oh no!" Sophia gasped, holding her sides. "I know I shouldn't laugh because I've had that happen to me before and I totally understand how mortifying it can be."

"What happened to you is actually what gave me the idea in the first place," Nadiah admitted. "I hope you don't mind."

"Of course she doesn't mind," Kat said. "But go on with the story — what happened next?"

Nadiah was really beginning to enjoy telling her story but when she got to the challenge of wills with the mud worms, she couldn't help noticing that both Olivia and Lauren looked sick.

"Skip the in-depth descriptions if you don't mind, please," Lauren said faintly.

"Yeah, it's enough for us to know Rast had to eat a live worm as big as his forearm," Liv said. "We really don't need details."

"I'm sorry," Nadiah said contritely. She hurried on, telling them how Y'dex had lifted and dropped her and Rast had caught her and saved her life. The girls exclaimed in horror and Liv offered the opinion that Y'dex should be "strung up by his balls." But it wasn't until she told about the last challenge, the challenge of blood, that Nadiah really began to blush.

"You shared blood with him?" Sophia asked softly and Nadiah nodded. Being bonded to a Blood Kindred, she knew her friend really understood the significance of the act. But the other girls seemed to sense it too. And when she spoke of the way she'd been pulled between the two males, all four of them made sympathetic faces.

"That must have hurt like hell," Kat remarked. "Being torn in two like that."

"It was the most painful experience of my life," Nadiah said softly. "I didn't think I could stand it. Didn't think I could free myself from Y'dex—it hurt too much. But when Rast shouted to me that he loved me, I finally found the strength."

"It nearly killed her, though," Sophia put in. "Tell them about seeing your dead grandmother, Nadiah."

"What?" Lauren's amber eyes were wide. "You saw who?"

Nadiah told them as much as she remembered about the experience but she couldn't help feeling like there was something she was leaving out. Something important. She wished she could sit and think about it for a minute but the other girls were hanging on her words. She had to finish her story. Oh well, she thought uneasily. Maybe it will come to me later...

"And then I woke up in Rast's arms," she went on. "Because he'd taken the other half of the blood bond into his own heart. But the magistrate didn't want to let us go even though Rast had won me fair and square..." She told about Magistrate Licklow's attempt to declare the challenge void and how her friends had stopped him by threatening to tell the Elders about his attempt to fix the challenges.

"Good for them!" Sophia declared. "I never liked that nasty Magistrate Licklow ever since he accused me of fondling him under the table."

"He what?" Lauren demanded and then, of course, they had to digress and talk about what had happened on Sophia's trip to Tranq Prime. When they had all finished laughing about that, Nadiah was finally able to finish her own story.

"So he carried me back to our ship and told me he loved me. And we've spent the last three days on the ride home, er, enjoying each other's company."

"Oh, no..." Kat shook her head. "You don't get off that easy. We can all see you have the same color eyes which Sophia informs us means you've still got your V card. But there's no way you spent three days and nights in one of those dinky little ships with the man you loved without doing something dirty."

Olivia nodded. "Details. We want details."

Nadiah could feel herself blushing to the roots of her hair and she twisted her fingers together nervously. "I'd be happy to tell you, uh, details, but I thought Sophia had something to say." She looked at her friend, pleading with her eyes. "Sophia?"

"All right." Sophia took a deep breath and Nadiah noticed that the other three girls immediately got quiet.

"You gonna tell us what's been bothering you the past few days, hon?" Kat asked.

Sophia nodded. "I am but it's not easy to say." She looked down at her hands. "I…I'm barren. I can't get pregnant."

"What?" the three of them shouted together.

"And you've known this how long?" Olivia demanded.

Sophia bit her lip. "Just a little while. I…I had Sylvan run some tests after Lauren found out she was pregnant and—"

"Wait a minute," Nadiah interrupted. "Lauren? You're…?"

"Going to have a little girl," Lauren said quietly. She looked happy but worried, Nadiah thought. "Xairn and I are very…excited." She glanced at Sophia. "I'm so sorry. I didn't mean for my news to bring you pain."

Sophia shook her head firmly. "Don't be silly, Lauren. I'm happy for you and Liv. I just…I wish I had good news too. But when I went to ask the high priestess about it—"

"The high priestess who died?" Olivia asked, interrupting her.

Sophia nodded miserably. "She had some kind of a fit or a vision. Talked about how my womb had been...had been closed for a reason. She said I must go and stand before the Empty Throne."

For some reason her words gave Nadiah a strange tingle along her spine. The Empty Throne, she thought. What is that? Something I forgot?

"I don't understand," Kat said, breaking her train of thought. "How can an empty throne heal you?"

"Not the throne itself, whoever sits on it," Lauren corrected. "But who sits on it?"

"That's just it, I don't know." Sophia looked unhappy. "And she never even promised it would heal me—she just said I had to go stand in front of it. It's somewhere on First World—the Kindred home planet, that's all I know. So Sylvan and I are planning a trip there as soon as...as... Oh my God, Nadiah," she exclaimed suddenly, looking at Nadiah. "Are you okay?"

Nadiah, as it happened, was not okay. From the moment Sophia had said the words, "empty throne," a strange feeling had been coming over her. A tingling sensation that started at her fingertips and grew to encompass her arms, head, and face. An al'lei, she thought, beginning to feel panicked. I'm going to have an al'lei. A waking dream. Oh, Goddess, please...

Suddenly Sophia's suite and the coffee table with the girls gathered around it disappeared. Nadiah found herself standing in a vast, empty space with rounded white marble pillars rising to the sky. A flood of pale green light seemed to be coming from somewhere overhead but when she looked up, all she could see was an immense stone chair made of the same white marble as the pillars. It was empty and unadorned but somehow it seemed to emanate with a strange power she could feel humming in her bones. If I got too close it would kill me! she thought and then a voice began to speak. A voice which Nadiah heard in her head...but also coming from her own mouth. Goddess, help me, she thought wildly. It, no she, is speaking through me!

"He comes. He comes and the Empty Throne shall be filled again," Nadiah heard herself say but the voice that came from her throat was not her own. It was deeper, filled with authority and power.

"Who...who comes?" Sophia quavered. "Nadiah, please..."

"He who is to fill the throne. There." Nadiah turned, or rather, a force outside her body made her turn, and pointed at the doorway of the suite.

As if on cue, the door opened and Rast stepped in.

"Hi," he said, smiling tentatively. "Excuse me. I hope you girls don't mind but I came to get Nadiah. I think I've found someone who might—"

"She is not for you, warrior," the voice coming from Nadiah's throat proclaimed. Helpless to stop it, she felt herself rise from her place at the table and stalk slowly toward that male she loved. "We have felt your energy across the vast reaches of space and believe you are the one. You must relinquish your claim in the female, Nadiah, and come to First World to be tried."

"What?" Rast frowned at her. "Is this some kind of joke? Why are you using that weird voice?"

"It's no joke." Sophia hurried to stand beside her. "She's having a vision," she whispered to Rast, her eyes huge and frightened. "Oh God, I hope it doesn't kill her!"

"Kill her? What are you talking about?" Rast demanded. He took Nadiah by the shoulders and shook her. "Enough of this now, Nadiah. Enough. Snap out of it!"

Nadiah only wished she could. But the al'lei wasn't over yet and the entity which had taken over her body was not ready to let her go.

"Take your hands from this female, for she is not for you," she heard herself saying—or someone saying through her. "You are meant for greater things, Adam Rast. A higher purpose calls you."

"What higher purpose? What are you talking about?" Rast demanded.

"You will come to First World," the commanding voice insisted. "You will come to be tried. If you take the oath and pass the trial, you will sit upon the Empty Throne."

"Look, you...whoever you are," Rast said evenly, staring into Nadiah's eyes. "I don't know who you are or how you got inside my girlfriend but you get out and leave her alone right now or so help me God—"

Nadiah heard a strange, hollow laugh issue from her mouth. "It is in the name of the Goddess, the Mother of All Life, that we call you. We are finished arguing. You will appear before the Empty Throne in First World before this solar week is out. If you do not, this female will die."

Suddenly, whatever or whoever it was left Nadiah in a rush. The room spun around her and she felt herself falling to the ground. Strong arms caught her.

"It's all right, sweetheart. I've got you," Rast murmured in her ear. "Are you okay now? Is that thing gone?"

"Yes...yes, I think so. I just feel so weak." Nadiah put a hand to her cheek. "And so cold. Why is it so cold in here all of a sudden?"

"It's not." Sophia was biting her lip with worry. "Rast, feel her forehead. She looks flushed."

Rast pressed a hand which felt like a block of ice to her forehead and pulled back cursing. "She's burning up! Was she sick before this happened?"

"No." All the girls shook their heads. "She was fine," Lauren said. "Perfectly fine."

Sophia put a hand to her temple. "I'm calling Sylvan right now. We'll find out what's wrong with her, I promise."

The next few minutes were a blur to Nadiah as Rast carried her to the couch and sat down, still holding her. Her head throbbed and her eyelids felt very hot and very heavy, as though someone had tied burning lead weights to them. The world greyed out for a few minutes and when it came back into focus she saw Sylvan looking at her with worry.

"Vashan fever," he was saying to Rast, who also looked upset. "A rare disease on Tranq Prime which only affects virgin females. I'm afraid it usually kills its victims within a week. But I don't see how Nadiah could have contracted it so quickly when—"

"A week," Sophia interrupted. "That's how long she said Rast had to get to First World."

"What?" Sylvan demanded. "Who..."

But the world greyed out again and this time the grey turned to blackness. The Blackness, Nadiah thought. The Blackness which Eats the Stars. It's coming...

And then...nothing.

Chapter Twenty-four

"I'm sorry to have to leave you so suddenly like this, old friend." Sylvan had a harried look on his face as he rushed around the med station, collecting equipment to bring on his journey.

"Don't worry about it. Nadiah is your kin — of course you have to take care of her." Merrick watched his friend with worried eyes. Sylvan didn't seem like himself. Of course, it wasn't every day that a much beloved younger kinswoman was suddenly and mysteriously stricken with a fatal, fast acting disease. Vashan fever, much like Blood Fever, infected only young, virgin females but it was even faster acting and more deadly. "Did she contract it on Tranq Prime?" he asked as Sylvan stuffed more instruments into his pack.

"She must have." Sylvan shook his head. "Of course, the symptoms don't manifest at once, but..." He broke off and put a hand over his eyes. "Oh Goddess, if only I hadn't warned Rast off her. The fever cannot attack females whose eyes have been changed. If only —"

"Stop." Merrick gripped his friend by the shoulder. "Stop beating yourself up over this, Sylvan. You were only doing what any Tranq Prime kinsman would do — protecting her virtue."

"I know." Sylvan looked up, his ice blue eyes anguished. "But it's her virtue that is allowing the fever to kill her."

"What were you supposed to do?" Merrick said roughly. "Offer her up to him on a silver fucking platter? You were doing what you thought was right. No one can blame you for that."

"I can," Sylvan said bleakly. "And I will, for the rest of my days if we cannot get her help."

"And you think the priestesses on First World hold the answer?" Merrick cocked an eyebrow at him.

Sylvan nodded. "They must. They are the only ones who serve beside the Empty Throne and that is where Rast was commanded to go. It's also the subject of the other prophecy—the one Sophia received. So we're all going together and bringing Nadiah to be healed." He clenched his hands into fists. "If she can be healed."

"Is there nothing you can do?" Merrick asked. "I thought if you caught the fever in its first symptoms—"

"That's the thing." Sylvan ran a hand though his hair. "There were no first symptoms. The fever came on her full blown. It was almost as though...as though she'd been cursed with it."

"Cursed with it? By the high priestess, you mean?" Merrick frowned. "How very fucking unsurprising."

Sylvan's eyebrows shot up. "You met the High Priestess of the Empty Throne?"

Merrick shrugged. "I told you I went on pilgrimage there—to First World—before I got attacked by the Trissies, right?" He scowled. "I was trying to, I don't know, get my mind right before I had to participate in your ceremony. Didn't want to bring you bad luck."

"What did she say to you?" Sylvan asked, looking at him intently. "Was it anything important?"

Merrick ran a finger down his scar, rubbing it where it bisected his eyebrow. It was a gesture he had when deep in thought. Actually, it was strange that he hadn't remembered the priestess's prophecy—or rather curse—until just now. But the deadly fight with the pirates, the worry over missing his friend's ceremony, and the excitement of finding Elise in the abandoned life pod had driven it all out of his mind.

"You shall find the bride you seek on your journey to help a friend seal his love. She who is meant for you waits wrapped in darkness — waits for your kiss to awaken her, warrior."

Yes, that was what the High Priestess of the Empty Throne had said to him. And then she'd gotten angry because he hadn't believed her. Angry enough to curse him, although she had denied it and said that he had cursed himself…

Merrick looked through the open doorway to the small room where Elise had been moved, stasis chamber and all for constant observation. Could the priestess have been talking about her? Hell no, that was ridiculous. Besides, she said he would find the bride that he sought and he wasn't seeking any damn bride. The whole thing was just a coincidence. Still…

"Well?" Sylvan demanded and Merrick realized he had been caught up in his own thoughts too long.

"I'm sorry, Brother," he said, shaking his head. "But I don't see how what she told me can help you. I will tell you to watch out for her though — she doesn't like being contradicted."

Sylvan sighed. "All right. I'll keep it in mind." He followed Merrick's gaze to the room with the sleeping Elise. "Don't worry about her, Merrick," he said, reassuringly. "I've programmed the stasis chamber for a controlled exit. That means when her body is ready, she'll come out of it on her own."

Merrick nodded. "I understand it could take a little while. I'll wait."

"More than a little while," Sylvan cautioned him. "It could be weeks or even months before she emerges. In fact, I think it's likely to be a very long time because of what she went through at the hands of the AllFather. Her brain isn't going to want to come to and deal with those memories."

"I'll wait," Merrick repeated stubbornly. "I'm acting as her protector. I swore to be responsible for her."

"I can relieve you of that duty at any time," Sylvan said. "No one would blame you if you wished to leave. As you said, you don't even know her."

"I said I'll stay," Merrick growled. "And that's fucking final."

Sylvan studied him silently for a moment and then nodded. "All right, old friend. I've instructed everyone at the med station on what to do and Olivia has promised to pay special attention to Elise every day. She's an excellent nurse—you can ask her if you have any questions."

Merrick nodded. "Understood."

Sylvan seemed to hesitate for a moment. "There's just one more thing," he said at last. "If—and it's a very big if—she starts to come out of the stasis before I get back, don't touch her."

"What?" Merrick frowned. "Why not?"

Sylvan shook his head. "It's a long and involved process—too hard to explain. But the time when she's coming out of stasis is a critical juncture. It could be dangerous for both of you to have physical contact at that point. Wait until she's all the way out and awake before you even hold her hand, all right?"

For some reason, Merrick felt a strong urge to disagree—but Sylvan was the one with medical training. He obviously knew best. "All right," he said grudgingly. "Hands off until she's wide awake—I got it."

"Good. Thank you for understanding." Sylvan squeezed his shoulder. "I must go. The ship is already primed and waiting."

"Good luck and the Goddess go with you," Merrick said. "I hope you're able to cure Nadiah."

Sylvan's eyes turned bleak. "I hope so too. If I can't, I will never forgive myself." And then he was gone.

Chapter Twenty-five

Luckily the trip to First World was very short — straight into the space fold and then a day to make orbit around the Kindred home world.

It was short in terms of crossing the vast distances of the universe, Rast knew. But to him, it felt incredibly, painfully long. Lying in a small bunk surrounded by cold packs, Nadiah alternately burned and froze. It was heartbreaking to hear her begging for blankets, whispering through fevered lips that she was cold, so cold, when Sylvan said her temperature was actually so high her brain was in danger of boiling in her skull.

So though he longed to give in and cover her in the warmest blankets he could find, Rast was forced to ice her down instead, stroking a cold cloth over her hot brow as she cried out weakly and begged him not to. Sylvan and Sophia had both offered to do the job but Rast refused. Nadiah was his responsibility now. For better or worse, in sickness and in health, he meant to do what he could for her…even if it tore the very heart from his chest to do it.

I'm right back to the blood challenge, he thought grimly as he changed her ice packs yet again for fresher, colder ones. Hurting her to help her. God, I hate this. Hate it so much.

"I'm sorry, Nadiah. So sorry," he whispered, leaning over to kiss her hot forehead before he put a fresh cold cloth on it. "I swear when this is all over I'll never hurt you again. Never."

"Rast," she whispered and at first he thought she'd heard him.

"Yes, sweetheart?" He cupped her cheek, searching her eyes anxiously for any sign of recognition.

But then her dark blue eyes clouded over and she started to shiver again. "Rast, please…Please help me. Cold. So c-cold…"

"I know you are, sweetheart. I'm sorry. This is the only way to keep your fever down." Not that the damn fever ever went away—they were barely keeping it in check and even as he watched, Nadiah seemed to be melting away to nothing in its hellish heat.

Rast's eyes stung and once again he swore vengeance. Whoever had done this to her—the owner of the mysterious female voice who had used Nadiah like a fucking short wave radio to convey her message—that bitch was going to pay and pay big.

"I'll kill her," Rast whispered to himself. The hand that wasn't soothing Nadiah clenched into a fist at his side. "Fucking kill her."

"Who will you kill?" Sophia was suddenly there, frowning uncertainly.

"Whoever did this to her." Rast looked up, his eyes feeling hot and red, as they had after the blood challenge. "Whoever made her sick. They're dead."

Sophia took a step back. "Oh my God, you really are Kindred. You're…you're going into rage."

"What was that?" Sylvan came back, frowning. "What did you say, Talana?"

"L-look at him." Sophia pointed at Rast, her voice shaking. "He looks just like you did back when…when you were trying to protect me from the urlich."

Sylvan frowned. "So I see." To Rast he said, "Take some deep breaths and try to calm down. We're about to visit a very holy and sacred place and you cannot appear before the priestesses in that state."

"I don't want to calm down," Rast snarled. "I want to hurt whoever did this to her. I want to make them pay."

"And I feel the same," Sylvan said evenly. "Nadiah is my kin – I love her as though she were my little sister. But you cannot go into the temple of the Empty Throne with murder in your heart. The priestesses will sense it and punish you."

"You think I give a damn for their punishment? For anything but her?" Rast saw everything through the red curtain now, even Nadiah's beloved face was painted with crimson.

"It is not you they would punish," Sylvan snapped. "Think of Nadiah. We are going into a place of healing – what if they refuse to heal her because of you?"

"What if they're the ones who did this to her in the first place?" Rast countered. "What about that?"

"Then they are the only ones who can undo it," Sylvan said heavily. "Please, Rast, we must not give them reason to refuse us."

Finally what Sylvan was saying penetrated the red haze of anger that seemed to hang around him like a burning curtain. *Nadiah. I have to calm down for her sake. Can't let the anger take me. Make me do things I'll regret later.* There was nothing he could do for Nadiah in his current state. Nothing but make an already desperate situation worse.

With a huge effort, Rast closed his eyes and breathed deeply. Then again. And again until he felt the anger leave him, leaking slowly away like air out of a balloon.

"Sorry." He opened his eyes and shook his head. "I don't...don't know what came over me. I just got so mad at whoever hurt Nadiah and everything went red..."

Sylvan nodded. "That's rage all right. It's a state a Kindred male goes into when he feels his female is threatened." He sighed. "But

I'm afraid it won't help in this case. We're dealing with much more than a physical threat here."

"What are we dealing with? And who?" Rast demanded. "Was it one of the priestesses of this Empty Throne thing? Who has the power to reach through space and make someone sick? Who—"

A beeping sound from the front of the ship cut him off.

"I don't know," Sylvan said, turning to go back to the controls. "But we're about to find out. Prepare yourself, Rast—we've achieved orbit around First World."

Chapter Twenty-six

First World was nothing like Rast had imagined it would be. Having been to the sacred grove aboard the Mother Ship, he'd thought that the whole planet would be a lush, deciduous forest filled with green and purple trees and carpeted with lavender and emerald grass. Instead, it was a desert world. A flat, sandy plane that seemed to extend for miles in every direction with no sign of life. Dotted here and there around the barren landscape were towering mesas that jutted from the sandy ground like mountains from the sea floor.

Some of the mesas seemed to have steps leading up their sides and most had colored smudges at their flat tops but they were too high for Rast to see what the smudges could be. Houses, vegetation—who could tell? But more than the far off mesa tops, it was the color of the ground—or rather the sand that caught his eye. When you gathered a handful of the stuff it looked to be no color at all—almost transparent, like tiny flecks of clear quartz. Yet, when the rays of the strange green sun shining down from above struck it, it turned every color of the rainbow—every color but green, that was.

Rast couldn't understand it. Shouldn't the green light make everything under it also look green? But somehow it didn't. They walked over cerulean blue and hot pink and magenta dunes. Aquamarine and chartreuse waves of sand washed over their feet like water in the ocean, even though Rast could feel no breeze. High above he could hear the sharp, distant scream of what he assumed was a type of hunting bird. Black specks soared through the cloudless sky high above—too high for him to make out anything more than their basic shape. It was a strange land—the rainbow desert with its massive mesas—stark and rich, desolate and beautiful at the same time.

"How long 'til we get to this Empty Throne place, anyway?" he asked Sylvan, who was guiding the hover-stretcher where Nadiah lay. Sophia was walking on the other side of it, silently drinking in the beauty of First World. "And why'd we park so far away, anyway?"

"We are making for the holy mountain, just over that ridge." Sylvan nodded at a distant turquoise and royal purple dune ahead. "And we landed where we did out of deference to the Goddess. It is said she is closest to this of all the Kindred worlds and she suffers no one who cannot fly of their own power to take to the skies around her sacred grounds. It is death to approach the holy mountain on anything but foot...or wing."

For some reason Rast's shoulder blades began to itch. "What—you have flying people out here?" he asked, shrugging his shoulders in an attempt to stop the irritation. "Now that must be a sight to see."

"So the legends say," Sylvan murmured, unperturbed. "But even if they're true, those old tales are ancient. No one has taken flight from the Goddess's mountain in over a thousand years—if they ever did at all."

"I'm gonna guess no to that one." Rast reached behind him, trying to scratch the damned itch but it always seemed to be just out of reach. "I mean, I'm no physicist but it's a simple matter of weight ratios. In order to support a six and a half foot tall warrior—assuming they were the same size you guys, uh, we are now—a pair of wings would have to be—"

"Enormous. Vast and beautiful—feathered with the light of the Goddess herself," a strong, feminine voice interrupted them.

"What?" Rast said, looking around. He soon saw the source of the voice—a female with long, curling emerald green hair and eyes that were solid emerald green to match with no white or pupil to break up the unnervingly blank expanse between her lids. She might have been forty or eighty or anywhere in between—it was impossible to say. The look on her face was not in the least welcoming.

All of them stopped dead as if by silent consent and Sylvan halted the hover-stretcher as well. "Priestess," he said, bowing respectfully.

Sophia and Rast followed his lead although Rast didn't like it. Not that he minded being respectful to a woman but this particular female looked like she was used to being bowed to and expected it. No, demanded it.

The priestess looked at him sharply. "It is my right to demand respect, Challa. As the High Priestess of the Empty Throne, I am due it in your thoughts as well as your actions."

Rast frowned. "Can you read my thoughts? Because I'd rather you didn't."

She looked at him with distain. "Only part of your mind is revealed to me. If you wish to change that, then shield yourself."

"Shield myself?" Rast demanded. "How the hell am I supposed to—"

"Your pardon, High Priestess," Sylvan cut in smoothly. "But Rast has only recently discovered he is Kindred. He was raised on the human world of Earth and has little understanding of matters of the mind."

"I am well aware of his origin." The priestess sniffed. "Though how he could remain among those primitives for so long without discovering that he was different is beyond me."

"His DNA was altered," Sylvan explained. "By someone—we don't know who—to help him fit in. When I gave him a shot with Kindred blood compounds in it, he began to show more signs of his true heritage."

"Yes. Such as the rage I felt directed at myself when your ship made orbit." The priestess frowned at Rast. "I will satiate your curiosity now, Challa. Yes, it was I who called you through the female that now lies upon yon stretcher. And yes, it was I who struck her down with the fever."

"Why, you—" Rast started toward her but Sylvan put out a hand to stop him.

It was Sophia who stepped forward instead. "Why?" she asked. "Nadiah is my friend and you'll never meet a sweeter, kinder girl. Why would you do something like that to her?"

The priestess made a dismissive gesture. "She is a weak vessel. Not worthy to be Lyzel to the High Counselor's Challa."

"I don't know what those words mean and I don't give a damn either." Rast was making an effort to control himself, but his voice still shook with barely repressed fury. "All I know is if you made her sick, you'd better heal her now."

The priestess shrugged. "I'm afraid healing her is beyond my power. I can raise the fever for a little while…" She made a careless wave of her hand and Nadiah coughed and sat up on her elbows, looking around in confusion.

"Rast?" she whispered through cracked lips.

"Oh, thank you!" Sophia smiled gratefully as she ran to embrace her friend. "Thank you so much."

"Do not thank me yet, child." The priestess frowned. "As I said, healing her completely is beyond my skill. The fever will return and in the end she will certainly die of it."

"What?" It was a full throated roar of rage and disbelief, torn from Rast's throat. He lunged forward and Sylvan intercepted him, obviously using all his strength to hold him back. "Let me go," he snarled, trying to get past the Blood Kindred. "Let me go, I'm going to kill this bitch."

If the priestess was worried about his threats, she certainly didn't show it. "Fear not, Challa, I only said that I could not heal her. But there is one here who can."

"Who?" Rast demanded. "Who, damn you?"

The blank green eyes opened wide and the priestess's thin lips curved into a cruel smile. "Why you, of course, Adam Rast. You alone can heal the little female." She nodded at the distant dune and the mountain beyond. "Come to the holy mountain and I will tell you how."

Then she disappeared.

Chapter Twenty-seven

Nadiah couldn't get over the breathtaking beauty of First World or the fact that she was conscious enough to enjoy it. She was still weak with fever but it was less now, as though someone had taken a roaring blaze and banked it carefully, ready to stir it to life again at any moment. She had a vague understanding that the strange high priestess — who seemed more overbearing than any other priestess Nadiah could ever remember meeting — was the one responsible both for her illness and her partial recovery. But every time she tried to think about it, her head began to ache.

In the end she decided it was better to just drink in the scenery and make small talk with Sophia, since Rast was apparently too upset to talk.

"This place is amazing," she murmured, squeezing her friend's hand. Sophia was walking along beside the stretcher where Nadiah still rode, though at least now she was sitting up. "I've heard stories of the rainbow desert on First World all my life but I never thought I'd actually see it."

"It is amazing," Sophia agreed. She was obviously making an effort to be cheerful but the worried look on her face ruined the effect. "Nadiah, maybe you should lie down again," she coaxed. "You still look so tired."

"I feel a hundred percent better though," Nadiah lied — it was more like fifty percent but she would take what she could get. "Besides, how can I lie down when there's something like that to look at."

She flung her arm out, pointing over the multicolored dune they were just cresting. Beside her, Sophia's breath caught in a gasp.

"Behold," Sylvan said quietly. "The holy mountain of the Mother of All Life."

It was indeed a mountain, and not a flat topped mesa like the rest of the towering landmasses that dotted the desert. The peak of it was incredibly high but Nadia couldn't see its tip—clouds, the only clouds she had seen in the otherwise clear sky—shielded it from view.

The rest of the holy mountain was bare of vegetation and seemed to be almost perfectly cylindrical with one exception. Jutting out from the side of it, about three fourths of the way up its cone, Nadiah saw a large outcropping covered in green and purple vegetation.

"The Healing Garden," Sylvan murmured in a low voice. "I thought it was part of the legends but it exists—it really exists."

"What? Where?" Rast turned to look at him and the desperation and pain in his truegreen eyes hurt Nadiah's heart. She wanted to hold his hand, to tell him she loved him and that everything would be all right. But he was walking ahead of her, beside Sylvan and she couldn't reach him. "There's a garden that heals people?" he asked her kinsman. "Where?"

Sylvan gestured at the outcropping covered in lush foliage. "There, I think. It's said that the Goddess walks there at certain times of the day. A drink from the fountain of the Healing Garden was said to cure any illness, no matter how severe."

"Then let's go! Right now!" Rast started to speed up from a walk to a jog but Sylvan caught his arm.

"Slow down, Brother. The whole thing may be just a myth—wishful thinking out of one of the old legends. And even if it's true, we can't reach it."

"What? Why not?" Rast demanded.

"Because," Sylvan said simply. "According to the legends, the only way to reach the Healing Garden is to fly there."

"Again with the flying people." Rast grimaced as if in pain and reached behind himself to scratch his back. "Damn it—I think I must be allergic to something in this damn place. My back is itching like crazy. It hasn't itched this much since you injected me with that hemo-booster."

"Is that right?" Sylvan looked thoughtful.

"Yeah, that's right." Rast sighed and appeared to decide to ignore his discomfort. "How do you think that priestess disappeared like that? We're still at least a mile from the mountain. Either she's a really fast runner or—"

"It was a projection of her mind." The new voice startled them all—Nadiah so much that she almost fell off her stretcher. Standing beside them was another, much younger looking priestess with more normal looking eyes. The irises were still a brilliant jade green but the whites of her eyes were normal and she had pupils which made her look less like a living statue. She was barefoot and wearing a simple white robe. Dark blonde hair, streaked with jade green, fell straight to the small of her back.

"Uh, who are you?" Sophia asked.

"And why do people keep popping up out of this damn desert?" Rast growled. "It's goddamn unnerving."

"I am Lissa, secondary priestess and a sand mover of the first order." The girl bowed. "Forgive me for startling you, but I heard one of your party was ill and thought you might like a ride to the mountain."

"Oh, we'd love a ride." Sophia nodded eagerly and then looked uncertainly at the priestess who was simply standing there. "Uh, where's your vehicle?"

"This is my vehicle." Lissa raised her hands and the sand around them suddenly firmed and lifted like a cresting wave.

"What in the seven hells?" Sylvan muttered, nearly losing his balance as the wave of sand started moving forward toward the mountain. He looked at Lissa. "How are you able to do this, Priestess?"

"Living so near the holy mountain enhances out natural gifts," the young priestess explained. "I am genetically endowed with my ability and being near the Goddess increases it."

"I have heard of such things," Sylvan murmured. "But I thought they were simply old legends."

Lissa laughed, a soft, tinkling sound that Nadiah liked at once. It sounded like small silver bells ringing. "There is more truth in the old legends than most people know, Warrior. You will see."

"Speaking of old legends, tell us about the Healing Garden," Rast said. "Is it true it heals anyone of anything? And how do you get to it?"

Lissa frowned. "I have been forbidden to speak of such things. And there is no time now, anyway. Look—the mountain approaches."

So smoothly did the wave of sand carry them, that it almost did seem as if the holy mountain was approaching them instead of the other way around. Nadiah saw that they were about to enter a high, arching entrance carved into the stone and that they were going much faster than she had at first perceived. She ducked her head reflexively as the sand wave rushed at the side of the mountain, but it set them down gently enough just inside the entry.

"Here I may not use my power," Lissa told them. "So we must go on foot. The High Priestess of the Empty Throne has summoned you all to a council in two standard hours time. This will give you time to rest, refresh yourselves, and change into proper attire. Come."

Rast didn't look very happy about the idea of changing into "proper" attire but he kept silent as they all followed the slender form of the young priestess down a series of twisting tunnels into the heart of the mountain.

Finally they came out of the dark tunnel into an oasis of light.

All of them blinked, trying to adjust to the brilliant sunshine after the gloom. Nadiah's eyes watered fiercely at the sudden change. They adjusted quickly, however, and when she looked around, she saw that the place Lissa had brought them really did look like an oasis.

They appeared to be in a sort of hollow crater in the side of the mountain which hadn't been visible to them from outside the sacred spot. There was a rippling blue-green pool in the center of the space edged all around with rainbow sand which stretched several yards in all directions. A grove of slender grey-green trees with pale lavender-grey leaves surrounded the sand. White material had been hung from their branches and it flapped and fluttered in the soft breeze. At one end of the little pool, someone had laid out a wooden table with food and drink on a white cloth.

"Rest and take sustenance," Lissa said, smiling graciously. "Bathe yourselves in the purifying waters and dress in the garments which have been provided for you." She pointed at the white material hanging from the trees. "I will return at the appointed hour to bring you to the temple of the Empty Throne."

"Hey, don't go," Rast said when she started to leave. "We have questions—a hell of a lot of questions."

"All will be answered at the council." Lissa smiled again and nodded. "Goodbye—for the moment."

And before Rast could protest further, she'd somehow melted into the surrounding hedge of trees and left them to their own devices.

There was nothing to do but follow the priestess's orders. Nadia didn't mind so much. She and Sophia took a quick bath in the cool waters of the pool while Sylvan and Rast kept their backs turned. At the silky, healing touch of the sacred water, Nadiah found herself refreshed and much more clearheaded. Finally, the last cobwebs of the fever were swept away and she began to understand what had happened.

"The High Priestess of the Empty Throne—she's the one who caused me to have the al'lei, isn't she?" she asked Sophia softly as they splashed in the water.

Sophia nodded. "I think so, hon. That's what she claimed."

"And she also made me sick." Nadiah could still feel the sickness inside her—like a hand closed tight. But soon the fingers would open, releasing the fever once more.

"In order to bring Rast here, yes." Sophia nodded again. "She said he could, uh, heal you."

"But how?" They were out of the water now and drying off, keeping their backs to the pool so the males could bathe in privacy. "How can he heal me?"

"I don't know, Nadiah," Sophia confessed. Her green eyes were troubled. "I really don't. Here—put this on." She handed Nadiah a long white robe which looked exactly like the one the priestess, Lissa, had been wearing. Nadiah thought of telling her tharp to emulate one but she had an idea the high priestess would know and become angry. Still, she was reluctant to be parted from her faithful garment completely. Whispering a command to it, she made it change into a pale blue sash which she wrapped around her waist. "There." She sighed. "I guess I'm ready to go."

"Then let's get something to eat," Sophia suggested. "Hey, Sylvan," she called. "Can we turn around now? Are you guys decent?"

"If you call this decent," Rast growled.

Nadiah turned around to see him and caught her breath. "Oh, Rast…"

Sophia laughed delightedly and ran to Sylvan. "You look like you stepped right out of a movie about the Greek gods."

"Yeah," Rast muttered. "Either that or a toga party. Why is it that everywhere I go outside of Earth I always end up wearing a skirt or a dress?"

He and Sylvan were both wearing the same kind of robes she and Sophia were, light, white material with no sleeves which gathered at the waist and then fell to the ankles. On them, however, the robes somehow looked masculine. But there was something about the robe Rast wore which bothered Nadiah.

"This is how I first saw you," she said, stepping forward to take his hands. Her ankle turned in the loose sand and she nearly fell but Rast caught her. It was a good thing because she wouldn't have had the strength to catch herself. *The fever. It's inside me, waiting to get out,* she thought. *Making me weak and clumsy.*

"What are you talking about?" he asked, when he had one arm firmly around her waist, supporting her. "I've never worn anything like this before in my life. Not even in my drunken college days."

"But I saw you," Nadiah insisted. "In the vision I had right before Sophia and Sylvan's joining ceremony. I saw you as you are now, wearing the white robes of a supplicant and standing in the temple of the Goddess. That was why I was so sure you were Kindred at first."

Rast sighed. "Well, you turned out to be right about that. Could you see anything else in your vision?"

Nadiah shook her head. "If I did I don't remember. But I do have a very strong feeling you belong here. This is the right place for you, Rast. I know it doesn't seem like it now, but it is."

"Guess I'll have to take your word for it." He shook his head. "But it sure doesn't feel right."

"Who's hungry?" Sylvan asked. He had gone to stand beside the small table and was looking down at the food which had been provided.

"I am," Nadiah said, and was surprised to find it was true. "I feel like I haven't eaten in a month."

"You look like you haven't either." Rast frowned and ran a finger along her collarbone. "That damn fever—burning you up from the inside out."

"I feel better now." She tried to speak brightly. After all, it was almost the truth.

"You're not, though." Rast looked worried. "Not yet. But you will be—I swear you will be no matter what I have to do to make it happen, sweetheart."

"I think we'll learn more about that in the temple," Sylvan said mildly. "In the mean time, we'd better get something while we can. I know all of us were too worried to eat earlier."

Nadiah was touched. "You shouldn't have put off eating just for me. Come on, Rast." She tugged at his arm. "I really am hungry."

He sighed. "All right. As long as it's not steamed brains or worm guts."

"I thought you liked my steamed vorteg brains," Nadiah protested. "You said they were the best you'd ever eaten."

"They were," Rast assured her. "But to tell you the truth, sweetheart, I don't usually eat brains."

Sophia smothered a laugh. "I get the feeling Rast isn't much into haute cuisine."

"You got that right," he growled.

"Very funny, Rast." Nadiah decided to let it drop although she promised herself to grill him later on what he really liked to eat. If there was a later. In the mean time, they gathered around the table which was laid with a simple white cloth and rough wooden bowls filled with what looked like tiny loaves of bread.

"Not much for variety, are they?" Rast murmured, looking at the nearly identical loaves. "Oh well, we didn't come here for the dinner service anyway."

"I think they look good. Better than fleeta pudding, anyway — no offence, guys," Sophia added to Nadiah and Sylvan. "Well, here goes nothing." She picked up a small loaf and took a bite. A strange look passed over her face. "Mmm! Tastes like…like tomato soup. And…and a grilled cheese sandwich." She took another bite. "And now it tastes like lime Jello." She frowned. "That's so weird — that was my favorite meal when I was a little kid."

"Really?" Rast picked up a loaf of bread no longer than his palm and bit off the end. "Cheeseburger," he said, frowning. "With extra ketchup. And fries...and a chocolate shake." His eyes widened. "My sister used to take me out on Thursday nights when our parents were working late that that was what I always got." He looked at the bread with wonder. "How does it do that?"

"It's like some kind of Willy Wonka mind-reading bread or something." Sophia took another bite and handed a tiny loaf to Nadiah. "Try it!"

Nadiah took a bite and her mouth was suddenly flooded with the tastes of her childhood. "Malabar pudding," she said. "And roast rump of vranna and tsitle berry juice."

Sylvan nodded, "I got the same except for malabar pudding—I always hated that."

They were so engrossed in the strange bread, which tasted different to each to them, that none of them noticed that the young priestess, Lissa, had returned until she cleared her throat.

"Oh, hello," Sophia exclaimed, turning to see her. "We didn't even see you there. This bread is amazing. How do you make it?"

"I am glad you enjoy it." Lissa nodded gracefully. "However, we have no time to tell you the secrets of our baking now. It is time—you are summoned to the temple."

"Oh." For some reason, Nadiah's mouth was suddenly dry. She swallowed hard and the last bite of bread went down her throat in a tasteless lump.

Rast didn't look happy about it either. "Come on," he said roughly. "Let's go. Might as well get it over with."

As they followed the young priestess out of the oasis of light and back into a tunnel filled with darkness, Nadiah felt a growing sense of unease. Somehow she knew something was going to happen once they reached the temple of the Empty Throne. And not necessarily something good.

Chapter Twenty-eight

The temple of the Empty Throne was located inside the mountain, in a vast cavern that made the huge grotto Rast had seen on Tranq Prime look small. But it wasn't dark or gloomy. Someone had drilled deep holes in the side of the mountain to let in the sunlight. Pale green shafts of light pierced the cavern, making mystical patterns on the sandy floor that led to the graceful white marble structure of the temple.

Tall, slender white pillars supported the roof of the temple and hundreds of white stone steps led upwards to a high, flat platform. Far back on the platform was another, smaller one—a dais with additional steps leading up to it. Sitting on the dais was a solid white marble chair with gold and silver lines running through it. The Empty Throne.

Even seeing it from a distance, the weird stone throne sent a shiver down Rast's back. It had an aura of power around it that seemed to radiate outwards and fill the entire huge space with a soft humming sound that was almost too low to hear. Like a generator, Rast thought. Only he had an idea that this particular generator could be dangerous—very damn dangerous indeed to the wrong person.

The throne's hum had a strange effect on him. His shoulder blades started itching again and every muscle in his body tensed, as though he was getting ready for a confrontation. But then the high priestess appeared again at the top of the stairs and everything else was driven out of his mind.

"You have come." Her voice tolled like a bell in the huge, echoing space and Rast thought she had a look of smug self satisfaction as she looked down, surveying them from the top step. Behind her, a group of younger priestesses stood silently, all dressed in white with green sashes tied around their slender waists.

"You didn't give us much choice," he snapped, frowning. "So here we are. Now tell us what this is all about. What was so important that you had to make Nadiah sick and force me to come here?"

The high priestess frowned. "A little respect, if you please, Adam Rast. You may be the one the prophecy speaks of but you are still addressing one chosen of the Goddess." She made a grand sweeping gesture with both hands. "Come up. You may all approach the throne but do not touch it on peril of your lives—even the one we seek if he is not ready to be found."

Without even asking, Rast knew Nadiah couldn't manage the steps—there were just too many of them and she was much too weak. Though she was trying to put a brave face on things and acting like she was feeling better, he could see the truth. The bruised looking circles under her dark blue eyes and the drawn look on her face let him know that she wasn't well. And she wouldn't be well unless he could somehow force the obtuse, entitled priestess who thought she was above all of them to cure her. Although how he was going to do that, he had no idea. Well, I can start by climbing the damn steps and getting in her face., he thought angrily.

There didn't seem to be anything else to do. Leaning down, he scooped Nadiah into his arms and started to climb.

"Rast," she protested softly as Sylvan and Sophia followed them up the steps. "You don't have to do this. I can manage."

"No you can't." He looked straight ahead, keeping the high priestess in his sights. "But you'll be able to soon. I promise you that, sweetheart."

Nadiah stopped protesting and laid her head on his shoulder. It reminded Rast of the way she'd relaxed against him after Y'dex had been yanking on their blood bond, during the trip to Tranq Prime. It made his heart clench to see that look of quiet submission on her face, that look which said she had been hurt before and knew she would be hurt again. He kissed her shining hair and made a silent vow to himself to make her better, no matter what.

The steps seemed to go on forever but at last they found themselves at the top. Rast set Nadiah gently on her feet, keeping an arm around her to make sure she didn't lose her balance.

"Phew!" Sophia exclaimed, panting as she reached the top step. "Like climbing up the side of a pyramid or something."

"Silence!" The high priestess's voice rang out harshly and Sophia's eyes went wide.

"Sorry," she whispered. "I didn't know the ceremony or whatever it is had already started."

Rast saw Sylvan squeeze her hand comfortingly. "Forgive us, your Holiness. We are here at your command. Would it please you to tell us why we were summoned?"

His respectful tone of voice seemed to please the priestess greatly. "Indeed, Warrior, I will tell you. But first I must share with you a story—a legend from our past...and, if we are not careful, a warning for our very near future. Turn from me now and look to the ceiling of the holy cavern. Watch as I relate."

All of them turned and Rast saw that the shafts of sunlight which dotted the cavern floor with golden green light had somehow been quenched. Now there was only darkness in the high, vaulted reaches of the holy cavern. But as he watched, the darkness was replaced with a picture. A picture of a man sitting on the Empty Throne.

Like the biggest IMAX in the whole damn universe, Rast thought, bemused. And on the heels of that, Hey, that guy looks a lot like —

"You. He looks just like you, Rast!" Nadiah breathed softly. "If you had black hair instead of light brown. Who is he?"

"The male you see here is Counselor Kall — the last Counselor to ever sit upon the Empty Throne," the priestess said, answering her question. "But then it was called the Seat of Wisdom. And he bore in his hand, the Eye of Foreknowledge." As if on cue, the male who looked almost exactly like Rast lifted a heavy silver scepter that looked to be taller than he was. At the top, the scepter was carved into a setting, almost like a ring holding a precious stone. But instead of a stone, the four fingers of silver held in place a…

"A soap bubble?" Rast frowned. "Why is he holding a bubble? And why doesn't it pop?"

"It is no mere bubble. The Eye of Foreknowledge is the third eye of a K'lil," the priestess intoned.

Sylvan frowned. "K'lil? I thought they were mythical. Do you mean the huge creatures that used to live on the fifth moon of Gilx? The ones no one could trap because they could always see the hunters coming?"

"The same." The priestess nodded. "The K'lil are extinct now. The Eye of Foreknowledge is a rare and precious gift, given by the Goddess herself that the First Kindred might know their enemies' minds and movements and thus defend against them. Only the Counselor himself can wield it."

As if on cue, the man who looked like Rast with black hair brought the bubble end of the scepter close to his face and looked into its shimmering, rainbow depths. Rast couldn't see what he saw there, but a look of fear and dismay spread over his face and he shook his head before looking up to call someone over.

A beautiful woman with long, golden brown hair came to join the man. Rast couldn't help noticing that except for the brilliant green streaks at her temples, her hair was the exact same color as his. She wore a long, loose fitting white gown but under it, her belly bulged prominently—she was pregnant.

"That is Zali, the chosen mate and Lyzel of Counselor Kall. Together as Challa and Lyzel, they interpreted the visions of the Eye and kept First World safe," the priestess said. "It was she he called to see the doom approaching them, although he did not wish to give her grief. Only she was worthy to help decide their fate."

The priestess looked at Nadiah as she spoke, making Rast wonder if there was some significance in the scene meant just for her. *Is she saying Nadiah's not good enough for me? But why the hell not? And what gives her the right to decide?*

"Of these matters we will speak later," the priestess said, giving him a dark look. Obviously she had caught part of his thought. "For now, simply watch."

Rast looked back at the scene and saw it was still unfolding.

The man and woman spoke earnestly and though Rast couldn't hear what they were saying, he could tell it was very serious. The woman put a hand to her cheek and a look of horror crossed her lovely face. The man offered her the scepter and, though it was clear she didn't want to, she looked into the soap bubble—or the Eye of Foreknowledge as Rast supposed he ought to call it—as well.

What she saw made her weep, tears running down her cheeks as she clutched protectively at her belly. She shook her head and Rast could almost hear her saying, "No, no it can't be true! My baby — not my baby!"

But the man simply nodded. She dissolved into tears and he held her while she cried.

Though he didn't know what it was about, Rast felt a lump in his throat. "What happened?" he asked. "Why are they so upset? What did they see?"

"I will show you." The priestess's voice was low and severe. "Prepare yourselves."

Suddenly the vast, dark space was empty. Then it was filled with a field of winking stars surrounding a small black ball. No, not a ball, Rast thought. It's a planet — a planet floating in space. But as the scene zoomed in, getting closer, he could see that the blackness of the planet wasn't stone or water — it was something living. Or many somethings — all writhing together in a shapeless mass that covered the planet's surface.

"Behold Hrakaz, home of the Hoard." The priestess spoke harshly but Rast thought he could detect fear in her voice. "Known to themselves as the Grimlax and to others as The Blackness which Eats the Stars. They are a vile, desperate, soulless rabble, intent only on devouring everything in their way and making everything as stark and barren as their own miserable rock of a planet."

"I can see that their whole planet is black with them," Sophia said timidly. "But why...why are they called The Blackness which Eats the Stars?"

"For this reason. Watch." The Priestess nodded at the scene. Suddenly, from the side of the planet, a ship thrust outward into space. And then another and another until the space around them was black with exiting ships, blotting out the nearby stars.

"Oh," Nadiah breathed and Rast could hear the fear in her voice. "They're looking for new worlds," she said. "I can feel their hunger."

"That is correct." The priestess gave her a grudging nod of approval. "The Hoard live on a planet in our solar system—only a few hundred million miles from the orbit of First World. They had long been known to us but Counselor Kall and his mate thought they only preyed on passing ships and would fear to attack a planet so large and well defended as First World. When they saw this..." She swept an arm to indicate the scene in front of them. "They knew differently. The Hoard were coming and there was little time to prepare."

"What did they do?" Sophia asked, her eyes wide. "How could they defend First World against so many?"

"The Challa and his Lyzel knew that both of them would die in the coming conflict," the priestess said. "It is one of the burdens a Counselor and his mate must bear—to know the hour of their own deaths. However, they had time to safeguard their son and send him far away—to a place they hoped the Hoard would never reach."

"They sent him as far away as possible," Sylvan said quietly, looking at Rast. "They sent him to Earth."

"What?" Rast suddenly understood what he was saying. "Sylvan, come on, you can't be serious. I'm not...those can't be my parents. Can they?"

"That is what we must prove or disprove, Adam Rast...are you the son of Kall and Zali, the last Challa and Lyzel of First World, or are you not?" intoned the priestess.

"I'm not," he said at once. "I mean, I can't be. Didn't you say this happened a long time ago?"

"A thousand years ago at least, if what Sylvan told me was right," Sophia said. "I don't see how he could be either," said, turning to Nadiah.

"A special ship was built—one equipped with a stasis chamber and faster than light ability," the priestess said. "It traveled through the fourth dimension—time, as well as space. So though a thousand years had passed on First World, by the time its occupant—the Counselor 's only son—reached his destination, he was still only two or three standard years old."

Sophia frowned. "But I thought, if you left someone in stasis too long it made them sick or over aged them or something once they got out."

"That's true if you leave them in with no breaks at all," Sylvan said thoughtfully. "But if you brought them out every once in awhile—say, even for a minute every day or two—they could stay in stasis almost forever with no ill effects."

"So it is possible." Rast suddenly felt weak in the knees. "Damn. Makes me wish I would've paid better attention in physics class."

"It is certainly possible," the priestess said. "And this is the year the Counselor was prophesied to be found on a foreign planet. It was said of him, 'He will know your ways as if born to them. There shall be wisdom on his tongue and truth and healing in his wings.'"

Sylvan frowned. "Rast, the way you took to piloting a Kindred ship. It amazed me—I've never seen anyone learn to fly that fast."

"And the way you were able to break the blood bond for me," Nadiah chimed in.

"Not to mention the fact that your blood tests prove you're Kindred instead of human," Sophia added.

"All right, all right." Rast held up his hands for quiet. "I get it. But what about the wings part—that's got to be a mistake—right?"

"There is no mistake." Suddenly the high priestess was right behind him. Before Rast could stop her, she grabbed the back of his white gown at the neck and ripped it straight down the middle, baring his back.

"Hey," he protested. "What the hell do you think you're doing?"

"Looking for that which is not there...but should be." The priestess ran one sharp green nail down his right shoulder blade and Rast shouted with pain.

"Whatever you're doing, stop it! That feels like you poured lighter fluid down my back and lit a match, damn it!"

"The wing shadows are there." The priestess seemed to be talking to herself, completely unconcerned with the pain she'd caused him. "But the wings themselves have not manifested yet."

"What wings?" Nadiah came around to see what the priestess was talking about and sucked in a breath. "It's just like my dream. My nightmare," she whispered. "Rast, your back...you have these long scars. And they're...it looks like they're moving..."

"Hey, stop it! Both of you!" Rast rounded on them and stabbed a finger at the high priestess. "I don't know what the hell you're talking about and I don't want to know," he snarled. "And I don't care if I'm the long lost son of your Counselor or Challa or whatever the fuck he was, either. All I want is to get Nadiah healed and get off this God forsaken planet."

The high priestess's blank emerald eyes narrowed menacingly. "I am afraid, Adam Rast, that both of your wishes are completely impossible. For you cannot heal your little female until you prove yourself. And if you prove yourself, you must never leave First World again."

Chapter Twenty-nine

"Ready to turn in?" Liv asked, looking fondly at her husband, Baird. He'd been yawning for an hour but he was still up, doggedly slogging through a book about parenting. The huge Beast Kindred warrior wasn't usually much of a reader but he was determined to do everything just right when their son arrived.

"Mmm?" He looked up, his golden eyes drooping with fatigue. "Sorry, Lilenta, what did you say? I didn't catch that."

"I asked if you were sleepy yet. Because I sure am—it was a long day at the med station without Sylvan to help." She stifled a yawn. "Not to mention that I had to field a call from Nadiah's parents demanding to talk to her."

"Oh?" Baird frowned. "And what did you say?"

Liv shrugged. "I told them she was making a pilgrimage to First World and wasn't available. They weren't too happy about it, either." She frowned. "And on top of all that, I had to keep checking on Elise Darden."

"Why did you have to keep checking on her?" Baird left the book on the couch and wandered over to her, scratching his bare chest. "I thought she was in the stasis chamber—she oughta be fine."

"She is, but the way Sylvan's got it set, she could wake up at any time." Liv frowned. "Not that she could so much as twitch a toe without your friend, Merrick noticing it. He's in there with her day and night—I don't think he ever eats or sleeps."

"Merrick is Sylvan's friend, not mine," Baird rumbled. "I didn't even know he was a hybrid until he showed up—Sylvan never told me. He doesn't talk about him much."

"Is that such a bad thing—being a hybrid?" Liv asked curiously. "I mean, I would think it would be good. You get the best of both worlds, right?"

"Afraid not, Lilienta." Baird shook his head. "More like you get the worst of both worlds. The Beast Kindred side gives you berserker rage—an animalistic joy in killing."

Liv shivered. "But you're not like that."

"I could be though," Baird said seriously. "If I thought you or the baby was threatened." He stroked her rounded belly gently. "But the same emotions that would set me off would also help me stop. For instance, I would become upset if I found I was hurting an innocent bystander and that would keep me from attacking them."

Liv frowned. "What are you saying? That Merrick wouldn't stop?"

Baird shook his head. "The Blood Kindred part of him makes him cold. Once the urge to kill is on him, he kills without mercy and without stopping until every last enemy is dead. He's got no compassion at all."

Liv put a hand to her chest. "A sociopath. You're saying he's a sociopath."

Baird thought for a minute, then shrugged. "I guess, in a manner of speaking. But only when he's fighting. And in Merrick's defense, I don't believe he wants to be the way he is—that's why he went to the temple on First World before Sylvan and Sophia's joining ceremony. He didn't want to bring them bad luck with his hybrid ways."

"That's good, I guess," Liv said doubtfully. "But are you sure it's safe to leave Elise alone with him? I mean, I don't even know the poor girl but she's so small and he's so huge. And after what you just told me I—"

"Don't worry about that," Baird said firmly, putting an arm around her shoulders. "Hybrid or not, Merrick is still Kindred. He won't harm a female in his care."

"She's safe here on the Mother Ship," Liv said, leaning against his solid, muscular frame and enjoying the warmth of his big body against hers. "So why is he still hanging around? Do you think he feels something for her? Maybe...could they be dream sharing or something like that, even with her in stasis?"

Baird shook his head. "I seriously doubt it, Lilenta. Hybrids aren't usually able to form bonds with females—they tend to be loners."

"What? Why not?" Even though she barely knew the huge, scarred warrior, Liv felt sad for him.

Baird shrugged. "Who knows? Maybe it's the Goddess's way of keeping them from overrunning the rest of the Kindred lines. An army of hybrids would be more destructive than the Scourge ever were."

Liv imagined an army of seven foot tall Kindred warriors overcome with unstoppable, berserker rage and shuddered. "I guess you're right. But if he can't form a bond with Elise, I don't understand why he's hanging around."

Baird shrugged again. "Maybe he feels responsible for her—he is the one who found her. Maybe he feels like he can't go until he knows she's well. Hybrid or not, he's an honorable male or Sylvan wouldn't think so highly of him."

"You're right about that," Liv agreed. "But for whatever reason he's staying, I wish he'd back off a little. He's making the rest of the staff at the med station nervous."

"Maybe if she had family to look after her he'd leave," Baird suggested. "Does she have anyone on Earth looking for her?"

Liv frowned. "We didn't think so at first but I got a call tonight from Detective Barnes tonight—he used to be Rast's partner back when they were on the police force together. He told me he'd located her mother and step father living in Oregon. Apparently Elise hasn't spoken to them in years but her mother was still upset to hear what had happened to her. She asked to be notified the moment Elise woke up."

"Hmm." Baird frowned. "Most parents would have been rushing to get up to the Mother Ship, demanding to see their child right away."

"I thought it was weird too," Liv admitted. "But I guess they're estranged for some reason—why else would Elise have moved across the country and stopped talking to them?" She stroked her belly protectively. "You don't think that could ever happen between us and our little guy, do you, Baird?"

"Of course not, Lilenta." He smiled and put his own hand over hers. "We're going to love and protect our son and raise him to be a strong warrior. He'll be the best of both of us." He kissed her cheek. "But I hope he has your eyes."

"Why?" Liv smiled and kissed him back. "Yours are much more striking. I still remember how I felt back when we were dream sharing and I saw you watching me with those molten gold eyes. It scared me to death but it excited me too."

"All of you excites me," Baird murmured. The sleepy look had left his eyes to be replaced by a glow of desire. Pulling her close, he kissed her gently but firmly on the mouth. "I wanna taste you," he growled softly, looking her in the eyes. "What do you say, Lilenta?"

"Baird!" Even though they'd been together for a good while now, his direct way of saying how much he desired her still made her blush a little.

"Come on, Lilenta," he murmured, still holding her eyes with his. "I want to lay you on the bed, spread your legs and lick your pussy until you come for me."

"You're such a pervert," she accused him, half laughing, half blushing. "Wanting to have sex with a pregnant lady."

"I can't help it," Baird protested. "That pregnant lady just happens to be my incredibly sexy mate. Besides..." He pulled her even closer. "How can I help wanting you now? You're so beautiful like this—all rounded and glowing. I swear if I'd know how damn gorgeous you'd be carrying our son, I would have made you pregnant sooner."

"Well it wasn't for lack of trying," Liv murmured, smiling. "You've certainly done your duty in that regard."

"Not nearly as much as I should." Baird kissed her cheek and stroked one hand over her full belly to cup her sensitive mound. "Let me taste you tonight, Lilenta. The book I was reading says a pregnant female should have lots of orgasms to be healthy."

"What?" Liv gave him a look. "You're making that up."

"No, I'm not," Baird promised. "I'll show you the exact page— as soon as we finish."

"Well..." Liv drew it out, making him wait. It wasn't likes she was going to turn him down and they both knew it. His mating scent and the warm, familiar way he caressed her body made her eager to spread her legs for him. It was fun to tease him, though. Fun to—

"Excuse me, Commander Baird?" A voice from the holo-unit interrupted them, much to Liv's surprise and annoyance.

"Who can it be at this hour?" she demanded. But as soon as the words left her lips, she had a new thought. "Is it Sophia? Are she and Sylvan all right? Do you think they had trouble on First World?'

"Only one way to find out." Reaching down, Baird snapped on the holo and a tiny blue dot hovering above the base quickly expanded to show the head of a Blood Kindred Liv recognized. He was one of the other nurses who worked in the med station with her and Sylvan on a regular basis.

"Glevan," she said, surprised. "What's going on? Is there a problem?"

"I'm sorry, Olivia," he said, nodding at her respectfully. "But Elise Darden is showing signs of waking up. The staff knows what to do, of course, but I thought you'd like to be informed. And…" He hesitated for a moment. "Commander Sylvan's, er, friend is growing agitated. I thought maybe if you spoke to him…"

"I'll be right there," Liv promised, glad she hadn't taken off her clothes yet. "Tell him to take it easy—everything is going to be all right."

"I hope so." Glevan looked worried. "Please hurry." He nodded again and the blue holo of his head winked out of existence.

Liv sighed and reached for her lab jacket. "Well, I guess your midnight snack will have to wait until later. Sorry, hon."

"Sorry, nothing." Baird was already pulling on a shirt. "I'm coming with you."

* * * * *

Hands clasped behind his back and a scowl on his face, Merrick paced beside the cot containing the stasis chamber. Not that there was much room to pace for legs as long as his—still he did his best. He had an idea that his restless movements, or possibly the look on his face was upsetting the med station staff, but he couldn't help it. As strange as it seemed, he literally could not sit still.

Will she be all right? Will she recognize me? he thought, staring down at the delicate features which were now contorted, as though in pain. Or will she forget our first meeting and scream when she sees me? Merrick pushed the thought away. After all, what did he care if the human girl didn't remember him from their brief first encounter? Why should it matter to him if his appearance frightened her or not?

It doesn't matter, he told himself fiercely. Why should I care? I don't even know her. I don't give a damn what she thinks. Just need to be sure she's okay for the sake of my honor. Once she was awake and ready to be claimed by her kin, his obligation was done. And then I'm out of here, he promised himself.

The lights on the side of the stasis chamber were glowing fiercely, and inside it Elise Darden was thrashing as though in slow motion. The opaque top of the chamber had melted away again, revealing her frail beauty and Merrick thought it was like watching someone move underwater—the stasis field was letting her go but slowly, oh so slowly.

He had an urge to touch her, to hold her again as he had when he first found her—but he had been forbidden from doing so. According to Sylvan and the rest of the med station staff, touching Elise while she came out of the enforced hibernation of stasis could be dangerous—both to her and to himself. He wished Sylvan would have explained why before he left, but his friend had been understandably distracted by other matters. All Merrick knew was that he must not touch her. So instead of taking action he watched, his huge hands curled into fists at his sides as she thrashed and moaned.

"Merrick, is she all right? I got here as soon as I could." Olivia was suddenly there behind him, a worried frown on her face. "What's going on? How long as she been like this?"

"Only the past quarter of an hour," Merrick gritted out. "She was moaning some before that but nothing like this."

As if on cue, Elise moaned and moved her head from side to side. Her long, black hair swirled around her pale face like a dark cloud.

"Oh dear." Olivia frowned and checked the lights on the side of the stasis chamber. "I wish Sylvan was here but everything seems to be normal. He did say there might be some agitation when she came out of it."

"Agitation?" Merrick snapped. "Look at her—she's fucking upset! Do something for her."

"She's doing everything she can, buddy." The low growl came from Baird, Olivia's Beast Kindred mate. "So why don't you calm down and—"

"Her vitals are dropping." Olivia sounded close to panic. "Baird, get Glevan and tell him I need a crash kit STAT."

The Beast Kindred left without a word and Olivia continued to work on the stasis chamber while being careful not to touch the thrashing girl inside. Merrick watched, every muscle in his big body tight. Was she dying? What was happening? And why the hell should he care so much?

Again he had the urge to reach for her—the feeling that if he could just touch her, skin-to-skin, everything would be all right. Instinctively he put out a hand but Olivia slapped it away.

"You know what Sylvan said—no touching," she said curtly.

"She needs me," Merrick grated out. He didn't know how he knew this but he did. The little Earth female's life was hanging by a threat but if he could just touch her—

"She needs you to leave her alone, you mean." Olivia's silvery grey eyes flashed. "Don't make me kick you out of here, Merrick. I don't care how big you are, the patient's safety comes first."

Merrick nodded curtly and stepped to one side, giving her more room to work. He took deep breaths, trying to hold the cold rage at bay, to keep the curtain of anger from dropping over his vision. He normally only felt like this when he himself was threatened. In fact, the last time he'd felt the rage for any female was when he'd been defending his mother from...He clamped down on the thought. No point thinking about that now. Got to concentrate on Elise. What's happening to her? Why the fuck do I want to touch her so much?

Elise's movements were weaker now but her moans had turned into words. "Please," she begged, her voice so soft Merrick could barely hear it. "Please don't hurt me anymore."

Must be remembering the Scourge...what the AllFather did to her. Merrick ground his teeth together at the thought. Sick bastard is fucking lucky he's already dead. Then Elise spoke again.

"Please," she whispered. "Don't...it hurts. I...I'll tell Mom..."

Merrick frowned. Mom? As in her mother? What the hell was that all about? He wondered what memory was surfacing in her confused brain. Was it somehow responsible for her rapid deterioration now that she was coming out of stasis?

Sylvan had said it might take her mind weeks, even months before it wanted to try and come forward to sort everything out. She'd been tortured and hurt so badly it was amazing that her body had decided to come out of the stasis now rather than taking more time to process the devastating experience. But maybe this memory, whatever it was, was too much to process.

Then Elise stopped talking and went still. The room was filled with a high, buzzing hum.

"Crap." Olivia sounded panicked. "She's flatlining. Where the hell is that crash kit?"

"Fuck this." Merrick shouldered his way past her, and scooped Elise from the cot. Pulling open his shirt with one hand, he pressed her naked body against his chest and held her there, willing her to live. He didn't know how he knew it, but he knew this was the right thing to do. The only thing that might save her.

"Merrick, no! Put her d—" Olivia stopped talking abruptly as the high buzzing hum, the alarm that warned of imminent death, cut off. "What the hell?" she whispered softly, staring up at Merrick. "What did you do?"

"Just touched her." Merrick cradled her small frame close, trying to give her his warmth, willing her to hold on, to live. "I told you," he growled. "It's what she needed."

A look of surprise and uncertainty crossed Olivia's face. "I don't understand it, but she does seem to be doing better."

"She's breathing, anyway," Merrick muttered, feeling the soft rise and fall of Elise's chest against his own. "That's a fucking improvement right there."

Just then, Baird and a Blood Kindred Merrick recognized as one of the nurses rushed into the small room. "Here's the kit, Olivia," the Blood Kindred said. "Is she—"

"She's not flatlining anymore." Olivia looked at Merrick with a mixture of wonder and worry on her face. "I don't know why but she came back when he picked her up."

"What the hell?" Baird demanded. "I thought you said Sylvan said nobody should touch her while she came out of stasis."

Olivia nodded. "That's what he said, all right."

The Blood Kindred nurse frowned. "Could he have been mistaken somehow?"

"I don't think so," Olivia said. "Sylvan knows his stuff."

"Then why—?"

"Shut up, the lot of you," Merrick growled, glaring at them. "Can't you see she's coming to?"

Indeed, Elise's big, brown eyes were open and she was staring up at him in awe. She seemed to be trying to say something but Merrick couldn't quite make it out.

"Tell me," he said softly, leaning down to put his ear next to her lips. "Say it again, baby. It's all right."

"He's coming," she whispered, her voice barely a breath in his ear. "He's coming back and this time he'll bring others. We'll all die. They'll eat the stars...all the stars."

"What?" Merrick frowned. "Who's coming back?"

Her eyes widened with fear and she looked past him, as though seeing something he couldn't. "Don't let him touch me again. He hurt me. I tried to tell but she won't believe me...She doesn't care. Only...only Buck cares. He tries to keep me safe. But he can't...not always."

"What is she talking about?" Baird said.

Olivia shook her head. "She's delirious—her mind is wandering." She looked up at Merrick. "Any chance you'll put her down so I can examine her?"

Grudgingly, he nodded. "All right but if she flatlines again, I'm picking her back up. Got it?"

"Sounds fine to me," Olivia said. "Come on, Merrick, she's out of stasis now so we'll move the tube. You can put her on the cot."

At her words, Baird and Glevan shifted the stasis tube out of the way, leaving a clear space on the small bed.

Slowly, carefully, Merrick laid her down. He couldn't bear to stop touching her completely, though. Crouching by the head of the cot, he kept one of her small, cool hands clasped firmly in his much larger one. Only because I'm her protector, he told himself. I'm responsible for her, that's all. Just trying to do what's best. "Okay," he told Olivia. "Examine her."

Silently, Olivia did as he asked. When she was finished, Merrick looked at her expectantly.

"Well? What's wrong?"

Olivia shook her head, a worried look on her face. "Nothing...nothing at all."

Chapter Thirty

"What the hell did you just say to me?" Rast demanded, staring at the High Priestess of the Empty Throne.

She raised an eyebrow at him. "Is it really so difficult to understand? You can only heal your little female by proving yourself to be the true Counselor we have been waiting for these last thousand years. And if you prove that you are said Counselor , you will never leave First World again—you will be bound to your home planet."

Nadiah felt her heart leap into her throat. As cruel as the words of the high priestess were, she could feel the truth of them. It was exactly as she had foreseen—Rast was going to be forced to make a choice. And if he chose to stay, he would never leave.

"It's true," Sylvan said, echoing her thoughts. "According to tradition, the Counselor is bound to First World, sworn to protect it and unable to leave it so long as he lives."

"Now hold on, back up a minute." Rast put up his hands. "I never signed on for any of this. I didn't notice any big flashing sign in your landing area that said 'No exit, ever.'"

"Very well, leave." The high priestess made a dismissive gesture. "It doesn't matter if your little female dies. She isn't right for you anyway—if she was, your wings would already have manifested."

"What are you talking about?" Rast's deep voice was a roar of frustration. "I don't have wings."

"No, but you should!" The high priestess's emerald eyes flashed.

"Excuse me," Sophia said timidly, stepping forward. "I, uh, don't want to start a fight but if the Counselor always has wings, why didn't we see any on the vid scene you showed us of Rast's father?"

"Normally the wings only manifest in times of great trouble — they come when they are needed and fold back into the Counselor 's body when they are not," the priestess explained in a stern voice. She looked at Rast. "By giving your female a life threatening illness, I had hoped to force your wings to come out, Adam Rast. But though they are clearly there, her plight has not yet caused them to burst forth. And until they do, you cannot claim the Empty Throne."

"Right," Rast said sarcastically. "Because obviously making the woman I love terminally ill is going to cause me to sprout wings."

"It had better." The priestess gave him a severe look. "If it does not, she will surely die. The only cure for her is to be found in the waters of the Goddess's fountain in the Healing Garden, high on the side of the holy mountain. And the only way to reach the garden is to fly."

Nadiah saw the stricken look on his face as his dilemma became perfectly clear. If his wings manifested in time, he could fly her to the Healing Gardens and save her life. But then he would be trapped — bound to First World by the very wings that saved her. If, on the other hand, his wings didn't manifest, she would die of the fever the high priestess had cursed her with. Rast would be able to leave, but he would do it alone for Nadiah would be dead.

"So," Rast said heavily. "The choice is stay here forever and cure Nadiah or leave and let her die."

"That is it, exactly." The high priestess smiled a cruel smile. "The choice is yours. You may have tonight to think about it and I will hear your formal oath tomorrow at sunrise on the high mesa." She glowered at him. "There your wings will surely manifest...or your female will die."

She turned to stalk away, moving toward the back of the temple, past the raised dais where the Empty Throne sat.

"Wait a minute," Rast called, running to catch up. "You know I'm not going to let the woman I love die. I've made my choice. So why—"

"This interview is over," the high priestess said, without turning. "I have matters to attend to. I must serve the throne."

Nadiah saw Rast look up. The bottom of the white marble throne was at the level of his head. Suddenly the priestess's earlier words to them echoed in her head. "Do not touch the throne on peril of your lives," she had said. Nadiah wanted to shout out a warning—Rast was so close—too close, but her mouth was too dry and the words wouldn't come.

"It's not over until you answer my goddamn question!" He reached for her shoulder, obviously meaning to spin her around. "I want to ask you why—"

"No more questions!" The high priestess whirled to face him. Planting both hands on his chest, she shoved him away.

"I—" Rast was knocked off balance. Nadiah saw him reach for something to steady himself...and his hand landed on the side of the white marble throne.

For a moment he was completely still and then his back bowed outward and an agonized gasp came from his lips. His whole body began to shake like a man being electrocuted, but still his hand stuck to the white marble as though it was glued in place. As though he couldn't let go.

Finally, Nadiah's paralysis broke. "Rast!" she cried and ran forward as fast as she could in her weakened state.

"No," Sylvan roared. "Don't touch him—it might cause a chain reaction!" He leapt forward and tackled Rast to the ground, breaking the connection between his hand and the throne. Rast fell, his head cracking against the white marble floor and Nadiah cried out at the sound.

She fell to her knees beside Rast as Sylvan hovered over him on the other side. "Is he all right?" she gasped, grabbing one of Rast's hands. It felt cool and unresponsive in her grasp. "Is he, Sylvan?"

Sylvan checked the other male's pulse and breathing. "He's alive," he said grimly. He glared angrily up at the priestess. "He could have been killed. You pushed him deliberately. Why?"

The high priestess stared down at them, her blank emerald eyes utterly pitiless. "I had to be certain he was really the future Counselor before I allowed him to ascend to the top of the high mesa tomorrow morning. Touching the throne, even briefly, would have killed anyone but the rightful candidate. Now I know it is safe to proceed with our ceremony tomorrow."

Nadiah shook her head. "But his wings—you saw the marks on his back. You had to know—"

"I know nothing until I see the wings manifest," the priestess snapped. "Which they would have already if you were the rightful mate and Lysell of the Counselor." She made a face as though she'd smelled something bad. "Clearly you are not. Now, I must go and meditate to clear my head for the ceremony tomorrow. Lissa will take you all back to the guest quarters and you may think of what I have said."

Turning again, she swept away, her white robe rustling on the bare marble floor.

Chapter Thirty-one

"She's coming around. Look, her eyelids are fluttering."

Olivia's soft words brought Merrick out of the half-doze he'd been in. Blinking his eyes, he sat up in the chair beside Elise's cot and looked over at her. Olivia had dressed her in a dark red healing gown — a stark contrast to her pale face and black hair. Sure enough, he could see her eyes moving under the lids. He hoped she would be in her right mind this time. It had been a long night and her earlier interludes of wakefulness had been brief and confused. He was beginning to wonder if her long stint in stasis had affected her mind.

As her small hand twitched in his, Merrick wondered what she would say this time. Sometimes when she woke, she begged him to keep her safe, to not let him hurt her again. At first he had thought the "him" she referred to must be the AllFather. But now he wasn't so sure. It seemed like maybe her mind was reliving an earlier trauma, an older hurt — perhaps one she'd buried? But he could never get details from her to find out.

Other times, she clutched at his hand and called him "Buck," which sounded like a male's name. Merrick had wondered about that — he didn't smell another male on her and Olivia said she had no mate on Earth — not one they'd been able to find, anyway. But still the name filled him with a nameless kind of rage. Though he tried to tell himself he didn't care, the idea that the little Earth female might be claimed by another male made him grind his teeth and clench his fists.

Don't be stupid, he told himself. She's not yours. She doesn't even know your name. She thinks you're 'Buck', whoever that is. And it's not like you want a female anyway. What could she do but slow you down and trip you up? But no matter what he told himself, his stomach still clenched every time she whispered that strange name.

His thoughts were interrupted when her eyes fluttered again and then opened. This time there was no pain or fear in them. Instead, she smiled tentatively up at him and put her free hand to her forehead.

"Hello," she whispered.

"Hey," he said roughly, then cursed himself for his abrupt tone. "I mean..." He cleared his throat. "How are you feeling?"

"Fine." She rubbed her forehead. "Tired. And thirsty."

"Here you go, hon." Olivia held a cup to her lips and Elise drank thirstily. A tiny trickle of liquid slid from the side of the cup and down her slender neck. For a split second, Merrick pictured himself licking it off. Then he pushed the idea away.

Elise finished the drink and nodded at Olivia. "Thank you." She turned her gaze to Merrick. "You're the one. You saved me from...from..." She shook her head. "I don't know from what but it was something awful. I didn't think anyone would come for me but you did."

Merrick shifted uncomfortably on the chair. "I found the pod you were in, drifting in space, and brought you back here—that's all."

She looked confused. "I was in a pod? In space? Well, thank you, I guess."

"You're welcome." He couldn't think of anything else to say.

"Have you been with me the whole time?" She nodded down to where Merrick was still holding her hand. "Keeping me safe?"

"Uh…" Feeling foolish, he yanked his hand away. "I had to. I found you so I'm responsible for your safety while you're here."

"All vitals are normal and brain activity looks good." Olivia smiled. "I think she's going to be just fine."

Elise looked around. "I'd feel better if I knew where I was. The last thing I remember is walking in the park by the marina in Sarasota—the one with the statue of the sailor and the nurse kissing. I was on vacation and…and everything else is a blank." She frowned.

Olivia's smile faltered a little. "Well, hon, a lot has happened since then. But the important thing to remember now is that you're safe. You're on board the Kindred Mother Ship, orbiting Earth."

"Really, the Kindred?" Elise looked at Merrick and gave a confused laugh. "You must be one, I guess."

He nodded briefly. "Yes."

"I always wondered about them—about your kind, I mean," Elise said. "But of course I never had to worry about being drafted by one of you."

Merrick's heart fisted in his chest. The only Earth females who didn't have to worry about the draft for Kindred brides were already mated or spoken for. But if that was so, why was there no scent of another male on Elise?

Olivia frowned. "You didn't worry about being drafted? Why not?"

"Why because…because of…" Elise frowned. "Isn't that funny? I can't remember." She looked down at her arms and frowned. "There seems to be a lot I've forgotten. How did I get these bruises? And why am I so sore?"

Merrick shifted restlessly on the chair and he and Olivia exchanged a glance.

"Some things are better left for another time," Olivia said. "Why don't you get some rest and maybe it'll come back to you later."

Elise frowned and sat up, looking more alert. "But I don't want to rest anymore. How long have I been out? My vacation time may be up already. Do you know what my caseload is going to be like when I get back home?"

"Caseload?" Olivia echoed.

"The number of cases I handle at work — I'm an attorney." Elise blew out a breath and pushed a stray lock of black hair away from her eyes. "Why is my hair loose? I never wear it down like this."

"An attorney, huh? Who do you represent?" Olivia asked soothingly, offering her another drink.

Elise took the cup without question, holding it on her own this time, and took a swallow. She made a face. "That's bitter."

"It's good for you. Have some more," Olivia urged. "And tell me about your job. I was a nurse down on Earth and I kept it up once I got here." She motioned at the med station. "Kindred anatomy is a little different from human anatomy so it was kind of a case of learning on the job."

"That's interesting." Elise took another sip and made a face. "Well, I'm a prosecutor with the Attorney General's office. Mostly I represent children because...because they..." She yawned and then looked at Olivia sharply. "Hey, what was in that drink?"

"Just something to relax you." Olivia stroked her arm. "I think you need a little more rest but don't worry, I'll contact your mother and stepfather while you sleep. They can be here when you wake up."

Elise's big brown eyes widened with panic. "No, don't do that! I don't…" She yawned again, obviously despite herself. "We don't talk," she finished, her eyelids drooping.

"Oh, I just thought maybe…" Olivia shook her head. "Never mind, I won't contact them. Just rest and you'll feel better in a little while."

"But I don't want to sleep." Elise's voice, which had turned sharp and businesslike for a moment, now sounded soft and childlike again. She looked up at Merrick appealingly. "When I sleep I…I have bad dreams. About him."

"About who, baby?" The endearment slipped out before Merrick could stop it. He told himself it was the look of fear on her face – it brought out his protective instincts. He had the urge to hold her hand again, the feeling that she needed to be touched, but he restrained himself. Or would have if Elise hadn't reached for him.

"Please," she whispered. "You'll stay with me, won't you? Stay and keep me safe?"

"Sure, I will." Merrick laced their fingers together noticing how her tiny hand was completely swallowed in his. "I'm your protector while you're here – It's my duty to keep you safe."

"Oh…good. Protector…just like…Buck." Her eyelids were drooping as the sedative Olivia had given her took effect.

On impulse Merrick leaned forward and looked into her half closed eyes. "Who's Buck?" he murmured. "You keep asking for him – who is he?"

"Buck?" She yawned and gave him a sleepy smile. "My favorite. He protected me. Always kept me safe until…until…"

But she was asleep again, leaving Merrick to wonder. Her favorite what? And he protected her until what?

Looking at her peacefully sleeping form, he wondered if he would ever know and decided he probably wouldn't. Really, now that she was awake and stable he ought to be on his way again, out into the universe. It was a vast place and he was sure he would never see Elise Darden again.

Merrick frowned. It was the right thing to do—the smart thing to do. There was no point in hanging around where he wasn't wanted or needed. He made the med staff nervous and Elise had parents and friends and coworkers on Earth waiting for her—a whole other life that didn't involve him and never would.

And yet, the idea of leaving her, of never seeing those big brown eyes again, made him uneasy. It was as though she stirred something in him—a tenderness he'd never even suspected was there. He couldn't help feeling that if he left her, he would never feel it again. Which would be good, he told himself grimly. Tender is just another word for weak. But still, he couldn't bring himself to leave.

Well, he needed to do some work on his star-duster, he decided. Now that he didn't have to be in the med station 24/7, he could see to his ship. That way he could hang around the Kindred Mother Ship just in case something else went wrong—which he was sure it wouldn't.

Merrick stretched and rose to go tell Olivia he could be found in the docking bay if she needed him. He could almost hear her sigh of relief already—she and the rest of the staff would be glad to get rid of him, that was for fucking sure.

Before he left, he leaned over to check Elise one more time. It was strangely hard to leave her, even knowing he was only going to another part of the ship. More weakness, he thought. Stop being a fucking idiot and go.

But somehow he couldn't stop himself from stroking her cheek one last time before he left.

Chapter Thirty-two

"Are you ready for this?" Sylvan asked, peering anxiously into Rast's eyes. "Are you feeling well enough to go through with the ceremony?"

"I'm fine." Rast winced and rubbed the back of his head. "Well, except for one hell of a headache from bonking myself on the damn marble floor. And the fact that that my shoulder blades are itching like crazy. But other than that, couldn't be better." He sighed. "Let's get it over with, okay?"

Sylvan nodded. "All right. I'm sure the priestess will be here soon."

They were standing in the oasis of light, as Nadiah called it, where they had spent the night. Sleeping had proved difficult because there were three moons instead of just one shedding their silvery light over the rainbow desert. It also didn't help that Sylvan kept waking him up to check his pupils and make sure he didn't have a concussion. Rast had finally assured him that he felt all right and managed to grab a few hours right before sunrise. But now that the sun was up he felt wide awake and edgy.

It was finally hitting home to him what he was about to do. He was going to take an oath never to leave this planet—to never go back to Earth again. As beautiful as it was, First World wasn't very welcoming. It felt familiar—as though something in his blood recognized it—but it didn't feel like home. Rast wondered if it ever would. Guess I have the rest of my life to find out, he thought glumly. Well, at least I'll have Nadiah with me.

The thought cheered him up immensely. No matter where he ended his days, if he had the woman he loved, it would be all right. Speaking of the love of his life, where was she? He looked over at the table and saw Nadiah and Sophia were sitting on the sand beside it. They were nibbling loaves of what Sophia had dubbed the "Willy Wonka mind reading bread" and talking quietly. Rast was disturbed to see that Nadiah had a drawn, unhappy look on her face. Was she feeling sicker this morning? Or was the thought of living on First World for the rest of her life getting her down, too?

"Hey, how does it taste this morning?" he said, walking over to take a piece of bread himself.

Sophia looked up. "French toast with butter and maple syrup…crispy bacon and…" She swallowed and took another small bite. "And orange juice."

"Sounds delicious." Rast smiled and looked at Nadiah. "What does yours taste like, sweetheart? Scrambled brains and fricasseed worms or what?"

Nadiah gave him a wan smile and shook her head. "Rast," she said softly, "I need to talk to you." She started to get up but her knees buckled and Sophia had to catch her.

She looked up at Rast with fear in her face. "She's light as a feather."

"Here." Leaning down, Rast swung Nadiah up into his arms. It disturbed him to see that she did, indeed, feel even lighter than she had the day before. "How are you feeling?" he asked anxiously.

"Fine," she gave him an exhausted smile. "Just…a little tired. And hot. It's so much hotter here than Tranq Prime."

"Yeah, I know. It's hotter than Florida too and that's saying something." Rast sighed. "But we'll get used to it. And you'll feel better as soon as we get you healed."

"Rast..." Nadiah looked down and drew an aimless pattern against his bare chest. After the priestess had ripped up the white gown he'd been forced to wear the day before, Rast had decided to hell with it and had gone back to wearing his jeans. But it was too hot for the long-sleeved shirt he'd come in by far, so he'd left it off.

"Yes, sweetheart?" he murmured, wishing she would look at him. "Something on your mind?"

"Yes, there is." Finally she looked up. "I don't want you to do this."

He frowned. "Don't want me to do what?"

"To take this oath. To swear to stay here the rest of your life just to save me."

"Nadiah," he said seriously. "Listen to me—if it's a choice between staying on this planet the rest of my life with you or living anywhere else in the universe without you, there's no contest." He looked into her eyes. "I choose you," he said softly. "And if there's no other way to save you than to be stuck here, well, I guess we'll both have to get used to living in the desert. What do you say?"

"I don't want you to feel trapped," Nadiah protested. "I don't want to be the reason you have to give up your whole life."

"I'm not giving it up—I'm just changing it a little." He gave her a crooked little grin. "Come on, what do you say?"

"Oh, Rast..." She smiled at last and the look on her face warmed him to the bones. He knew he would do anything to see that look— the love and tenderness shining from her deep blue eyes—anything at all. Even live on a foreign planet the rest of his life.

"I love you," he murmured and kissed her gently on the mouth.

"It is time." The soft words made him break the kiss and Rast looked up to see that the young priestess, Lissa, had reappeared and was standing at the mouth of the tunnel.

"We're ready," he answered for all of them.

"Are you?" Lissa looked at his shoulders and frowned.

Rast frowned back. "I know what you're thinking but sorry, no wings yet. My back itches like hell but so far not so much as a single feather." He felt a touch of anxiety. "They should come out during the ceremony, right?"

"Certainly. Of course." Lissa nodded but Rast thought there was a troubled look on her face. "Come," she said, beckoning them. "I must lead you a different way this time — up to the high mesa."

* * * * *

Nadiah allowed herself to be carried until they reached the bottom of the mesa. But when she saw the narrow stone steps cut into the side of the rock, winding higher and higher around the vast natural stone structure, she begged Rast to put her down.

"There are too many steps," he objected, frowning. "You can't possible climb all the way up there, sweetheart."

"Yes, I can." Nadiah lifted her chin, and looked at him defiantly. "Because I have to. It's too narrow, Rast. You can't carry me — not without both of us falling." She shivered at the thought. She had always hated heights and the towering mesa was higher than anything she'd ever been on.

Rast sighed. "It is narrow. Too bad they're no guardrail for safety."

"Forgive the crudeness of the steps," Lissa murmured, coming up behind them. "The mesa has not been used regularly for hundreds of years. And even when it was, the steps were not the way most used to get to the top."

"What, you've got an elevator around here?" Rast asked. "Because that would be nice."

She frowned. "I refer, of course, to the fact that the Counselor usually flew to the top of the high mesa and took his Lyzel with him. But what is this 'elivador' you speak of?"

"Oh," Sophia jumped in. "It's a sort of box with cables on the top that runs up and down between floors in a tall building. You press the button for the floor you want and it stops there and you get out. It's much faster than climbing the stairs."

Lissa looked thoughtful. "I have no 'elivador' as you call it, but I might be able to make something like it. Tell me," she said, looking at Nadiah. "Would you trust my powers to raise you to the top of the mesa? I have never reached so far myself but I am certain I could do it."

Nadiah took another look at the narrow, crumbling steps that wound around the steep face of the stone wall. She imagined herself clinging to the wall like an insect, inching her way up, step by step, while the hot desert wind gusted through her hair, trying to pull her back down to the sandy rainbow floor. No—I can't do that. It's too much, too high. She nodded gratefully at the young priestess. "Of course I trust you. Thank you, Lissa. Thank you with all my heart."

The young priestess blushed with pride. "You are welcome—it is my pleasure and privilege to serve you. Would you please all group yourselves together?"

Sophia and Sylvan came up behind them and Rast picked up Nadiah again, over her protests. "Forget it," he murmured, under his breath. "If we're going a thousand feet straight up into the air on a platform of moving sand, I'm keeping you close."

Nadiah gave up without much of a fight. To be honest, she was glad he insisted on holding her. Being able to close her eyes and put her head on his shoulder greatly mitigated her crippling fear of heights.

"Get ready," Lissa said quietly and then the sand firmed under them as it had before and slowly began to rise.

"Wow," Nadiah heard Rast murmur. "This view is amazing."

A quick peek showed that he was right—it was amazing the way they were slowly lifting up into the clear blue sky and leaving the multicolored desert below them. Amazing and extremely frightening. Quickly she shut her eyes again and buried her face in Rast's shoulder.

"You will get used to such sights quickly when you soar above the clouds," Lissa said softly.

"You mean when my wings, finally sprout." Rast sighed. "God, I can't believe I just said that. Somebody call the loony bin and reserve me a room."

"The wings are no joke, Rast," Sylvan said from behind them. "According to legend, they're made of the same corporeal material as the Goddess herself—they are a part of her, grafted onto her most trusted servant, if you will."

Rast sighed again. "Yeah, well, I'll believe it when I see it."

"If you will forgive me for saying so, you do not sound very happy about the idea of gaining your wings or living here on First World," Lissa murmured. "Perhaps our planet does not seem beautiful to you?"

"Oh no, it's lovely," Sophia protested politely. "It's just, well...I don't think Rast expected to have to stay here, you know, forever. Not that he doesn't want to," she added hastily. "He and Nadiah both, I'm sure they'll be happy once...once they get used to it..." She trailed off and Nadiah was positive she was blushing—though she wasn't about to open her eyes and make sure.

"I am certain they will be very happy," Lissa said quietly. "It does take some getting used to. I myself am not native to this world.

I came—was forced to come—to join the priestesshood here, though I didn't want to. You could almost say I was exiled to First World, just as you and your female are, Counselor ." She nodded at Rast.

"Oh really?" Rast sounded interested. "And where did you come from?"

"My parents were part of the Tarsian trade," Lissa answered. "My father was a First Kindred and my mother was a female of Tarsia. It was she who decided I should come back to my father's home planet and dedicate my life to the service of the Goddess."

"Was there no one to speak for you?" Sylvan asked. "No one to protest your exile?"

My..." Lissa paused slightly. "My...forgive me, I'm not certain what word you would use but for the purposes of my planet it was my older brother. He spoke for me but he was overruled."

"I have heard of that trade," Sylvan said. "But I thought most of the Council was against it—they said there weren't enough of your people yet to make a good genetic base."

"So they did." Lissa nodded. "But a few Kindred warriors defied them and came to us anyway."

"What does it matter how many people there are?" Sophia asked.

Lissa's voice dropped. "I think the Council feared there would be...inbreeding. And given the particular abilities of my people, any genetic flaws that resulted would be...dangerous."

"Dangerous?" Sophia asked. "Dangerous how?"

The young priestess sighed and Nadiah thought she sounded terribly sad. "My people are...different. The male warriors that result from the trade are not well accepted among the other, established Kindred races."

"I didn't even know there was a whole other branch of the Kindred. Why aren't they accepted?" Sophia said.

Sylvan cleared his throat. "The Tarsian Kindred have certain...powers. They are called the Touch Kindred by the rest of us."

"The Touch Kindred? Why?" Sophia wanted to know. Nadiah wanted to know too, so she was glad her friend was asking. All the rumors she'd heard about the Touch Kindred were ominous and a little frightening but she'd never actually met one before.

"The male warriors of my kind have the ability to manipulate things outside themselves in the way I manipulate and use the sand," Lissa said hesitantly.

"Oh, like telekinesis," Rast said. "I've had as much as I want of that shit." Nadiah felt him shudder and knew he was remembering the challenge of wills where he'd been forced to eat a mud worm.

"In a way," Lissa admitted. "But their powers are more... internal."

"Using their mental powers, they are able to 'touch' or manipulate the body of another. Specifically, they can 'touch' a female they want," Sylvan said, taking over when it became obvious the young priestess was too embarrassed to continue.

"Exactly," Lissa murmured and Nadiah could hear the shame in her voice.

"But...why is that a bad thing?" Sophia sounded confused. "It sounds like once they meet the woman they want to bond with, it would be, well, amazing."

"Their talents wouldn't be a problem if the Touch Kindred didn't have such unpredictable temperaments," Sylvan said. "But they tend to be volatile and erratic in the extreme. I'm afraid their abilities are not always used in the appropriate manner. For which the Council has banned them from the Mother Ship."

"That was one reason my mother insisted I come here," Lissa said. "She said she wanted a more stable life for me than the one she'd had." She laughed and it sounded very bitter to Nadiah. "You must admit, we have an abundance of stability out here in the deserts of First World."

"That you do," Rast murmured and Nadiah felt him shift from foot to foot restlessly.

"But...is there no hope for your people then?" Sophia sounded sorry for Lissa. "No way they'll ever be accepted by the other Kindred?"

"They are trying," the young priestess said. "Our population is quite large now and the rules which regulate who one may be joined with are quite strict."

"My understanding was that they were positively draconian," Sylvan murmured. "Is it true that you aren't allowed to be bonded to a person within your own clan?"

"Yes," Lissa murmured. "We must seek a mate outside our clan family. Even if there is no blood relation, a relationship between members of the same clan is considered disgusting and unthinkable. Completely taboo."

"But that's ridiculous," Sophia protested. "That's like saying you can't marry anyone from your home town just because you happen to live in the same place."

"It is the way of my people," Lissa said simply. "Or it was when I was one of them. Now I am simply a priestess and I have no more contact with my clan or..." She choked slightly. "Or anyone who is in it."

Despite what was happening in her own life, Nadiah couldn't help hearing the hurt in the other girl's voice. She'd make a good friend, she thought to herself as they rose slowly through the air. I'll have to remember that when all this is over. Maybe I can give her a zan-daro—what Sophia calls a 'make-over' and cheer her up. If they let priestesses have make-overs that is…

"Hey, looks like the elevator is almost at the top floor," Rast said, sounding worried. "Guess we'd better go get this over with."

At that, Nadiah dared to open her eyes again. She was treated to the dizzying sight of the multicolored desert floor hundreds of feet down below her as they hovered, seemingly in mid air on a paper thin layer of sand. With a gasp, she closed her eyes again and pressed her face to Rast's neck. Breathing in his dark, spicy scent made her feel a little better but she would still be glad once they were back on solid ground.

"Yes, here we are," Lissa said. "Thank you for trusting my abilities. I am sorry the journey took so long."

"Not at all," Sophia assured her as they all left the sand and stepped onto the mesa. "You should be in an elevator when some kid has pressed all the buttons and it stops on every floor! The ride you gave us was much smoother than that."

They all murmured their thanks and then Rast whispered to Nadiah, "It's okay, sweetheart. You can look now."

Nadiah opened her eyes and saw that the top of the mesa was covered in low maroon grass and blue bushes. The bushes formed a ring around the outside edge of the mesa though she thought they served more as a warning than a barrier. They weren't tall enough or thick enough to actually stop anyone from falling off.

At the far end there was some higher vegetation—two of the familiar purple and green trees Nadiah remembered from the sacred grove—grew close together, forming a kind of backdrop for the high priestess who was standing in front of them. She was frowning already—apparently she didn't approve of the way they'd reached the top. She probably wanted us to crawl up the steps on our hands and knees, Nadiah felt a rush of shame for the uncharitable thought but there was no denying that the high priestess had wronged her greatly. Considering the fact that she'd given Nadiah a deadly fever and was forcing the male she loved to stay in on First World the rest of his life, it seemed Nadiah could be forgiven a few snarky thoughts.

"Well, here we go," Rast murmured, looking down at her. "Are you ready?"

"As long as you are," Nadiah whispered. But she couldn't help feeling that something was wrong. She couldn't quite put her finger on it but something, somewhere was out of place. No, not something—someone, she thought. But how could that be? Besides themselves, the only people on the mesa were the high priestess and four of the other, lower priestesses including Lissa. So how—

"Come forward, supplicants." The high priestess's voice rang out, breaking Nadiah's train of thought. "Come forward and meet your fate."

* * * * *

Rast didn't like the whole 'meet your fate' thing—it sounded way too ominous considering the oath he was about to take. Still, there was nothing else to do but go forward. Nadiah asked to be put down and he set her gently on her feet but kept hold of her hand in case she tripped over the long maroon grass. Her growing weakness worried the hell out of him and he wondered how much longer it would be before the fever came back full force and carried her away.

No, can't think like that! he told himself sternly. That's not going to happen. I'm not going to let it happen! Unfortunately, the only way he could stop it was to suddenly sprout wings. And even though his shoulder blades itched like crazy and everyone else seemed to think it was perfectly possible, there was still a corner of Rast's mind that doubted. Still a part that asked, seriously, they expect me to fly?

He was a practical, driven man who had never been into any kind of science fiction or fantasy. Now he found himself right in the middle of the kind of scenario he would have scoffed at if he'd seen it in a movie or read it in a book. Here he was—the long lost son of a planetary ruler who had died a thousand years ago in a conflict with creatures so evil Rast couldn't even imagine them. And now he was coming back to claim his rightful throne and prove himself worthy of ruling by growing wings and flying all over the place. To Rast it seemed like a dream—or some ridiculous mindfuck. It was just too damn hard to believe. But I have to believe, he told himself grimly. If I don't, if I can't do this...

He looked over at Nadiah and couldn't finish his thought. She looked so frail and the dark circles around her eyes were like rings of bruises. Knowing that she wanted to walk to the priestess herself, Rast resisted the urge to pick her up again. But, God, all he wanted was to hold her close, to keep her from slipping through his fingers. To make her well, to make everything all right. Please, he thought, uncertain of who he was praying to but praying all the same. Please help me heal her. I love her so much! That has to count for something...

"Come no closer." The priestess held out a hand and they came to a stop about ten yards from her. Behind her, the two sacred trees rustled their thick branches in the high desert breeze.

Rast frowned as the warm wind blew his hair back from his forehead. What's that smell? Something familiar... familiar and unpleasant...Who...?

"We are gathered here today," the high priestess intoned, breaking his train of thought. "Gathered to bear witness to the oath of a new Counselor. The first Counselor that First World has had in a thousand years."

At this, the row of priestesses to her left hummed softly, as though in musical agreement. Rast wondered if that was part of the ceremony and supposed it probably was. It reminded him of a bumper sticker he'd seen once which said, The problem with real life is, it doesn't have any background music.

Suddenly he realized that the high priestess was speaking to him and he'd missed it. To his relief, she beckoned to him and he simply stepped forward, bringing Nadiah with him.

"No, Challa," the high priestess frowned. "Did you not hear me? I told you to come forward alone."

"Uh, sorry." Rast dropped Nadiah's hand but before he did, he looked back and gave Sylvan a significant look.

Understanding crossed the Blood Kindred's face and he and Sophia stepped forward as one, standing on either side of Nadiah to support her frail frame.

"Are you ready now?" The high priestess sounded impatient.

"Yes." Rast lifted his chin. "Yes, I'm ready," he repeated loudly.

"Very well. Then repeat after me. I, Adam Rast, being of the true blood of Counselor Kall of the First Kindred, do solemnly swear and avow before the Goddess and all her creation that I will protect First World."

Rast repeated the words and thought he was done but there was more — much more.

The priestess continued, "I will guard it, guide it and through the use of the Seat of Wisdom and the Eye of Foreknowledge, I will attempt to keep it and all of its habitants safe from harm or terror."

Dutifully, Rast repeated but the oath still wasn't over.

"I will choose a proper Lysell to help me bear these burdens and a fitting mate to bear me sons, that the blood of the Counselor of the First Kindred shall never die out. And…" The priestess gave him a significant look. "I shall nevermore leave but make First World my one and only home."

The words seemed to stick in Rast's throat but somehow he got them out. He felt a rush of anger at the priestess who was forcing him into this. After all, if she hadn't made Nadiah sick he would have had a choice. And though he didn't mind visiting his planet of origin, he certainly wouldn't have chosen to live here. Especially knowing he was supposed to rule over the whole thing—although from what he could see of the desert, there wasn't a whole lot to rule over.

The first thing I'm going to do when this is over is get Nadiah out of here, he vowed to himself. We'll take a tour of the whole damn planet—anything to get away from this desert. I may have to stay on First World but I'll be damned if I spend one minute more than I have to with the green eyed monster over there.

The blank green eyes of the high priestess flashed and he knew she'd picked up on some of his thoughts but Rast didn't give a damn. The only thing that mattered now was getting through this so he could save Nadiah. He was glad the ceremony seemed to be moving to its conclusion, although he was still wondering when his wings were supposed to sprout.

At last the priestess spoke a kind of benediction—"Unto thee, oh Goddess, Mother of All Life, we entrust these sacred vows along with the light of our eyes, the love of our hearts and the understanding of our minds. Unto thee be all glory given forever and unto the end of time."

Rast repeated dutifully and all the priestesses, who had been humming throughout the entire ceremony, murmured, "So be it."

"So be it," Rast echoed, nodding. When no one said anything else he looked at the high priestess. "Uh…is that all?"

"We are finished." She nodded gravely. "You have taken the vows and will be the next Counselor of First World."

"All right, well…" Rast craned his neck, trying to look over his shoulder. "So then where are the wings? Why can't I fly?"

The high priestess frowned. "You cannot fly because your wings still have not manifested—a clear sign that the female you have chosen is not fit to be your mate or the Lyzel to your Challa." She cleared her throat. "Seeing that is the case, I myself will undertake the roll."

"What?" Rast shook his head. "Oh no, I don't think so. I don't care what you say or how holy you are, I'm not sleeping with you, lady."

"Please. I do not seek to breed with you." She made a face, as though such an idea were completely distasteful. "But the Counselor must have a Lyzel—a female counterpart. Someone to represent the Goddess, someone to consult and see into the Eye of Foreknowledge with him. Traditionally, the office of Lyzel is filled by the Coucilor's mate but in this case, I think we will have to separate the rolls."

"Separate the rolls? What are you talking about?" Rast demanded.

"I am simply saying that though it is a heavy burden to bear, I am willing to take on the responsibilities of Lyzel. You can, of course, choose a mate for carnal relations from among our priestesses." She indicated the row of priestesses standing beside her. "Worry not for all of them are virgins and any would be a fitting match for the Counselor ."

Rast was beginning to get really angry at this point but somehow he managed to keep his fury in check. "Nadiah is the only woman I want," he growled. "And she's the only woman I'll accept as my mate and Lyzel."

"Impossible." The high priestess frowned. "The Lyzel is always a priestess. This Tranq Prime girl has had no training in the ways of the Goddess and she is of the wrong bloodline to bear your heirs. She must be put aside in favor of a more suitable candidate."

"Why, you...If you think—" Rast began but Sylvan took a step forward and put a hand on his chest.

"With all due respect, your holiness," he said in a low, angry voice. "Nadiah cannot be put aside. She and Rast already share a blood bond—a very strong one. Breaking it would kill my kinswoman which is not acceptable."

The high priestess frowned. "A blood bond, hmm?" She beckoned to Nadiah. "Come forward, my child."

Rast wanted to stop her but Nadiah had already stumbled forward, almost as though she couldn't disobey the summons. "Please," she whispered. "Rast and I love each other. We'll stay here but please don't try to part us."

The priestess ignored her. "I will look into you now," she proclaimed. "I will examine this bond and see what may be done about it." Taking Nadiah's face between her hands, she stared with her blank, emerald eyes into Nadiah's deep blue ones.

Rast saw Nadiah shudder and worried that whatever the priestess was doing was hurting her. But after only a minute, she released Nadiah who stumbled and would have fallen if Lissa hadn't run forward to catch her and put an arm around her waist.

"A fresh bond and one which isn't sealed yet," the high priestess announced. "I can break it easily and graft it to another male, ensuring that this little female will live—so long as you are able to fly her to the Healing Garden, Challa." She eyed his still wingless back disapprovingly.

"I don't want the bond grafted to anyone else," Rast growled. "Nadiah is mine. Besides, who would you even find to graft it to in this place? As far as I can see Sylvan and I are the only males for miles around."

"She can graft it to me, of course." As if by some evil magic, the thick branches behind the priestess rustled and a familiar figure appeared from behind the sacred trees.

"Y'dex!" Nadiah's already pale face went suddenly snow white with fear.

"Hello, my lovely." Y'dex's thin lips pealed back into a nasty grin, his pale blue eyes bulging greedily. "Didn't I tell you it wasn't over between us?"

"Nadiah, get over here!" Rast lunged forward but Y'dex was closer. But before Rast could reach her, he was right behind Nadiah with one long arm snaked around her waist and fishbelly-white fingers wrapped around her throat.

"I think not," he murmured, smiling unpleasantly. "From the moment I heard that my little Nadiah was going to First World, I knew I had to come and claim her. Your own parents told me— wasn't that kind of them, my lovely?" he asked Nadiah who didn't answer.

"How did you even get here?" Sophia demanded. "I thought only the Kindred Mother Ships had the ability to fold space."

"I'm sure you'd love to know that." Y'dex smirked. "Let's just say the Kindred aren't the only ones with interstellar jumping abilities now." He squeezed Nadiah's neck until she gasped and then released her slowly, grinning at Rast.

"Take your hands off her," Rast growled, his vision going red.

"Why should I?" Y'dex sneered. "I'll touch her as much as I want. After all, Nadiah is mine."

Hearing his own words echoed back at him and seeing another man's hands—Y'dex's hands—on his female's body, made Rast feel like he was losing his mind. A fury so strong it was almost insurmountable rose within him, threatening to drown him in a tidal wave of angry red.

"Hold," he heard Sylvan murmur and felt the big warrior's restraining hand on his chest. "Going into rage won't help you now," Sylvan whispered fiercely. "You have to keep control of yourself, Rast. Keep control of yourself and the situation or everything is going straight to the seven hells."

He's right. Sylvan's right. Everything's going to go to hell if I can't keep it together. With a huge effort, Rast swallowed the anger that wanted to engulf him. Taking a deep breath, he looked at the high priestess. "I can see what you're trying to do," he said grimly. "But it isn't going to work."

The high priestess frowned. "Whatever are you talking of, Challa?"

"I'm talking about this. All this." Rast made a motion with his arms as though to encompass the whole planet. "There hasn't been a ruler here for a thousand years so you, being high priestess, are ruler by default. A pretty sweet gig if you get off on being the queen of the desert. And I think you do, your Holiness."

The high priestess's face had begun to grow red. "I never..."

"But then I showed up on your radar and suddenly you realized you're going to have to share. Not only with me, but with my chosen wife too. Now instead of being first in line, you're going to be bumped down to third. Bet you don't like that a bit, do you?" Rast growled.

"I have never even thought—" she began. But he wasn't done yet.

"So you decide to get the woman I love out of the way—either by illness or by letting this slimy, sadistic bastard take her back to Tranq Prime. That way you figure you'll have the second spot all sewed up." He laughed angrily. "Hell, maybe even the first spot if I'm too grief stricken to rule. Why, I'm sure you'd be more than happy to sit on that damn electric chair of a throne and look into the fortune telling soap bubble for me. You'd rule and judge and make pronouncements until you were blue in the face—all on my behalf. Am I right?"

"Only the Counselor may sit upon the Seat of Wisdom and use the Eye of Foreknowledge," the high priestess said stiffly. "Although as Lyzel I would, of course, rule in your stead if you were to become incapacitated. That is the way it has always been."

"You don't say? What a fucking shock." Rast glared at her. "Well there's about to be a change right now. For starters, Y'dex is going to give me Nadiah back right now. If he doesn't, my first move as ruler is to demote you to last place on the feeding chain."

The priestess went suddenly pale. "You would not do such a thing. You could not!"

"As ruler of the whole goddamn planet I can and I will," Rast growled. "I don't know who makes the beds and scrubs the toilets around here but you can be her personal maid and that's where you'll stay, your Holiness, for the rest of your miserable life.

Because there is no fucking room for advancement for a nasty, conniving bitch like you on my planet."

She glared at him. "You speak out of turn, Adam Rast. You still have no wings to prove your rights. Until and unless your wings manifest, you are nothing but the Counselor in waiting, unable to sit on the Empty Throne or make judgments about anything."

"Wings or no wings, I don't give a damn." Rast stabbed a finger at her. "If any harm comes to Nadiah, I'm holding you directly responsible." He looked at Y'dex. "Give her back. Now."

Y'dex smirked. "I think not. I have the backing of the High Priestess of the Empty Throne for my claim to Nadiah. She's already promised to officiate at our joining herself."

"No!" Nadiah struggled weakly in his grip but he only laughed.

"Oh yes, my love." He laughed nastily. "Oh yes."

Rast glared at the priestess. "This is worst than I thought. You already made a deal with him before we even started here today?"

"He arrived shortly after you did and made his case." Her thin lips curved into a cruel smile. "I judged the matter and found that the honorable Y'dex was in the right and you were in the wrong. This Tranq Prime female will be his...now!"

As she spoke she made a swift tearing gesture with both hands. Rast felt a horrible wrenching sensation deep inside—it was as though someone had suddenly yanked one of his teeth from its socket without warning. Looking across at Nadiah, he saw that she felt the shock as well. She staggered, one hand pressed to her heart. Y'dex laughed and let her fall to the ground.

"Rast...the bond." Nadiah was on her knees, the maroon grass the color of dried blood against her white gown. She raised a hand to him but it was too late—the fragile blood bond between them had been severed.

"Nadiah!" He wanted to go to her but he was suddenly weak, all the strength leaking out of him as he lost the vital connection with the woman he loved. I knew it, he told himself angrily. Knew I should have sealed the bond when I had the chance. If I'd listened to my gut instinct, all this could have been avoided. But it was too late for regret — he had to do something now, before it was too late.

Rast forced himself to stand straight and stagger forward. "Nadiah, hold on," he rasped, holding out a hand to her. "Hold on, we'll get it back."

"That you will not." The priestess looked at Y'dex. "What are you waiting for, you fool — take the bond into yourself. Make her yours at once."

"I'm...trying." Y'dex had a look of deep concentration on his pale face. "Almost got it but... it's...slippery."

"No!" Suddenly Nadiah was on her feet. She stood swaying in the tall grass and Rast wondered how she even had strength to remain upright. He was afraid that any minute she might faint after losing the all important bond. "No," she said again, looking at Y'dex. "I...I'd rather die."

"What are you talking about, you little idiot?" he sneered. "You're not going to die. The priestess will lift the fever and you'll come home with me to Tranq Prime where you belong."

Rast couldn't believe what he was hearing. "So you lied about that too?" he demanded, staring at the high priestess. "All along you had the ability to heal her? To undo the damage you did?"

She shrugged. "I did what I had to in order to tie you to First World. Your vows cannot be unsaid and to break them now means death." A slow smile creased her ageless face. "With a new Counselor installed on the Seat of Wisdom, the whole of First World will have to listen and heed my decrees. Many have abandoned the old ways—it is time they were brought back with a vengeance."

"That's all you care about," Rast accused her. "Power."

She smiled. "What else is there? And speaking of power, without your wings, you have none. I'd advise you to fine a nice room in the lower halls and spend your days in quiet meditation. Leave the little female to your rival and the ruling of First World to me."

"I'll never—" Rast began but a curse from Y'dex cut him off.

"Nadiah, you little fool! Come back? What are you doing?"

Rast tore his eyes from the high priestess and saw something that made his heart jump into his throat. Nadiah was standing on the very edge of the mesa, beyond the boarder of blue-grey bushes. She was swaying, barely holding on to one of the slender, vine-like branches and looking like a strong breeze might blow her over the side at any minute.

"Nadiah," he whispered. "Please, sweetheart, be careful."

"I'm sorry, Rast." Her lovely dark blue eyes were filled with despair. "But I'm not going back to Tranq Prime. I...I'd rather die than do that. Than be without you and be stuck with Y'dex."

"Nadiah..." Y'dex was slinking toward her, the look of intense concentration still on his face. "Nadiah, come here. I command you to come here right now." Suddenly, he lunged for her.

With a cry, Nadiah stumbled back, trying to elude his grasp. And then, without a another sound, she fell off the edge of the mesa and into the wide blue sky below.

"Nadiah!" Her name was torn from Rast's throat—a cry of despair and devastation. Without thinking what he was doing, he ran forward, toward the spot where she'd disappeared.

"Rast," he heard Sylvan shout. "Rast, you can't!"

He paid no attention. The itching in his shoulder blades had become a fierce burning now, as though someone had doused his back in gasoline and set it alight. But Rast didn't care—didn't care about anything but getting Nadiah back. Or dying with her if he couldn't.

Without hesitation he dived over the edge of the mesa, aiming for the rapidly descending female form in the fluttering white gown. He felt his shoulder knock into something solid as he went and dimly heard a hoarse gasp in his ear. But only part of him registered that Y'dex was also falling, screaming and flailing as he went. Most of his mind was completely occupied with the idea of getting to Nadiah.

Have to get her. Have to hold her, he thought disjointedly as he streamlined his body, making himself into a living arrow aimed at his target. He didn't know why but it seemed very important that he feel her in his arms one last time. Even if they were both destined to smash into the desert floor below, he wanted to do it with Nadiah pressed to his chest as she whispered his name.

They were both falling fast but he weighed considerably more and soon he was right beside her in mid air. The ground was coming up rapidly to meet them and he knew he had only seconds before they made impact.

"Nadiah!" he shouted and she turned her head, a strangely serene look in her dark blue eyes. Rast held out his arms and suddenly she was in them, her white gown fluttering in the wind like so many feathers.

Feathers, he thought and wondered why it should seem so important.

"I love you," she mouthed and he nodded and held her close.

This is it, he thought as the sandy ground reached up hungrily to greet them. This is where we di—

Suddenly the ground swooped away and they were sailing upward again. Rast was dimly aware of something extending to either side of them, something shining and silvery and nearly translucent in the green sunlight. What the hell? he thought, frowning. Are we hang gliding somehow? But where did the glider come from? And how—?

"Rast!" he heard Nadiah laughing in sheer delight and looked to see her grinning at him. "Your wings," she shouted over the wind whistling in their ears. "You have wings—you saved us!"

"Wings?" He was dimly aware that the horrible burning pain in his back was gone and yes, the strange hang glider like things on either side of them did appear to be attached to him somehow. He could feel the drag of the wind, the push and pull of the air currents deep in his shoulders as they glided along. But he wasn't making any kind of effort to fly—it was almost as though he didn't have to. As though the wings that had miraculously sprouted from his back knew how to take the initiative and keep him aloft themselves. Except…how the hell could that be?

Don't worry about how, whispered a little voice in his brain. Worry about what comes next—what you can do to cure Nadiah. Looking to his left, he saw they were flying close to the holy mountain. In fact, they were almost at the level of the Healing Gardens now. That's it, he thought. That's where I need to take her. Have to get her to the fountain so she can drink and be healed.

The minute he thought it, the wings stroked through the sky and their position changed subtly. Holding Nadiah close to him, he searched for a good landing place. It was time to do what he'd set out to do in the first place—heal the woman he loved.

Chapter Thirty-three

Nadiah was dizzy from the great height she and Rast were soaring at. Dizzy but exhilarated too. Though they were much higher than they had been on top of the mesa, she felt no fear. She was safe in the arms of the male who loved her. Safe and serene.

The moment was both beautiful and surreal. They went gliding through the air with Rast's huge, silvery wings stretched to either side of them, the feathers flashing in the sunlight. The sky vaulted overhead like a huge blue bowl and far off the sharp cries of avian hunters rang out. Nadiah had never felt such joy. *This is how it's supposed to be between the Challa and his Lyzel,* she thought. *This joy, this pleasure and love and excitement. He takes her flying often—it's one of the things that bonds them together.*

She didn't know how she knew that, but somehow she did. This flight—this mating flight—was a sacred ritual between the Counselor and his female. It had been lost for centuries but now that Rast was here, back where he belonged, it could be resurrected, like all the old customs.

Looking down she saw Sylvan and Sophia waving at them and the high priestess standing there with a stricken expression on her face. *She never expected him to get his wings,* Nadiah thought and knew it was true. *She wanted him tied to First World for the extra power it would give her but she thought she'd be able to use him as a puppet while she was the power behind the throne—literally.* Well, that wasn't going to happen. Rast wasn't the type of male likely to allow another to dictate to him. Maybe the high priestess should look for another line of work.

"There—the Healing Garden," Rast said and her attention was torn from the high mesa and directed to the lush, verdant garden which grew from the side of the mountain. Another oasis, she thought. An oasis of healing.

And it was healing she desperately needed. Now that the first wild exhilaration of flight had worn off, she was beginning to feel both the fever and the severed bond. The fever made her shiver with cold one moment and hot as an oven the next, while the broken bond felt like a deep blood vessel in her soul which had been cut. From its ragged end, all her strength was rapidly leaking away.

"Rast," she whispered. "Hurry. Please hurry."

"Going as fast as I can, sweetheart," he promised as they hovered over the small patch of green and purple jungle. "I've just never done this before. Not quite…sure how to land."

But as he spoke, the wings seemed to sense his desires. The silvery feathers cupped the warm desert air gently and slowly, they descended. Soon Rast's feet touched the ground and the wings folded surprisingly small and flat against his back.

"Nice… landing," Nadiah murmured. She wanted to examine his new wings, to look around the Healing Garden which reminded her of a wilder version of the sacred grove back on the Kindred Mother Ship. But her run to get away from Y'dex and the rush of excitement during the flight had used up her last reserves of strength. Grey and black blotches were appearing in her vision which made it hard to see…hard to think. Dimly she was aware of her own raspy breathing.

"Hold on, sweetheart." Rast sounded nearly panicked as he held her close to his chest and began striding through the underbrush.

"Just got to find the fountain. It's gotta be around here somewhere — this place really isn't that big. I just..."

He stopped suddenly and Nadiah wondered why. "Rast?" she whispered, having to force out the words. "Rast is...is everything...all right?"

"No," he whispered brokenly. "No. Oh, no."

She wanted to ask what was wrong, wanted to comfort him and tell him she loved him no matter what. But the grey and black blotches had grown until they obscured her entire field of vision.

Nadiah didn't want to faint — she was afraid if she did, she might never wake up again. The idea of never again opening her eyes, of never seeing Rast's smile or hearing his deep laughter made her want to cry. Please, she thought. Please, I don't want to go. I'm not ready. Not ready to leave him.

But though she tried desperately to stay with him, the combined weakness of the fever and the severed blood bond were too much. Her last sight was of Rast's eyes — his truegreen eyes which had marked him as a Kindred from the first, even before his blood. Rast looked back at her and she saw those eyes were filled with tears.

Then she saw no more.

* * * * *

"No! No, it can't be. No!" Rast pounded the stone side of the empty fountain with helpless rage. It wasn't just empty, either. The elaborate structure — which was carved with all kinds of alien beasts he didn't recognize — was bone dry and looked like it had been for centuries.

"A drink from the fountain of the Healing Garden was said to cure any illness, no matter how severe." The words echoed in his head, teasing him — mocking him. A drink — she just needs one drink. But there was none to be had.

Well then, I'll heal her myself. Maybe if the bond is restored I can give her some strength, keep her going a little while longer until I can make that priestess bitch cure the fever. Closing his eyes, Rast concentrated with all his might—reaching out to the woman in his arms, trying to find the connection that had so recently been between them. Before, on Tranq Prime, he'd been able to feel the blood bond with no problem. But this time there was…nothing. Just nothing. It was like feeling around in a dark room for a light switch that wasn't there.

He didn't know how long he tried before he realized it was useless. Before he simply held her close, his tears falling on her pale, unmoving face.

She was gone and there was no bringing her back.

He looked hopelessly at the dry fountain. There would be no healing drink for Nadiah—no sudden and miraculous cure for the woman he loved. Everything that had happened—their frantic flight to First World, his unbreakable vows to stay there always, the desperate dive to the sandy floor of the desert—all had been for nothing.

Nothing.

His last foolish hope had been dashed to smithereens the way he should have been when he dove off the mesa. As he would have been if the wings hadn't suddenly manifested at the last possible moment.

Fucking wings, he thought savagely. What good are they now? What am I supposed to do with them except look like a freak? Twisting his head, he stared over his shoulder to glare at them bitterly.

Though they had moved seemingly of their own volition earlier, now the wings were folded flat against his back. In fact, they seemed almost ready to melt back into his skin making him wonder if they might be reabsorbed by his body whenever they weren't in use.

Use them now.

Rast jumped. It sounded like a thought but the idea had clearly come from outside of his head. From somewhere in the Healing Garden.

"What?" he said. "I mean, hello? Is anybody there?"

Only silence greeted his words and he felt like a fool. Who was he talking to? He was going crazy with grief, so upset he was hearing voices. He—

Use your wings. Enfold your beloved.

Okay, that time he had definitely heard something and it wasn't just in his head.

"How?" he asked and then answered his own question by flexing his shoulder blades. The huge, shining wings came out at once, as though they had been waiting for his summons. To Rast, they felt like an extra pair of arms and hands sprouting from his shoulders. Imagining them like that, he concentrated on getting them wrapped around himself and Nadiah's still form, lying in his lap.

Soon he and Nadiah were deep in a rustling nest of silvery, incandescent feathers. They formed a barrier against the world, a shield around himself and the woman he loved that nothing could get through.

Rast found that image strangely comforting. And he also found that something new was happening—something that seemed to involve not just his wings, but his entire body.

As the wings came together and their feathers interlocked, a strange rush of power came over him. It started slowly, as a tingling in his toes. Then it made its way up his calves and legs and thighs. By the time it hit his hips and chest it was rushing upward in such a dynamic, electric burst he thought the top of his head might fly off. It didn't though, he just felt different...filled with...something, some power, he didn't understand.

"What the hell?" he muttered, flexing the wings again. The power rushed up and down his body in bursts and he was dimly aware of having the hardest erection of his entire life. The strange electricity built and built until he felt like sparks might start shooting from his fingers and toes if it didn't dissipate soon. What was going on?

It is the power of your wings. Use it. Channel it into your beloved. This time the voice sounded slightly more urgent, as though Rast didn't have much more time.

"Channel it into Nadiah?" he said doubtfully. "But what if I hurt..." He trailed off as he looked at her lifeless body. Her chest no longer rose and fell and he was fairly sure if her heart was still beating it was only a faint stutter in her chest, soon to be silenced forever. The woman he loved was beyond hurt now. He had nothing to lose by trying.

"Here goes nothing, sweetheart," Rast whispered to her. Taking a deep breath, he cupped Nadiah's pale cheek in his hand and willed the power to surge from himself into her.

Please, he thought as he pushed the power into her. Please, I don't know who you are but please let this work.

At first there didn't seemed to be any effect except that he felt the power flowing from him into her, like a full cup pouring into an empty one. Only his own cup never ran dry—the power generated by his wings kept it flowing, always flowing.

Then the current seemed to shift somehow. To Rast's astonishment, he felt the power targeting the hidden, hurt spots inside Nadiah. It found the viruses causing her fever and eradicated every microscopic one of the little bastards. It filled her lungs with air and started her heart beating again. And then the current of healing power found the broken bond—not only Nadiah's end but Rast's as well. As he held her tight, he felt the warm, soothing flow as the current knit the two ragged ends together like an expert seamstress mending a garment.

When the last stitch pulled tight and they were back to where they'd been before the high priestess had interfered, Nadiah took a deep gasping breath and opened her eyes.

"Rast?" She sounded confused but completely herself. "Rast, I had the strangest dream."

"So did I. Thank God it came true." He blinked back tears. "Or the Goddess, I guess. Thank the Goddess."

There was no answer but he felt a sense of approval, as though the owner of the voice he'd heard was listening. There is a Goddess, he thought wonderingly. And whoever she is, she wants Nadiah and I to be together—together forever. He felt another, even stronger surge of approval and knew it was true. Somehow, even though they had been born on different planets in different galaxies, he and Nadiah had been made for each other. She was the only one who could complete him, the only one who could make him whole. And he was the only one who could do the same for her.

"Rast?" Nadiah was looking up at him anxiously. "Are you all right?" she asked.

"Are you?" he asked, giving her the question back.

She frowned, appearing to take some internal inventory. "Actually, I feel...wonderful. I'm still a little weak but the fever's gone." She looked at him uncertainly. "Did...did you do that?"

"I don't know," Rast said honestly. "Maybe not so much me as something—someone working through me...through the wings." He nodded at them.

"The Goddess," Nadiah breathed, her eyes shining. "But...are you all right? You have such a far away look in your eyes."

"I'm fine," he said firmly, pulling her closer. "Perfectly fine now that you're okay and our bond is back in place."

"Yes, I feel it too." She shifted in his arms. "It's back just the way it was before that awful priestess cut it. Thank the Goddess Y'dex wasn't able to regraft himself to me. Ugh." She shuddered. "I don't think I could have stood that."

"Don't think about him now," Rast said. Leaning down, he kissed her gently on the mouth. "Don't think about anything but us, here, now, alone."

To be honest, he wasn't quite sure that they were alone, but the presence in the garden seemed to be completely benevolent. He didn't think the Goddess would mind if he held the woman he loved.

"We are alone, aren't we?" Nadiah smiled. "Finally."

"Mmm-hmm." Rast kissed her again. "No parents to disapprove, no slimy ex- fiancée to get in the way," he murmured. "No one at all to interfere..."

"No one to interfere with what?" Nadiah asked a little breathlessly.

"With this." Rast traced with one finger down her jaw and throat and around to the low scooped neck of the gauzy white priestess gown she was wearing. "You know," he murmured, "I never realized how thin this material is. I can practically see right through it."

"Rast." Her cheeks were beginning to get pink with embarrassment and he thought how wonderful it was to see them flushed with life and health instead of fever.

"Sorry," he murmured. "I can't help it. You're just so beautiful."

"You're not too bad yourself...for a male with wings." She smiled at him and then nodded at the surrounding wings. "I like this you know—it's like having our own little private space right in the middle of the garden." She stroked the sleek, iridescent feathers gently with her fingertips.

A shiver of pleasurable sensation ran through Rast's entire body, surprising him. It felt like a warm, gentle hand was stroking him, caressing his entire body whenever Nadiah touched the wings.

No, not just the wings—my wings, he thought. As strange as it might seem, he was beginning to think of the new feathered appendages as being part of him—part of his body.

Nadiah must have noticed his reaction because she pulled her hand away. "Did that hurt?" she asked, looking at him anxiously. "You shivered and I thought—"

"No, really, don't stop. It felt good." Rast gave her a hungry look. "Really good."

Nadiah stroked him again, petting the individual feathers. "They're so amazing. They saved us, you know—if they hadn't come out—manifested at just the right time...."

"I know." Rast arched his back as the warm stroking sensations increased. Looks like I've just grown a whole new erogenous zone, he thought. A damn big one.

"Did you do it on purpose?" Nadia asked. "I mean, did you consciously think about making them come out when you came after me?"

Rast shook his head. "No, that was the last thing on my mind. All I could think about was getting to you—holding you one more time before... well, before the end, I guess."

Her eyes widened. "So you just dove after me, thinking you were going to die?"

He shrugged, making the feathers rustle. "I guess so. I just knew I couldn't be without you."

"Oh, Rast..." Leaning forward, she buried her face in his neck for a moment. "I love you," she whispered brokenly. "Love you so much."

"I love you too, sweetheart." He kissed the top of her head and cradled her close, breathing her in, loving the feel of her in his arms.

At last she sat up and wiped her eyes. "Sorry." She sniffed. "I just...I can't believe you would..." She shook her head, unable to continue.

"It's okay," Rast assured her, stroking her hair. "Everything is going to be okay now. I promise."

She gave him a slightly watery smile. "I think you're right."

"I know I am."

"But the wings..." Nadiah began stroking them again. The delicate feeling of her fingers caressing him was driving Rast crazy.

"Yeah, what about them?" he asked hoarsely.

"Well, they came out when you came after me," Nadiah said, sounding thoughtful. "Do you think...does that mean I am the right female for you after all?"

"Sweetheart, you're the only female for me," Rast assured her. "You know that, don't you?"

"Now I do." She gave him a tentative smile. "For awhile there, though, I was worried that I might be impeding your progress. You know, keeping you from answering your higher calling as the Counselor of First World."

"You could never do that." Making a decision, Rast cupped her cheek and looked into her face. "Enough about my wings—let's talk about your eyes. Have I told you what a beautiful color they are?"

Nadiah bit her lip. "Yes," she whispered. "Several times, I think."

"Because it's true—your eyes are the most gorgeous shade of blue I've ever seen." He paused for a moment. "But I never want to see it again."

"What?" Nadiah looked at him uncertainly. "What do you mean, Rast? You're scaring me a little."

"I mean..." He stroked her cheek tenderly. "After our time together here in this garden, I never want to see that shade of blue again. I want to change it. I want to change you."

"Oh, Rast..." Understanding bloomed on her face and her cheeks were flushed with pleasure. "Are you sure? I thought you wanted to wait until we were joined."

"That was before," Rast told her. "I wanted to prove to Sylvan that I was a man of my word—to let him know he could trust me to take care of you."

"I'm sure he can't dispute that now." Nadiah smiled. "Not after you dived off a cliff for me."

Rast grinned. "Actually, now I don't care what he thinks. What anybody thinks. Remember how I told you that I always follow my gut instinct and it never plays me wrong?"

She nodded. "You said you trusted your intuition. Why?"

"Because I had a feeling, back when we were coming home from Tranq Prime—a feeling like if I didn't claim you then, that I might lose you. I ignored that feeling and look what happened—this whole mess with the crazy priestess could have been avoided if I'd just listened to my instinct."

"That's true." Nadiah nodded. "But you also never would have come to First World and learned your true identity. And you never would have gotten your wings either. That would have been a shame." She ruffled his feathers again and Rast groaned with pleasure.

"God, that feels amazing. I think it gets better every time you do it."

She laughed. "Good. I have a whole new way to touch you."

"And I want to touch you in a new way too," Rast reminded her gently. He couldn't keep the need out of his voice, the hunger he felt to touch her, to take her. "I need you, sweetheart," he murmured, kissing the side of her neck again. "Need to be inside you."

Nadiah shivered with pleasure. "I want that too. In fact…Rast, can I tell you something?"

"Anything," he assured her. "Anything at all."

"All right, well, this might sound strange but now that I'm better I feel so…so…"

Suddenly Rast knew exactly what she was feeling. It was as though, when they were touching her, the wings gave him powers of perception that extended from his own body directly into hers.

"Hot?" he finished for her, raising an eyebrow. "Wet?"

Nadiah blushed and nodded. "I know it's not right. I was nearly dead just a few minutes ago but now…well, it's like my entire body is tingling. And I need...I need...I don't know what I need," she ended in obvious frustration.

"I do." Rast gave her a lazy smile. "Will you let me give it to you? Will you let me change the color of your eyes?"

"Yes," she whispered. "With all my heart, yes. Do...do you think we can do it like this? I mean, surrounded like this?" She indicated the protective way his wings still encircled them.

"I'm sure we can. In fact, I want to." Rast gave her a hungry look. "It feels right this way. It's like I have you all to myself. Like we're in our own private world."

"I feel that way too," Nadiah murmured softly. Pressing forward, she rubbed her breasts against his bare chest.

"God, sweetheart!" Rast groaned. He could feel the tight little buds of her nipples though the thin white material of her gown. It made him feel like he might explode if he didn't take her soon.

"I want you to change the color of my eyes," she said. "I want to give myself to you completely."

"Good, because I can't wait anymore" he growled and took her mouth in a ruthless, hungry kiss that made her moan and cling to him even tighter.

Mine, he thought as he had so often before, but this time it was true. He was going to make it true and claim her properly. And Rast swore to himself that when he was finished, no one would ever be able to take the woman he loved away from him again.

* * * * *

Nadiah couldn't wait to be naked with him. She shed the thin white robe and her blue sash tharp and tossed them away to land in the Healing Garden. Rast got rid of his jeans as well and then she sat in his lap and leaned back, enjoying the feel of his wings stroking her naked skin.

Both of them groaned at the soft brush of feathers against flesh and Nadiah knew Rast was getting as much pleasure out of the contact as she was. It was as though some kind of current was running between them—a current of power and pleasure that built and grew stronger with each touch.

Goddess, wonder if I could come like this? she thought as the feathers brushed the tight buds of her nipples and slipped softly between her legs. It seemed entirely likely that she could but she didn't get a chance to find out. Because just then Rast's big, warm hands replaced the feathers, caressing her breasts and cupping her hot pussy mound.

Nadiah moaned as she felt two thick fingers spreading the lips of her pussy so he could stroke her slippery petals.

"Mmm, you are wet, aren't you my little numala?" he murmured hoarsely.

Nadiah felt herself blushing, the hot blood rushing to her face. But there was no way she could deny it. "Yes," she whispered. "I...I can't help it."

"Don't want you to help it. You think you're wet enough to take me?" Reaching between them, he grasped his thick shaft and slowly, teasingly, rubbed the broad head against her open pussy.

"Oh!" Nadiah gasped and threw back her head as his cock slipped hotly over her swollen clit. "I...yes, I think so," she whispered.

He shook his head and slowly withdrew his shaft. "If you're not sure, you're not ready."

"What? No, don't stop!" Nadiah protested. "Please, if you'll just—"

He laughed softly. "Don't worry sweetheart, I'm not stopping. I just need to spend a little time getting you ready."

"Oh?" Nadiah began to smile again. "And how…how are you going to do that?"

"Like this." Suddenly she was lying on her back on the ground, though she could barely feel the green and purple grass because of the soft, incandescent feathers that cushioned her body.

"Is this okay?" she asked a little anxiously, indicating the wings. "I mean, does it hurt when I lie on them?"

"Not at all." He smiled. "It feels like…almost like I have another set of arms to hold you with. I like it."

"I like it too," Nadiah confessed, arching her back and rubbing her shoulders against the feathers until he groaned.

"That's enough of that," he murmured with mock sternness. "Now it's my turn." He was leaning over her, between her thighs as though he intended to make love to her then and there. But Nadiah thought he had a different idea.

It turned out she was right.

He began at her lips, taking her mouth in long, slow, hot kisses that made her moan and want more. But Rast was in no hurry. It seemed to take forever for him to lick a ticklish trail down to the hollow of her throat and then make his way to one of her aching nipples. By this time Nadiah was reminded of his preference to "take it slow." She only hoped she wouldn't go insane by the time he finally reached the area south of her navel.

But Rast surprised her. He sucked both her nipples briefly, nipping them gently to make her squirm, and then began to lick a path down her trembling abdomen almost at once. Nadiah felt the power surge between them again as he split her thighs wide and rubbed his rough cheek against her pussy mound.

"So good," he groaned softly as he bathed in her scent and marked her with his own. "God, you smell so good, sweetheart. So hot and wet and ready for me."

"I am ready, please Rast..."

She didn't have to beg for long. Spreading her wide with his fingers, Rast flattened his tongue against her sensitive inner pussy and took a long, loving taste.

Nadiah cried out and bucked up to meet him, reveling in the sensation of his hot mouth on her tender cunt.

"Beautiful," Rast murmured and kissed her pussy gently, almost as though he was kissing her mouth. "You have the most beautiful little virgin pussy, sweetheart. It's so pink and innocent looking. But at the same time you're all swollen and wet so I can tell what you need."

"What...what do I need?" Nadiah asked breathlessly.

"Why, more kisses of course." Looking up briefly he gave her a teasing smile, and then returned to the business at hand. This time he dropped tiny, soft kisses all over her mound and pussy lips before finally going back to her core.

"Rast, please!" Nadiah begged. Somehow she found her hands were buried in his hair, tugging with abandon as she tried to lead him back to the place she needed him most.

"Patience, sweetheart," he murmured, grinning. "Take it easy. Take it slow."

"No!" Nadiah wiggled her hips and moaned as he lapped her again, taking time to circle her clit with the tip of his tongue until she thought she was going to go mad. "No, I don't want to wait anymore. I want you inside me now."

Rast gave her a teasing smile. "Your wish is my command." Spreading her thighs even wider with his broad shoulders, he bent his head and Nadiah felt something hot and wet thrust into her slippery entrance.

"Goddess, Rast!" she moaned as he thrust his tongue even deeper into her cunt. This wasn't what she'd meant but it felt amazing just the same. She loved the feel of his tongue moving in and out of her, fucking her so deliciously. And it was evident Rast loved tasting her. He growled hungrily as she pressed against him, trying to get even deeper contact with his tongue. Nadiah felt his arms wind around her legs and his fingers gripped her thighs to hold her in place as he lapped and sucked and tonguefucked her until she could barely breathe.

"Oh...oh please...please..." She couldn't help begging, couldn't help the low, broken moans that came from her throat. She was so open for him, so vulnerable and yet she wanted to give more, to bare her very soul to him as she was baring her body. She tugged at his hair with trembling fingers and bucked hard against his mouth, pressing up to meet the rhythm of his tongue inside her cunt. She was close, so close to coming but she needed something...something more.

If only it was just a little harder...if only it could go a little deeper...

As though sensing her need, Rast pulled back panting, and looked in her the eyes. "I think you're ready now, sweetheart. As ready as I can make you, anyway. And you're close, aren't you? Close to coming?"

Nadiah nodded. "So close. Please, Rast..."

"I knew you were." He licked her open pussy again and gave her a lazy smile when she moaned. "The only question is, do you want to finish with my tongue inside you...or my cock?"

It was no contest. "Your...your cock," Nadiah whispered. "Please. Your cock. I need you inside me so much, Rast. I swear I'm ready now."

"Yes, I think you are." Sliding up the length of her body he kissed her mouth, giving her the sweet, salty taste of herself on his tongue. Then he wrapped his arms around her and sat up, bringing them back to where they'd been before with him sitting on his knees and Nadiah facing him in his lap.

"You're sure this is the way...the way you want to do it?" Nadiah asked uncertainly. "I thought maybe you'd want to be on...on top of me."

"Not the first time." Rast shook his head. "I want to take this slow and easy and really be able to look into your eyes while we make love."

"Then, please, Rast. I can't wait any longer," Nadiah moaned softly. Her desire for him was so great that the urgency she felt to have him in her was almost painful.

Rast seemed to sense it because he didn't try to draw out the foreplay anymore. "All right then, sweetheart. Look down a minute."

Nadiah looked and caught her breath at the erotic sight. Rast had grasped his shaft in one hand and positioned himself so that the broad head of his cock was poised just at the entrance to her wet channel.

"On the count of three I want you to lower yourself down," he told her softly. "Come down as fast or as slow as you want, just don't hurt yourself. You've never done this before so it might feel a little tight."

"I don't care about that." Nadiah pressed against him, watching as the thick head of his cock began to slide into her open pussy. "Don't care about anything but having you inside me."

"Hey." Rast gave a hoarse sounding chuckle. "You're supposed to wait for the count, remember?"

"Then start counting," Nadiah told him. "I need you in me."

"All right then, my eager little virgin," he murmured. "One...two..."

"Three," Nadiah gasped and pressed down with her hips, taking half of his thick shaft inside herself in one swift motion.

"God!" Rast's deep voice was tight and his fingers dug into her ass reflexively.

"Oh!" Nadiah gasped at the same time. For her part, she was feeling both pleasure and pain. It felt amazing to finally have Rast inside her, even if it was only halfway. But there was no denying the sharp, stretching feeling she got from having such a thick shaft lodged deep inside her.

Rast must have seen the pain on her face because he looked at her anxiously. "You okay, sweetheart?"

"Fine, just...give me a minute," Nadiah gasped. She held perfectly still, concentrating on the feeling of his thick girth filling her. After a moment the pain receded leaving only the pleasure of having him inside her. "Better now," she told him, smiling. "I, uh, guess maybe I shouldn't have done that, huh?"

"Maybe not." Rast's voice was slightly strangled. "You want me to pull out?" he asked. "We could —"

"No." Nadiah shook her head emphatically. "I want you inside me. I need you, Rast. I just...I'll try to go slower for the, uh, second half." They both looked down to where his thick shaft was impaling her, stretching the entrance to her pussy wide.

Rast gave a low groan at the erotic sight. "Got that's hot, sweetheart," he murmured. "So fucking hot to see my cock stretching your sweet little pussy open like that."

"I like it too," Nadiah admitted breathlessly. "But I'd like it better if…if you were all the way in."

"Come down, then." Rast gave her a look of pure lust. "Come down all the way and let me fill you up." He kissed her softly on the mouth. "But slowly, this time, all right? I want to watch while you take my cock all the way inside your pussy."

His hot words coupled with the gentle kiss made Nadiah feel like she was burning up inside. With a little moan, she braced herself on his shoulders and slowly let the tight muscles of her thighs relax.

She wasn't sure it would work, wasn't sure he would be able to enter her if she wasn't pressing down to force the issue. But Rast had done a damn good job preparing her and though she was tight, her pussy was incredibly wet and slick, ready and eager to finish the job she had started.

Biting her bottom lip, she slowly relaxed and watched as the rest of Rast's thick shaft disappeared inch by thick inch into her pussy. It was an incredibly hot sight but even better was the feeling of completion, of oneness she felt with him when the broad head pressed against the end of her channel to kiss the mouth of her womb.

This is how he'll do it, she thought, feeling her stomach flutter with anticipation. This is how he'll change the color of my eyes.

"You're right, sweetheart," he murmured and Nadiah realized she'd spoken the thought aloud. "But first we have a little business to attend to. First I need to fuck you."

The hot words and the way he looked at her when he spoke, his deep voice gravelly with desire, made Nadiah feel like she might go crazy if he didn't fulfill his promise soon. "Then do it," she whispered, wiggling her hips tauntingly. They both moaned at the delicious friction her action caused. "Do it because I want you to, Rast. Because I need you to."

"I need it too, sweetheart," he admitted. "Are you ready? Nothing hurts?"

"It feels amazing," Nadiah admitted. "It doesn't hurt at all. I just want more."

He grinned at her hungrily. "That's good because 'more' is exactly what I'm going to give you." Then, gripping her ass, he lifted her slowly until his thick shaft was almost all the way out of her. "Here we go, sweetheart. Hold on tight, it's going to be a wild ride."

They both moaned as he slid back into her, pressing hard and deep to fill her to the core. He held still for a moment and Nadiah felt him throbbing inside her, stretching her even when he wasn't moving. Then, when she didn't protest, he pulled out and thrust into her again, harder this time, as though the need to claim her completely had overcome him.

Nadiah was overcome with need too. She moaned and gasped as he pounded up into her, pressing hard against the end of her channel with every thrust, building the pleasure that was growing inside her like an explosion waiting to happen—like a bomb waiting to go off. All around her body she could feel the feathers caressing her naked skin, teasing her nerve endings to even greater heights of pleasure, somehow forming a new, intense connection between herself and Rast she had never imagined was possible.

"Oh, Goddess…Oh, Rast!" Closing her eyes, she gripped his broad shoulders hard and spread her thighs even wider, trying to be open enough for his deliciously hard fucking. "Feels so good…so right."

"No, open your eyes."

"What?" His command surprised her. Nadiah looked at him and saw that his own truegreen eyes were blazing with lust and desire.

"Keep them open," Rast directed, thrusting even deeper and harder into her as he spoke. "I want to see…don't want to miss the moment when they turn."

"All…all right," Nadiah whispered. Leaning her forehead against his, she looked into his eyes, giving her all, making herself as open as she could as she worked her hips to the rhythm of their mutual pleasure.

""That's good," Rast growled softly. "Can't wait…to see it. Can't wait to make you come."

Nadiah didn't think she had far to go. The intensity of having him inside her, filling her and the jolting burst of pleasure she felt with each hard thrust as he pressed against the mouth of her womb was quickly pushing her over the edge. She just needed one more thing, just needed…she wasn't sure what she needed, but something to make her lose control completely. "Please, Rast," she gasped. "Please, I'm so close. I just can't…quite get there."

"I'll take you there, sweetheart." Rast moved one large hand from her ass to slide around in front where they were joined. Nadiah moaned as he found her pussy and the broad pad of his thumb came to rest directly on her sensitive clit. He stroked gently but firmly over her swollen button, sending shards of brilliant pleasure that radiated from her clit to every single part of her body.

Suddenly Nadiah couldn't take it any more. The feeling of being filled...of being fucked, taken and owned by the male she loved overcame her. The bomb which had been ticking inside her from the first suddenly went off—an intense internal explosion of pleasure. As if that wasn't enough, the feeling of Rast's feathers against her skin somehow magnified it, making her feel the orgasm in every part of her body at once.

Nadiah was lost—utterly lost and drowning in a sea of sensation. "Oh," she sobbed. "Oh yes...yes...Goddess, yes!"

"That's right, sweetheart, come for me," Rast growled. "Come hard, love to feel you coming all over my cock." He pulled out and then thrust into her one last time, shoving his shaft as deeply into her as he could. Then Nadiah felt him swell even bigger and suddenly he was coming, bathing the mouth of her womb in hot spurts as he held her tight against him.

A strange feeling began inside her. A feeling like she was melting from the inside out. A rush of heat enveloped her body, starting at her core, where Rast was inside her to the hilt, and ending in her eyes which felt like they were glowing like hot coals.

"Oh!' Nadiah gasped and clutched at Rast's shoulders. It wasn't a painful sensation but it was an intense one—once more, made even more intense by the soft feathers of his wings brushing every part of her naked body. Goddess, so good, her mind babbled. So good, so good, so good!

"I agree with you, sweetheart—it's incredible," she heard Rast murmur and realized that he was talking inside her head.

"Rast?" She looked at him in wonder as the intense pleasure finally began to ebb. "Rast can you...can you hear me?"

"Yeah, I can." He sounded surprised and a little confused. "Is this normal after sex?"

Nadiah felt the brush of feathers against her skin again and suddenly understood. "Not after regular sex—only after bonding sex," she sent through their new link. "It's the way Kindred warriors tie their females to them for life and every branch of the Kindred do it differently. Blood Kindred have to bite, Twin Kindred have to both take a female at the same time, Beast Kindred have to have their mating fist involved...I don't know about regular First Kindred but with you, I think it has to do with your wings—having them around me while we made love made a difference. It gave us a much deeper connection."

A look of cautious joy came over his face. "You mean this is really it? Nobody can ever separate us again?"

Nadiah nodded, feeling his joy overflowing through the link and filling her heart as well. "We just made a bond even deeper and stronger than the blood bond," she told him. "One that can only be broken by death. We'll be together forever now."

"I could have told you that before, sweetheart." Leaning forward, he took her mouth in a hot, possessive kiss. "Because I'm never letting you go ever again. By the way...your new eye color is beautiful. Even better than the original, if that's possible."

"Is it?" Nadiah put a hand to her cheek as though she could feel the new color. "What is it? What does it look like? Have my eyes gone a shade lighter?" She was certain they must have—her eyes were already such a dark blue they couldn't have gotten darker.

But Rast shook his head. Frowning, he cupped her cheek and studied her eyes intently. "Not lighter so much as they've changed to a whole different color," he murmured aloud. "Kind of a bluish-green."

"Blue-green? Really?" Nadiah was surprised. Of all the Tranq Prime females she'd ever know, none had ever had their eyes change to a whole different hue. Usually they just lightened or darkened a shade or two after the female in question surrendered her virginity.

"Yeah…" Rast smiled. "If I had to describe it I'd say…it's a perfect mixture of your old eye color and mine right now. It's beautiful—reminds me of the deep sea." He looked at her anxiously. "Is that all right?"

Nadiah gave him a trembling smile. "It…it's more than all right," she whispered as emotion overcame her. "Don't you see, Rast—I'm yours. I was meant to be yours all along and no one can say any different now. The proof…all the proof we'll ever need is here." She tapped the corner of her eye. "Right here."

He looked at her, bewildered. "Then why are you crying?"

"Because I'm so ha-happy." Nadia sniffed and tried to get herself under control. "I'm sorry I just…I feel like I belong to you now. And it makes me feel so safe and good and right."

"Oh, sweetheart." Rast pulled her close and his feathers rustled with the motion. "If you belong to me, then I belong to you too," he told her, his voice rough with emotion. "I'm yours and you're mine and nothing is ever going to come between us again—I swear."

Nadiah hugged him tight and buried her face in his neck. Another wave of emotion overcame her and she wept freely, unable to help herself. As the tears of happiness dropped from her new eyes, she knew Rast was right—they would never be parted again.

Chapter Thirty-four

Elise woke up with the strangest feeling that she had forgotten something—something very important. She looked around the small room she found herself in. It was comfortable and warm, but still very obviously a hospital room. The readout of her vitals above the bed she was in showed that. Beside the bed was a chair—an empty chair. Elise frowned. It wasn't supposed to be empty—she was sure of that. But who was supposed to sit in it? And what hospital was she was in?

Where am I?

The answer came back almost immediately. *The Mother Ship. The Kindred Mother Ship. But how did I get here?*

This time the answer wasn't so quick and easy. There was a frightening blank that made her break out in a cold sweat. Then, slowly, her memory started to fill it in.

She'd been walking in the park in Sarasota, the one with the Unconditional Surrender statue. It was based on the old picture from World War Two, where the sailor had the nurse bent over his arm and was kissing her senseless.

Okay, yes, I remember that.

She'd been looking at the statue, thinking that it was simultaneously romantic and unrealistic. Unconditional surrender, indeed. As if you could ever really give yourself so totally to someone else…Elise knew she couldn't. That way lay only pain and disappointment. She'd learned at an early age that you couldn't depend on anyone but yourself—had learned the hard way after— no, stop. Don't go there.

A picture appeared in her mind. A picture of an old-timey bank vault, one with a door that was a solid foot of stainless steel. Thick, heavy—nothing could get through it. Or out of it.

Keep it in the vault, she thought. Don't think about it now.

Elise nodded to herself. Yes, some things were better left in the vault. Now, as to her faulty memory—what had happened next?

I was looking at the statue. I was thinking about James and how he and I would never act like that. How we would never...

She frowned. Who was James? The name sounded familiar but no face rose from her mind to link to it. Instead, she saw a scarred man with one blue eye and one gold. Just like Buck.

She smiled. Buck, she remembered. He was good—no need to put that memory in the vault. Her stepfather had always complained that he was an ugly son-of-a-bitch but Elise hadn't minded the way he looked. Buck kept her safe—protected her. As long as he could, anyway...

Elise shook her head, the memories rattling in her mind like dice in a cup. She had to get back on track. Forget Buck and her stepfather for now—that was the distant past—ancient history. The question was, why would she be staring at the kissing statue and thinking of someone she didn't know? Someone called James?

No, the real question is, what happened next?

Closing her eyes, Elise tried to remember.

A cheese grater. Felt like my whole body was put through a cheese grater—torn apart into a hundred tiny shreds. Then I was sucked back together inside someplace...someplace dark. There was metal everywhere—metal so cold it burned. It burned me because I was naked...

The memories were beginning to come now. Faster and faster and they weren't good. But now that they had started, Elise didn't know how to stop them.

There was a huge screen above my head and a machine with wires. Wires that hooked into my skin.

Elise looked down at her arms and saw the scars. They were tiny and pink, as though they'd only recently healed and most were so faint she could hardly see them. But they were definitely there. She stared at them, feeling sick.

That was where he put the wires. The wires that ran under my skin. And made pictures appear on the big screen—awful pictures. He opened the vault...dragged things out...things I didn't want to think about. Memories...secrets...

High, ugly laughter filled her ears and a hissing voice whispered in her head, "Ssso tasty, my dear. Your pain...ssso deliciousss..." Burning red eyes filled her vision and a boney, scabrous claw reached for her. But worse than that were the memories flashing on the huge screen above her head. Memories of what had happened so long ago...

No...No!

"What is it? What's wrong?" The nurse with blonde hair and grey eyes came rushing into her room and Elise realized she'd shrieked the last word aloud. But she couldn't help it, couldn't control herself. The flood of images wouldn't stop. The memories she'd buried so carefully had been dragged out of the vault like rotting corpses pulled from their graves. If she let them they would drown her, would drag her down with their putrid, decayed fingers locked around her throat...

"Buck!" she gasped, reaching out blindly, trying to find him. "Please, I need Buck..."

"I'm here." The tall man with the scarred face and eyes like Buck suddenly burst into the room. He was so huge he seemed to fill it completely and he came to her at once. Anyone else would have found him frightening but Elise remembered finding shelter in his arms. Whoever he was, he would keep her safe—he would protect her. She knew it instinctively to the core of her being.

The blonde nurse looked at the huge man in surprise. "How did you know she was awake?"

"I felt it." He didn't sound very happy about it. "I could feel her needing me all the way across the fucking ship. Got here as fast as I could." He looked at Elise. "You okay?"

"Please—" She held out her arms to him, like a child begging.

To her relief, the man didn't hesitate. He scooped her out of the bed and held her close. He was wearing a thin black sleeveless shirt that exposed his muscular arms and chest. Elise threw her arms around his neck and pressed her face to the hollow of his throat. His skin was warm and his scent was instantly comforting. Dark, smoky, animalistic, with a hint of fur and musk—all the smells she associated with safety.

Safe, I'm safe now, she told herself trying to regain control. All right—everything is going to be all right.

"You're all right now," the big man said, echoing her thoughts. "What happened, baby? Did you have a bad dream?"

"No." Elise shook her head, still pressed against his chest. "I...I woke up. And I remembered."

"What did you remember?" he rumbled. "What he did to you?"

"I don't think—" the blonde nurse, who was still in the room began. But the man shook his head.

"Let her. It has to come out sometime."

Elise shook her head again. "It wasn't just what he did. It was...he made me remember what I wanted to forget. All the things that happened when he...when my—" She stopped herself abruptly. The vault. Keep it in the vault. Put it back, keep it safe. Don't think about it. Yes, that was what she had to do.

"When what?" the big man asked but Elise didn't answer. Inside she was gathering the ugliness which had been dragged out—a double armful of pain and hurt—and shoving it back into the old-timey bank vault at the back of her mind. With a sigh of relief, she slammed the door and locked it, twisting the dial to set the combination only she knew. So vivid was the image, she could almost hear the click of the tumblers falling.

"I'm all right," she said out loud and was reassured to hear the calm in her own voice. "I...I'm going to be fine. It's gone now. I'm safe."

"Of course, you are," the blonde nurse soothed. But when Elise looked up, she thought she caught a look of disapproval on the scarred man's face.

"Packed it away, huh?" he rumbled. "All right, if that's how you want to deal with it."

"It is." Elise cleared her throat and realized she was still clinging to him like a frightened child. But I'm not a child anymore. I'm not that hurt, scared little girl who went running to Buck for comfort after...She shook her head. No, keep it in the vault. The point is, I'm a grown woman and I don't even know this man.

No, she didn't know him, yet here she was, sitting in his lap wearing only a thin red hospital gown. What's wrong with me, acting like this? I'm an attorney, damn it—one of the toughest prosecutors in Tampa. Hell, in all of Florida! And here I am, acting like one of my clients after they've been traumatized and abused. Come on, Elise—get hold of yourself!

The self-pep talk worked. Elise sat up straight and dropped her arms to her sides. "I...uh..."

"You wanna go back to bed now?" The scarred man cocked a black eyebrow at her. His hair was short, she noticed—skull-cut close to his head. But it looked like it would be as black as his brows if he let it grow out.

"Yes, please." Elise nodded. "I...I'm so sorry for climbing all over you that way. I was...I guess I was a little hysterical."

He didn't deny it or try to downplay it. Nor did he try to help her off his lap. "Yeah, you were." He shrugged, his massive shoulders rolling with the gesture. "Not surprising, considering what you went through."

"I'm over that now," Elise said quickly.

"Oh yeah?" He frowned. "That was fucking fast. Do you even remember what you just got over?"

"Merrick—" the blonde nurse began but Elise was already talking.

"I was taking a vacation in Sarasota when I was abducted," she said. "I was...the man who took me had red eyes. They glowed. It was very..." She swallowed hard. "Very frightening."

"I bet." The man nodded. "Go on."

"I was naked." Elise looked down at herself, at the thin red gown she was wearing. She really needed to get off the strange man's lap but somehow telling this was easier when he was near and he didn't seem to mind holding her.

"Go on," he said again when she paused too long.

Elise cleared her throat. "He...he hooked me up to a machine. The wires went under my skin. Here...and here and here...all over." She indicated the tiny, pink scars on her skin. "It hurt. And the machine...it showed things."

"What things?" the man asked.

"I don't remember," Elise said at once. The vault. Keep it in the vault! She swallowed again. "Bad things, I'm sure. Frightening things. Anyway, it doesn't matter now because I got away. I found a place to hide in. Someplace little and snug where he couldn't find me."

"You found a stasis chamber," the scarred man rumbled. His voice was so deep it sounded like someone rubbing two stones together. "It put you into suspended animation. If I hadn't found your life pod, floating around in the trash dumped from the damn Scourge ship, you'd still be out there."

"Suspended animation?" Elise put a hand to her throat. "I don't understand. What—?"

"The stasis field slows down all your bodily functions dramatically," the blonde nurse explained. "That's why we missed you before—there were no life signs coming from the pod you were in. Lucky for you, Merrick decided to check it out anyway."

"Merrick?" Elise looked up at him. "Is that your name?"

"The one and only." One corner of his mouth lifted in a crooked smile and she got the feeling it wasn't an expression that crossed his face often.

"And you're Kindred," Elise said, beginning to remember things from their last conversation. "You said...you said you'd protect me."

He nodded gravely. "I found you out there so I'm responsible for you. At least until you're able to go home—back down to your planet." He didn't seem very happy about the idea.

Elise felt a sudden, sharp stab of distress. "So...I'll go home and you'll stay here? I'll never see you again?"

He cocked an eyebrow at her again. "Why, you wanna play house? I'm not exactly the kind of guy you bring home to your parents."

"I wouldn't bring anyone home to them," Elise said without thinking. "I haven't spoken to my mother in ten years." Then she shut her mouth. Why had she told a complete stranger such an intimate, personal detail about herself? And why was she still sitting on his lap? "Excuse me," she said stiffly and tried to get up.

Her body didn't want to cooperate. She stumbled and nearly fell. Merrick caught her neatly and picked her up. "Take it easy, baby."

Hot blood rushed to her cheeks. "I'm not your baby. Please put me down," she demanded in her frostiest tone.

"All right." He deposited her neatly in bed, making her feel like a stupid little girl. "Guess we're not playing house after all."

"I guess not." Elise tried to gather her dignity but it wasn't easy considering she was still wearing nothing but a hospital johnny. "Where are my clothes?" she asked, looking at the nurse this time. "Can I get something else to wear? I'm not sick and I'd rather not dress like I am."

"Well, we prefer that our patients wear the healing robes we put them in—this fabric was specially developed by the Kindred." The nurse pointed at the sleeve of her crimson robe. "It's actually infused with antibacterial cultures. But I'll try to find you something for the trip home, at least. You're what...a size four?"

"I'm a six." Elise looked down at herself, swimming in the red gown. "Or...I used to be," she said doubtfully. "Maybe a four would fit now." She let out a shaky laugh. "Wow, the kidnapping and terror diet really works—who knew?"

The blonde nurse smiled at her. "A sense of humor—I like that. Don't worry, I'll find you something to wear back to Earth." She bustled away, leaving Elise alone with Merrick.

"Well." He stretched, his fingertips easily touching the high ceiling. "Looks like you're doing fine. Guess I'll be going too." He turned away and Elise knew she ought to let him go. But somehow she couldn't. She just couldn't.

"Wait!" she said before she could stop herself. "Wait, please."

"Yeah?" He turned back to face her, an unreadable look in his mismatched eyes.

"I'm sorry," Elise said in a small voice. "I didn't mean to snap at you. I...I can get a little prickly when I'm feeling threatened."

"You don't have to feel threatened around me." His rough voice grew somewhat softer. "I'm here to protect you—remember?"

"I remember." Unable to stop herself, Elise held out a hand. She felt an unutterable sense of relief when Merrick took it and entwined their fingers.

"So," he said sitting down in the chair beside the bed. "You want to talk? Or just rest?"

"Just rest, please," Elise said humbly. He looked like a felon or an escaped prisoner but she had never felt such peace and safety as when he took her hand. His touch was soothing somehow. Healing. All better now, she thought and yawned. She realized with surprise that she was sleepy again. Why was she so tired when she needed to get back down to Earth and get things in order? Her caseload alone—

"Let it go."

"Huh?" She frowned in surprise. "What did you say...Merrick?" His name felt strangely right on her tongue.

"Whatever you're thinking, let it go. It can wait." He squeezed her fingers lightly. "For now, just rest. You can do that, can't you baby?"

This time she didn't get angry or upset at the endearment. It seemed...sweet. Roughly charming, like him. "Yes," she said at last. "Yes I guess I can."

"Good. Close your eyes. Relax." He leaned back in the chair, crossed his legs in front of him, and closed those strangely compelling eyes. His tall, muscular frame looked almost lanky in repose.

Elise followed his example and relaxed back against her pillows. She wished he was holding her again—it would be better if he was closer, if she was touching his skin. But for right now, holding his hand was enough.

What would be better? she asked herself. There didn't seem to be an answer. She only knew that touching him felt good, felt right. But more than that—it felt necessary. Like she needed to touch him. Elise pushed that idea to the side—it was silly to think she had to touch a man she'd barely met. It was time to rest. And now that everything was safely back in the vault, she could sleep.

But what if the vault opens again? What if the door swings wide and lets everything out?

The sudden thought made her eyes fly open and her heart start to race.

"Easy," Merrick murmured and she realized he was watching her from half-lidded eyes. "Take it easy, Elise."

She bit her lip. "I'm sorry. I just thought—"

"Relax. If you have a bad dream I'll wake you up."

She looked at him with gratitude. He understood. "You...do you promise?" she asked, feeling like a little kid again.

He nodded. "Swear." He squeezed her hand gently and Elise had the fleeting thought that she wished he could get into the bed with her. She was certain she'd be able to sleep without nightmares if he was curled up around her, spooning her protectively.

The adult part of her mind rejected the idea at once. She'd only just met him—she couldn't ask him to share her bed. Plus, she didn't think he'd fit. He was positively the biggest person she'd ever seen in her life—not that it bothered her. She was used to being the shortest kid on the block so she didn't let size intimidate her...

"Stop thinking so hard and sleep," he said. "What are you thinking about, anyway?"

Elise yawned despite herself. "Just that you're too big to fit in the bed with me." Then, realizing what she'd said she added, "Not that I want—"

"I do." He looked at her speculatively. "Wish I could crawl in there with you. I'd like to hold you again."

Elise felt her cheeks getting hot. "I...I'd like that too," she admitted in a low voice. "But I don't know why—I barely know you."

"I know." He looked troubled for a moment. Then he shrugged. "Oh well. Worry about it later." He gave her that lopsided smile again and yawned, which exposed surprisingly long canine teeth. They looked almost like...

"Fangs." Elise yawned too. "Do you have...fangs?"

"Uh-huh." He nodded. "I got a lot of frightening things about me, baby. You scared?"

She shook her head. "No. Somehow when I touch you I'm the...the opposite of scared. Why is that?"

He shrugged again and squeezed her fingers lightly. "Don't know. Doesn't matter now — go to sleep."

"But..." Elise yawned again. "I don't mind fangs," she mumbled, closing her eyes. "Just like...Buck's."

"Who the hell is this Buck, anyway?" she heard him say but sleep was already claiming her and she couldn't answer. Concentrating on the comforting feel of his hand holding hers, she drifted away.

Chapter Thirty-five

A soft murmuring sound woke Rast from a deep sleep. He blinked and looked around. It was still night and he and Nadiah were in the middle of some kind of jungle or forest. He could smell the plants and hear their leaves rustling against each other in the soft breeze. Multiple moons shone down from the night sky, illuminating the area which looked like a lush wilderness.

Rast blinked. More than one moon—what the hell? Where are we? He sat up, rubbing his eyes, and felt a strange pull in his left shoulder blade. Looking down, he realized why—Nadiah, looking angelically content, was lying on his wing.

Oh, of course. My wing.

He lifted her gently and put her to one side so he could flex the feathered appendage before it suddenly hit him—he had wings! Wings.

"Oh my God!" he said aloud, looking around the Healing Garden. "It wasn't a dream. I really do have wings." He flexed them both and the feathers rustled softly, making an almost musical murmur as they moved.

But not as musical as the sound which had woken him up. Standing, he followed it a few feet away to the center of the garden. It seemed to be coming from the stone fountain—the one he had cursed earlier when he thought Nadiah was going to die because it was dry.

However, as he approached it, Rast saw that it wasn't dry after all. The strangely carved alien animal heads that sprouted from it had silvery streams of water flowing from their mouths and the basin was filled to the brim. Rast stopped where he was, wondering if he was dreaming. Could this be true? Had there been some kind of rain that filled the fountain? But why hadn't it woken him and Nadiah up?

You may approach, Counselor .

The voice—low, feminine, and authoritative—nearly startled Rast out of his skin. It was the same voice which had told him to use his wings to heal Nadiah. But though he looked high and low, he couldn't find its source.

You may not see me, Counselor . To look upon my face is to die for a mortal, the voice said. Now come, approach the fountain.

Not sure what else to do, Rast obeyed. Though it was only a few steps, it seemed a very long and strange journey to the side of the stone basin. When he finally got there, he just stood, looking around.

"Uh...I'm here," he said at last, wondering if the owner of the voice had left.

So I see. The voice sounded amused.

"Are you the Goddess?" Rast asked, deciding to cut straight to the point. "I mean, excuse me if you're not but—"

I am called by many names. Goddess is one of them. Mother of All Life is another, the voice said. Here in my garden, I am Healer of All Wounds.

"Healer, then," Rast said, bowing his head respectfully. "I suppose you're the one who healed Nadiah. Thank you."

Actually, it was you who healed your female, the Goddess told him. By the power of your wings. Know this, Counselor —there is great power in them but it must be used only for good, for healing.

They are given you for that purpose, and that you might fly to my garden to commune with me when you have great need.

"Oh, uh...so are we going to have daily planning meetings or something?" Rast asked. "Because now it looks like I'm supposed to rule this whole fucking—uh, excuse me—freaking planet and I don't have the first clue how to start."

You must rule as you see fit, with wisdom and grace.

"What about all this stuff about me being a Challa and needing a Lyzel?" Rast asked. "I only want Nadiah but she's not a priestess or anything."

Nadiah has something more important than training as a priestess. I gifted her with the Sight that she might help you in this new undertaking.

Rast felt a sense of relief. "I'm glad to hear you say that. But the whole thing with the high priestess and growing wings and nearly losing the woman I love—you have to admit that's a hell of a first day on the job."

Do you regret your vows to serve and guide First World? The Goddess sounded almost sad. Do you wish to be released of them?

"Well, I..." Rast cleared his throat, not certain what to say. "I never expected to have to stay here forever. Not that it's not a beautiful place..."

Its beauty will soon be erased, along with all other beauty in the universe if it is not guarded carefully.

Rast frowned. "What do you mean?"

Look into the fountain.

Suddenly, the streams stopped pouring from the animal heads and the water in the basin went as smooth and dark as black glass.

Not sure what he would see, Rast leaned over the stone basin, searching its inky depths. At first there was nothing but then…

"Hey, that's the planet the high priestess showed us," he exclaimed, frowning. "The one with the…what do you call it—"

The Hoard. The Goddess's voice was hard and cold now. They seek to destroy and devour all that is light and good and pure in the universe. And First World will be their first target. Their memory is long and still they hate the First Kindred for their near extinction over a thousand years ago.

"But what can I do about it?" Rast asked. "I'm no military genius."

You are uniquely suited for this office, the Goddess said. It is in your blood.

"And if I refuse?" Rast asked, his heart beating in his mouth. He half expected to be struck down by a lightning bolt for his question. But the Goddess only said,

Look into the fountain again.

Rast looked and saw the black masses of the Hoard once more. They were leaving their world in droves, blotting out the stars with their sheer numbers. The Blackness which Eats the Stars, he thought.

Indeed, the Goddess murmured. But watch…

Rast kept staring into the basin as she directed. The sky around the black, dead planet was dark with the ships of the Hoard— hundreds—no, thousands of them taking flight every minute. Then, in a single instant, they all disappeared.

Rast frowned. "Where did they go?"

Keep your eyes trained on the fountain. You shall see.

Rast did as she said and was surprised when the view changed. Instead of the bleak world of the Hoard, he now saw a new world – a pale gold globe bathed in the glow of two small suns. The view grew closer and he saw that it was covered with peaceful looking cities and quiet farms. The inhabitants were tall and thin with blue fur and backward bending knees. They reminded Rast a little of llamas which had learned to stand upright and use technology.

Behold the Pardos, the Goddess whispered. You will probably never meet them. They live across the universe in a galaxy far from this one and their genetic make-up is too different from the Kindred to make a viable trade.

Just as well, Rast thought. Can't imagine wanting to have sex with a llama woman.

They are different from both Kindred and the humans you grew up with, the Goddess said. Different but peaceful. They have no weapons of warfare, no way of defending themselves. Watch.

Rast watched. The view pulled back again and suddenly the sky around the peaceful golden planet was filled with black ships, swarming with the Hoard. They descended on the planet en mass, covering its surface in the same way they had covered their own planet. The round, golden surface was black with them, like an apple riddled with rot. They're a disease, Rast thought. A cancer growing and growing – they'll kill everything.

Shrieks, cries, and moans of agony drifted up from the golden planet and he realized he was right. The Hoard were systematically covering the entire globe, leaving mass destruction in their wake.

This planet will be despoiled and all its inhabitants dead before the setting of its suns, the Goddess said. And then the Hoard will look for new worlds to devour. They will find them, too – for darkness ever seeks to extinguish light.

The scene changed again. This time it was Earth in the basin of the fountain. Rast recognized the familiar blue and white globe at once—he could even see the long peninsula of Florida, his home state. Then, suddenly, the sky around Earth was black with ships.

"No," Rast whispered numbly. "No, they can't."

They can and will. They are seeking to destroy and this planet you think of as your home burns brightly as a beacon of civilization in the blackness of the universe. The Hoard will seek out all such planets until there is nothing left. The Goddess's voice was cold with certainty.

"When is this going to happen?" Rast demanded. "I have to warn them!"

No warning will help. Prevention is the key. The Goddess's sigh was a warm breeze stirring the branches full of green and purple leaves. I have shown you a possible future. It is up to you, Counselor , to see that it does not become the present.

"But how?" Rast demanded, exasperated. "How am I supposed to prevent this…this universe-wide genocide from occurring?"

Stay at your post. I will not always be able to commune with you but you must sit on the Seat of Wisdom and look often into the Eye of Foreknowledge. These are the tools I have given you and the Counselor s before you—I know you will use them well.

"What am I looking for? How will I know when I find it?"

You will know.

"Why can't you just tell me?"

Because the future is fluid and ever changing. It is affected by the million different choices made every second of every day. And because some hearts are shadowed, even from me.

A new picture appeared in the fountain. A man—Rast supposed it was a man, anyway—tall and broad shouldered as any Kindred with thick black hair and a neatly trimmed black goatee and mustache framing sensual red lips. When he smiled, white, even teeth were revealed. Teeth that looked every so slightly too sharp. His eyes were a solid silver with no pupil at all.

"What is he? Is he one of the Hoard?" Rast couldn't take his eyes from the man in the fountain. Behind that handsome face there was a blackness—a roiling, hungry evil like a mass of snakes which could never be satisfied, which would never stop eating.

He is Draven, the Goddess murmured. The leader of the Hoard. His power for destruction is unmatched in the universe. Your father wounded him badly—drove him underground. But a thousand years have regenerated him completely—now the Hoard grow ever stronger and their appetite for destruction grows with them.

"Great," Rast said flatly, still staring. He had the feeling if this guy looked at you in just the right way, you might fall down dead from an aneurysm or wake up the next day with a tumor the size of a baseball lodged in the base of your spine. Babies would cry until their noses bled and old men would have heart attacks wherever he went. Yet, he would also be able to walk around in broad daylight, looking perfectly normal and carrying that cloud of evil wherever he went.

He is one of the soulless ones—what you would call a demon, the Goddess said. The most powerful one the universe has ever seen. And he is hungry, Counselor —ever hungry.

"Yeah, I get that," Rast murmured, still staring. Suddenly the demon-man turned his head and those his pupiless eyes bored into Rast's own, making him gasp. "Turn it off! Turn it off—he can see me."

He can sense you. *The vision in the fountain faded and the water began flowing once more.* He knows there is a new Counselor on First World—the first in a thousand years. And he knows you are your father's son—it makes him wary and cautious—slow to act. This is the only advantage you have. *The Goddess's voice was becoming faint.*

"So I'm just supposed to keep an eye on him?" Rast asked. "I mean, I'm not allowed to go fight him, am I? I'm not allowed to leave the surface of the planet."

To leave First World is to lose your wings forever. *The voice was fainter still.* You will find others who are suited for this battle as well. Find them and gather them to you. They will help you learn what Draven is planning—his strategy and secrets. Even now he is searching for the key—the key to unlock the universe for his designs. He must not find it!

"But...but how will I know them?" Rast asked. "The ones who are supposed to help?"

You have ever been a finder of the lost. *The Goddess's voice was little more than a whisper now.* It has been your calling from the first. Use it now along with the knowledge and wisdom I will send. For now, I must go.

"But Goddess—"

Be vigilant, Counselor . Guard First World well. For if it falls, the universe will follow.

And then she was gone.

Chapter Thirty-six

Nadiah woke and yawned, stretching her arms above her head to get the tingly feeling out of her fingertips. She looked around for Rast and saw him pacing a few yards away, his new wings tightly furled against his back. In that position they were almost completely invisible as the feathers molded to his body and took on the coloring of his skin. She reflected that unless someone knew his secret, they would never guess he had the power of flight.

"Hello." She rose and went to him, smiling. "I guess we must have fallen asleep. I can't believe we spent the whole night up here."

"Yeah, we really wore ourselves out, I guess." He turned to face her but his smile was troubled.

"Rast..." Nadiah put a hand on his arm and noticed that his wings quivered with her light touch. "Are you all right?" she asked anxiously. "You seem unhappy."

"I'm just a little worried, that's all." He cleared his throat and smiled at her. "I had...well, I guess you would call it a vision last night. I, uh, met the Goddess."

"You did?" Nadiah exclaimed. "What did she say?"

"Pretty much that I'm meant to be here and so are you." He smiled at her briefly. "But also that there's big trouble coming. Not just for First World but for the whole goddamn universe if we can't stop it."

"How can we stop it?" Nadiah asked.

He shook his head. "I don't know. I only know we're supposed to be vigilant and find people to help us." He pulled her close suddenly and looked into her eyes. "And that we're supposed to be together."

Nadiah looked at him hopefully, her heart beating hard. "The Goddess said that?"

Rast nodded. "You're supposed to be my Lyzel, all right. She said the reason she gave you the Sight was to help me guide First World." He frowned. "And it looks like it's going to need a lot of guidance in the very near future."

"That's all right." Nadiah hugged him hard. "We'll do it together." Then she pulled back and looked at him, biting her lip. "But…what about the high priestess?"

Rast smiled grimly. "Oh, I think I can handle her. In fact, I don't think we should wait a minute longer to do just that. Are you ready to go?"

She nodded. "I guess so. I'm famished and Sylvan and Sophie are probably worried sick about us."

"Then let's go ease their minds." Rast swung her up into his arms and spread his wings. Their great, feathered lengths glinted in the green sunlight, dazzling Nadiah's eyes. "Come on," he said, smiling at her. "Let's fly."

* * * * *

"Look, there they are!" Sophie pointed to the winged shape cresting the horizon, relieved to see it wasn't just another one of those huge black birds of prey that swooped over the desert from time to time.

She and Sylvan were standing in the guest area, which she thought of as the oasis of light, and scanning the skies anxiously. They'd both seen Rast's wings come out and watched as he scooped

Nadiah out of the sky and spirited her away to the Healing Garden. But afterwards as they waited and waited for the couple to come back, Sophie had begun to worry and wonder. A thousand thoughts had crossed her mind. What was going on in the Healing Garden? Had Rast been able to save Nadiah? What if he hadn't been able to save her and he was too grief stricken to leave the lush garden?

Sophie hadn't wanted to share these ideas with Sylvan—the strain of worrying about his younger cousin was evident in his face. But it was impossible to keep some of her fear from leaking across the bond they shared as a married couple. And she couldn't help feeling his fear through the same link. All in all, the two of them had spent an extremely restless night, barely nibbling on the Willy Wonka bread even though it tasted wonderful, as always.

So it was with great relief that Sophie watched Rast circle above them and land lightly in the oasis with an obviously healthy Nadiah held securely in his arms. She felt Sylvan's relief as well and flashed him a smile which he returned whole heartedly.

The minute the couple touched down, Sophia ran to them. "Oh Nadiah, thank God! I was so worried!"

"We both were," Sylvan said, coming forward.

"We're sorry for making you worry." Nadiah looked sheepish as Rast set her down. "All the uh, excitement sort of wore us out and I guess we fell asleep after I was healed."

"Excitement, hmm?" Sylvan studied her closely for a moment and then smiled. "Of course, I see. And may I be the first to congratulate you on the new color of your eyes. I don't think I've ever seen a transformation more spectacular."

Nadiah blushed all the way to the roots of her fair hair. "Oh, Sylvan..."

"I know we're not married—er—joined yet," Rast said. "But I promise you, Sylvan, we will be before the day is over."

"You'd better hurry then—it's almost lunch time now." Sophie laughed and took Nadiah's arm, pulling her toward the food table. "Come on, you must be starving. I know 'excitement' always gives me a big appetite."

Nadiah blushed again and smiled. "I am pretty hungry," she admitted.

"Then let's eat!"

"There is no time for food now." They all looked up to see Lissa standing there in her plain white priestess robe. "Forgive me," she continued. "But you are summoned to the temple."

"Is that right?" Rast came forward, frowning. "And by whose authority are we summoned?"

Lissa bit her lip. "By the High Priestess of the Empty Throne. I'm so sorry, Counselor ," she added in a rush, bowing reverently. "I told her it was blasphemy—that you could not be ordered about now that your wings have manifested. But she insisted that I summon you."

"It's all right, Priestess." Rast nodded at her formally. "We will all go to the temple. But it won't be the Temple of the Empty Throne for long—I am going to take my rightful place."

Sophie stared at him in surprise and saw Sylvan doing the same thing. Yesterday, Rast had seemed extremely reluctant to assume the mantle of leadership that his vows demanded he take. Today there was something different about him. Something almost...royal.

"He has been visited by the Goddess," Sylvan murmured, taking her hand. "I know that look. Deep had it after he survived his encounter with death."

"Do you really think so?" Sophie breathed as they followed Lissa. The dark network of tunnels under the mountain was beginning to seem familiar.

Sylvan nodded. "I do."

It didn't take long to reach the temple. As before, the high priestess stood on the topmost step, looking down on them, a haughty expression on her face.

"So, Adam Rast, you have returned," she said as they approached the foot of the stairs. "I am glad you had the good sense to answer my summons."

"I didn't come in answer to your summons, Priestess." Rast's deep voice rang in the vast, hollow space that housed the temple. "I have come to take the throne my father left me."

Swinging Nadiah into his arms, he spread his vast, iridescent wings and took off with a mighty down stroke that blew Sophie's hair into her face. When she managed to get a clear view, she saw Rast and Nadiah soaring upward toward the vaulted ceiling. He brought them down gently and with precision directly in front of the high priestess. So close, in fact, that she was forced to take a step backwards.

"Come on, we don't want to miss this." Sophie grabbed Sylvan's hand and they hurried up the many steps. As they reached the top, Sophie saw that Rast and the priestess were having a kind of stand off — she was bodily blocking the way to the huge white marble throne.

"A fine display," she said, scowling. "But the wings prove nothing."

"Is that right?" Rast cocked an eyebrow at her sardonically. "Because just yesterday you were saying they proved everything."

"It is well that you have returned, Adam Rast," the priestess said, standing her ground. "But the fact is, you are a time traveler — a relic of our distant past. You have no knowledge of the First World of today. Or any world but the remote, primitive planet you were raised on."

"I think I can manage," Rast said dryly. "I'll just have to do a little on the job training." He started to step around her, but again the high priestess blocked his path.

She looked down her nose at him and announced, "I have had a vision from the Goddess just last night — I fear that the Empty Throne must remain empty."

"Oh?" Rast growled, clearly losing patience. "Because that's not what she told me when I met her in the Healing Gardens. She said the entire universe is in peril and told me I have a job to do." He grabbed Nadiah's hand and pulled her forward. "Along with my Lyzel, that is."

The high priestess went positively pale and her blank emerald eyes narrowed. "You cannot displace me with one such as that. She has no training in the ways of — "

"She has the Sight," Rast interrupted her. "Given to her by the Goddess to help me rule and guide First World. Nadiah will be my Lyzel and you'll either be third in line or you'll be last. Your choice, Priestess."

"I...I..." For a moment it seemed like the priestess had lost her voice but then she rallied. "You cannot claim your place without a test — without proving you are worthy."

"Okay, fine." Before she could stop him, Rast strode around her and climbed the dais that led to the Empty Throne.

Sophie's heart was in her mouth and she could see the worry on Nadiah's face as well. Yesterday when he'd barely touched the marble throne he had almost died. But Rast seemed to have a new confidence. He walked with the air of a man who knew exactly what he was doing and feared no consequences for his actions.

He reached the throne and, without hesitating an instant, turned and sat on it. There was a low gasp from all assembled, Sophie included, but nothing happened. Rast simply sat there, looking completely at home with his vast wings extended on either side of the throne. For the first time, Sophie noticed deep notches in the white marble between the back and arms of the chair. For his wings, she thought, understanding. So they don't get cramped when he sits.

At last Rast spoke, breaking the silence. "Well?" he asked, staring down at the priestess. "Good enough for you?"

It had to be good enough—Sophie was sure even the belligerent priestess couldn't dispute that Rast was in his rightful place now. But she hadn't counted on the woman's stubbornness.

The high priestess crossed her arms over her chest and frowned. "So the Empty Throne did not kill you. It still doesn't prove your female should be Lyzel."

"Oh no?" Rast frowned and nodded at Nadiah. "Come up here, sweetheart. Don't worry—it won't hurt you," he reassured her when Nadiah looked uneasy. "I won't let it."

Nadiah lifted her chin and there was a glint in her new blue-green eyes. "I know," she said and ran lightly up the steps of the dais to stand beside Rast. She put one hand firmly on the white marble arm of the throne and Sophie was relieved to see that absolutely nothing happened to her.

"Good." Rast nodded at her approvingly. Then he turned to the high priestess. "All right, your turn, your Holiness. Come on up and stand on the other side of the throne." He patted the other broad arm of the throne. "This one's all yours."

The high priestess didn't budge. "I will do no such thing. A Lyzel is not required to touch the Empty Throne to prove her place."

Nadiah spoke up unexpectedly. "But she is required to work with the Counselor and not against him," she said. "And this is the Empty Throne no longer, Priestess. For now that the rightful Counselor sits upon it, it shall be known once more as the Seat of Wisdom."

The high priestess glared at her. "You dare to address me in such a manner! You, who have no formal training in the ways of the Goddess!"

"I know enough to stand by Rast and help him guide First World," Nadiah shot back.

Very well..." The priestess drew herself up, her blank emerald eyes glittering. "If you know so much you will recollect that the final test of the Counselor is a healing. He must heal one who is in need here in the temple, before he can claim his place."

"I already healed Nadiah last night," Rast pointed out, frowning.

"That was done out of sight and not before the throne," the priestess countered quickly. "In all probability it was the waters of the Goddess's fountain that healed her."

Rast glared at her. "That fountain was bone dry when we reached it. Without the healing abilities of my wings, Nadiah would be dead right now and I'd have you to thank for it."

"Prove it then," the priestess challenged. "Prove that you have the healing abilities that only the true Counselor may claim."

Rast frowned. "I would but there's no one to heal." He pointed at her. "And before you get any bright ideas about giving someone else a terminal illness, let me warn you that if I catch you making anyone sick ever again I will personally throw you out on your ass and you will never be welcome back again."

The priestess went pale. "Very well. But if you won't allow me to make anyone ill, I don't see how you can prove your claim."

"I do." Nadiah stepped forward and beckoned. "Sophia, my dear friend, come forward."

Sophie, who had been watching the exchange between Rast and the priestess with breathless excitement, suddenly felt her heart begin to pound. "Oh, Nadiah," she began uncertainly. "I don't know—"

"I do," Nadiah said with loving sternness. "Didn't you say that your womb had been closed for a reason? This is the reason, Sophia. Come forward now and fear not to be healed by the Counselor ."

Sophia looked at her in wonder. Could this really be the giggly teenaged-acting girl who used to say "Omigoddess!" all the time? The girl who had gossiped with her about Sylvan and given her a zan-daro or make-over when they first met on Tranq Prime?

Nadiah had matured so much in such a short time. She truly was no longer a girl but a full grown female who had come into her own. And when she spoke, her words had the ring of a higher authority about them.

"The Goddess," Sylvan whispered through their link as Sophie made her way up the steps of the dais that held the throne. "Nadiah speaks with her power now. She'll make a fine Lyzel to Rast's Challa."

"They're a perfect match," Sophie agreed, as she finally reached the top of the dais and stood before the throne.

She wasn't sure what came next and she was afraid to touch the white marble chair—after all, she wasn't the one getting married to the rightful ruler of the whole freaking planet. It might zap her if she wasn't careful.

"Be at ease dear friend," Nadiah murmured, touching her arm gently. "And prepare yourself to be healed."

Before Sophie could ask any questions about what being healed entailed, Rast rose from the throne and stepped toward her. "It's all right," he said when he saw her frightened look. "It won't hurt."

"I don't care if it does." Sophie raised her chin. "As long as it means I can have a baby. Sylvan and I want one so much."

"Of course you do." Rast smiled at her and stepped closer. "Just hold still. It's all in the wings."

Sophie opened her mouth to ask what he meant and then she was surrounded by a soft wall of iridescent feathers. She wasn't aware of Rast at all, though she sensed he was there somewhere. Mostly she simply felt encompassed on all sides by the warm, soft, glimmering wings. "Oh," she whispered breathlessly. "Oh, they're beautiful."

"And functional." Rast's voice seemed to come from far away. "Just hold still," he murmured. "And let me concentrate."

Sophie did as he said, holding as still as she could though at first she felt nothing. Then, a warm tingling sensation started in her toes and rushed up her legs. She gasped as it arrowed inward and lodged itself deep in her pelvis like a glowing ball of heat between her hips. "Oh, my," she murmured as the tingling and the warmth grew and grew until it was almost overwhelming. Just as it grew so intense she thought she couldn't take it anymore, it suddenly ebbed away, leaving her feeling shaky but more completely well than she had ever been before.

"There, that's it," Rast muttered and suddenly the curtain of feathers was withdrawn.

"Th-thank you." Sophie took a tottering step forward and nearly stumbled down the steps of the dais. Luckily, Sylvan was there to catch her.

"How do you feel?" he murmured, putting an arm around her waist and supporting her down the remaining steps. "Are you all right?"

"I feel wonderful, actually," Sophie admitted. "Just...just amazing."

"But are you healed?" he asked.

"She is." Nadiah answered the question, her clear voice ringing out in the vast, echoing space. Sophie recognized the look on her friend's face at once.

"Look," she whispered to Sylvan. "She's having a prophecy!"

And indeed, Nadiah was. When she turned to look at Sophie, her new blue-green eyes had gone a pure emerald and her voice was deeper, richer and more authoritative somehow.

"Sophia, my daughter," she said, inclining her head graciously. "Your faith has been rewarded. I say to you now that your womb shall be full of life. You and your male, Sylvan, shall have sons upon sons to comfort you and bless your union."

"Thank you." Sophie bowed reverently. Behind her she heard murmurs of surprise from Lissa and the other assembled priestesses who had been standing silently throughout the entire confrontation.

"The Goddess," they were saying. "The Lyzel is now the mouthpiece of the Goddess! Hear how the Mother of All Life speaks through her!"

"How dare you!" The high priestess rounded on them, a snarl of hatred on her face. "It is I who am the mouthpiece of the Goddess. She speaks only through me."

"No longer, Priestess." There was a caged power in Nadiah's voice now — or in the voice which was speaking through her, Sophie thought. "You," she said, pointing at the priestess. "Have misused the power I granted you for the last time. I hereby rescind that power and cast you down from your office as high priestess. From this day forth, you will be the lowest of the low — the meanest novice who comes to learn the ways of the temple shall be above you."

"No," whispered the priestess and Sophie saw that the solid emerald hue was leaking from her eyes. It left behind two very ordinary light brown eyes with no green at all in them. Her hair also turned, from a rich green to a drab, dishwater blonde. Lines appeared on her face and she suddenly looked old. "Please," she whispered. "Please, Mother of All Life. You...you are a gracious Goddess...a forgiving goddess..."

"There are some things I cannot forgive," the Goddess said through Nadiah. "You have lied in my name, you have blasphemed by speaking such lies here in my holy mountain in the very temple you were sworn to guide with humility and love. You have used the power I granted you for harm instead of good — sickening this little one I am speaking through almost to death."

"It was the only way," the priestess protested. "Please, Goddess, I had to bring your chosen servant, the new Counselor , to First World."

Nadiah's face drew into a disapproving frown. "You did so only because you thought you could control him and thus increase your own power over the planet. Do not lie to me — I know your heart!"

"Please, Goddess..." the priestess began but Nadiah held up a hand.

"And last but not least, you have laid a curse upon one I sent to you for guidance. Great was his burden and weary his load of guilt. Yet instead of granting him healing and forgiveness as he asked, you cursed him with a future filled with pain and suffering."

"He was a hybrid," the priestess protested. "His blood wasn't pure enough to receive your blessing, my Goddess."

"It was his humbled heart I was interested in, not his bloodline." Nadiah said. "Now go. Get to the barracks below the mountain and begin your new duties. I will have you in my temple no longer."

The priestess—or former priestess, Sophie supposed—opened her mouth to reply but only a choking sound came out. Her drab brown eyes filled with terror and she turned and fled, running down the temple steps so fast it was a wonder she didn't fall and break her neck.

There was a soft moan and Sophie turned to see that Nadiah had collapsed into Rast's lap. She looked faint and was holding her head.

"Nadiah?" Rast murmured. "Are you okay, sweetheart?"

"I...I'm fine." She shook her head and looked up. "I just had another al'lei, didn't I? What happened?"

It was Lissa who answered. "The Goddess spoke through you." She looked at Nadiah reverently and then turned her attention to Rast. "My Counselor , may I be the first to pay homage to the two of you, the rightful Challa and Lyzel of First World." She bowed low before the throne.

All of the other priestesses bowed as well and Sophie, thinking it was only right, copied their gesture. From the corner of her eye, she saw Sylvan bowing too and smiled.

"Bet you never thought you'd be bowing to your baby cousin. The little girl you used to sing to sleep at night when she had a nightmare," she sent through their link.

"No, I didn't," he sent back. "But I'm happy to pay Nadiah the respect she deserves. She and Rast have come through the fire to get here—they deserve our deference and esteem."

Sophie thought he was right, but they didn't get the chance to bow for long.

"Rise," Rast said, smiling at them all. "Sylvan and Sophia, you don't need to bow like that. And Priestess Lissa, you rise too. I am naming you the new high priestess, effective immediately."

"Me, Counselor ?" Lissa rose, looking both surprised and confused.

"Yes, you," Rast said firmly. "Don't look so surprised—I think you'll be well suited for the job."

"I...thank you."

Sophie thought the young priestess looked troubled but she only nodded respectfully. But Rast still wasn't done.

"As your first task in your new position," he said, beckoning to her. "Is to perform a marriage, er, joining ceremony between myself and Nadiah."

Lissa's green eyes grew wide. "Truly? You wish me to perform it now?"

He shrugged. "Why not? No time like the present."

"But...but Counselor , a joining between the Challa and his Lyzel should be filled with pomp and ceremony. The candles and flowers alone—"

"We don't want any of that," Nadiah interrupted her, smiling. "We just want to be one in the eyes of the Goddess."

Lissa swallowed hard and nodded. "Very well," she murmured. "If that is your command, Counselor , I shall be happy to obey it."

"Wonderful." Rast took Nadiah's hand and the two of them came down from the dais. "Well, let's get going," he said. "And then somebody show me where the Counselor sleeps." He winked at Nadiah who blushed and smiled shyly back. "I can't wait to start the honeymoon."

Chapter Thirty-seven

"Oh, I am so glad you're home, Sophie!" Kat flopped down on the sofa between Lauren and Olivia with a groan. "These two pregnant ladies have been running me ragged."

"Oh, hush." Lauren elbowed her good naturedly. "We're not that bad."

"Well, you're not, I'll give you that," Kat conceded. "But Liv is just awful. She's all 'Fetch me this, get me that, I need ketchup for my pickled seaweed sandwich...'"

"Seaweed sandwich?" Sophie made a face. "That sounds terrible."

"It's very good for the baby," Liv said huffily. "And besides it really does taste amazing with ketchup."

"Ugh." Lauren shook her head. "Don't, okay? Just the smell of that nasty stuff—"

"Well, it's better than raw meat," Olivia pointed out, grinning. "Which is all you seem to want, cuz."

"Raw meat?" Sophie said doubtfully. "Is that good for the baby?"

"It is if the baby's half Scourge," Lauren said, patting her still-flat belly. "She's a carnivorous little thing. It's funny—I never used to want my meat anything but well done but now steak tartar is my favorite dish."

Liv sighed. "I'm sort of jealous of you, having a girl. I already love my little guy but I can't help wishing that someday I could have a girl to dress up in cute little frilly dresses..."

"And have tea parties with," Kat put in.

"And take for mother-daughter mani-pedies." Sophie smiled at her twin. "Remember how Mom used to take us out on girl days?"

"Of course I do." Olivia wiped a tear from her eye. "Crap, Sophie, don't make me think about stuff like that when I'm all hormonal."

"I'm sorry, womb-mate," Sophie said contritely. "But I have to be honest, I don't know that you'd want a Kindred baby girl. They seem to have a pretty heavy load to bear."

"Oh?" Kat raised an eyebrow. "How so?"

"Well," Sophie said, sinking down on the ottoman opposite the couch. "They're so rare there's almost no chance they'll have sisters to play with for one. And for another, they all seem to end up being priestesses, whether they want to or not."

Liv frowned. "I did notice there seems to be an expectation that they'll enter the priestesshood and serve the Goddess."

"I met a girl like that on First World," Sophie said. "Her name was Lissa — she's one of the Touch Kindred."

"Whoa — wait a minute." Kat held up a hand. "There's a whole other branch of the Kindred we've never even heard of?"

"I've heard of them," Lauren said unexpectedly. "Xairn told me. They were another splinter group of warriors who went against the will of the Council to form a trade — pretty much the same thing that happened with the Scourge."

"Oh? What else did he say?" Sophie was interested. "All I heard was that they could touch things and people with their minds."

"Mmm, sounds sexy." Kat grinned.

Lauren shrugged. "I guess, if you're into that. I prefer to have my man's hands on me, not his mind."

"No, you didn't!" Liv laughed. "Lauren, you're bad."

"No, just honest." Lauren smiled. "But to answer your question, Sophie, I don't remember much of what he said about the Touch Kindred. I did get the idea that the Scourge and the other Kindred feared them though. I don't know why."

"Well, I have to admit that Lissa had some pretty spectacular powers," Sophie said thoughtfully. "I mean, she could move mountains of sand around with her mind. But I felt really sorry for her, anyway. She didn't really want to be there on First World—she said her mother had exiled her there. Her older brother spoke up for her but he was overruled. At least..." She frowned. "I think he was her older brother. The Touch Kindred seemed to have some funny ideas about familial relationships."

"To prevent inbreeding," Lauren said. "I remember now—Xairn did say something about that. There weren't enough of them to begin with and they intermarried too much. That was what caused the touch gene to become dominant in the first place. They're trying to breed it back out again now so the Kindred High Council will accept them and allow them on board the Mother Ship. "

"Oh, so that's why they're so picky about who you can and can't marry over there," Sophie said thoughtfully. "Makes sense, I guess."

"So they want to come on the Mother Ship? I don't know that I'd want to be in such close quarters with a bunch of guys who could reach out and 'touch' me anytime they wanted to, just by thinking about it." Olivia shivered.

"Which is exactly why they're not recognized by the Council and banned from the ship," Lauren said. "You know how protective and possessive Kindred men are." She smiled. "And that goes double for Scourge."

"There would be fights breaking out all over the place!" Sophie exclaimed. "You know, even when Rast healed me and Sylvan knew he was doing it for my own good, he told me later that it was really hard for him to let me get so close to another male without doing something about it."

She'd already told them about the healing and Nadiah and Rast's joining, but now, of course, they had to discuss it all over again.

"All I can say, is hurry up and get preggers, womb-mate," Olivia said when they had exhausted the topic of Nadiah's simple but elegant ceremony with Lissa presiding. "My little guy and Lauren's little girl are going to need company."

Sophie laughed. "I'll do my best. In fact..."She blushed. "Sylvan and I have already been trying on the trip back home. You wouldn't believe how creative he can get, even in one of those cramped little ships." She looked at Kat. "What about you, Kat? All aboard the pregnancy express—where's your ticket?"

"That's one ticket I'm not ready to get punched yet, thank you very much," Kat said tartly. "Besides, who's going to wait on all the pregnant ladies if we're all pregnant? Somebody has to be available to make the pickled seaweed sandwiches and pass the ketchup."

"Don't," Lauren and Liv said together.

"You're making me so hungry," Liv added.

Lauren groaned. "Just the thought makes me want to puke."

Kat and Sophie laughed together and Kat said, "See what I mean? This is what it's been like. And with you gone there just weren't enough minions to go around." She sighed. "I swear, when you get pregnant too, I'll have to clone myself."

Lauren looked pale. "Don't say that, Kat. I was cloned you know. It wasn't much fun."

"Sorry, hon." Kat patted her knee. "I forgot all about that. But didn't you say they were all — what did you call them — seed clones? Temporary?"

"All but one." Lauren shivered. "One of them was exactly like me. She even had my memories." She shook her head. "I have nightmares about that sometimes — wondering what became of her. I just can't imagine what it must have been like, being left behind in that awful place but feeling like she belonged back here. She must hate me just for being me."

"That's so creepy." Sophie made a face. "Let's talk about something else."

"Like what?" Liv asked. "You've already told us every single detail of Nadiah's adventure on First World." She sighed. "It's so sad she can't ever leave again."

"No, it's Rast who can never leave," Sophie corrected. "Not unless he wants to lose his wings."

"I know something you didn't tell us," Kat said. "What ever happened to Y'dex?"

"She told us that," Liv said. "He fell off the ledge when Rast jumped after Nadiah, right? So he must have gone kersplat all over the ground." She put a hand to her mouth. "Oh God, how disgusting. I think just made myself sick."

"Actually, he didn't splatter all over the ground," Sophie said. "We never saw him hit bottom. Of course, everybody was watching Rast and Nadiah instead and it was awhile before we thought to look."

"So what happened to him?" Lauren asked. "Did you ever find the body?"

Sophie shook her head. "Huh-uh. But Sylvan saw one of those huge black hunting birds they have on First World flying away with something in its beak. So it's possible..."

"That Y'dex ended up as bird chow," Olivia said. "Yuck, now I really am going to be sick."

"Serves him right," Kat said, frowning. "Going all the way to First World to try and break Rast and Nadiah up after he lost the challenge fair and square. How did he even get there?"

"We don't know," Sophie admitted. "He said something about the Kindred not being the only ones who had interstellar travel abilities or something like that." She frowned. "But according to Sylvan, it takes enormous amounts of power and really complicated technology to fold space—I don't see how he could have done it and followed Nadiah from Tranq Prime all the way to First World in one of those little ships."

"He could have used wormholes," Lauren pointed out. "Xairn did when he took me to get our DNA altered."

"Maybe so," Sophie said thoughtfully. "I guess that would make sense. But then why would he brag about his 'interstellar abilities?'"

Kat snorted. "Honey, why does any man brag? He was probably trying to impress Nadiah. Not that she'd ever go back to him—the slime."

"Well, however he did it, I guess his secret died with him," Lauren said.

Sophie nodded. "I guess so. There's no way anyone could have survived that fall." She looked at Liv. "And now you have to fill me in on what's been going on in the Mother Ship. All I've heard about so far are you and Lauren's weird pregnancy cravings. There must be something else going on."

"There is," Liv said, trying to sit up. Her belly was getting bigger by the day. "Ugh, in another two months I won't be able to move, I swear," she panted.

"What's the news, oh rotund one?" Kat asked, giving her a hand.

"You're going to pay for that remark once you finally do get preggers with twins," Liv snapped. "But anyway, Elise Darden is awake and she and Merrick are really hitting it off."

"Oooh." Sophie smiled. "That's wonderful! But I thought he wasn't supposed to be able to form bonds because he's a hybrid?"

"I thought so too," Olivia said. "But something is definitely going on between them. He'll hardly leave her side for a second—he even watches her while she sleeps. And it's not a one way street, either—the minute she wakes up, she looks for him. If he's not there—which is rare—she gets really upset. And here's the thing— he knows she's upset, even if he's halfway across the ship. He can feel it and he comes running."

Kat frowned. "But that's not possible without some kind of a bond. Are you sure they're haven't done the bonding sex hanky-panky in her hospital bed when you weren't looking?"

"Positive," Liv said, frowning. "You know all the med station rooms are monitored. The point is—this type of connection between them shouldn't be possible."

"What does Sylvan say about it?" Sophie asked.

Liv shook her head. "Well I just told him last night when you guys came in. He seemed concerned but he said he'd have to do more research before he could address it."

"So that's why he was reading that huge long medical paper about the 'extended effects of stasis sickness' into the wee hours last night," Sophie exclaimed. "I could hardly get him to come to bed. I tell you, if we hadn't had so much fun on the trip home, I would have been really upset." She pointed a finger at Olivia. "Luckily for you, womb mate, I was too tired to care."

Liv held up her hands in a "don't shoot" gesture. "Hey, just doing my job." She frowned. "I'm just worried about Elise. Merrick can take care of himself but she's been through so much."

"We all know how she feels," Lauren said quietly. "You tell her if she needs someone to talk to about what she went through, we're here for her."

"That's sweet, cuz." Liv smiled and reached across Kat to pat Lauren's hand. "I'll let her know. But to be honest, I think she just wants to forget." She shivered. "Can't say that I blame her."

Lauren nodded. "Well, if she wants to talk, my door's open."

"I'll let her know before she goes back down to Earth," Olivia promised. "She's healing remarkable quickly. I don't know if it has to do with Merrick or not but she's really bouncing back from her ordeal very well."

"Maybe she just has a good nurse." Sophie leaned forward and gave her twin a quick hug. "The best."

"Aww…" Liv hugged her back. "You really mean that, womb-mate?"

"Of course I do." Sophie smiled.

"Then…do you think you could make me a sandwich? Pretty please?" Liv begged. "The pickled seaweed is in the fridge and the ketchup's on the counter."

"And on that note, I'm leaving," Lauren said.

"Why?" Kat grinned at her. "You need to get home and whip something up for dinner?"

Instead of blushing and laughing, Lauren looked troubled. "Very funny, Kat. But you can stop teasing—there's no whipping or spanking or handcuffing going on at my place at the moment."

"Oh no—that's bad," Liv exclaimed. "Is everything all right, Lauren?"

Lauren sighed. "Well yes, and no. I'm super excited and happy to be pregnant but Xairn seems…conflicted. And ever since we got the pink flower, he won't touch me. I think he's afraid he'll hurt the baby."

"What?" Kat shook her head. "Did you tell him she's probably only the size of a lima bean right now?"

"Yeah, send him over to Sylvan if you want," Sophie said. "I'm sure he can explain."

"It's not just that. It's…" Lauren shook her head. "I'm not sure what it is. But I'm hoping it will all work itself out pretty soon."

"Well, you know you can talk to us anytime, right cuz?" Liv asked. "In fact…come here." She reached across Kat to give her cousin a hug.

"Help!" Kat exclaimed. "I'm being squished! Attack of the pregnant ladies."

"The very hormonal pregnant ladies," Lauren said, sitting back and sniffing. "Why does being pregnant make you so emotional? I haven't cried so much since I was a teenager."

"Hormones—they make you do crazy things." Liv swiped at her eyes. "Like right now, I'm even willing to forgo my seaweed sandwich if you want to stay."

Lauren sighed. "No, I really have to go. Xairn will be back soon and I need to do a new batch of cupcakes while I still have the energy." She looked at Kat and Sophie. "Either of you non pregnant ladies want to be my sous chef? I could use an assistant."

"I'll come," Sophie volunteered. "Sylvan won't be back to our suite until late." She frowned. "He's talking to the Council about something Rast told him."

"What?" Liv asked.

Sophie shook her head, feeling troubled. "He didn't say exactly. Only that there's some kind of threat to First World. It sounded pretty scary."

Kat frowned. "Well, I'm sure the Council will know what to do. I guess it's a good thing Rast turned up when he did."

"The Goddess works in mysterious ways," Sophie said seriously. "I just wonder what she's got up her sleeve for us next."

"Who knows," Olivia said. "But whatever it is, you can be sure it won't be boring. Come on Kat, since Sophie is helping Lauren you're on sandwich duty."

Kat groaned. "Again? All right but someday you'll pay for making me handle that nasty pickled seaweed."

"I promise I will," Liv said sweetly. "Just as soon as you've got your own two buns in the oven, Mrs. Twin Kindred."

They all laughed and got up to go. But as Sophie hugged everyone again and followed Lauren out the door, she sent up a silent prayer for Rast and Nadiah that everything would be all right. Though they were light years away from First World, she couldn't help feeling like whatever was happening there might spill over into their part of the universe as well.

"Keep us safe, Goddess," she whispered. "Keep us safe and our children too." Secretly, she stroked her flat belly where even now a seed might be sprouting. She promised herself she would ask Sylvan to do a pregnancy test soon. Very soon.

Chapter Thirty-eight

Merrick watched over Elise as she slept. She was curled on her side in the healing cot, her cloud of black hair obscuring her face. For a moment she was restless, twisting in her sleep and moaning.

Bad dream, Merrick thought and it was no wonder. She'd packed away what had been done to her by the AllFather as quickly as possible. He'd watched her do it and he knew there was no way she'd been able to process her pain before she shoved it to the back of her mind and locked it up. It worried him but at the same time he understood. Some things didn't bear remembering—some pains went too deep. Toxic memories could incapacitate you if you let them and Elise had simply made the choice not to let that happen.

We're a lot alike, he thought. No one would think so to look at them but it was true—despite their very opposite looking exteriors, inside they were both survivors.

Elise moaned again, something that sounded like a plea. Reaching down, Merrick pushed the cloud of hair away from her face and stroked her soft cheek. She quieted at once and cuddled against his hand, murmuring something that might have been his name.

Merrick felt a strange stirring in the region of his heart. What was this feeling which had crept up on him so suddenly? Why did he want to touch her all the time? Why did he hate to leave her, even for a moment?

And what was he going to do when she left the Mother Ship and went back to her old life on Earth?

Don't think about that, he told himself uneasily. Besides, all you're feeling is a male's natural protectiveness toward a female he has sworn to keep safe. It was a Kindred trait, one that apparently, not even his mixed heritage could breed out of him. He was going to have to get over it, and very soon too. Elise was healing remarkably fast—much faster than was normal for humans according to Olivia.

"She'll be ready to leave in a day to so," she'd told Merrick earlier. "Maybe even sooner. Do you want to escort her down to Earth?"

"I don't know. Let me think about it." He'd shifted uneasily from foot to foot. The thought of taking Elise back down to the small blue and white planet and just leaving her set off all kinds of alarm bells in his head. It was stupid and foolish but he couldn't help feeling that she wouldn't be safe there. That something might happen to her the minute he left her.

Don't be a fucking idiot, he'd told himself. It's her home planet—she'll be fine. Better off, probably, once she sees the last of you. But no matter how much he lectured himself, the idea that he would never see her again tied his stomach in knots.

Olivia had left him to consider his decision hours ago but he'd been unable to do so. He just wanted to spend the time they had left watching over Elise, memorizing her delicate features, soothing her when a bad dream troubled her sleep, and hearing her soft voice when she called his name...

Listen to me, he thought, withdrawing his hand. He slumped heavily on the chair beside her cot, frowning. I sound like a fucking love-sick bride hunter—one of those pure blooded idiots pining for their one true love or some shit like that. That's not me—I'm strong. I don't need anyone.

Well maybe she needs you, whispered a little voice inside his head. Did you ever think of that?

Merrick pushed the thought away uneasily. Elise Darden had a very successful life and career down on Earth. From what he could gather, she was busy from morning until night working in the planet's legal system—mostly on the behalf of children who had been wronged or abused in some way. There was no way she needed him—no way she had room for a hybrid giant who was scarred both inside and out in her busy life.

Elise turned over again, showing her lovely profile and Merrick sighed. It would be easier to leave her and go back to his own life if he didn't feel any kind reciprocal affection from her. But he did. It was there in the way she looked at him, the way she said his name when she was awake. Also the way she kept touching him.

It seemed that every minute they were together Elise had to have a hand on his arm or her fingers entwined with his. Once or twice when her nightmares were especially bad, Merrick had scooped her up and held her close to his chest. That, he found, was best of all. Elise rubbed her cheek against him and nearly purred when he held her—like a feline begging for a caress. Merrick couldn't deny he loved that, just as he couldn't deny the way he felt when he held her close.

Complete. I feel complete. It was true. He felt complete and happy in a way he hadn't been since he was a very young child and his mother hand held him in the same way. In fact, if he thought about it, that early time in his life was the last time he'd experienced any kind of prolonged physical intimacy with anyone. Back before the bad times started, he thought. Before my real father died.

Not that he had strictly paternal feelings for Elise Darden. To the contrary, every time he touched her, he got hard. Even the lightest brush of her hand would make his shaft thicken and the mating fist at its base throb with desire. There was a mixture of innocence and sensuality about her that made him crazy. It aroused a protective heat in him he couldn't understand.

You don't have to understand it, he told himself as she stirred again and her eyelids began to open. You just have to get over it. Look at her—all her bruises are healed and her wounds are nothing but barely visible scars. She'll be leaving soon—maybe even today. It's time to let her go.

So why did he feel sick at the thought of losing her?

Her eyelids fluttered again and then opened, showing her warm brown eyes fringed thickly with black lashes.

"Mmm. Hi," she murmured, looking up at him. "Have you been watching me sleep?"

"Yes," Merrick admitted hoarsely, unable to lie. "Just wanted to make sure you had good dreams."

She frowned. "If I had bad ones I don't remember them. You must have chased them all away." She reached for his hand at the same time Merrick was reaching for hers and their fingers entwined automatically. Elise sighed contentedly. "That's nice," she murmured, squeezing his hand. "I don't know why but it is."

"Yeah." He nodded. "Yeah, it is. So…" He cleared his throat, not wanting to say what came next.

Elise seemed to catch on to his mood at once. "What is it?" She sat up in the cot, looking at him anxiously. "Is everything all right?"

"Better than all right," Merrick said gruffly. "Olivia says you're good to go home soon. Back down to Earth," he added unnecessarily and then kicked himself. Don't be a fucking idiot—of course she knows where she lives!

"Back to Earth, huh?" Elise gave him a weak smile. "Sounds like a science fiction movie or something." She sighed. "In fact, my whole life sounds like science fiction lately."

"You think so?" Merrick raised an eyebrow at her.

"Well sure—just think about it. Girl on a vacation is kidnapped by bad aliens. Girl gets taken away and..." Elise swallowed hard and shook her head. "Anyway, she manages to escape, only to trap herself in a stasis tube. Which she's rescued from by the good guy and—"

"The good guy?" Merrick interrupted. "Me?"

"Sure." Elise nodded. "You found me. You saved me. You protected me, comforted me...of course you're the good guy."

"Okay, sure. I guess." He shrugged and laughed uneasily. "Just to let you know, that's not a name I've ever been called. Not with a past like mine."

"I don't care about the past," Elise burst out, surprising him with her sudden passion. "I only care about the future. Merrick..." She leaned toward him, her brown eyes earnest. "I...I don't want to go back. Not if it means leaving you."

"Elise...baby..." His heart knotted in his chest.

"I mean I know that sounds stupid," she rushed on. "We haven't even known each other that long. I don't know your last name or where you come from or even what kind of Kindred you are..."

"Hybrid," he said hoarsely. "I'm a hybrid. Half Blood, half Beast. And I was raised on Tranq Prime but I got outta that fucking hell hole as fast as I could."

She gave him a trembling smile. "I feel the same way about Portland. Portland, Oregon—that's where I was raised. That's why I moved way across the country to Florida. I like it a lot better there."

"But not enough to go back to it?" Merrick raised an eyebrow at her. He was trying to stay calm, to keep things in perspective. But damn if his stomach wasn't clenched like a fist and his heart pumping overtime as Elise confessed how she felt.

"Not...not without you." She shook her head. "I know I sound stupid and desperate and believe me, this is not like me. I'm tough—I'm the one they bring in on the worst trials to scare the defense, to make those slime ball child molesters and abusers confess or run for cover."

Merrick smiled. "You're so tiny. I can't imagine you being very scary."

She lifted her chin. "Just because I don't look scary on the outside doesn't mean I'm not frightening as hell on the inside, you know."

"I bet." He nodded, admiring her spirit. She was really going out on a limb here, admitting how she felt about him. Telling him she didn't want them to be parted.

"But when I'm around you..." Elise shook her head. "I can't explain it. I can't even understand it. But I...I need you, Merrick. I feel like there's something between us." She looked down at their clasped hands, his large fingers entwined with her much smaller ones. "I feel like such a fool telling you this—"

"Don't." He scooped her out of bed suddenly and held her close to his chest. "I feel it too, baby. I don't know what it is but it's there."

"Oh, thank God." She put her arms around his neck and pressed her face to the hollow of his throat. "I'm so glad. I thought you didn't feel the same."

"I shouldn't," Merrick said roughly. "But Goddess damn it, I can't seem to help it. I don't know why."

"I don't either." She nuzzled against him, breathing deeply. "God, you smell good."

"You smell pretty damn delicious yourself," Merrick murmured. Her scent was fresh and delicate and devastatingly feminine. It filled his senses and went straight to the throbbing shaft between his thighs. Gods, but he wanted this little female. Wanted to possess her and never let her go. If he hadn't been a hybrid he almost would have thought he was forming some sort of a bond with her. Of course, that was impossible. And they weren't dream sharing or anything. So why—

"Elise? Oh, excuse me." Olivia started to back out of the room but Merrick stopped her with a shake of his head.

"It's okay. Is there a problem?"

"No, it's just...there's a call in the viewing room for Elise."

"A call?" Elise sat up frowning. "From who? My boss? Is he upset?"

Olivia shook her head. "No, we contacted your employers soon after we brought you aboard and found out who you were. They know that you'll be out for awhile. But this man...well..." She bit her lip uncertainly.

"What man?" Merrick felt the short hairs on the back of his neck rise and a low, possessive growl built in his throat.

"He says..." Olivia looked at Elise, her gray eyes troubled. "Well, he says he's your fiancée."

End

Epilogue

Draven made himself comfortable on the lush, Strovian mink lined couch, enjoying the feel of its soft fur tickling his skin. He took pleasure in sensual comforts and wasn't ashamed to admit it. The couch, for instance, had come from a planet his people had despoiled over a thousand years ago—yet it was still soft and supple. Still perfectly delightful to sit on and he should know—he'd spent the last half millennium here, gathering strength. Trying to heal from the nearly fatal wounds that Kindred bastard, Kall had given him. He'd only recently awakened from his healing sleep and he was not happy.

The hand stroking the couch curled into a fist but there was no change in his expression. His odd silver eyes, like two blank coins, stared straight ahead as though he was deep in thought...or lost in madness.

Suddenly there was a timid rapping at his outer sanctum door.

"Come," Draven said, using the pain speech which inflicted agony on anyone who heard it. He didn't know who was on the other side of the door and he didn't care. It was his pleasure to give pain to whomever he wished. And it had been a long time since he had taken that pleasure.

The door opened and an imp, one of the lowest of the Shmeel tribe, stepped inside. "Your pardon, Master," it squeaked, rubbing its dirty grey claws together nervously. "But the prisoner is here."

"Is he? Excellent—bring him in."

The imp winced as the words sliced its mottled greyish skin and black blood flowed sluggishly from the wounds. It was wise enough, however, not to say anything. It only bowed and opened the door wider. "Come," it said, nodding at those who were waiting in the hallway. "The master says bring him in."

Two burly trolls of the Xa tribe dragged a tall, lanky male with white blond hair into the room. He was wearing the traditional clothing of Tranq Prime, Draven noted—a purple furred tharp and boots to match. They made quite a contrast with the prisoner's pale skin.

"What are you doing? Take your filthy paws off me," the male demanded angrily. "I am a Licklow of the largest grotto on Tranq Prime. Release me at once."

"We release you...if Master says. Not before," growled one of the trolls. The other simply champed its tusks menacingly, drool running down its beefy chin to fall on its bare chest.

Draven made a motion to the trolls. "You heard our guest—he wishes to be released. Do so at once."

"Master says, we obey." The trolls let go of the prisoner at the same time but since they'd been holding him about a foot off the ground, he fell in a heap at Draven's feet. He got up at once, dusting himself off and glaring at Draven.

"I don't know who you think you are but I am very displeased by my treatment here."

"I'm so very sorry!" Draven exclaimed. "You must forgive my subordinates—the undertribes are so crude. You there," he said, directing his attention to the already wounded imp. "Get our guest a drink at once."

The imp winced as more wounds opened on its filthy hide and scuttled to do Draven's bidding. It poured a stream of blood-colored wine into a jewel encrusted cup and ran to offer it to the prisoner. He took it gingerly, Draven noted, making sure not to touch the imp's skin, and sniffed suspiciously before taking a sip.

"It's good, is it not?" Draven smiled charmingly. "Pressed from the grape over a thousand years ago. An excellent vintage and well aged. I, on the other hand, am going to have quite a different libation."

Rising, he took his own cup, the twin of the one the prisoner held, and walked toward a cabinet at the center of the room. Inside, bound, gagged, and naked was a female Varian. Her three full breasts thrust outwards from her chest, their dark blue nipples tight with need.

The prisoner put down his cup and stared, wide eyed, as Draven stroked each breast in turn, taking his time in choosing his vintage. The middle breast seemed the fullest so Draven placed his cup beneath it and palmed its smooth, pale blue surface almost tenderly.

"Wine is all well and good," he told the Tranq Prime male as he gave the full breast a savage squeeze. The Varian female moaned with pain. Draven ignored her and squeezed again, forcing the breast to flow. "However, sometimes one wants something a little stronger. A little…sweeter." He pinched the nipple to get the last drops of rich purple milk and then took a sip. "Ahh, delicious. Even better than Lagosian wine, I think."

"Did you just say Lagosian?" The Tranq Prime male frowned. "But Lagos is a dead planet. It was despoiled by the Hoard over a thousand years ago."

"Exactly." Draven nodded and shut the cabinet, muting the Varian's cries. He strolled back to stand in front of the prisoner. "Now do you know where you are?"

The male's skin went suddenly even paler. "I...it can't be — not Hrakaz! I thought I was still somewhere on First World. The last thing I remember is falling and then..."

"One of my underlings caught you and brought you here." Draven smiled and took another sip from his cup. "It saved you from splattering all over the desert floor — you're quite welcome for that, by the way. Although you may not be too quick to thank me if you can't answer my questions."

"What questions?" the male demanded, drawing himself up and lifting his chin. "And what gives you the right to question me?"

"Well, I did save your life," Draven pointed out pleasantly. "I wouldn't think you'd mind answering a few questions. You know — just as a favor, between friends?"

"But, I—" the prisoner began.

"However, I can see you're determined to be stubborn." Draven put his cup on the ornately carved table by the couch and smoothed his thumb and forefinger along his perfectly trimmed mustache and down his goatee. It was a habit he had when he was feeling thoughtful...or bloody. "Such a shame," he sighed. "I do dislike unpleasantness."

"Now, wait a minute..." The prisoner's bulging blue eyes were suddenly filled with fright.

"Hold him," Draven told the trolls. "Body and head." They grabbed the male's arms before he could move and one of the trolls gripped his white blond hair with its thick, sausage like fingers. It pulled tight until a squeak of pain was forced from his lips. "Very nice." Draven nodded and took a step toward the prisoner so that they were face to face.

"Stop!" the male gasped. "Please..."

"All in good time." Draven smiled gently. "Now," he said, cupping the male's sweating cheek lightly in his palm and positioning his thumb over one bulging blue eyeball — the left. "You have a choice, my friend. You can either lose one eye...or both."

"I...I don't understand." The prisoner was obviously trying to keep his courage up and failing miserably. "What are you talking about?"

"I'm talking about the fact that you've been rude to me several times already in our brief conversation," Draven told him sternly. "That alone will cost you an eye. However, if you think you can behave yourself and answer all my questions in a civil tone, I might spare you the other. Just because I'm feeling generous today."

"What...what do you want to know?"

"Maybe I can tell you what I already know and you can fill in the blanks." Draven smiled pleasantly and stroked the prisoner's trembling eyelid lightly with the ball of his thumb. "What do you say?"

"Yes, yes. I say yes," the male promised hoarsely.

"Good. Aren't things more pleasant when we all use good manners?" Draven stopped stroking and rested his thumb more firmly on the male's eyelid. "Now, it is known to me that First World has recently gotten itself a new ruler. A new Counselor to watch over and protect it. Yes?"

"Yes, yes!" The male nodded and Draven felt the eyeball roll under his thumb like a marble. "Same off-worlder bastard that stole my female," he went on. "He came and challenged the blood bond for her — took her away."

"Dear me, that sounds like a rather unpleasant business." Draven shook his head and made a tsking sound with his tongue. "But as to this new Counselor , my spies have been monitoring First

World—they saw him come. Saw his wings manifest just in time to save the girl—now that was a good catch, wouldn't you say?"

"I..."

"A rhetorical question, I assure you." Draven pressed a little harder on the male's eyeball, eliciting a muffled shriek, and continued. "Anyway, it's an understatement to say I wasn't pleased to see him come—but I wasn't exactly surprised either. There's a prophecy, you see. There's always a prophecy when it comes to the Kindred." He made a bored motion with his free hand. "But this one speaks about the lost son of the Counselor coming home to rule once he sprouts his wings and finds his Lyzel, etcetera, etcetera, ad naseum." He made another circular gesture with his free hand.

"Now, I, of course, have a small score to settle with the new Counselor . Mostly because of what his father did to me quite a few years before your time, my friend." He smiled and pressed the eyeball again. The prisoner tried to flinch back but the troll behind him held him in place. Draven was pleased—you could go on all day about how stupid the Xa tribe was, but no one could match them for brute strength.

"Please." The prisoner was shaking now and sweating much more freely. Draven couldn't tell if the clear liquid running from his eye was sweat, tears…or something else. "Please, I beg you."

"And I'm begging you to be quiet and let me finish my story." Draven pressed harder. "How many times do we have to talk about manners? It's very rude to interrupt." He sighed. "Well, as I was saying, I have a score to settle with the new Counselor but First World is not my only interest. Far from it."

He waited, but the prisoner said not a word.

"So rude," Draven admonished him. "You could at least ask what my interest is."

"I didn't know…I thought I wasn't…wasn't supposed to," the male whispered through trembling lips. "S-sorry."

"I'll forgive you this time," Draven said, removing his thumb.

The male nearly sobbed. "Thank you. Thank you."

"Don't thank me yet." With careful precision, Draven placed the tip of his thumb and index finger at the corners of the much-abused eye. The bulging blue ball rolled frantically in its socket, filling with fear once more. Before the prisoner could start whining again, Draven went on.

"As I was saying, there is more at stake than simply First World." He nodded at the Tranq Prime male encouragingly. "And you say…"

"What…what's at stake?" the male gasped hoarsely.

"Very good!" Draven was pleased that the prisoner had taken his cue so well. "What's at stake you ask? Only the entire universe, my friend. Of course," he added thoughtfully. "It will take us years and years and years to conquer every known civilized planet, but we can start with the Kindred worlds and move on from there. We have the time and the numbers. The undertribes multiply so fast. Why, did you know that among the imps and trolls, the females are actually born pregnant? It makes fucking quite unnecessary—not that it stops them." He laughed. "It's most amusing is to see a troll fucking an imp. The size different makes it quite a challenge as I'm sure you can see." He nodded at the tiny three foot imp standing to one side and then to the eight foot trolls holding the prisoner's arms. "But I digress…"

Digging his finger and thumb into the corner's of the prisoner's eye, he pinched lightly, drawing a strangled gasp. "What I wanted to ask, friend," he said, smiling into the wide, terrified blue eye. "Is exactly how you got here. You see, my spies saw the Kindred ship come—right through the fold, as always. Folding space…a useful technology if you want to move a huge ship with many armed warriors from one fixed spot to another," he mused. "But it requires enormous amounts of energy and it's not quite as useful if one aims to move many smaller ships to many different points in the universe at different times. For that, we need something else. Something else entirely."

"I came by wormhole," the prisoner gasped. "Wormhole, I swear it. That's why I didn't come through the fold."

"Yes, my friend, but I've checked the star charts over and over. You didn't come through a known, existing wormhole. You came through a small and extremely stable rip in the space-time continuum that was never there before. And as soon as you exited it, it promptly disappeared." Draven pinched harder, putting stress on the fragile, slippery structure beneath his thumb and finger. "Can you explain that to me?"

"New…ship," the prisoner groaned. "Got it from…Trissian navigator. Don't know…how…it works."

"Ah yes, a Trissian," Draven mused. "Still known for their thieving ways, I see. But the question is, who did he get the ship from?"

"Said he…modified it himself," the Tranq Prime male whimpered. "Got the plans from a spy probe during…a raid."

"And who was he probing?" Draven massaged the eyeball cruelly, pinching hard to tug the bulging blue eye from its socket.

The prisoner gave a hoarse scream. "I don't know! I don't know! I swear to the Goddess, I don't know!"

"Mmm, that's unfortunate for you, my friend," Draven murmured, still tugging at the reluctant left eye. "Because you see, we've examined your ship and the mechanism seems to have burned out. It's a twisted hunk of junk—there's just no way to find out how it works—or worked, anyway." He dropped his hand abruptly and wiped his fingers on his immaculately tailored Frenez skin slacks. "I'm growing tired of this. Is there really nothing else of use you can tell me?"

"I'll tell you anything," the prisoner babbled, blinking his wounded but still intact left eye rapidly. It was leaking clear fluid and Draven doubted the male would ever have full vision in it again, but that wasn't his problem. "Anything at all," the prisoner repeated, sobbing.

"Yes, but do you have anything useful to tell," Draven said impatiently. "You see, my spies saw a star-duster doing the exact same thing you were—making its own worm holes—not too long ago. Unfortunately, the imp on duty neglected to tell me of this very interesting anomaly until it was too late and the ship was gone." He laughed charmingly. "Heads rolled on that day—I can tell you. And I do mean that literally. There's a most amusing game one can play with imp heads and a hungry tantor…but I digress again."

He sighed. "To make a long story short, I would be most interested in obtaining this new technology. I'm certain you can see why. It would be infinitely useful in moving ships around in space and one wouldn't have to have a huge power source to fold space or rely on the known, unstable wormholes which are really too rare to be of much use anyway. And you could pop up unexpectedly anywhere in the universe you wanted without warning. Now wouldn't that be fun?"

"Don't know." The prisoner was blubbering now. "Don't…don't know. Tell you anything. Can't think…can't see…"

At this mention of his vision, Draven frowned. "Yes, thank you for reminding me. I did promise to take one of your eyes, did I not?"

The Tranq Prime male shrank back against his guards in horror. "B-but you d-did," he stuttered. "Can't see...left eye all...all b-blurry."

"Well, if you're still getting something from the left, I supposed I'd better take the right." Swiftly, Draven cupped the sweating cheek and dug the tip of his thumb into the prisoner's right eye. There was a feeling of pressure and then a soft pop as his thumb pressed through into the warm, wet, jelly-filled socket.

The Tranq Prime male howled in agony and jerked, trying to get free. White goo leaked from the socket and the ruined right eye lay on his cheek like a crushed grape. A blue grape, Draven thought with satisfaction as he withdrew his thumb and wiped it fastidiously on a napkin handed to him by the imp.

"I think our business is done," he said, nodding at the trolls. "Take our prisoner back to his ship and let him go. We'll see how well he does flying blind."

The trolls dragged the Tranq Prime male away, still blubbering and the imp shut the door behind them. Draven picked up his jeweled cup and took another sip of the smooth purple Varian milk. He really had to think of some way to find out who that original star duster had belonged to. Either that or find the Trissian pirate who had scanned it. If he was going to attack and despoil all the Kindred worlds in one fell blow, he had to have that wormhole generator technology.

"All good things to those who wait," he murmured thoughtfully. "But I won't be willing to wait much longer,

Counselor . I have a debt to pay—one that's been collecting interest for a thousand years.

To be continued…

The End

If you've enjoyed this book, please take a moment to leave a review for Revealed on Amazon at

www.amazon.com/dp/B007DCYR3O

Good reviews help readers decide to try new books. And more readers means I can keep writing for a living and feeding my readers' Kindred cravings. ;)

Now continue the saga with Book 6, Pursued, Merrick and Elise's story.

Also by Evangeline Anderson

You can find links to all of the following books at my website:
www.EvangelineAnderson.com

Brides of the Kindred series

Claimed (Also available in Audio and Print format)

Hunted   (Also available in Audio format)

Sought   (Also Available in Audio format)

Found

Revealed

Pursued

Exiled

Shadowed

Chained

Divided

Devoured (Also available in Print)

Enhanced

Cursed

Enslaved

Targeted

Forgotten

Switched (coming 2016)

Mastering the Mistress   (Brides of the Kindred Novella)

Born to Darkness series

Crimson Debt (Also available in Audio)

Scarlet Heat   (Also available in Audio)

Ruby Shadows (Also available in Audio)

Cardinal Sins (Coming Soon)

Compendiums

Brides of the Kindred Volume One

  Contains Claimed, Hunted, Sought and Found

Born to Darkness Box Set

  Contains Crimson Debt, Scarlet Heat, and Ruby Shadows

Stand Alone Novels

The Institute: Daddy Issues (coming Feb 14, 2016)

Purity (Now available in Audio)

Stress Relief

The Last Man on Earth

YA Novels

The Academy

About the Author

Evangeline Anderson is the New York Times and USA Today Best Selling Author of the Brides of the Kindred and Born to Darkness series. She is thirty-something and lives in Florida with a husband, a son, and two cats. She had been writing erotic fiction for her own gratification for a number of years before it occurred to her to try and get paid for it. To her delight, she found that it was actually possible to get money for having a dirty mind and she has been writing paranormal and Sci-fi erotica steadily ever since.

You can find her online at her website www.EvangelineAnderson.com

Come visit for some free reads. Or, to be the first to find out about new books, join her newsletter.

Newsletter – www.EvangelineAnderson.com

Website – www.EvangelineAnderson.com

FaceBook – facebook.com/pages/Evangeline-Anderson-Appreciation-Page/170314539700701?ref=hl

Twitter – twitter.com/EvangelineA

Pinterest – pinterest.com/vangiekitty/

Goodreads – goodreads.com/user/show/2227318-evangeline-anderson

Instagram – instagram.com/evangeline_anderson_author/

Audio book newsletter – www.EvangelineAnderson.com